I dedicate this to my Mother and my Sister. Mom, for always encouraging my writing. Lil Sis, for always yelling at me to hurry up and finish a novel already. I love you both. Thank you so much.

&

To Grandma

Acknowledgements

First and foremost, I acknowledge my Lord and Savior.

To the Etching in Time Writing Community, and our amazing coordinator Shannon Martin, thank you guys so much for pushing me to keep writing, to have confidence in myself and to not be so afraid of stepping out of my comfort zone.

To Tira Wilson, my beta-reader who waited so patiently for me to turn in complete manuscripts, who told me how much she was enjoying it and couldn't wait to read the finished version. I finished it Tira!

To Wanji Kihanya, my writing-partner-in-crime. You were a cornerstone of finally getting this novel done. Your constant encouragement and support drove me many times to put pencil to paper, or my fingers to the keyboard. Thank you.

To Angelyne Ngo, aka my sweet potato, my very first fan. Thank you for all the cheerful and encouraging talks we've had over the years.

Last and not least, to everyone who ever told me to keep writing, who told me they were interested in reading my story, teachers, professors, therapist, classmates, random people I talked to at grocery stores and on the sidewalk, thank you and I hope you enjoy!

The Other Side 4

The Other Side

A. E. Costello

The Other Side 6

1

August 1st
Friday

My sternum was ripped from my collarbone to my bellybutton, like unzipping a jacket. My ribs were cracked and spread wide to the air. My heart floundered to keep pumping blood, the wind brushing over the exposed muscle's frantic flexing. My lungs heaved, in and out, in and out, struggling for each breath. My stretched windpipe forced out booming screams.

My right arm was snapped off at the forearm, as my head whipped from side to side, I could see the abandoned limb out of the corner of my eye. My hand was limp and the fingers splayed. My bone stuck out sharp white in contrast of the red blood and pink meat surrounding it. The bone was gnawed with large serrated cuts slashed into the paleness, tendrils of yellow tendon trailing on the ground.

One shout pierced into my ears just as the pain increased.

"He's starting to Change!"

Black markings wiggled over my skin, a burning sensation following as thick gray fur pressed up through my pores. My ribs snapped into place as meat and flesh pulled over it. The gaping hole in my chest sealed together then bubbled as the smashed organs inside took new shape. My torn forearm stretched and lengthened, creating fresh bones that ground together. The fingers thickened into paws, the nails curved into claws.

My screaming cut off and choked as my vocal cords twisted, roughened. I gurgled as my skull elongated, my mouth and nose melted into one then broke open to release a howl out of my newly formed muzzle. My spine bent forward, then a tail swiped out from the base, my arms and legs hunched over as fur swiped over my new form.

Then it all faded away, as I jerked and twitched, the wolf receded and left my human body behind, laying on a pool of blood and fluid, breathing hard but alive, no wounds. My eyes burned gold with the new life birthed inside of me.

Just as dark shrouded my senses, I heard one last sentence.

"He's one of us now."

* * *

August 6th
Wednesday
First Student Day

After being mauled by a werewolf over summer break, I was sitting in Lakeside Village Comprehensive High School's main office meeting my principal with my father at my side. Apparently now that I'm no longer human, I had to report to the school about my Change.

Principal Lisa Hamilton typed at her computer, adjusting my student profile. She had to change my status from Human to Shifter.

"So, when exactly did the Change take place?"

I stared at the floor between my shoes and didn't answer.

Dad said, "August 1st ma'am."

"And you didn't get a vaccination beforehand?"

Dad answered. "Xon doesn't have any shifter friends so we didn't really see the need. Besides the shifters in this town are mostly prey shifters, they aren't aggressive like the predator types, so it wasn't like he was going to be attacked or bitten by friends playing too roughly."

Principal Hamilton's brows raised. "Then how did-?"

When I still didn't say anything, Dad spoke up. "He was attacked out of town, in California. I'll admit I wasn't there at the time, but a werewolf attacked him and tried to kill him, however he survived and was Changed instead."

I touched my chest over my heart at Dad's words. I still remembered the sensation of air touching my beating muscle, the scent of my own dying flesh.

Dad looked at the principal. "Is there any problem that my son is now a werewolf? There are other shifters at this school, so he shouldn't be treated any differently, right?"

"There are only five other werewolves here." She said with a sigh. "Now six including your son. They've made their own little group and we have several shifter faculty members. If you're worried, don't be. The shifters really tend to look after their own. As for humans, no one wants to anger a werewolf so he shouldn't be targeted for bullying or anything like that. Also the Dominion is one of the staff members here, so that should also ease any misgivings."

Dad prompted, "The…the Dominion?"

Principal Hamilton nodded. "Yes, that is an authority position within the shifter community, appointed by them and for them. Mr. Richard Forrest, as the Dominion of Lakeside Village, he simply is the leader of all the shifters here. His control doesn't stretch to the city of Mountain Ridge. If Xon has any problems, which he shouldn't, then Mr. Forrest is the shifter to go to."

Dad nodded and placed a warm hand on my shoulder. "Okay Xon? That doesn't sound too bad, right?"

I nodded, my tongue swollen too much to talk. Instead, a weak whine left my nose and throat. It didn't sound like a human noise, it was high and wavered then lowered into a rumble. An animalistic noise. A dog noise. Wolf. Not human.

Principal Hamilton looked awkward, she bit her lower lip then averted her eyes. Dad paled under his dark skin, giving him a ghastly grayish color before he coughed and stood up.

"Well, if that's all, I need to get back to work."

A. E. Costello 9

Principal Hamilton stood too. "That's fine, I'll escort Xon to class. Get your book bag."

I picked it up and slung it over my shoulder then followed Dad out of the office.

Dad put his hand on my waist and said to me, "Try not to be so nervous. I'm sure your friends will still be your friends and won't think any different of you. Just be yourself and everything will be fine. Remember, the Lord guides the young. Proverbs 3:5-6, *trust in the Lord with all your heart and lean not on your own understanding, in all your ways acknowledge him and He shall direct your paths.* So be calm and trust God, alright?"

I nodded again, still unable or just unwilling to speak. Dad was always like that, he had a scripture for everything.

Dad sighed but then Principal Hamilton joined us, so he gave me a tight hug then left.

Principal Hamilton walked me to my American Literature class and knocked on the door before entering.

Ms. Cannon, the teacher, looked up and smiled at first. "Xon! I was wondering where you were…"

Then her voice trailed off as she looked at my face, and into my eyes.

Every shifter has some sort of telltale, the one physical trait on their body that gives away their not-human status. For wolves, in the black expanse of the pupil that's empty in a human, there's a bright gold spark in the midst. It's not in the exact center, it's off to the side and it can move around as well as get bigger and glow brighter. It's the sign of the wolf that now lives on the inside. Mine bloomed wide, making my pupils shine like the sun.

Whispers swept around the room. The other kids I had been sharing classes with my entire life now looked pale, shocked and unsettled.

Principal Hamilton cleared her throat. "Enough talking please. Yes, Jaxon Reeves was Changed into a werewolf over summer break, but that doesn't change who he is on the inside. Please treat him with the same courtesy and respect as you have before when he was still human. Laura, you can continue class. Xon, take your seat."

I sat down and thumped my book bag to the ground and faced front. Principal Hamilton left and closed the door behind her. The room, before swamped with whispers, was now silent.

Ms. Cannon looked away from me and addressed the class. "As the principal said, treat Xon the same as you always have. Just because he's now a different species, it doesn't mean he's any different than he was before. Now, let's get back to our subject at hand, American Literature."

Her throat undulated as she swallowed hard, I picked out the quickening of her pulse. I could hear the *swish, swish* of the blood rushing in the veins, the *thump, thump* of her heart beating.

I didn't know any werewolves and seeing how weird she was acting, maybe Ms. Cannon never had a wolf in her class before. Or it must be the fact that the last time she saw me I was a human and now I'm staring at her with the burning gaze of a wolf.

As I sat there, staring at the floor, my wolf lifted his head. I sensed him with my mind's eye. Like when you're daydreaming and even if your eyes are open and you're looking at something real, such as the clouds or trees, you could still see whatever it was you were imagining about. Well I could see my wolf, the animal now inside of me, just the same. He was looking around, sensing outwards, taking in his surroundings. As he did, I understood everything he was taking in.

I smelled the classmate next to me, I turned to look at him as my wolf took it in like layers. The first layer was the guy's base scent, the scent of his species. He had the human scent, unclean meat. The uncleanliness wasn't in the sense of spirit or personality, but it was an off-putting smell that discouraged my wolf from feeling like he was food or something to eat. Nobody wanted to eat something that smelled dirty like that. After the base scent came the basic scent which was is either male or female, he smelled male, strong and musty. Then the next layer was his personal scent, the scent that labeled him who he was as an individual. Onions and hay. All of that just came from his skin. Then came the smell of his clothes, his hair, his breath. The clothes smelled like detergent, lavender and vanilla. His hair like oil and dead skin. His breath, orange juice and spearmint gum.

"Xon...Xon. Xon! Jaxon Reeves!"

At my whole name, I snapped back and looked over at Ms. Cannon who had been calling me. Flushed in the face, her lips pinched together, she said, "Stop staring at Greg and pay attention! Otherwise I'll report it as visually threatening him!"

I blinked and looked back at Greg. He was ice pale and had slid to the edge of his seat like he was *this* close to jumping up and running away. The room was silent again and a quick glance around revealed everyone was staring at me. But only one other person had the gold spark. The kid on the other side of me, he watched me with the long stark stare of a wolf assessing another wolf. His eyes were bright green and in his dark pupils was the shining gold glint of his wolf spark. This was the first day of school, I had no idea there was a werewolf in my class.

I smelled him just as well as I did Greg. His base scent, thick and heady like the outdoors, werewolf. Then his basic scent, forest and musky, male wolf. Personal scent, warmth like sunshine and sharp like lemons. I didn't know his name but I knew his scent and I would recognize it anywhere. I wouldn't forget Greg's or this new wolf's scent.

I faced front and focused on the teacher as she began to talk. My neck itched. I glanced over at the other wolf student; he was watching me again and his wolf spark flickered, jolted, like his wolf had noticed mine. I couldn't *see* his wolf in his own body but my wolf bared his fangs.

Who is this guy? Why does he keep staring at me? Does he want something? Is he starting something?

The werewolf student blinked then looked down at his desk. Something hard and hot burned in my gut and I looked away too. I didn't hear a word for the rest of the class as my wolf scented and logged information of every student in class.

The girl in the back row, she wasn't human either judging by the lack of the unclean meat smell. Her base scent was like burnt fruits and fresh fungus. It took my wolf a few seconds to catalogue the scent as bat. The boy by the farthest window, he was human but he also smelled odd, stark, bitter, he was a cigarette smoker.

When the bell rang and Ms. Cannon gave out the homework, I grabbed my book bag and left. The smell of the hallway smacked me in the nose. The collective scent of human beings flooded my nose, that unclean meat, it clogged up the entire building. I smelled not just their skin, but their breath, hair and clothes all had a scent to it. Before I hadn't noticed it because it was like my wolf had been asleep or something, but now he was aware and taking note of everything.

"Hey, Xon! Xon!"

I turned my head at my name but even as I heard that, I heard everything else and its cousin. The hallway was *loud*. The scraping and thudding of everyone's footsteps on the tiled floor, the rustling of shirts and pants brushing as people moved through the crowd, even the buzzing of cell phones and the tiny animated voices of that kid over there playing his Vita.

I stood still.

Dear God, why didn't You let that bastard Rocky kill me? I was dying, my body torn apart, there was no reason for me to survive that attack. Now I'm still alive but the suffering isn't over. Shit, why is this happening to me?

"Xon, dude didn't you hear me calling you?" Zaheed stopped in front of me, his brows raised. Zaheed's breath smelled like milk and cheerios, his curly hair was giving off the stench of car grease. His father ran a mechanic shop. "I mean, you looked right at me but you didn't wave or smile."

The bell rang, once when the shrill sound was just alarming enough to make you hurry to class, now it sounded like a bullhorn blasted directly into my eardrums.

Holy shit, I did not know that turning into a werewolf would jack my senses up by twelve million degrees. I need to go back to Cali and ask Toni more questions about this because this is almost too much to deal with.

"Wait dude…" Zaheed trailed off as he was looking into my eyes. His skin drained pale, from his normally sandy brown color to yellowish milky white. "Your…your eyes man."

I looked away but I knew it was too late, he had already seen it. "Yeah, I know. Just last week."

Zaheed whispered, his voice strangled and high. "Wh-what do you mean, *just last week*? You…you're like…a shifter now?"

I nodded, looking at the floor. I didn't want to see his expression but that didn't matter because I could smell his emotions. Stinging onions, confusion. Piss, fear. A crumpled and weak scent of emotional pain. A wet muddy smell, sadness.

Zaheed asked, "So that's it then?"

I glanced at him, taking in the strain on his face, his mouth tugged downwards, eyes damp though he wasn't crying.

"What do you mean? It wasn't my choice."

The warning bell rang, we had three minutes to get to class.

Zaheed nodded, a jerky wobble of his head and walked away with swift hurried steps.

I walked to my class, staring straight ahead.

Great. Zaheed is afraid of me and he'll definitely tell the rest of the guys. Not to mention everyone in my last class are probably spreading the news right now.

In my classroom, Algebra II, the teacher Mrs. Ellis was already writing a ridiculously long math problem on the board.

The classroom floor stunk, a gagging nauseating spin of everything anyone's shoes have stepped on now stamped onto the tiles. As if the floor wasn't enough, I could smell the unwashed book bags, the used textbooks and the collective stench of unclean meat humans.

There was only one person in the room who didn't smell like that, an Asian guy leaning backwards in his chair and chatting with two girls. His base scent was like herbs and cashew, some sort of large bovine but not a cow. He was a shifter but my wolf couldn't name the animal this guy turned into. I didn't see a telltale in his eyes.

Putting that information away for later, I looked for my friends that shared this class; Aydan and Regan Nicholson, twin brothers. They were already at their seats in the back. I preferred to sit at the front during math class because it was hard and I needed to pay close attention if I expected to pass.

I walked over to them. "Hey guys. How was your weekend?"

"Oh...hi Xon." Aydan made a weak smile, compared to how he usually grinned so wide you could see all of his gums, now his smile was very small and didn't last but a second. He had this faint pissy scent, nervousness. "It was um, fun. We went to the movies with the other guys. Ah...Zaheed told us. We didn't want to believe him. Dude, is it true?"

I lowered my eyes, trying to hide my wolf spark with my lashes. "Oh...yeah. It's a new development, but you know, I'm the same person."

Regan coughed. "You're a shifter Xon. You're not even human. How is that the same?"

That hurt.

Not human? If I'm not human, if I'm not the child of God...then what am I? Who's child am I then?

My knuckles cracked and my nail beds itched. I got a whiff of my own scent, burnt and dry, irritated.

"Xon, stop talking and take your seat." Mrs. Ellis called from the front of the room. "You're holding up class, sit down."

I went to my seat and sat down with a heavy exhale. I slumped over, dropped my book bag and covered my face. Once my hands covered my nose, I smelled myself, my personal scent. Tea leaves and ground pepper. It was a calm soothing familiar scent, it was like jumping into my bed and rolling up in my covers, it was *my* scent, just me and I could easily accept it.

Dear God...my friends don't even like me anymore. They're saying I'm not human but God, you created humans, you created me as a human. If I'm not human, if I'm not Your creation...then who created me? Did You really abandon me? Once I became something else, am I no longer Your child? I'm so confused Lord God. Please, help me. Amen.

"Xon, Xon. Jaxon Reeves!"

At the sound of my full name, I jumped and looked up.

Mrs. Ellis had her arms crossed. "I told you to put your hands down but you ignored me. I'm not going to start class with you being disruptive. Keep your hands away from your face and pay attention, understood?"

I nodded. "Yes Mrs. Ellis."

She strode to the front of the room.

It was like on one hand, my life was normal. Getting up, going to class, interacting with my teachers. On the other hand, it was completely out of whack. Smelling everything, hearing everything, my friends mistrusting me, there was no way that anyone would actually *want* to be a werewolf if this was what life was going to be like.

The Other Side 16

The class began and I went through the motions, doing the worksheets and taking notes but my mind wasn't comprehending or retaining anything. The bell rang, Mrs. Ellis told us what exercises to do in the book and I walked out. Any other time, I would have walked with Aydan and Regan to lunch and we'd meet with Zaheed and Daewon.

I started down the steps to the cafeteria and was nearly knocked on my ass.

If I thought the students, the hallways and the classrooms smelled nauseating, none of it had prepared me for the olfactory horror of the cafeteria. Over there, the giant buckets of garbage cans with people dumping their rotten food inside, there was the smells of vomit and spit gum, soiled napkins. Even with that, my wolf raced to start cataloging the smorgasbord of scents. The first thing he did was start separating the human scents from the not-so-human ones.

I smelled a pair of siblings, male and female, they smelled like grass and leaves with the boy having the extra masculine scent of hot wind. They were gazelles. I scented another set of siblings, twins this time. They smelled dusty and breezy, my wolf was quick to acknowledge that these two were tabby cats. There was a male who smelled like seawater; dolphin. There was another boy, he smelled salty and fishy but this guy I actually knew. Dave Powell, the president of the SSGA or the Shifter Student Government Association. I knew he was a shifter but I hadn't known what type. My wolf knew this scent, he was a swan.

Now that my wolf had successfully sorted out all the students, it was time that I delved into actually finding something to eat. Each of the five lanes serving food all had their specific round of scents.

First lane, beef tacos. The ground beef was soaked in grease, the soft tortilla had been over-grilled and was giving off the stark scent of charred flour. The shredded cheese smelled like it was at least three weeks past the

A. E. Costello 17

expiration date, the lettuce smelled wilted from sitting out for too long, the slimy tomatoes piles of red mush.

My stomach pitched towards my mouth like to make me hurl so I exited that lane for the next.

Pizza. Wait. This is what pizza smells like to a werewolf? Really? Back then pizza smelled like heaven. Somehow, by turning into a wolf, pizza had turned into a twisted hell of what was once good memories. The bread smelled strongly of the oven it had been in, the oven that must not have been cleaned in a century. The tomato sauce was over-baked, the melted cheese gave off this wet milky odor, even the pepperoni smelled like it had been shaved from an old warthogs back.

I stumbled away from that lane.

Three more lanes left. Please, let something be edible!

It was cheeseburgers. You know what, fine. Meat, bread and cheese, you can't go wrong. Yes, the bread smelled old and moldy, the cheese wasn't melted because the burger was ice cold, I didn't care. I got the burger, a scoop of cardboard French fries, a cartoon of acid fruit punch and checked out of the line.

"Hey Xon!" Walking up to me with his large Afro and bright white smile was my best friend for most of my life, Daewon Harris.

I turned my head away, hoping to hide my wolf-shined eyes from him.

He sighed and clapped my shoulder, making me jump.

"It's not like I don't know already," he said. I quickly looked at him, shocked. Daewon tsked his teeth at me. "Your mom is best friends with my Mom, remember? Miss Kyra told her, so I know. Besides, Zaheed, Aydan and Regan also told me."

I said, "But…do you still want to be my friend?"

Daewon's eyes widened. "Bro, I've known you since we were in diapers. So what you howl at the Moon now, as long as you don't bite me or anything, you're still awesome."

A smile wiggled its way across my face.

Daewon laughed and threw his arm around my head, forcing my face into his shoulder in a hard quick hug before he pushed me away. Even so, I caught his scent in that quick moment. Despite the unclean smell, he smelt like my friend, which was like a watered down version of my own scent. Like mine.

"Dumbass," he said cheerfully.

I chuckled then asked him, "Have you seen Melody around? She lives across from you, you ride the same bus."

Daewon shrugged. "Ah she didn't ride the bus this morning, and we don't share any classes this semester. Still, if I know, wouldn't Melody already know? I mean, this is a small town, and she is your girlfriend. Your parents must have informed her parents too. Anyway, come and sit with us, let's eat."

I nodded and walked with him to a round table by the large plate-glass windows that took up the far wall. Aydan, Regan and Zaheed were seated with their food, while there was an empty seat with a tray there, and a second empty seat.

Daewon dropped himself down in front of his tray, and pulled out the seat next to him. I put down my tray, but Regan hooked his ankle around the leg, and jerked the seat against the table before I could sit down.

I said, "Regan?"

"Listen," said his twin, Aydan. "We...we've already decided." He glanced at the other two, then lifted his chin at Daewon. "We don't want Xon sitting with us."

Daewon sat up straighter. "What? Guys, Xon is-"

"Not human," said Zaheed in a low tone. "And I don't really feel comfortable with him sitting here. Besides, majority rules. Xon can't sit with us."

These guys and I had been friends since last year, and it was Daewon who introduced me to them.

Daewon said, "Xon can sit here, he's our friend."

Regan looked me in the eyes for a moment and I looked back. He paled and jerked his head away.

"There's no way I'm eating with him," he said, his fists clenching on the table. His scent thickened with the piss of fear, yet mired in it was the minty aroma of truth. He meant what he was saying. "I can't sit here with him staring at us like that."

Zaheed and Aydan nodded, also not meeting my eyes.

"Fine," I said, picking up my tray. "Don't," I said as Daewon moved to stand up. "You can sit with them. I'll see you later."

"Xon!"

Daewon called after me as I walked away. I went and sat down alone, at the far end of a crowded table where there were two empty seats. I stared moodily at my food, not feeling like eating a bite.

Then my mind's eye flickered. The wolf in me raised his head, sniffing and then my stomach grumbled. He was hungry and wanted to eat.

I pushed the vision, the feeling, back. I didn't feel like eating, I was so fucking pissed.

The wolf's hunger came right back, the urge was like knives in my stomach, my throat grumbled and pain pricked my forehead. If I didn't eat, it would make me sick. The wolf in me wouldn't even let me not eat.

I downed the burger in two bites, gobbled the French fries and finished off the juice in a quick gulp. It all dumped into my stomach and was digested immediately. My wolf curled up and went to sleep, satisfied.

So now it's not just me, as in Xon, but there's another me, the wolf on the inside. The wolf has its own feelings and needs that have to be met, along with the ones I already have. Not to mention, I get that each emotion has its own scent. I've learned what fear and truth smells like. Ok...maybe that is a little cool. I know one thing, no one is going to be able to lie to me again, ever.

I walked up the cafeteria steps and opened the door to the men's room. My eyes sunk closed, my knees weakened at the battering ram that knocked into my face, nearly whamming me unconscious. When I was human, before the Change, I was aware the men's room smelled but it wasn't like the atrocity I was smelling right now. My nose burned hot like I was trying to inhale lava, my eyes pricked with pained tears.

"Hey!" A guy protested from behind me. "Are you going in or not? You're blocking the door!"

I don't want to go in. I don't want to!

My bladder clenched; I had to go in or I'd piss my pants. Pulling my shirt collar up to cover my nose, I walked straight toward the closest urinal, struggling to undo my buckle. I had to do my business and get out, now! I finished as quickly as possible, washed my hands then hightailed it out of there.

I entered the hallway and I smelled her first. A warmed feminine version of my own scent, mixed with the personal scent of melted butter and fresh bread. She walked around the corner, Melody Summers, my first girlfriend that I've been dating since eighth grade.

"Melody," I sighed, walking over to her while rubbing my damp hands down the sides of my jeans. "I was hoping to see you."

She turned her head, soft blonde curls bounced against the nape of her neck. A smile was on her face at first as she looked at me with bright blue eyes but it dropped once my wolf spark flickered in my pupils.

"Xon." Melody stepped back, and her creamy skin blanched gray.

"Yeah," I said with a short smile, rubbing my close-cropped hair with one hand, the other hand I curled into a fist behind my back. "I wanted to talk to you, you know, explain some things."

Melody turned her head away. "I...I can't talk to you. I...I have to break up with you..."

I froze and only her name edged out through my lips.

"My parents Xon, they don't want me to even be around you anymore." Melody sniffed just as I smelled the salty metallic of tears. Her scent clouded with a heavy dank scent, unhappiness, mired in a wet slimy mold scent of hopelessness. "They believe that...werewolves are demons."

I gasped. Mr. and Mrs. Summer's warm smiling faces flashed before my eyes. We went to the same church, that was where I had met Melody before going to high school.

Demon?

Melody ran her arm over her face, and fully turned her back. "I can't say if you're really a demon Xon...I don't know how a human being can turn from a human into a wolf, and it doesn't sound of God at all. The idea of you just...what if you get angry and attack me? You have fangs and claws, and...your eyes...those eyes aren't the eyes that I remember before you left for California. You...I just can't."

She sprinted away and I didn't call her back, I just stood there numbly as the bell rang, signaling the end of the lunch period.

* * *

U.S. History with Mr. Malone, an ex-military hard ass who spoke like a drill sergeant and tended to yell. I took my normal seat, third row by the window. I looked out, my view was of the courtyard.

There was the fountain in the mid-center, it had been so heavily vandalized with graffiti, laundry soap and vomit that the water was turned off and there were caution signs around it. My enhanced eyes could pick out the individual tags on the cracked dirty marble, black jagged spray paint of nicknames and numbers. Farther back was the field, just an expanse of tall grasses, undeveloped land. On three sides were trees. Lakeside Village was inside a forest, a large section had been mowed down and the village built there. Most of the forest remained, our town snuggled inside of it with a river that cut through and separated our village from the neighboring city, Mountain Ridge with a bridge connecting us together.

The wind blew outside and drowned out Mr. Malone's loud bark of a voice. Instead, I could hear the twittering of birds, the thud of heartbeats, saliva rushed over my tongue and my pulse ached, throbbed. A sharp prick, a tingle, at the very back of my head, like something shifting. The wolf lifted his head and leaned forward, pressing against my control.

I tore my eyes away from the window and stared at my desk. I didn't want to think of the forest anymore, didn't want to imagine peeling my skin off and letting the wolf run free. I bit down on my tongue to hold the urge back but the bright flash of pain only jolted excitement down my spine. My heart expanded, a gasp filtered its way past my itching teeth.

No, no, no, no. I chanted. *No, not now. Go back, go away, go to sleep.*

The wolf didn't listen, fur tickled underneath my rolling skin, my fingers tensed up and released claws, slashing from my nail beds, curved and shiny ebony like freshly polished switchblades.

"Jaxon Reeves!"

My head jolted back and my eyes spread wide.

Mr. Malone stood in front of me, arms crossed and his thick brows furrowed. "Enough sleeping in class! Your whining noises and kicking the floor are disturbing my lecture. Now keep your head up and pay attention. Understood?"

I nodded, realizing the entire class was staring at me. My head had been down on the desk as I fought back the wolf so he thought I had been asleep. Mr. Malone went back to the front of the class and I stared at my lap. My jeans had ten furrows from my claws slicing into the fabric like butter. I had cut my skin, blood stained the ripped fabric but I had no wound.

I rubbed my nose. *Try and calm down, focus on paying attention.* When I lowered my hand, I breathed in deep and scented a shifter. Mr. Malone's back was turned, so I looked around for it. The kid all the way in the back, he was wearing a hat and sunglasses, both of which were not allowed in school but Mr. Malone hadn't said anything about it. I could smell him, his base scent was hot and tangy, horse.

Something hard hit me in the head. I jumped and caught it before it fell. It was the cap to a dry erase marker. I looked up.

Mr. Malone glowered at me. He spoke through gritted teeth. "Face front and pay attention Reeves. If I have to speak to you again, I'll give you detention, understand?"

"Yes Mr. Malone."

I handed him back the cap and focused on my work. Even so, I was stunned by how my new heightened sense of smell could find out anything about anyone. Also how many students here that were shifters that I had never taken notice of. I wondered if they could all smell me just the same.

When U.S. History was over, I slowly headed toward my last period, Psychology. Ms. Hughes was at her desk, flipping through the textbook. Today the desks were arranged in groups, four or three circles together. There were already names on each desk. My stomach fell.

Jaxon Reeves. Melody Summers.

I didn't even read the other two names.

Why. Why did she do this? Why.

"Xon." Ms. Hughes got my attention. "Sit down please."

I sat after a moment. Melody barely got in the room as the late bell rang.

Ms. Hughes gave her a warning look. "That was cutting it close Miss Summers."

"Sorry," Melody gave her the sweetest smile then her shiny blue eyes scanned the room, noticing the set up. Then she saw the last remaining seat with her name on it and her gaze bounced to me, my desk next to hers.

"Miss Summers, sit down. You're holding up class." Ms. Hughes's eyes sparked with impatience and her crisp singed smell revealed it.

Melody's normally smiley face slumped then she straightened her shoulders and sat down next to me, getting out her binder and textbook.

My wolf sat up, looking over the slender white curve of her neck, the soft blonde curls at the dip below her skull, how her slow calculated breaths rose her breasts close to the neckline of her shirt. I inhaled and her scent swept over me. Rose and cherry perfume, coconut hair gel, her lemon fabric softener scented clothes, her meat-stink human smell, all of it charged up my nostrils and stabbed me in the brain. I covered my face with my hands and turned away, instead sucking down my own scent, calming myself down.

Ms. Hughes was talking and I managed to lift my head up to try and pay attention. "After his accident, Phineas Gage was reported to have a major shift in his personality…"

Melody next to me, she did her best to completely ignore me, and not look my way. She also shifted her body as far away from me as she could without falling off her chair. Her scent shifted with an faint ammonia smell of anxiety with strings of wet muddy scent of sadness. I wanted to comfort her, just tell her, say something, anything, to let her know that I'm not a demon, and I'd never get angry and attack her. Just because I had a wolf, that didn't make me more violent.

The wolf lifted his head again but I shut that door, not wanting to urge on another near Change again, not with Melody sitting right next to me.

Ms. Hughes passed out handouts. I had missed the instructions she had made, and Melody was talking with Wesley and Karen. I think they had tried to get my attention but seeing as I was unresponsive, they were working without me.

Wesley was human, but the girl next to him, Karen, she wasn't. Not only that, I recognized the warm deep scent that I've come to label between siblings. She was the sister of the guy in my U.S. History class, the horse who wore a hat and sunglasses even though it was against the rules. Her horse scent was different from his, hers was a cool sweet scent, female.

Too much. Too much is going on. I don't want to deal with this.

I closed my eyes and let the classroom drift away, my head laid down on the desk. The handout stuck to my face, it smelled like the copier it had been printed from and Ms. Hughes's hands; they smelled like oil, nail polish and dead skin.

Everything smells.

I could hear the classmates talking over me but nothing was making sense, the heartbeats, the breathing, the sighing.

Everything is loud.

My spine tensed, my toe joints snapped in my shoes. I wanted the forest, the tickling grass, the fluttering trees.

Mrs. Hughes's hand laid on my shoulder, her long fake nails pressed on my skin. "Xon? Do you want to go to the main office? Are you sick?"

I wasn't sick, in fact I was probably more healthy than I had been in my entire life. The wolf in me purged my abilities to get sick, natural immunities came with the werewolf health care package. But if going to the office would get me out of this room, then hell yes.

I nodded and slowly lifted my head, when I spoke my voice sounded like I was ready to hurl, lower and tightened. "Yes…I want to leave now."

Ms. Hughes looked concerned but said, "Alright, go to the office and lay down. Maybe Mrs. Mitchells will let you call home, but seeing as this is the last period, there's not much point. Sure you can't just hang on until the final bell?"

I didn't even want to try. I wanted to leave, I had to get out of this building. I stood up, shaking my head and picked up my book bag. I wanted fresh air, skies, grass, trees. The concrete, the tile floor, the walls all around me, the sickening meaty stench of humans, all of it was driving me mad.

I headed towards the front door when I smelled blood, rushing straight into my nostrils by a gush of cooled air from a vent. Unlike how human skin smelled like unclean meat, the smell of blood was intoxicating, like the scent of food to a starving man, like the scent of honey to a honey bear.

I had to have it.

The Change clutched my stomach and it shifted, jerked. I lifted my shirt to bare my abdomen and saw the skin rolling and bulging, my ribcage made a cracking sound and my spine bent forward. I dropped my shirt and covered my nose, but the vent on the ceiling blew cool air toward me, the smell of human blood riding on it. Like a bug attracted to glowing light, I turned around and followed the smell down the hallway. My eyesight enhanced. I could see the individual flecks of paint on the walls, the threads making up the banners of the school organizations hanging from the ceiling, the pixels of skin of the sports teams photographs in the trophy cabinet to the side. The colors were more extreme, brighter and vivid.

I followed the smell to the main office and looked inside through the glass cutout on the door. It was a kid sitting on the bench against the wall across from the desk. He had a massive nosebleed, coming down his mouth and chin, deep red sparkling blood. He was overweight; his whole body must be full of blood. If I could just taste some then-

"Hey, Xon, are you going in or not? You're in the way."

I turned around and faced Zaheed Mohammed, my friend who had rejected me earlier today.

He stared at me and paled, his sandy skin color turning dank yellow. "Jesus, Xon, what's up with your eyes? They're yellow…"

Shit, my eyes are still in wolf form!

I closed them and thought hard about being human, chasing back the smell of blood and the want to eat, to feast. I visualized my own eyes, light brown and concentrated on it until I felt a sharp prick. I opened my eyes and I could tell from the dimmer colors and the lesser focus on things far away and small, that my eyes were back to normal. Even so, I could tell my vision was much better than before I had become a werewolf, I could see sharper, crisper.

Zaheed stepped back several times, and swallowed hard. His scent flooded so strong with the scent of piss, it was enough to make my eyes water. Still, I blinked it away and fixed my shoulders. I needed to set some things straight.

I said, "Zaheed, I know I'm a werewolf now, but that's literally the only thing that's changed about me. I'm still the same person."

Zaheed laughed hollowly. "Oh, right, the same person? You're not human anymore, so how are you still my friend? Your eyes changing are just the start. Claws, fangs, super strength. What happens if I piss you off, huh? You can rip my arm off no problem."

My lips tightened for a moment. "Zaheed, that's insane. As a human, have I ever tried to attack you when I get angry? I took taekwondo for a year, remember? I know how to control my emotions."

Zaheed shot back. "Yeah, as a human! Now with a wolf, you won't have that control anymore! You're nothing more than an animal in human skin!"

In the shocked silence after that, the door opened behind me.

Mrs. Mitchells peered at us, "Boys, why are you standing in front of the door? Do you need something? Otherwise go back to class."

I lied, looking up at the ceiling and my fingers wrapped around each other. "Mom is picking me up, she's outside. I was coming to say I was signing out."

Mrs. Mitchells frowned. "You know she has to come inside and sign you out. Hey! Get back here!"

I ran out the door and dashed down the steps. I dropped my bag, picking up the pace. A hand grabbed the back of my collar and heaved me back. It was like getting a noose snatched up around my windpipe and I gagged from the strength of the grip.

The hand whirled me around and it belonged to the Chemistry teacher at my school, Mr. Richard Forrest, one of the shifter faculty members and the Dominion of Lakeside Village. He was tall, just underneath my six foot, his body thick and bulging with a beer belly, he had a gravelly voice, a hot temper and no patience. He was known for being a bald, grumpy old man and quick to give detention.

He stared at me with beady eyes from under brown bushy eyebrows. His eyes were black, his pupils and irises merged into one dark abyss. "Where you heading off to so fast Mr. Reeves? Maybe you didn't notice, but class is still in session. So get your book bag and get back inside."

Even though I knew before Changing that Mr. Forrest was a shifter, now I could tell because he *smelled* inhuman. His base scent smelled very pungent, harsh, ragged, like he was pure wildness on the inside. Like an aggressive strong animal stuffed behind the thin human skin. I didn't know what animal he shifted into but there was something about Mr. Forrest, his incredibly strong grip, the hard stare of his solid black eyes, I knew this guy was no joke. The wolf inside of me was backing away, like I instinctively should be afraid of him. But *why?*

I rubbed my neck, my collar had abraded my skin and at my touch the pain went away. I thought werewolves were supposed to be the strongest shifter. The strength in Mr.

Forrest's hand had been unlike anything I had ever felt in my life.

I asked, "W-what are you?"

Mr. Forrest's eyes narrowed as a tiny red dot burst into life in the black expanse of his pupils, bright like hot acid. "I will not repeat myself Mr. Reeves. Get your shit and get back to class. I know how new wolves are, you're antsy and the forest calls to you, calls you to go running to it but rules are rules and the rules say school ain't over just yet. Get inside, *now*."

That last *now* was guttural and gruff, a sound so rough and raspy that human vocals shouldn't be capable of sounding like that. His nose wrinkled back, his lips turned black and shriveled up as he bared thick fangs, they were so large in his human mouth that it should have been cartoonish but there was nothing funny about it. His fangs were sharp and jagged, like machetes carved out of mountains.

Fear shot down my spine and I barely managed not to straight out piss my pants. Still, I couldn't stop my legs from trembling, from how my body began to shake, sweat pouring down my tingled skin. My wolf scrambled backwards like he wanted to run and hide behind my spine. So I grabbed my book bag and rushed back into the building.

I didn't want to go to class after just walking out, nor did I want to see Melody so I went to the library instead.

The librarian looked up to see me and frowned. "Shouldn't you be in class?"

"I got permission." I lied, averting my eyes and my foot scuffed the carpeted floor.

The librarian tilted his head, St. Croix stamped on his staff id.

He said, "You're looking a little heated up. You should go see the guidance counselor. You know which one I mean."

I did know who he meant. There were two guidance counselors at our school, one for humans the other for shifters. It wasn't discrimination but if a student shifter is having problems that humans cannot have then only an adult shifter would be able to help.

I sighed but I knew St. Croix, he wouldn't just let me laze around in the library for the remaining thirty minutes of class. I went to the counseling office and opened the door; the bell attached to the doorknob jingled.

It was a medium-sized room with several arm chairs, a table stacked with magazines, the walls plastered with posters reading encouraging slogans like, *If you can believe, you can achieve* and *shifters are humans too!* That last one was on a door that had been covered with little sticker paw prints of different types of animals, so there was no doubt who was behind that door.

A man sitting at the desk by the door, he looked up, saw me then pointed at the animal-themed door without saying anything, looking into my eyes then away. I sighed again and walked over. The name card on the door read Jayanti Sher.

"Come in," said a woman's voice before I could even knock. I didn't have to be freaked, she definitely heard me the moment I came in.

I opened the door; the office was little more than a closet. A short desk was shoved against the far wall with a rolling chair behind it and two chairs in front, the tiny plastic ones for little kids because a full-sized chair wouldn't fit in this cramped space.

I stepped back as my wolf reacted with bared teeth and raised hackles. Without any windows, there was no sight of trees or clouds, there wasn't even a vent so no fresh air. It was a hell dimension with no access to nature.

The woman at the desk smiled. "Ah. Jaxon Reeves. I knew you'd be showing up soon, a brand new wolf. You entered my register this morning. I keep requesting an office with a window as shifters don't like to be confined but anyway." She shrugged and then stood up. "Let's move outside, shall we?"

As she walked towards me, I took in her smell. Her base scent, hot, humid, jungle. The wolf labeled it. Tiger. My mouth went dry. She was short, barely came to my mid-chest, but what Ms. Sher lacked in stature she made up for in curves. Toss in her full mouth, large heavily lashed brown eyes, dark gold skin and long straight reddish black hair, Miss Ma'am should be a beauty queen, not stuck in an airless guidance counselor's office.

Taking my eyes off her plentiful assets, I lead the way out of the room.

Ms. Sher closed the door behind her and said to the man, "Finney, I'm taking him outside."

Mr. Finney nodded and turned back to his book. Ms. Sher opened the door and took me right back to the front steps where I had been when Mr. Forrest caught me. I could still smell him, that harsh pungent odor hung in the air, stained on the steps.

Ms. Sher's nostrils flexed and she moved down to the lawn where the air was a little cleaner and after smoothing down her skirt, sat down right there on the grass. I kept my eyes off those golden legs and sat down across from her. A check on my watch revealed there was little under twenty minutes of class left and honestly, I'd rather spend Psychology out here with a beautiful woman than inside with my former girlfriend and a teacher who smelled like nail polish and hair spray.

She started. "So Jaxon."

"Xon." I said. "People only call me Jaxon when they're mad at me. If we're cool, everyone calls me Xon."

She smiled, her brown eyes glowed with a sudden green glint, like emerald light flashed over her irises. "Xon then. And you can call me Jayanti. So, I can tell you are newly Changed. May I ask the situation that took you from your birth state?"

I kept looking in her eyes, hoping to see her telltale again. "I don't really like to talk about it, but a werewolf attacked me, he tried to kill me. Before I could die, the Change took over and healed me. It happened the last week of summer break, so five days later I'm at school like nothing happened."

"But something did happen Xon," said Jayanti. She was looking me straight in the eyes and didn't flinch when my gold spark reflected in her deep black pupils. She didn't pale, she didn't smell afraid or confused. She was a shifter like me and I was a normal person in her eyes. "You've made that wild strange exotic *shift* from one species to the next level, from a human to a higher being. It's intense but-"

I had to cut her off. "A higher being ma'am?"

She smiled. "Jayanti."

"Miss Jayanti." I said. "What do you mean a higher being?"

"We're two-sided." She held up two fingers. "We have this human or skin form." A wave of her hand gestured to her body. "And the fur form."

She held that same hand out to me, and it bubbled, like hot oil when water is dashed in it; her skin wrinkled back and thick fur burst over her hand. Her fingers thickened as silver claws shot out from the beds and her palms turned black and padded. Just like that, sitting on the end of her wrist, was a tiger's massive paw. Her other hand held up her human wrist, which looked like a toothpick dangling on the end, ridiculous and unmatched.

"This form is superior to the human, the one-sided."

The tiger paw wiggled, flexed and like watching a tape rolling backwards. The digits shortened, the pads softened then paled, the fur receded as skin slid over the appendage. Then there was her slim gold-skinned hand just like before. It was as if the shift into a tiger's paw had never happened.

I had stopped breathing at some point and my heart pounded like I had just run a marathon. I had known

Jayanti wasn't human since before I met her. She was the shifter's guidance counselor, she smelled like a jungle and she had the telltale in her eyes but *that*, that right there nailed it all in.

She wasn't human.

And now I'm not human.

Tears burned as I struggled to understand that thought. I didn't know about shifters being *higher* than humans but was she right that I wasn't human at all? She said I made a shift from my birth state, from human to shifter. So if I'm not human...then what am I really?

I don't understand God. The bible doesn't say anything about You creating people with the ability to turn into animals. Does that mean someone else created us? But there is no one else but YOU right? You are the Creator of everything, so how, how is this possible? Am I no longer Your child? You really did abandon me, forsook me the moment I was Changed from human to shifter. Its because You hate me, is that it? I don't get it, God. I don't know what to think anymore.

The bell rang, class was over and it would only take mere moments before this lawn was overrun with the meat-stink of humans.

Jayanti stood up in a smooth flowing motion and brushed off her skirt. "You can come see me anytime Xon and I'll be more than happy to put your fears at ease. Remember, just because you're a shifter, it doesn't mean you're a different person. Consider yourself an *enhanced* version of yourself. See you."

She smiled at me as green light flickered from her irises. She turned and walked into the building.

Students rushed out of the doors, laughing and talking while the buses rattled and heaved up to the sidewalk. The air immediately began to stink and I stood up, getting my book bag. I turned to get to my bus and a girl stepped right in front of me, I nearly tripped over her.

I didn't know this girl's name, though I recognized her from the halls. She always had her long hair in a different style of braids. Now she was full on confronting me when before she never looked my way. She spoke quietly enough that I knew no one else around could hear but what she said made me freeze.

"So, you're one of us now. When did that happen? Last I checked, you were human."

I swallowed and I took in her smell. She smelled completely different from the rest of the humans at my school. I had learned that humans smelled like meat, unclean meat really, as if they were a dead deer or pig that had been left in mud for too long, off-putting food. This girl smelled like a sweet musky odor, like a woman who's been rolling in rose petals and honey. It was attractive and it meant one thing. She wasn't human either.

My throat was dry. "Did you smell that?"

"And saw it." She said. "You're twitchy, eyes flicking every which place. Your nose is wild, flexing and inhaling and your fingers are tense. You're a cub waiting to fling yourself out of your human skin and run for the forest. It's all over you kid, freshly Changed and can't even think straight. So, when?"

Her irises were a mysterious shade of bright hazel, like honey. Her black pupils shined with the gold spark in the depths, her wolf staring out at mine. My wolf jolted back and forth, alternating between baring his teeth and ducking his head down, like he couldn't decide between aggressive or submissive. His confusion had my skin bristling hot and my breath was cold, my throat tightened.

I whispered, "Who are you?"

"The name is Skylark Cloud." She held out a hand. "Call me Sky, not Lark. And your name?"

I clumsily shook her hand. My hold was weak and sweaty, her grip was steel-tight, easily able to crush bone. My stomach jumped and I couldn't speak as my wolf's hackles raised and he slumped backwards, tail tucked between his thighs. He didn't know what to make of her, a lady wolf. She wasn't weak or innocent, but had sought me out and confronted me. So was she an enemy or was she a friend?

Sky's eyes went wide. "Why are you so scared of me? Was it a woman who Changed you? I mean, I'm short, like a foot shorter than you. I'm not a threat. Relax, okay, jeez. Just wait until Shane sees you. Hell, he'll beat you up just for the joy of it."

My throat tightened even more, until my voice croaked like a bullfrog. "S-Shane? Who's Shane? Is he...like us?"

Saying *us* was like swallowing something nasty. Us. As in not human. Us. Not just me, not just her, but Shane, and the others. More than one. I'm not insane. It happened. It's real.

Sky crossed her arms. "Man you are one shaken up pup. We usually meet up at the playground in Lakeview Park. You can come with me, I was on my way. Come on."

Lakeview Park was in walking distance from the high school but just about everything in Lakeside Village was in walking distance.

Sky didn't talk so neither did I as I walked behind her. I kept my eyes away from her swaying hips, unsure if she would be able to tell if I was staring or not.

The park was over a small incline then settled into a tiny valley, like God had pressed his thumb into the ground. The developers had paved the three hills down into the park, which skateboarders used to ramp off into the sky like they were birds with wheels. With the trees that surrounded the valley and the tall grasses, the wolf stopped pacing inside, stopped trying to chase me off into the forest to be away from the school and the airless hallways and the stink of humans.

Because school had only just let out, the playground was mostly deserted. There was an older couple sitting on the bench, the man reading a newspaper and the woman engrossed in a hardcover book. Grouped at the monkey gym were three other boys; I didn't know any of them. Sky jumped from the top of the stairs to land at the bottom of the valley, easily thirty steps. Then she turned and looked up at me. She didn't speak and she didn't have to.

My wolf's hindquarters lowered, tensing. He was being challenged, he liked it and he wanted to do it too. I ignored him and walked down each step.

Sky was already at the monkey gym, leaving me to walk over by myself. As I walked, I took note of the other three. I could already guess who Shane had to be. He was tall, two inches taller than me and muscular. His skin tanned from the sun, his head graced with wavy blond hair and his eyes were bright sky blue. Right in the midst of his black pupils burned the wolf spark, the gold color shining brighter than sunshine.

The other boy was Hispanic with straight black hair, his skin was colored lightly toasted brown and he was on the chubby side. He immediately gave me a kind smile and his wolf spark glowed like a miniature star in the blackness of his pupils.

And the last boy, who was the smallest, his head topped with brightly dyed neon green hair. There was a small smile on his face but he was sporting a black eye, the skin mottled purple and drying blood from a cut under his eye spotted his skin. Yet even as I stared, the cut was sealing together, the purple color fading to a dark blue then paler. After about three seconds, the green-boy's skin was clear and peachy-colored again. He used his finger to pick off the dried blood, revealing perfectly healed skin underneath.

The first boy chuckled. "You look like you have never seen accelerated healing before."

"He's very new," said Sky. "Like yesterday or something new. Right?"

I shrugged, scuffing my sneaker into the colored rocks. The gravel was pink, blue, green and yellow. It looked blinding. It looked like vomit. My stomach pitched and I looked up again.

The other boy held his hand out but lowered it when I jerked back. "My name is Javier Eduardo de Calderón Méndez, you can call me Javier. What is your name?"

His voice was accented and he spoke very proper English, like he had studied it in formal education. Add in his pressed black slacks, white collared shirt and the tie tucked under his chin, he dressed for success, like school was his profession.

"Jaxon Reeves." I got the words out around my heart beating in my mouth. "Everyone calls me Xon it sounds like Zon but you spell it with an X."

I had thought he was going to attack me, when he lifted his hand like that. As a human, I wouldn't have been scared, he wanted to shake hands, it was obvious. But my wolf took it as an aggressive gesture and flinched, which made *me* flinch.

The older white boy, no doubt Shane, snorted then stood up off the ladder. "Xon huh? So when were you Changed new kid?"

He was over six-feet and had the heavy muscles at the chest and arms of someone who lived and breathed at the gym. I now saw the small blood stain on his right knuckles and knew where the other kid got his black eye from.

He's not to be messed with. He's the leader and I'm a nobody.

I stepped back, my wolf huddled, his tail wrapped around his leg, ears lowered. My knees slightly bent, my shoulders hunched towards my ears. All body language so he'd know I wasn't a threat. My tongue twisted, I couldn't speak.

Sky nudged me, saying, "Relax. Answer the question, he's not going to hurt you."

"I might," said Shane with a drawling lazy tone, his half-smile bared a canine sliding into a fang, his blue eyes tinged olive. In his pupils the wolf spark flashed. "He's pissing me off."

I swallowed hard then said, "The last week of summer break. Five days ago to be exact."

"And here you are on the first day of school." The green-haired boy laughed. "I can't believe you came to school like nothing happened. I'd be hiding in my closet for at least a month. I'm Connor Hawkins, by the way."

He laughed again but a strange scent was coming off his body that didn't match. He had a musky scent, but it wasn't as heady and thick like how Shane smelled, or even me. It was softer and wispy, young. A pup. Over that though…it was dank, heavy. My wolf sniffed then supplied me the information. It was *unhappiness*. Even though Connor was laughing and smiling, he was sad. The strange thing was the fact the sad smell was stamped on Connor's skin, like a personal scent.

How can someone be so sad that the scent stains their skin?

Shane crossed his arms, the muscles that pressed against his shirt sleeves made me back up again. He smiled, his blue eyes satisfied. He knew he had intimidated me and liked it. Something small and hard in my gut burned.

He said, "Shane Armstrong and I'm Changed too, three years ago. Only Javier here isn't."

"Isn't what?"

"Changed." Javier smiled. "I am a natural wolf." He saw my blank look. "It means I was born a werewolf. I have never been human. So if you were bitten, then what happened after that?"

I said, "I don't remember much…there was so much pain."

Sky's brow crinkled. "If it was only a bite, then there's some pain but not enough to black out your memories."

"I wasn't just bitten." I explained. "Rocky tried to kill me. He ripped my insides out, he tore my arm off, broke my collarbone. I passed out after the Change, I slept the rest of Friday and most of Saturday. So that's why I don't remember a lot."

Javier watched me carefully. "This Rocky…what happened to him?"

I shrugged. "I don't know. I didn't see him again so I'm sure they locked him up or punished him somehow."

"Oh there he is!" Connor called, making me jump. He waved his arm. "Here comes Leo. What took him so long, fool."

I turned in time to see a very long boy loping down the steps, he took them five at a time. His legs looked like stilts, his arms were just as long, his shoulders broad but thin, his chest sunken in, his neck so frail like I could break it with just a flick of my finger. He was stretched out and pulled thin. It was the wolf from my first class. The same guy who kept staring at me, he was the first wolf I had encountered.

"That's Leonard Dawson, call him Leo," said Sky.

As he walked, the wolf stalking toward us, I stumbled backwards and I bumped into Shane, stepping on his shoes. He cursed and pain slammed into the back of my head, I hit the gravel before I realized he had punched me. I clasped my head, blood coursing over my fingers and down my neck. Yellow and white burst in my eyes, my skull throbbed and under my hand the broken plate cracked.

He fractured my skull. One hit. Jesus Christ, that's strong! If I hit him back, maybe I could break his jaw with one hit.

"God, really Shane?" Sky protested. "He's new! He didn't mean to!"

"Fuck off Sky, these are limited edition Air Force 1's! He's lucky I don't do worse!"

Worse came as Shane kicked me in the ribs with a force like his sneakers were a jet-propelled wrecking ball. The bones snapped like toothpicks, crumpling into my lungs. I coughed up blood and curled into a ball, placing my arms over my head to try and protect it, pulling my knees to my chest to cover those organs. I knew very well how a wolf could tear open my chest cavity and bare my insides to the air. It was a sensation I never wanted to feel again.

"That's enough dammit!" Over my head I heard scuffling, sounded like Sky pushed Shane back.

I didn't know, I kept my eyes closed and focused inwards.

Heal. Heal. Heal.

My wolf was shaking and making low whines. My legs twitched with the idea to run but I didn't dare because Shane would definitely chase me and hurt me worse. Someone laid on top of me, I jerked to escape.

Javier said softly in my ear, "It is me Xon. I am healing you, feel it?"

A warmth seeped through my body, more than the hottest setting on a blow-dryer. Boiling heat coiled through my veins, heading straight for where it hurt the most. My ribs crunched back into place, my skull stitched together and I was okay, I was better.

Javier stood up then brought me to my feet with one hand. I was six-feet and two hundred pounds. Javier wasn't even five-five and overweight. It was the wolf in him that let him do that.

Dried blood crusted on the back of my head, my neck and staining my shirt. There was some blood dotting my chest from where I coughed it up. Connor ducked underneath the monkey bars, crouched down in a ball. Leo was behind me, he hadn't gotten too close when Shane attacked me.

Shane stood over by the swings, looking irritated and bored at the same time. Sky stood nearby me and her fingers were strapped with large ebony claws, lethal stiletto blades slicing from her nail beds. Yet her hands were small and the fingers looked dainty, her wrist thin. Compared to the giant Wolverine-style claws braced at the tips of her fingers, it looked unreal.

It was quiet for a moment, the air was shimmering, heated with blood and sweat. I didn't know if I should run, hide or try and apologize to Shane.

Instead I looked at Javier. "How did you do that?"

Javier gave a small smile. "What I did is called the heat transfer, or simply the heat. The heat is a near magical transferring of healing ability from one wolf to another. Each wolf has his or her own heat, it is how we heal ourselves so quickly. But if a wolf is having trouble healing, then another wolf can transfer their heat over, helping that wolf heal. So that is what I did for you Xon. Sky, you can relax now."

Sky stood up straighter, her head lifted and her shoulders relaxed. Her claws seeped backwards and turned pale pink and settled on her fingers as normal fingernails. If I hadn't seen it, I would have never thought those nails could become talons.

Wow...we really aren't human. Javier used magic to heal me, Sky can grow claws at will, Shane is incredibly strong. An entire new world has opened up before me and in this world... where is God? Where are You in this?

Leo stepped up and placed a hand on Sky's shoulder. She was still glaring over at Shane, Leo snapped his fingers in her face. She blinked and turned away. Sky looked at me and my stomach clutched. Her eyes weren't that hazel color anymore, now they were a crystal silver, so pale she looked like should have been blind but with the intensity of her gaze, it was more like she was looking right through me. Then she slowly lowered then raised her eyelashes. Her eyes were hazel again.

Whoa... A slow breath sighed out between my teeth. *I thought Jayanti Sher's eyes were beautiful...Sky is on a whole new level.*

Shane was coming back. I stepped backwards again and my spine stiffened. I wanted to run but at the same time with the others here, maybe I didn't have to run. Sky could fend off Shane by herself, so what happens if we all stood up together? Shane was the leader for the clear fact that he was the strongest, I had learned that already. If Sky can fend him off, then add in me and the other three, we could all take Shane together, couldn't we?

Shane strolled over, not looking worried or upset or that he had attacked me. He went and leaned against the ladder of the slide, arms and ankles crossed. "So you're back Leo. Why were you late?"

Leo didn't respond, his body didn't shift, he didn't blink or smile, his scent was the thick headiness of a male wolf. His emotional scent was faint ammonia, that was anxiety and a burnt dry whiff…irritation.

Sky sighed. "He's not going to talk Shane. He's mute, leave him alone."

Shane flicked Leo's shoulder, he moved to the side. "Hey, I'm talking to you. Why were you late showing up today? Speak up, I can't hear you."

Leo walked away to stand over by Connor by the monkey gym, yet he didn't turn his back on Shane, he walked backwards to keep Shane in his sight the entire time.

My phone's alarm beeped, it was 4:15pm. At this time I would be home from the bus and getting started on my homework. Mom got home by 5:30pm and if she saw that I wasn't working on my homework or that I wasn't even home she'd start breathing fire the moment she saw me.

I said, "I have to get home. See you tomorrow…I guess."

"Definitely," said Javier with a nice smile, waving.

Connor lifted two fingers in the peace sign.

Leo gave me a nod.

Sky said, "Take care of yourself Xon. Oh, first, let's share cell numbers."

I handed over my phone and she put in several contacts. While she did it, I kept one eye on Shane.

Shane didn't say anything, watched me with a set hard look in his eyes that contrasted to the pleased smirk on his mouth. His scent was the heady male wolf, orange citrus of amusement and even a sharp oily scent, confidence. He had beat me, he had dominated me, he knew it and he liked it.

Sky handed me back my phone and I picked up my book bag from the ground, it was dusty, had rocks and a few droplets of blood on it. I slung it over my shoulder and backed away without taking my eyes off Shane like Leo did. I walked backwards all the way back to the steps before turning and running up. This time I naturally bounded to take ten steps at once, I blinked and I was at the top. I looked back, Shane had grabbed Connor and was giving him a hard noogie, his arm around Connor's neck looked like the muscle of a boa constrictor. Connor's blue face attested to it. Sky was shouting at Shane again.

What a weird group of people...but they're all wolves, like me. They know what I've been through and Javier even used like magic on me. I didn't know werewolves had magic, I didn't even know you could be born a werewolf, a natural wolf. I knew wolves were strong...but Shane...he fractured my skull with one punch and broke my ribs with one kick. It's the first day of school and all of this drama already!

I slowly walked home, everything that had gone on whirling about in my head. When I got into my bedroom, I tossed my book bag to the floor, dropped onto the bed and the black curtain of sleep fell over my mind as my face hit the pillows.
* * *

A shrill scream cut into my mind, like getting a fistful of glass thrown into my ears. I sat up straight and saw Mom standing in the doorway of my bedroom, her expression strained with horror.

"What?" I stood up, going to her. "What's wrong? Why are you screaming like that?"

"Ja-Jaxon." Her voice was weak and shaking. "You...you're covered in blood."

Oh yeah. I never even cleaned up.

I touched the back of my head. My wound was healed but dried blood was sticking to my skin, with crusts on my neck and my shirt.

"I got in a fight." I said, rolling my shoulders at the itchiness. I pulled my shirt off and used it to rub at the back of my head and neck, rubbing the reddish black flakes off my skin. "But I'm fine now."

My mother, Kyra Melissa Reeves, stared at me with her solid brown eyes as if she had never seen me before.

"What?" She whispered. "A fight? You? Jaxon, what do you mean you got in a fight? Since when are you violent? Yes, you took taekwondo during your freshman year but-"

I interrupted, "It wasn't a *real* fight, I met some guy and he got a little too rough. It looks really bad because it's a head wound, it bled a lot but it's not serious. I'm fine, really. See?" I knelt in front of her and bowed my head, using my hand to brush away more flakes. "See? I'm fine."

Mom's soft hand touched my scalp. Her voice was still quiet and horrified. "Jaxon...you're *more* than fine...you're not even injured. There's not a bruise or a scar or anything like you've been hit at all." Her voice hardened and her tipped nails nicked my skin. "Are you telling me the blood on your shirt and skin wasn't your blood? What did you do to the other boy, you head-butted him?"

Her voice rose, gone was the concern and fear, now replaced suspicion and anger.

"You don't lie to me Jaxon William Reeves. What happened at school today? Don't think I don't know you skipped school early. I got a call from your teacher that you said you were sick and left her class thirty minutes early, then you lied to the receptionist I was picking you up and waiting outside. Since when are you a liar Jaxon Reeves? Now you say that you got in a fight? So where did you go? You went somewhere to fight? Since when are you into fighting? I will tell your father about this. Now do your homework and you can forget dinner tonight."

She slapped my head away from her, I sat back and watched as she slammed out of the room. I sighed and rubbed my head, more dried crusts crumpled onto my shoulders. I stood up, tossed my bloodied shirt into the trash and took a shower. When I came out, my father was sitting in my desk chair, examining the evidence.

He glanced up as I walked in, a towel hitched around my waist. He turned away by swiveling in the chair so his back was towards me. Just the fact he didn't even leave to let me get dressed told me I wasn't going to sneak out of a lecture.

Jackson Grant Reeves didn't normally lecture me in the way Mom did, his version of dealing with me when I got into trouble was a laidback calm conversation. It wasn't Dad who gave me the beatings growing up, that's for sure.

Can I still get beatings now? I've felt how strong some shifters are, Mr. Forrest and Shane for starters. Mom is a human being, can her hitting me even compare in pain to them?

Sighing, I pulled on sweatpants and a tank top. I sat on my bed, gearing up for the lecture.

I said, "I'm dressed."

Dad swiveled back in the chair and held up the bloodstained shirt. "Explain this Jaxon William Reeves, and in a way that makes sense." His dark molded face was held firm.

Full name, I'm really in trouble. And his expression doesn't look good either.

I didn't want to lie, in fact, I knew I had to lie but I sucked at lying. My body gave me away every time, licking or picking my lips, can't make eye contact and I shift my weight from foot to foot. Dead giveaways and just about everyone who knows me knows them. So even though I don't like to lie I can't anyway. But what the hell could I say?

Well Dad, I met the group of werewolves at my school and their leader beat me up. Yeah, that'll go over real well. He was worried enough about me already and if I tell him that I got into a fight with another shifter my first day, he'll flip his shit. No, its best I don't tell him, for his sake.

Dad's dark brown eyes narrowed just a centimeter. "Jaxon, I'm waiting on an answer. I won't ask you again."

I bit my lip then said, "I told Mom already. Didn't she tell you?"

Dad wasn't put off. "I've spoken with your mother, yes. Now I'm talking to you."

Dammit.

I rolled my eyes up to the ceiling, then to the wall my bed was pressed against. A huge poster of Toni Jaa graced it right above my headboard. His head bowed, black hair matted with sweat, a twisted white headband tied tightly around his forehead. His arms held out and the fists touching, wrapped with tightly knotted rope over the knuckles and palms, covering his wrists. With his tensed body and the water running down his chest, I thought it was a very powerful statement, a fighter at rest but ready to lash out any second.

That brought to mind what happened at the park. Shane.

My jaw gritted and bunched; my gums itched, threatening fangs. My hands curled into fists and claws pricked into my palms.

Dad spoke quietly, as if not to encourage my obvious anger. "Who made you so angry Xon? Did you get in a fight with someone?"

I let out a hollow laugh. "Oh man…you couldn't even call it a fight. I got my ass handed to me."

I looked over at Dad, seeing the worry on his face. The anger seeped away, the beginnings of the Change retreated.

I said, "Listen, it's not that serious. I met this guy and we got a little rough. I ended up hurting my head and it bled a lot but I'm fine, I'm better. Mom overacted, she thought I was like in a knockdown drag-out fight or something. It really wasn't that serious."

Dad sighed and ducked his head down, his large blocky fingers rubbed at the stubble growing on his large shiny dome. "Your mother told me that you don't have a scratch on you. And I also saw you just now, your body condition doesn't match the blood on your shirt. You said he got rough, but how much of this blood isn't yours?"

"It's all mine." I said. "I didn't hit him, he hit me. And hey, relax."

I said it quickly as Dad stood up in one movement. Dad was six-two, had fifty pounds over me in thick muscle. When he moved so fast it always made me feel like he was ready to kill something, especially since he was normally so calm and laidback.

I said, "I provoked him so it's really my fault."

Dad blinked then looked at me like I had turned into some stranger, his facial expression incredulous.

"Say what? Xon, is that what I've taught you about confrontations and violence? I don't give a damn who started it, you don't let someone hit you. And if you said you didn't hit him, then that means you said something that bothered him, right? That doesn't give him license to hit you so hard you bled like a pint. Remember Xon, the Lord our God says in Proverbs 3:31, *do not envy a violent man or choose any of his ways*."

"It wasn't a pint." I said, knowing it was a lame comeback but I didn't have anything else to say.

Dad was right, of course he was. But he's only right...because he's human. As a wolf, I knew what went down and I can't explain it. When I stepped on Shane's shoes, it wasn't really because they were expensive. It was because I was in his space, my body on his crossed boundaries. He hit me to get me off him then to make sure I knew my lesson, he kicked me. It hurt, I bled and broke bones but I got it. Shane was the leader, period. That small hardness in my gut burned again, hot enough like I had swallowed a blazing coal. My wolf shifted, lifting his head with ears pricked.

Dad spoke quieter this time. "Whatever happened Xon, I can tell you're not willing to share. Fine. Don't come home like this again. You scared the shit out of your mother. You've got detention tomorrow, so make sure you serve it. I also don't want to hear you've been cutting class again either, or lying. The semester just started Xon and I don't like where it's going already. You hear me?" Then he sighed and rubbed his brow. "Maybe we let you go back to school too soon. We can keep you out for another week or so, and maybe you'd want to see someone, to talk to I mean."

I shook my head. "No, I don't want to get behind in school. And I don't need a therapist, I'm figuring it out on my own."

Dad didn't look convinced. "Jaxon…"

"I'm fine Dad, really." I looked at him with a firm nod. "I get it, I'm sorry. I'll do better, I promise. No more fights or missing class or anything. I promise."

"I don't want promises Xon." He opened the door and looked back at me. "Words are only as strong as the actions that go with them, understand? You can promise and apologize all you want but if your behavior doesn't match up then they're useless. Xon, remember what God says on keeping your word. Numbers 30:2, *if a man makes a vow to the Lord, or swears an oath to bind himself by some agreement, he shall not break his word; he shall do according to all that proceeds out of his mouth.* You understand? You say something then you need to do it. Honor your words Xon."

"I know Dad." I said. "I know and I'll do it."

He's raised me with those words. His talks always included a little preaching and I appreciated it. Yet now that I'm not human, does a book for humans even apply to me anymore? I couldn't say that to Dad; he'd totally lose it if I told him that because I'm a werewolf I'm not God's child.

Dad gave me a lazy two-fingered salute then left, closing the door behind him, then he cracked it and said, "Your mother decided you can't have dinner, but if you do your homework I'll bring up something later. Don't tell her though."

The door closed again.

I got my book bag, sat at my desk and realized I hadn't written down a single homework assignment from any of my classes; in fact I had ditched Ms. Hughes' Psychology before class really started. Mom will flip all over again when I told her I didn't have my homework assignments.

I sighed, kicked the book bag away from me and went to lounge in my beanbag chair by the window. I curled up and closed my eyes. The wolf wrapped himself into a ball too, fur brushing underneath my skin, my tail pulled over my hindquarters, my ears cuddling against my scalp. I smelled the forest, heard the chirping and chittering of prey. What the wolf wanted more than anything was to run away, just run hard and fast, feel the power rushing through him, the strength of his bite and hear the song of his howl.

I just want to be human again.

2

August 7th
Thursday

I spent the entire night in the beanbag chair and woke up to the stringent ringing of my alarm. A covered dinner plate was on the desk, I could smell green beans, hamburger and rice from across the room. I stood up and ate it ice cold. I took another shower. Dressed in jeans, a blue t-shirt featuring Garfield gorging on lasagna and wearing black Converse Weapons on my feet, I was ready.

Book bag over my shoulder, I headed downstairs, one hand brushing my hair with a short hard bristle brush. I didn't have a lot of it, I kept it shaved rather close but it would still look nappy if I didn't take care of it.

Dad stood at the door adjusting his shoes, Mom was already gone by the time I got up for the day. He looked at me as I came down, his brows cinched over his stark eyes.

"No more fighting, right Xon?"

"Right Dad." I smiled at him even as my wolf whined. Who knew if Shane would keep his hands to himself.

Dad looked suspicious as his eyes narrowed but said, "Okay, I'm trusting you. Have a good day son."

He patted my shoulder and we left together. The bus picked me up at the stop sign down the street, so I waved and jogged there. Two other guys were picked up at that spot, Jarrod Fletcher and Gavin Houston. I shared Psychology with Jarrod but we never talked that much.

Jarrod leaned against the stop sign. He had very pale green eyes, ghost-white skin and ginger-colored hair. Gavin's head was down as he played on his Vita, like always, and he rarely made eye contact. This time though, they both looked at me.

"What?" I asked but my voice had an extra rough quality to it, a growl, inhuman.

Jarrod's thin orangey brows pulled together. "You totally walked out of class yesterday."

"I was sick." I lied, looking to the side and rested my weight on my right foot then my left. It was true that I *felt* sick but physically I was perfectly healthy, the wolf in me made sure of that.

Gavin snorted and went back to his game, muttering out the side of his mouth, "Phony."

I ignored him and cocked my head to the side.

I said, "The bus is coming."

Jarrod frowned and checked his phone. "Nah, the bus doesn't come for another five minutes. It'll never arrive early, Mrs. Dorris is slow. She'll probably be late."

I bit my tongue before I said *the bus is coming because I can hear it coming.* Jarrod was right, it would be about five minutes before the bus pulled up, but I could hear the engine grinding, the wheeze of the brakes and even the collective shouts and screams of the passengers. I could hear it from so far away because it was so loud. If I focused really hard, I could probably start listening to sounds inside of the houses lining the sidewalk.

I closed my eyes and realized I could hear small things too. Gavin's breathing, it was abnormal. He took in a breath, it held for several tight seconds before relaxing. His heartbeat too was irregular, it skipped beats or stopped for a half second before continuing. Now I knew why he never took part in gym or physical activities, always playing his Vita instead. He was sick, I couldn't tell why or what was causing it. I took a slow inhale. His scent, that meat-stink of human was altered, there was a mouthy sour smell to it, like spoiled milk. He smelled like sick prey, like infected meat.

I covered my mouth as my eyes flashed open and backed up, turning away. Gavin and Jarrod were staring at me like I had done something insane.

I looked away again but now that I had Gavin's scent logged, I focused on Jarrod next. He did *not* have the meat-smell of humans. I slowly turned to look at him again and shifted through his scent while I stared at his eyes, watching for the telltale.

"It's not in my eyes." He said that just as I accessed his base scent, his shifter scent. Like grass and warm earth, like hot running blood and rapid breathing. He smelled like real prey, like something my wolf wanted to chase, to tackle and catch that elusive pulse between my teeth until it ran quiet.

Jarrod actually smirked at me. "I'm a Cervidae, a white-tailed deer. See?" He turned his hand over and revealed a white irregular triangular mark on his palm. "Not every shifter's telltale is in their eyes."

The bus rumbled up from around the corner and coughed to a stop at the sidewalk, then the doors wheezed open. Gavin got on the bus, not saying anything or looking back.

Jarrod still had that strange smile on his face and he got on the bus and I did too.

I stumbled backwards, my nostrils flared. The bus smelled like meat-stink, sweat and dried gum.

Mrs. Dorris grumbled, "Sit down. I can't sit here all day."

I slumped onto the closest seat next to me and scooted to the window, wanting to suck in clean air. I jerked it down as far as it would go, knowing if I forced it I'd break the metal hinges. By the time the bus had heaved to a stop at the school's front sidewalk, I had a wicked headache from the sensory download. My nose had cataloged all the kids on my bus and my wolf logged it to memory. If I ever smelled any of those scents again, I'd know exactly who it was even if I didn't know what they looked like.

All I wanted was some fresh air, the forest, the grass, anything but being in a metal rocket with grinding gears and coughing breaks. I tumbled down the steps then I leaned against a tree and took in heavy breaths. The bell rang and I ignored it, sitting down at the base of the tree, eyes still closed. I wrapped my arms over my head and placed my face on my knees. My scent swept in and wrapped around me like a comforting blanket, calming, safe, familiar.

Dear God...are You even listening to me anymore? I keep talking to You and it's like You're ignoring me. I was staring at Gavin like he was food, like he was prey, and same with Jarrod. That's NOT human. If I'm not human, if I'm really something else, is that why You won't talk to me? Does being a shifter mean I can't be Your child anymore?

A hand touched my shoulder and I jerked back, inhaling. Heady, musky, wolf. Sunshine and lemons. I opened my eyes and saw Leo from yesterday looming over me, he had to be about six-three. His face was blank, expressionless, like he wasn't feeling anything. But his scent *had* emotions to it, he smelled faintly like piss, nervousness, and a fruity scent of curiosity. I never actually got introduced to Leo. All I knew was that he was really tall and apparently mute.

When my eyes met his, the golden spark in his pupils winked at me, his wolf acknowledging mine. Leo tilted his head at me then walked away, stopped and looked over his shoulder, then lifted his chin at me again. Clearly I was to follow him.

I sighed and stood up, adjusting my book bag over my shoulder. I came with him.

"Where are you taking me?"

Leo didn't answer, didn't shrug or make any motion that he heard me at all. The answer was American Literature with Ms. Cannon, he stepped back to let me in first.

Jeez, I guess friends don't let friends skip class.

Ms. Cannon frowned as we entered. "You're late boys. Hurry up and sit down before I make you go to the office for a tardy slip."

I took my seat and Leo took the seat right next to mine.

Why did he force me to come to class? I just wanted to be alone.

Ms. Cannon was talking but I was watching Leo. He must have felt my gaze because he looked at me. His irises were green, a jade green and the gold spark flickered, his wolf again noticing mine. My wolf lifted his lip, baring a fang. I didn't know Leo or what he wanted or why he made me come to class. Why didn't he leave me alone?

"Jaxon, what is selective omniscience?"

Ms. Cannon moved to stand in between me and Leo, staring down at me. She caught me not paying attention.

I didn't say anything, my mind still on Leo. And how did his wolf notice me like that? How was my wolf able to send a response? I didn't literally *see* with my eyes the interaction, I just sensed it.

Ms. Cannon's brow furrowed. "Jaxon Reeves, I asked you a question."

I looked at my desk and said, "It's when the narrator usually only sees through one character."

"Correct. Xon, how about you face forward and stop staring at Leo, are we clear?"

I nodded, not speaking.

Ms. Cannon paused, I knew she wanted to say something as her scent changed to thick dank smoke, like smog. Worry.

"I'm fine." I said as she took a breath. "It's nothing. I'll be fine."

She placed a hand on my shoulder. "If you need to talk, just let me know."

Her putrid meat smell wafted into my nose and choked my throat. I stood up and hurriedly left the room. The scent of humans was just too nauseating to take. I never heard other werewolves or any other type of shifter complaining how badly humans smelled, so either it was just me or everyone else had learned to ignore it.

I was outside, racing for the forest when a hand clasped me around the arm and jerked me back. I spun on my heel while throwing a punch. Leo caught my wrist in time, my knuckles stopped an inch from his lip. He pulled my arm down and walked me back to the school steps, he sat me down and took a seat next to me. He didn't speak.

I asked numbly, "You don't talk, do you?"

Leo shook his head. His scent was strong with faint ammonia, fruity and citrusy; anxious, curious and excited. Yet his face was empty as blank paper. For some reason, even though Leo felt emotions, he wasn't able to express them. Still, he was trying to help me.

I asked, "Were you Changed? Did the wolf bite your vocal cords out? Is that why you can't talk?"

Leo nodded, then shook his head and shook his head again.

Yes. No. No.

I paused then asked, "When you were…new. Was it this bad?"

Leo didn't move or make an expression but from the slight way his eyebrows cinched, and his fingers curled into his palms, I knew he was thinking.

Finally, Leo held out his hand and tilted it from side to side.

So-so.

I rubbed my forehead, closing my eyes and breathing in the fresh air. The wind blew the call of nature. All I really wanted was to run away to the forest where I could be free.

Leo placed his hand on the back of my neck and squeezed. My wolf squirmed then went still, caught. My breath held and I slowly exhaled; I opened my eyes. Leo watched me closely, he cupped his hand at his chest and brought it up towards his nose slowly, taking a deep breath. I mimicked him, doing the breathing exercises with Leo tightly holding my neck, keeping my wolf in check.

After a minute, he let me go and stood up, then held out his hand. I took it and let him stand me up. Then we walked back to class.

Ms. Cannon tossed us a look but didn't interrupt class as we sat back down. I got out my binder and was able to think again, it was like Leo had forced my wolf into a cave, someplace where he couldn't bother me.

When class ended, Leo walked me to my next period, Algebra II. I stopped before reaching the door. Leaning against the wall before the door was Shane. His shoulders touched, while the rest of his body stretched out adjacent, bearing his weight on his heels. He turned his blond head as we approached, and his blue irises tinged olive around the edges.

At the sight of him, my body stiffened, my wolf bared fangs. Leo put his hand on the back of my neck again and held tight, reining me in. The wolf snapped his teeth and growled but he didn't move, couldn't move. Heat flushed through my veins but the Change wouldn't come over me.

Shane's eyes narrowed as a twisted smirk came over his face. "You look like a little pup, bearing his teeth while shaking in fear. I'm here to check up on you, a new wolf in school."

"I'm fine," I said, swallowing back a growl.

How is he talking like he cares when he shattered the back of my skull the other day?

Shane chuckled, the sound low and hoarse in the back of his throat. "You still got a lot to learn about respect. *Boy.*"

That did it.

I lunged for Shane, hands reaching for his throat but he leapt back, dodging the attack. Leo jumped onto my back, forcing me to the ground. My arms cushioned my head from hitting the floor, I grunted as all the air was forced from my lungs. Girls screamed, a few boys cursed in surprise. Leo kept his knees on my lower back, his hands pinned my shoulders down.

"Hey! What's going on here?" The Calculus teacher, Mr. Dorman stormed up. "What's going on here? No fighting!"

Leo stepped off me and jerked me to my feet in one fluid motion. The movement was slick, unnatural like he had muscles in places humans didn't. Mr. Dorman's eyes widened and he let off a sour scent of uneasiness.

Leo's hand clasped back onto my neck, and I breathed heavy, saying, "We weren't fighting. I tripped, that's all."

While I said it, I looked at the wall and bit on my lower lip.

Dammit, he'll know I'm lying.

Mr. Dorman looked at Shane then back at me. "Well from what I saw, it looked like you tried to grab Mr. Armstrong here by the throat. And if it wasn't for Mr. Dawson subduing you, you could have seriously hurt him."

Shane snorted. "Reeves, hurt me? He can't lay a finger on me." Shane looked at me with olive-tinged blue eyes. "You need to learn your place."

He walked away without looking back.

"Don't be late to my class Mr. Dawson," said Mr. Dorman, watching us shrewdly. "I'm letting you off with a warning Mr. Reeves, don't *trip* like that again, understand?"

Mrs. Ellis came to the door. "Xon? Why are you hanging outside, come in. Oh, John, is everything alright?"

"It's fine Elsie. Get to class Mr. Reeves. Mr. Dawson with me." Mr. Dorman walked away as the late bell rang.

Leo let go of my neck but hesitated, looking at me.

"I'll be okay." I said, offering up a half smile, it was so crooked and half-hearted it died, leaving my face strained. "I'll see you later, after school, okay?"

Leo's eyes darkened, he wasn't fooled, his scent was like a dead fire. Disappointed. He pointed to his watch then at me before walking away. I got it, he'd be back when class is over and he'll probably walk me to the cafeteria.

Mrs. Ellis was looking at me so I came inside and sat down. Aydan and Regan were near the door, they must have been watching. Aydan's skin paled as Regan whispered to him. My super-sharp ears caught it.

"Did you see that? He really isn't human."

Mrs. Ellis said, "Boys, to your seats please. I can't start class with you being disruptive."

Tossing me awkward looks, my once-friends took their seats at the back. I sat in front and made an effort to pay attention. I really couldn't afford to keep walking out of class and not getting down the homework. I'm a junior, if I mess up now it'll make senior year more difficult.

When the bell rang, Leo was standing outside, leaning on the wall. Aydan and Regan watched me walk over to him. When Leo placed his hand against my forehead, then under my chin, as if feeling my temperature, they both made sick smiles.

I lowered Leo's hand, muttering, "C'mon man, chill out."

Leo lifted his shoulders and hands.

My bad.

Aydan and Regan walked behind us to the cafeteria. Standing at the bottom of the steps was Zaheed, my other former friend. We were all so stoked we had the same lunch, thought it would be great. Now I wished they'd go away.

"Hey Leo! Hey Xon!" A bright flash of green disrupted my vision and I blinked to see Connor waving from the steps. "Come on, there's sloppy Joe today!"

Leo loped down the steps, his long legs taking four at a time. I trotted behind him, not looking over at the group of guys who used to be my friends.

The three of us moved as a unit into the sloppy Joe lane. The scents seared my nose but I focused my eyes on the mound of meat and sauce the lunch lady Judith was sloshing onto the trays.

Connor went first, saying with a chipper squeal, "Fill 'er up!"

Judith smiled and gave him one scoop on his bun. Connor pouted with his lips puckered and brows furrowed. Judith sighed dramatically but with a sweet smile, added another scoop. I held out my tray. Judith gave me one scoop.

"More."

Judith frowned but plopped a second scoop onto the bun.

"More."

The meat smelled appetizing enough but that tiny little handful wasn't going to feed the beast. My wolf drooled, everything in him was urging me to hurry up and eat it, eat it all, eat everything. Judith was fat, rolls at her chin, neck and shoulders. Full of blood, of meat. Leo clasped my neck just as I realized I had taken an unconscious step forward.

Judith put the top on my bun, saying in a high sharp tone, "Next!"

Leo got a sloppy Joe and with his long-fingered steely hand gripping the back of my neck, steered me to the check out lane where Connor was waiting on the other side. I paid for my food with my lunch number and found myself sitting with Connor and Leo at the far side of the cafeteria.

Connor and Leo began to wolf down their food but I hadn't had a chance to get started when Shane bounded down the stairs into the cafeteria. His eyes were focused right on me, and I don't think he was about to stop.

I leapt from the seat in a movement so fast the air snapped around me. My vision altered to high-definition, focused on Shane's stupid mocking face. Leo had his arms around my chest and Connor's arms were around my neck; they had both grabbed me in the split second left before I could tackle Shane. Connor was standing on the table, my sloppy Joe kicked to the side.

The cafeteria had gone silent, everyone's eyes on us. Then the chant rose.

"Fight! Fight! Fight! Fight!"

Connor gasped in my ear, "Don't do it Xon! Don't!"

Leo grasped my arm nearest him and pulled it tight behind my back. A sharp yelp left my mouth.

Mr. Dorman arrived on the scene. His face pinched like he smelled something disgusting. His scent shifted into wet ash and dead fire. Disapproving and disappointed.

"Come with me Jaxon Reeves." He looked at Leo. "You too Mr. Dawson."

Connor stabbed a finger at Shane, who was losing the fight to keep the smile off his face. "What about him? He started it!"

Mr. Dorman didn't miss a blink. "Mr. Armstrong is underneath the Dominion's jurisdiction. Mr. Forrest will deal with him, you don't have to worry about it. Mr. Dawson, Mr. Reeves, with me. Mr. Hawkins, you can come too."

Shane's smile slipped right off his face, leaving a cold dark visage. He watched as Leo frog-marched me away with Connor bringing up the rear. Leo's hands clenched so hard on my upper arms my bones felt like they'd snap. The tight grip did its purpose, I didn't turn back, I didn't try to attack Shane again.

We went up the stairs and towards the right. The main office and administrative office were a few strides away from the cafeteria.

Mr. Dorman opened the main office door; letting Leo walk me in first with Connor following.

Principal Hamilton just happened to be coming down the hall from the offices in the back. She paused when she saw our procession.

She said, "John, does this have anything to do with what you mentioned earlier?"

"Jaxon Reeves tried to attack Shane Armstrong *again*." Mr. Dorman crossed his arms. "If it wasn't for Mr. Dawson and Mr. Hawkins, this wouldn't have ended without bloodshed."

A quick smile flashed over my face as I imagined Shane sprawled on the cafeteria floor, a bloody ragged hole where his throat used to be, the floppy fold of flesh held in my jaws.

My stomach jerked, twisted and I bent over, gasping as my face contorted. The Change rolled over me, urged by my violent thoughts to kill. Leo let go of my arms only to grab me again, turning me into his chest and hugging me tight. He was thin, weak and I grasped his waist, trying to fling him off. My arms buckled, my nail beds burned.

"Hey! Hey!"

"Stop it!"

"Let go of him!"

Human voices touched then bounced off my ears. I heard the wolf howling, crashing through my defenses, then Connor jumped up and sunk his teeth into the back of my neck, his hands holding onto my shoulders. Immediately a teacher struggled to break his hold but Connor held on. The grasp combined with Leo's tight hold, the feeling of being protected by my fellow wolves pushed my wolf back and I relaxed.

My knees went out and Leo bent with me to the floor. Connor took his teeth out of my skin and he hugged me around my shoulders. For that moment, it was just us there, three wolves, holding, hugging, comforting.

The main office was completely silent, and I didn't even want to imagine what this had looked like. My eyes closed and I placed my face in Leo's neck, I was too tired to deal with all this, the effort of continually forcing my wolf back had drained me.

Everything slowly faded.

* * *

I woke up laying on a cot in the nurse's office. The lights were out and the door was cracked, the windows open letting in steaming summer air. I didn't move then rolled my eyes to the side to check the clock hanging on the wall. It was a little past 12pm. Lunch was over, I should be in Mr. Malone's History class.

I sighed and covered my face with both hands, inhaling my scent.

God...this can't go on. Leo and Connor can't be there for me all the time and I can't keep getting into trouble. Something has got to give.

The wolf in me flicked his lip up to bare his teeth in a primal smile. Something had to give but it wouldn't be him; I'm a werewolf now and that can't change, can't go back. I could kill myself, yes but the thought of it made my stomach hurt.

The door opened and Principal Hamilton peeked in as she flipped the light. Her face was pale.

"What?" I asked.

"Your eyes...they were." She shook her head, not saying it. "Your father is here Jaxon, do you feel okay to talk to him?"

Oh great, here we go...he's going to be pissed.

"Yes." I said, steadying my shoulders.

Principal Hamilton disappeared then my father walked in. He was still in work clothes, his hardy Timberland boots crusted with dust and dirt. His ragged denim jeans sported a new rip in the knee but his skin wasn't hurt. His t-shirt sleeves rolled up to the shoulders, streaks of some sort of oil or tar stained his large muscles.

When his eyes met mine, I whined. "Sorry Dad."

"Don't make puppy noises or puppy eyes at me Jaxon William Reeves." His voice wasn't raised, he didn't curse or snap, but the hard quality to his voice caused me more pain than if Mom was here to slap me. I had broken my promise to him, I didn't keep my word.

"I said sorry." I insisted, trying to keep the whine out of my voice again as I hunched my shoulders and bowed my head. "It just...I mean...I was."

There was no way to say the wolf made me do it or I want to rip Shane's throat out. I couldn't explain at all.

Dad took a seat on the nurse's chair and rolled it up in front of me. He touched my chin but I jerked away, glaring at the floor. None of this was what I wanted. Everything had been perfect before I went to Cali. I had my crew, Melody was my girlfriend and we all knew junior year was going to be on point. Then I went to visit Aunt Kysha in LA, I met Leah who I shouldn't have been talking to in the first place when I had Melody back home. Rocky flipped his shit and did his best to kill me, then Toni patched me up and sent me home. I didn't ask for this and I didn't want it either. My wolf snapped his teeth. He couldn't speak in words, he was an animal but I knew he disagreed with me. He wanted to keep trying.

Dad said, "Xon? Can you please tell me what's going on? Why are you acting like this?"

"It's nothing." I said after a few tense seconds. "I'm just fine."

"Son, I don't know who you think I am but you can't brush me off. You came home with a bloody shirt yesterday and I've been told you had to be held back by your friends twice today before you could jump on this kid named Armstrong. Now look, you haven't told us anything about what happened between you two. Not to mention, you were going out with Melody and-"

I leapt up. The shout that left my mouth sounded like the howl of an angry wolf. "I DO NOT WANT TO TALK ABOUT MELODY!"

Dad stood up, his large body deft as a cat and he put his large finger in my face. I leaned back, stunned at the sudden move.

He spoke in a deep stern voice, "Jaxon William Reeves, don't you ever raise your voice to me like that again. Now sit your stupid ass back down and let me finish talking, understand?"

I slowly sat. I looked at his shoes and didn't speak, didn't nod my head.

Dad let out a heavy sigh. "My God Xon, I don't know what's going on in your head, your body. You are a werewolf and I'm doing my best to understand but you've completely changed from my son into someone else. You're moody, violent, snappish and now you're in this puppy pouty mood. Listen, the Summers have ordered you to stay away from Melody, and I know you're hurt about losing your girlfriend, but son, that doesn't give you the right to go around starting fights."

"I didn't start any fight." I muttered, not looking up from the floor. "I told you. Shane got a little rough but-"

"Who exactly is Shane Armstrong to you? Who is he?"

I swallowed hard, realizing I'd end up revealing more than I should.

"Some guy."

I started to say vaguely but Dad cleared his throat, sounded like grinding rocks together.

I said, "Shane is the guy who hit me the other day, but it's not serious."

Dad said, "You told me you provoked him. Now you're saying you didn't start the fight. According to Principal Hamilton, you initiated the attacks on Armstrong, and that your friends had to hold you back. I don't condone lying and neither does God. Proverbs 12:22, *lying lips are an abomination to the Lord.*"

I glared at him, heat rising under my flesh. "I'm not fucking lying! Shane is-"

I shut my mouth at the frozen look on Dad's face. I had cursed at him, and with Dad's code of respect, I'd be lucky if he didn't hit me in the mouth.

I let out a long breath, cooling off. "I'm sorry I cursed Dad, I didn't mean to get so heated. I'm not lying, honestly, I'm not."

Dad stood up, not looking at me. "You should go back to class Jaxon, and you have detention to serve after school. I'll see if it's me or Kyra who'll pick you up later on."

"Dad, I'm sorry." I started but he walked away. I stood up, unable to keep the whimper down as my eyes watered.

Dad sighed. "Don't cry Xon, please. I've tried to find out what's wrong but you won't tell me. I get fed up so you start crying. I can't figure you out. What do you want me to do?"

"Nothing."

I laid back down on the cot and rolled so I was facing the wall. I curled into my personal ball, my own scent, my own arms, my own safety. If Dad said something, I didn't hear it.

* * *

I was shaken awake probably not long after Dad left, because the clock said the time was only 12:30pm; U.S. History was still in session. I got to wash my face then Mrs. Mitchells told me about my detention after school, and that I had a second detention for tomorrow. The first was for skipping school yesterday, the second was for the fights that I had almost started. I doubted Shane was going to get in trouble for being the one who ticked me off in the first place.

I went to class and the room silenced as I walked in. Everyone stared at me like my head was on fire.

I took my seat and took out my books like nothing happened, not looking at anyone.

"Attention! Face front, eyes on the board." Mr. Malone's voice was rough and demanding, so after a few seconds everyone listened.

I struggled to pay attention but all I could think about was my problems. My wolf, my father and that asshole Shane. It was like everything was not only piling up but intertwining with each other. The wolf was a huge hindrance on its own. Besides the heightened senses that were driving me out of my mind, he made me want to Change and kill Shane. He even made me curse at my father then cry. It was like nothing could be normal anymore. And what was the worst thing of all was that God had probably abandoned me the moment I turned from His human child into a shifter.

The bell rang and while people stood and got ready to go, they were either watching me or talking about me, sometimes both.

"Xon totally tried to kill Shane today."

"I was there, in the hallway and at lunch, tried to jump on him. Isn't Shane supposed to be the leader of the shifters at this school? Doesn't that mean Xon is going against his boss?"

"Xon got sent to the office and everything. I heard he was going to get arrested but his Dad namedropped to get him out of it."

"Say what?"

I left, not wanting to hear them start talking about Dad's past. Dad had moved on from that time in his life and he wouldn't namedrop either. He would want people to take him as he is now and not who he used to be.

Leo was in the hallway, he looked into my eyes, assessing me. I knew the only reason he didn't touch me was because of the other people watching. Leo shrugged then tilted his head, and came with me as I walked to Ms. Hughes Psychology class.

I stopped.

Daewon and Melody stood by the door. Daewon was close to her, only a foot or so back, with his head lowered down near hers to keep their conversation private. However even though he was talking low, I could easily hear from where I was standing.

"Can't you even try and talk to your parents about Xon? He's not a demon. He's the same guy as always, he hasn't changed."

Melody turned her head to the side, her arms clenched tightly over her chest. She didn't speak.

Daewon sighed heavily and looked towards me, probably seeing me out of his peripheral vision. He smiled and gestured to me. Melody turned, saw me and slid away from Daewon and into the classroom before I reached them.

"I've been trying to get her to get her parents to change their minds," he said, leaning against the doorframe. "We can talk, but once I bring you up, she shuts down."

"You don't have to do that for me Daewon," I said softly, sighing and rubbing the back of my neck. "You told her I haven't changed…and I'm struggling *not* to change…but I…I'm not sure if I'm really the same person."

"You are to me," he said as the bell rang.

He clapped my shoulder then jogged away. Leo inclined his head to me and left for his class.

I walked into the classroom and took my seat.

Ms. Hughes called the class to attention. Melody sat on the far row by the windows and two seats up. She had those large blue eyes flicking towards my direction but then adjusted to face front.

I got out my books and listened as Ms. Hughes explained Freudian theory, talking of the Oedipus complex and the Electra complex. I wondered what type of theory explained this problem I was having with Melody and her freaking parents. Even though things weren't going too well for me, the struggle of balancing this new wolf in me and my old self, I knew I wasn't a demon. What was really insane was how the Summers haven't even talked to me personally, and Melody wasn't trying to explain anything either. So it's that easy for them? We've been going to the same church for years, we were practically raised in church together. How can they write me off as a demon like I mean nothing to them?

"Jaxon Reeves!"

The strident call made my mouth click together with a clear snap. The entire class was staring at me, except Melody, who had her hands over her ears, blonde head ducked towards her desk.

Ms. Hughes faced me, arms on her hips and two high blushes on her cheeks. "How dare you sit there growling like that! You're disrupting class and I can very well send you to the office for vocally threatening Melody!"

I swallowed back a rough comeback. I hadn't *meant* to growl at Melody, I was fed up with my own situation, grumbling to myself but the wolf was growling and that made *me* growl. The wolf was me and I was the wolf. But no. I didn't want this, I didn't want to be the wolf anymore. There had to be a way to make it stop, to make it go away. Fine, I get it. If I'm a wolf and all my wolf wants is to run to the forest, then fuck it, let me just go to the forest already. He was driving me insane and ruining my school life, so I had to give in.

I stood up and packed my bag.

Ms. Hughes's eyes widened. "Jaxon? Just what do you think you're doing? I didn't send you away, sit down."

"I'm going to the office." I lied, bending down to fake-tie my shoes so she didn't see me not making eye contact. "You're right, I threatened Melody. I probably need another detention."

"Oh no you don't mister." Ms. Hughes moved to block the door. "You're just trying to sneak out of class, you don't have any intention of going to the office. Sit down, get your books out and pay attention."

I stood up and loped to the door. Ms. Hughes spread her arms out so both hands touched either side of the frame. I could run her over; I could trample her into the ground underneath my paws, rip her apart with my claws. All of the pent up aggression burned in my eyes as I stared down at her.

"Get out of my way."

Ms. Hughes gasped and darted to the side, her scent ripe with fear and shock, piss and lemon. The class crowed "OOOH" behind me but I didn't look back. I left the school. Forget detention, forget the promise and apologies I made to my father. I had to stop this, I had to end this.

My book bag dropped somewhere by the SCHOOL ZONE sign, then my shoes and my socks, even my shirt. I blended with the wind, my wolf's heart swelled, with each stroke of my legs I propelled myself deeper into the run. There wasn't anyone on the sidewalk, no cars drove by; it was the middle of the day, people were at school or at work.

I hit the edge of the field then plunged into the forest. My jeans shredded off as my wolf leapt out and I slid from one form to the next. My hands thickened into paws, my legs buckled then stretched as my spine bent forward and lengthened. My head grew heavy on a thin neck before it thickened. My nose grew out as my mouth rose to meet it, pulling into a muzzle. Large triangular ears swiped to the top of my head. Fur rippled over my flesh and the wolf was finally free.

I kept running, running deeper and deeper into the forest until the anxiety went away, until my heart stopped pounding and I no longer struggled to escape from my own skin.

I slowed to a walk and panted, my chest heaving.

So this is what it means to be a werewolf. At least, I think so. I abandoned school and now I'm wandering the forest in a wolf body.

I slumped down against a tree and closed my eyes. I hadn't laid there long when my ears flicked at rustling. I opened my eyes and saw a furry light brown face peering at me from the bushes. The eyes were greenish brown and settled between a long muzzle. It was another wolf and he smelled like sunshine and lemons.

I scrambled to my feet as Leo stepped out from the bushes. Just the fact he was right behind me told me he must have been following me from the start. I was so freaked out that I didn't notice.

I stared at him.

[Why did you follow me?]

He didn't answer, not that he would have. He instead jerked his head to the side and walked away, expecting me to follow him. I breathed out from my nose but did so. If anything he was probably taking me back to the Village; it wasn't like I had any idea where I was right now.

We walked in silence but the silence was only the lack of speech. The forest was alive with noise and life. The birds chittered as they hopped from branch to branch, the leaves whistled as the wind blew through, the small feet dashed over the grass.

My stomach grumbled just as a whine rumbled from my throat. The wolf wanted food and to hell with the cafeteria's fake offerings. He wanted real food, prey, blood and meat. The worse thing about it, I wanted it too. I wanted to feel something alive and kicking, struggling beneath my claws, to taste fresh meat in my mouth and have my fangs slice through soft flesh.

Leo looked over at me as my ears flattened to my skull and my legs crouched over the ground. I met his eyes and the whine came back, imploring.

[I'm hungry. I want to hunt.]

Leo's ears flicked up high and his shoulders writhed from side to side then he pawed at the rich earth, his tail swiped against his legs. I could tell he was indecisive and he probably wanted to go back to school but then his stomach growled too. At that noise, I took in Leo's wolf form. He was just as stretched out and skinny as his human body. He had long legs and a flat body, like a skeleton with his light brown fur pulled tightly over it.

It was true that I didn't know how to hunt but I turned and headed back into the forest with Leo trotting behind me. At first we walked around aimlessly with our stomachs grumbling until I got a whiff of something. I stopped and lowered my head to the scent.

The scent was like Jarrod, at least, the smell of prey but it wasn't the same because Jarrod had smelled like a person too. This smell was like grass and must, animal, male, young. Deer. Prey.

I took off after it and Leo kept up with me at my side. We moved swiftly, our paws didn't damage the earth, our passing compressed the grass and moved on, like shadows during the day. The scent enhanced until I slowed to a stop in a bunch of prickly bushes. Just a few feet in was a deer, coltish legs and a wedge-shaped head balanced on a long neck. His ears flipped up and he looked around. I hunched down to the grass and so did Leo. We both breathed slowly from our nostrils and the thick bushes hid our bodies.

The deer paused then turned back to his meal.

I jumped out, Leo next to me and the deer sprinted away.

Not fast enough.

My paws clobbered the little beast around its hindquarters and back, while Leo's fangs hooked over its leg. Together we pulled it to the ground. While it desperately tossed its head, I snatched up its throat and tasted hot lifeblood pouring down my mouth, the pulse kicking its way down. Leo had already started tearing up chunks from its behind. The throat claimed, I honed in on the chest. The forest was quiet save the rips of meat from bone and the gobbling of hungry mouths.

I feasted on the deer like I had done it before, cracked open rib and thigh bones with effortless snaps of my jaws, clawing open the abdomen so the steaming bloody organs tumbled onto the wet grass, digging my snout into the scooped cavity to lick the carved expanse for any giblets leftover.

It must have only taken about ten to twenty minutes, but when I stood back, the deer was gone. Nothing left but a pile of bones and grizzle laying on top of slick red grass. Leo rooted through the smear for any crumbs. My wolf curled up on the inside, satisfied.

I slumped to the ground too, my stomach bulged out to spread from my chest to my crotch, full of slowly digesting food. Eating small portioned cafeteria food that's easily devoured was nothing compared to eating prey, eating organs and fur and bone marrow. I was stuffed and needed to sleep this meal off.

Leo finished scavenging then came next to me, laid his head over my neck and relaxed into sleep. My eyes closed next and I slept.

I woke up naked with an equally naked Leo in my arms. I sat up and stretched, jostling Leo off me. Leo tumbled over and lay still then slowly looked over at me, rubbing his eyes. He blinked, his bright green eyes calm. He smelled like me, like grass, like a shared meal and a shared bed. He smelled not like family and not even like friendship, I didn't know this scent. But the wolf did.

I reached out to him, grasped his arm and pulled his wrist under my nose for my wolf to log. Leo didn't fight me, he let me do it. I smelled Leo's personal scent again, lemons and sunshine. Then came the scent of laying on bloody meaty grass, and some of my scent was on him, but that bond scent was there, the bond of running together, hunting together, eating together and sleeping together.

Pack.

My wolf didn't have a voice, he couldn't speak in a human language but I heard it in my head, in my own thoughts. Something about what Leo and I had done together had bonded us more tightly than blood of family or close friends. It had gone beyond our human flesh into our wolf spirit. He was my Packmate now.

I let him go and Leo sat up, stretching his arms way over his head. I stared at his upper body. His collarbones stuck out and lifted against his skin like a plastic coat hanger, thin and fragile. If I flicked it his bone would snap. His ribs were countable, I could run my finger down his chest and bump across each one.

Leo blinked at me and tilted his head to the side. His scent shifted to the fruity tinge of curiosity.

"You're like anorexic man." I said, brushing at bush leaves sticking in his tuft of curly pale brown hair. "Don't your parents feed you at home?"

Leo's face drained blank and his eyes became lifeless. In that instant, he changed from being my Packmate to some dead-faced mannequin. His scent switched from curious to a throat-clogging suffocating scent…despair.

I asked softly, "Leo…are your parents dead?"

Leo looked somewhere past my shoulder but he nodded with a short jerk of his head.

My throat tightened but I asked next, "Does anyone live with you? Do you have a guardian?"

Two head shakes.

"Did you ever have a guardian? After your parents died, you didn't immediately take care of yourself, right?"

He nodded and nodded again.

"Is your guardian dead too?"

Another head nod.

"So you're saying that your parents died, you got a guardian to watch you then they died too, and now you live alone?"

He nodded.

I asked, "Is that why you don't talk? Because everyone you loved died? Did you have siblings?"

Leo nodded, nodded and nodded.

My stomach balled into a knot, my skin flushed cold.

I asked, "So your siblings are dead too?"

He nodded again. His shoulders shook as tears dropped to the ground but no sound left him. He didn't move, he sat there, frozen.

I asked, "How did they die? Did someone kill them? Was it a werewolf who killed them?" A horrid idea came to my mind as Leo just kept nodding. "That's how you were Changed, wasn't it? A werewolf attacked you and your family...you were the only one who survived, everyone else died. And because of that, you stopped talking, too traumatized. Right?"

Leo's body melted. His skin slid off his bones that cracked and popped into new positions. His muscles made slick sounds as they slid over and wrapped around his new form, fur breathed over the body and a wolf laid there, shivering and wheezing like it was dying.

I didn't know what to do but then my wolf instincts took over. I bent over and shifted from human to wolf as easily as blinking or taking a step. Fur covered my skin, my body morphed from two-legged to four-legged.

I laid down next to Leo. He trembled, his breathing ragged like he was having an asthma attack. I used my paw to pull him into the thick fur at my ruff and chest then curled my legs up around him, cuddling him against me. His thin body was cold and mine was radiating heat. Leo tucked his muzzle under my chin and his paws pressed into my chest and abdomen, taking in my comfort. I laid my head over his neck and my throat flexed, my chest inflated then a long gentle sound emanated from deep within me. It wasn't a growl or a whine but more melodic, soft and tender.

A croon.

My wolf was singing a lullaby to Leo's wolf, a gentle whisper for healing, for peace, for renewal. Leo's shaking slowed into stillness, his breath relaxed and then he only made tiny snores. My eyes closed and we slept again.

This time when I woke up, the sky was black and dotted silver with stars. The forest hooted, chirped, and rustled with nightlife. I had no idea what time it was, where my clothes were or what my parents were thinking. To them, they would know I wasn't home and had never come home after school. I hadn't called or sent a text; I could be anywhere doing anything.

Anything included having a naked boy with his arms and legs wrapped around me while we laid in the forest next to a pile of picked over bones.

I sat up and gently eased Leo off me onto the grass. His eyes opened and he laid there without trying to get up.

I said, "We should really be getting back."

Leo rolled onto his stomach and as he moved, his flesh peeled back, fur brimmed over him as his legs and spine jerked, flexed, then he stood up as a wolf. He stumbled and looked disoriented as his body wavered from side to side and his eyes were heavy-lidded. Then he shook himself and blinked a few times, adjusting.

I got on my hands and knees, then called my wolf to the surface. This time I could see him. His coat was gray, the fur on his chest and down his belly was light gray. His eyes were bright yellow.

Leo was waiting for me, watching me closely with his ears pricked.

I looked around. I had never been in this part of the forest before. But I had an idea, to trace my way back by following our scents. I snuffled my nose in the ground until I smelled my scent trailing away with Leo's next to it. I followed it and Leo came to my side.

[This is crazy Leo.] My thoughts projected towards him and because his ears flickered, I knew he could hear me even if he wouldn't respond in words, or couldn't. *[Have you ever gone hunting before?]*

Leo shook his head and his tail swiped from side to side, the brushy end of it smacked my tail. I playfully snapped at his foreleg. Leo jumped then he tackled me around my neck, his teeth gnawed my ear. Yelping, I wiggled to get him off then knocked him to the ground. My teeth grasped for his neck while he batted at my muzzle and shoulders with his paws.

I got Leo's neck in between my jaws and squeezed with a rough growl. Leo went limp in surrender, his tail flat to the ground and closed his eyes. I let him go and he rolled to his feet. His tongue lolled out for a second in a quick smile, then we kept walking together.

Even in the dead of night, the forest was alive. The leaves crunched as small insects feasted. The moonlight reflected red and green eye-shines of nocturnal stares. Chuffing and grunting of sleeping animals filled the air. The Moon and the Stars gave the only light, barely shining through the heavy cloak of the dark yet my wolf vision stayed hyper-focused. I could see the veins in the leaves pulsing with water, the cracks in the bark with sticky sap seeping through, even the piles of ant hills and hard balls of mice droppings.

I didn't know how long it took, but we arrived to the edge of the forest at the empty field. The ruins of my jeans and underwear were strewn about, left where my shifting body shredded them. I didn't know where my shoes, socks and shirt were, I had tossed them away while running for the forest.

Leo's clothes laid neatly piled under the base of a tree. He trotted over and began to Change. I didn't bother Changing, I had no clothes I could put on and I wasn't about to walk back naked.

Dressed, Leo turned to me and his brows slightly raised before settling level over his eyes.

[I can't go home naked.] I thought to him but Leo's scent stung sharply like onions, confusion. [You can't understand me, can you?]

Leo stared into my eyes then looked away, rubbing the back of his neck. Yeah, it was clear he didn't know what I was communicating. I guess telepathy in wolf form didn't cross over into human form.

So I Changed back to a human, saying, "I can't go home naked. I have to go back as a wolf."

He nodded and walked away then glanced back at me.

Guess I'm supposed to follow him?

I did so after Changing again. Walking at Leo's side as a wolf, I realized just how large my wolf form was compared to a human being. Leo was six-feet-three and my head came to his elbow. I knew that shifter animals were larger than the real animals but still, that's huge.

Leo walked silently even in his sneakers; he was stealthy for such a tall lanky guy. And now he was the closest friend I had besides Daewon. My former buddies had turned against me, I didn't have Melody anymore and somehow Leo had taken it on himself to make sure I'm doing alright. How he knew I had abandoned class and followed me into the forest, I didn't know but I was grateful.

Leo bent down and when he stood up he was carrying my sneakers, which were ripped at the soles where my feet had busted out of them. He collected my ragged socks and then my shirt, which had a tear from the collar to the middle. My book bag was there too, which Leo also grabbed and slung over his shoulder.

Well, Mom's gonna be pissed. I destroyed an entire outfit. And we left the ruins of my jeans back in the field. Nevermind the clothes, how will I explain coming home in a giant wolf body?

Leo dumped the ruined clothing into a dumpster then kept walking. He was going the opposite way from my house. I paused then went with him. Oh! If I went to his house, I could borrow his clothes. While I definitely weighed more than him in muscle, he was only a few inches taller. Jeans and a t-shirt would be fine.

Leo loped up a cracked walkway and I stared at the ramshackle hovel that he was calling home. The house's paint was chipped, one of the windows had a hole in it like some kid slammed a baseball through it, the blinds were broken, and his grass was dead. He opened the door, it hadn't even been locked, and disappeared inside.

I entered after him and glanced around, wondering if the outside was an indicator of the inside. He had furniture at least. There were clothes everywhere, plus cartons of microwave dinners and takeout boxes. How Leo ordered takeout when he didn't talk, I didn't know.

He disappeared into a room and I listened to him rummaging about, then he came back with very shaggy cargo pants and a giant t-shirt that would even swallow Dad.

Wow, Leo is really awesome. He keeps my wolf calm, he stops me from attacking Daewon twice, and now he's giving me his clothes. I asked God for help and then enters Leo. So...God didn't actually abandon me?

I Changed forms and got dressed. "Thanks Leo. You're a life-saver. I'll head home now."

His scent shifted from tingling oranges, happiness, to that of wet mud, sadness.

"Hey." I tossed him a smile. "You can come too. Meet my parents. I'll need you as an alibi for why I've been missing. I still don't even know what time it is."

I went into my book bag and got my cell phone to check. Oh shit, it was ten at night!

"Come Leo, I gotta get home stat!" I ran out.

Leo kept behind me as I raced through Lakeside Village. The Village was locked up tight, everything closed at nine-thirty in these woods. The streetlights were bright with little bugs circling around in worship, the storefronts had the word sign CLOSED and all the cars were in driveways or on the curb.

Home was a large three-story house with a connecting two car driveway. I had a car too but I hadn't driven it since I got back from California. Both of my parent's cars were parked on the pavement while mine was in the garage.

I flew up the lane and tested the doorknob, it opened, unlocked.

I shouted into the stillness. "I'm home."

Lights clicked on upstairs then Dad bounded down the steps. He looked like a giant angry bull-mastiff and even though I had a wolf, seeing that enraged look on his face, I stepped back.

"Dammit Jaxon William Reeves!"

Dad caught me around the neck and hugged me tightly.

"I thought something terrible happened to you!"

He grabbed my shoulders, shaking me.

"What happened? The school said you ran out! We looked for you and found your clothes torn off in the street. The shifter guidance counselor told us to leave them so you could find your way back. Kyra is losing her mind and..."

Dad finally saw Leo standing in the doorway.

His eyes narrowed. "Is that Shane?"

"No way Dad." I had to laugh. "This is Leo." I reached for Leo's arm and jerked him forward. "This wolf here keeps saving my ass."

Dad's brows went high and he looked into Leo's eyes. Leo's gold wolf spark flickered as if in greeting. Dad stepped back, his breath hitched.

"He's my Packmate." I said. "I've been with him this whole time, so I'm fine."

"You seem energetic." Dad pointed out and then held out his hand to Leo. "Grant Reeves. And you are?"

Leo didn't offer his hand, blink or move.

"Oh, his name is Leo Dawson." I introduced him again. "And he doesn't talk Dad. Uh..."

I trailed off. How do I tell Dad that Leo had his entire family mauled by a werewolf and he was the only survivor so now he's traumatized and can't talk or facially emote? That was more Leo's business than anyone else's.

I said, "He's had a hard life so he has trouble communicating. But he's really cool, I promise."

"Grant? Who are you talking to?" I heard Mom from the second landing but she was in the hallway and I couldn't see her from where I stood by the doorway. "I'm certain its not our son, because our son has run away from home." Her voice was soft and gentle, which only meant she was so pissed she couldn't even scream.

Dad winced then asked me, "Are you hungry Xon, Leo? Why don't you go into the kitchen and help yourselves, I'll talk her down."

"Oh I don't think so Jackson Grant Reeves!" Mom could be fleet as a deer and it only took her two seconds to race down the steps. "You don't hide him from me!"

Mom was all of five feet tall; a tiny package stuffed full of jalapeños and corrosive acid. She charged at me, hands raised for a beat down.

"Mom I can explain!" I dodged her first attack and stepped on Leo's foot. He jerked back, knocking into the side table, broke through it and hit the floor, clattering mail, keys and other knickknacks around him. Instead of getting up, he laid still in the mess and closed his eyes. More than anything, he looked like he had been knocked out though actually he was showing that he was submissive.

"Leo." I touched his shoulder and then grasped his arm. "Stand up, Mom won't hurt you."

Mom looked ashamed for a moment, and her bitter and sour scent matched it. Then she straightened up and lifted her chin as I got Leo to stand up. "Who is this? I demand you tell me where you've been Xon. And where did you get those clothes?"

"This is Leo Dawson, he's my friend. I've been with him; these are his clothes."

It was best to answer her questions as quick and plain as possible.

Mom's arms crossed. "Why did you leave school Xon? Again."

I rubbed the back of my neck. *Because my wolf was driving me insane with the need to go to the forest. There's no way Mom will accept an answer like that.*

Mom's eyes narrowed. "Boy, you've got five seconds. Four. Three."

"I went to the forest." I said, knowing another slap would be on the way if I didn't answer. "I know its hard to understand but my wolf, like, my other side, he wanted to go to the forest and he's been kicking up a fuss ever since I came to school so I went to get him to relax."

Mom stared at me like I was speaking gibberish. "What? That sounds like a load of bullshit to me Jaxon Reeves! You are a person with a fully functioning mind and you are telling me that your wolf is like a secondary mind? And this wolf gives you urges and commanded you to go to the forest?"

"Yes!" I didn't mean to shout but her hand swiped out for my face. Dad caught her wrist and gently lowered it.

"Kyra, just listen to him." He said. "We…we have to be understanding. This is a new situation for all of us."

"Understanding? Understanding of what exactly?" Mom snatched her arm from Dad's hold. "That our only son is some sort of wild animal? That he leaves school and tears off his clothes so he can go running naked in the forest? That's what you want me to understand?"

"Mom, I'm sorry, I just-"

Mom put her hand up for silence. "I'm going back to bed. Jaxon, you have two detentions for leaving school and a third one for skipping detention yesterday. If you get another detention or skip again, you're getting suspended and let me tell you something."

She looked at me, her sweet brown eyes the color of dried blood and her mouth twisted. "I don't want you to mention that beast to me ever again. You are my son and that's all I want, just you. I'm going to bed. Grant, don't wake me up."

She went up the stairs without looking back.

Dad let out a long breath and leaned against the wall then looked at the shattered remains of the table with the scattered keys and mail. "Well I've got to get this cleaned up. Is Leo staying over? It's pretty late and it's a school night. Did he ask his pa-?"

I quickly cut him off. "Leo can stay if its okay with you. Come on Leo, I'll show you my room."

Still holding his arm, I tugged him up the stairs, calling back, "Goodnight Dad."

"Night son." Dad's voice was subdued and I would have tried to smell him but mine and Leo's scents were overpowering from a night spent outside in the forest. I'm surprised Mom didn't yell at me to take a shower like she used to whenever I came home from playing outside. She must have been too angry about me not coming home to care about how bad I smelled.

"You can take a shower first." I told Leo as we reached my room on the third floor. I opened the door to the connecting bathroom. "I'll take out something you can wear to bed, okay?"

Leo nodded and went in then closed the door behind him. I took off his clothes and folded them up then put on some shorts. I got out shorts and a shirt for Leo and put it on the bed. Then I went downstairs to get something to bring up for us to eat. The hunt's meal had been digested by sleep, now I was hungry again.

Dad was tying up the garbage bag of broken wood and dust as I came down.

He said, "I thought you were going to bed."

"Hungry."

I headed straight to the freezer. My eyes brightened up like the sky with a full Moon. Meat. All the meat. The freezer was stocked with turkey legs and turkey wings, pot roast, ground beef, chicken tenderloins, breasts, thighs, legs and wing sections. It was enough to make my wolf sit up and beg.

I snatched out some packages of legs and wings, placing them on the counter then dove in to get more.

"No Xon, that's for dinner." Dad grabbed the meat and started to put them back. "If you want something to eat, get a snack from the pantry closet. Go on, shoo."

I couldn't tell Dad to shut up and let me eat the meat, so I slunk off to the pantry cabinet. There was snack food, like fruit gummies, cereal bars and plenty of cookies and chips. I grabbed as much as my arms could hold and went upstairs.

Leo was laying across my bed with his face deep in my pillow. I didn't hear him snoring so I didn't think he was asleep.

How can he breathe like that?

"Hey, I got snacks." I said, dropping the goods onto the bed.

He sat up. The only other reason I can assume he had his face in my pillow was because he had been smelling it. I didn't know how to take that so I ignored it.

"Don't eat it all. I've got to shower."

He nodded even as he was tearing open a potato chip bag. He shoved the chips into his mouth with both hands.

And I thought I could be weird some times.

I dropped the shorts I had on and got into the shower. It smelled like Leo but only faintly, as the water and soap washed away his scent. I somewhat mourned the loss of the forest smell; it felt like comfort, like welcoming. Clean and dressed, I went back into the bedroom. Leo was more than halfway through the snacks, now munching on both Oreos and chocolate chip cookies.

"Dammit Leo! I told you not to eat it all!" I shoved him onto the bed and quickly rescued the last five or six bags of snacks. "You little pig!"

Not trying to fight back, he laid on the bed and rubbed his flat stomach.

"Don't you eat at home?" I asked him around swallowing mixed fruit gummies.

He closed his eyes and shrugged.

If he doesn't have a guardian and he definitely doesn't have a job, then how does he have income to even buy food for himself? But I saw the food containers on the floor, so he's getting money from somewhere. Does the school know that Leo is fending for himself? How did his guardian die? Leo has had so much loss in his life that he can't even talk or show emotions anymore, yet he has enough room in his heart to give it towards helping me out.

The snacks demolished, I gathered up the remains and put them in the trash. Leo hadn't moved from his splayed position on the bed and now I was pretty sure he had fallen asleep.

"Get under the covers." I pushed at him while tugging down the comforter.

Leo wiggled underneath then went still again. I got under too but instantly felt uncomfortable. Not because Leo was there and with two guys its awkward but the exact opposite. It was because I had so many clothes on and couldn't feel his skin. It was a strange sensation; removed, distant, cut off. I needed to feel my Packmate; I wanted to know he was there with me. The clothes were a barrier, disconnecting me from him. Leo also started to writhe and twist as if to wriggle the clothes off him.

In the forest, we slept close together, skin to skin and it felt normal, like that was how it was supposed to be. As wolves our fur touched, as humans our skin touched. That's the way I wanted it.

Without speaking, clothes came off. Leo rested his head against my shoulder, his arm over my chest. That was more than enough, just to feel his skin, hear his breathing. My eyes closed and again I slept.

3

August 8th

Friday

The sound of a door slamming woke me up. I smelled my mother's vanilla rose perfume along with the hot spiciness of anger. I rubbed the gook out of my eyes. My bedside clock flashed the time in pale yellow. It was barely six am, I still had another hour to sleep. Then I realized what probably caused my mother to storm out in anger. The comforter had been kicked off to the floor and the sheet was dangling off the corners of the bed. Leo and I were naked and limbs tangled. I was comfortable, warm and safe.

I sighed and sat up. I couldn't go to sleep like nothing was wrong. Leo's arm slid from my chest to land in my lap and I moved it over. He stirred then his eyes opened, bright green and lazy.

I rustled his curly hair, saying, "You ready to go to school?"

He shook his head then pulled a pillow over his face, going limp again. Our smell was enhanced, the combined smell, the one that labeled as Pack. Eating together, sleeping together, that bond that deepened from our human selves into our wolf selves. It was a scent I wanted to wrap around me like a blanket on a cold night, I wanted to dive into it. I also wanted to spread it. I wanted someone else to have this scent, to join in the camaraderie that I had created with Leo.

Connor. Sky. Javier. Shane?

I didn't know about Shane. He had beaten me the first time I met him and he wasn't friendly. Did someone like that deserve to be in a Pack?

The door opened and Dad peeked in. He saw me and Leo naked and he closed the door with a quiet click. Dad knew I was straight but the scent I smelled behind the door was both the hot spices of anger and the wet mud of sadness.

Dammit.

A. E. Costello 85

I got out of bed and put on clothes for school then went after Dad. I found him in his study. The study was off the living room, a part of the hallway that led to the backyard door. I went in.

"Dad. Can we talk please?"

His chair was swiveled to face the wall, his large bulky body bent over like the world was on his shoulders.

His voice was tired and heavy. "Talk about what son? About what I saw happening in your bed? All I know is Leviticus 18:22. *You shall not lie with a male as with a woman. It...is...an...abomination.*"

My teeth snapped together with a sharp sound like knives clashing.

I said as calm as I could. "Dad, I didn't touch Leo in anyway that you're thinking. We're Packmates, like I told you."

"Xon I don't have a flying fucking clue what *Packmates* means." Dad's voice growled more than mine and I had never heard him take that harsh tone with me before.

I took a step back in shock, the lemon scent came off my skin.

I said in a soft voice, "Dad...I thought you understood."

"Goddammit Xon!" Dad stood up and slammed his fists on the computer desk. "You don't think I'm *trying* to understand? You're getting into fights, you keep running out of class, you've got *three* detentions in two days of school! Then you stay out all night, you come back funky as shit and now you're sleeping in bed naked with other dudes! What do you think I understand, huh? What can I possibly understand? I know my bible Xon, at the start to the end of my day all I have is my bible and everything you're going through is putting me to the test! Now this. God, Xon, I don't know what to think anymore! So what do I know? What do I understand? You have to explain it in a way that makes sense Xon, for God's sake. For my sake."

I won't cry. I don't have any need to cry. It's my wolf, my wolf is a punk little bitch and he's sad that Dad is yelling.

I sucked in a steady breath from my nose. "Dad. I've been as honest with you the best I can be. Leo and I, I'm trying to explain this. He took me under his wing. He really has been trying to help me. He's kept me sane, reeled my wolf back when I thought I'd go wolf shit on Shane. Last night, yeah, I ran away from school to the forest because I needed to get out of my human skin. I don't know how to explain it, it's like cabin fever, only within my own body. I had to escape my body and I finally flipped. Leo came after me and we ended up going hunting and sleeping in the forest for a while. So I brought him home so he could be like my alibi, so you'd believe where I had been. Yeah, we slept naked in bed, it felt right, felt normal. *Nothing happened* Dad, nothing. We just slept, that's all. We're Packmates, we're bros, okay?"

Dad stood straight and looked me in the eyes, his dark and intense. "Xon, I've had bros before, I've slept over with other men before. But we *never* slept naked in the same bed."

"Dad!" I groaned and banged my head into the doorframe out of pure frustration.

The wood cracked and bent inwards.

"Oops."

I grasped it and tried to pull it back into place but my grip shattered the frame and some of the wall crumbled.

"Fuck."

I picked up the pieces and looked at Dad helplessly.

He stared at me then burst into laughter. Smelling his bright orange citrusy scent of amusement, I sighed in relief, glad this dark upset talk was over.

"I'm sorry." I said, dropping the broken wood and plaster into the trash bin. "I'll fix it."

"No you won't because you suck at home improvement. I'll fix it. Look Xon." Dad looked serious again. "Your mother…she doesn't want you to talk about being a werewolf and she doesn't like that you're…acting different. She just wants you to be yourself, to be her son."

"I am her son." I said. "And I'm being myself, my personality hasn't changed. I have…I have another side to myself that has to adjust. With Leo and the others, I'll work it out."

Dad's brows raised. "The others? Principal Hamilton said there were six werewolves at the school, including you."

I held up my fingers. "Me. Shane. Sky. Leo. Connor. Javier. Yup, six."

Dad crossed his arms and leaned against the desk. "So Shane is the one who hit you hard enough you bled so much?"

"It wasn't that much." I said but that hard coal burned to life in my gut, my wolf growled and the sound replicated in my throat, like a car engine rumbling but more animalistic, deeper, throatier. Not human.

Dad's eyes widened and his scent dashed with the pissy scent of fear.

"I guess I'm a little pissed about it." I said to explain away the inhuman noise. "But I understand why it happened and it won't again." I gave him a smile. "I won't let him knock me around, you taught me better than that."

"And didn't pay for taekwondo lessons for nothing either." Dad checked the time on the wall. "Alright son, you should get some food in you and get ready for school. You're behind in homework as well."

I winced, thinking about classwork and how I had frightened Ms. Hughes last time. At least it was Friday and I'd have all weekend to catch up.

"Right Dad."

I saluted him, he waved me off and I went upstairs. Leo was still in bed. He had switched to lay along the width of the bed, so his shoulders, head and legs were hanging off the sides and his arms spread wide across. I stared at him then grabbed the covers and tossed them over his waist.

"Wake up Leo, it's time to eat then school."

He snorted, a sleepy confused sound then managed to sit up. He blinked and rubbed his face.

I said, "Wash your face and brush. I have an extra toothbrush you can use. Then we can get something to eat before we leave. Hey, Leo!"

I snapped as it looked like he was laying back down again. He jerked up straight and nodded, then got out of bed, reaching for his clothes from yesterday. We got presentable then went downstairs. Dad had cooked some pancakes with turkey bacon. Leo glanced at Dad, as if for permission.

Dad nodded, waving at the table. "Go and eat, I made it for you boys."

Like a dog let off his leash, Leo inhaled the pancakes. He took the spatula Dad used to make the pancakes, gathered a stack of pancakes on it and shoved the food into his mouth.

"Leo!" I snatched the spatula away from him and growled. "Act like you have some sense. Use a fork and sit down, you fool."

Dad, staring, made Leo a plate and handed him a fork. Leo didn't look ashamed or even smelled embarrassed, just went straight back to eating like he hadn't eaten in a century. I wasn't sure if he could breathe with the way he was stuffing his mouth full like that.

Dad gave me a look that said, *you gonna eat like that too?*

I grinned and made my plate. "Don't worry Dad, I may have a wolf but I remember my manners."

While Leo and I ate, Dad poured us both glasses of orange juice that we drank quickly.

Dad checked his watch. "It's past seven-forty, you'll miss the bus if you two don't leave now."

"Alright. Come on Leo, we gotta paw it." Seeing Dad's facial expression shift, I quickly said, "Uh, hoof it."

Leo waited for me at the door, I had to put on a different pair of shoes as I had ruined my last pair.

Dad caught my arm before I could head to the bus stop. "Xon, please, stay in school the *whole* day, serve your detentions, and no fighting. Got it?"

His voice was low and serious, he watched me like he was waiting to see my truthfulness.

"Dad, I got it." I nodded. "I'll be late, okay?"

He let me go and said, "I trust you Xon. Your word Xon. Numbers 30:2."

"I know Dad." Just then, the bus roared past. "Shit! Leo, run!"

I ran off and Leo came with me. The bus was down the street, Jarrod and Gavin already boarding.

"Wait! Mrs. Dorris, wait!"

The bus heaved away from the sidewalk just as I reached it and I banged on the door. It bent inwards and shrieked in protest. The bus jerked to a stop and the kids on the bus screamed, some in laughter but others in earnest fear. The doors groaned as they opened, the windows cracked and the plastic distorted.

Mrs. Dorris stared at me as I hopped on, Leo behind me. "You…you just…it's not poss-"

As she said it, she noticed my wolf spark glinting brightly. She paled and slumped back against the driver's side window, swallowing so hard it sounded like she was trying to gargle donuts. Her fleshy body wobbled from her thick head down to her large ankles, she looked like a human sized pile of Jell-O.

Leo caught my arm just as I realized I had been leaning into her, staring at her and the bus was dead silent.

Mrs. Dorris was ice white. "I'll, uh, I'll have to report this as visually threatening me."

"Report it then." I said, moving to sit by a window and lowering it so I would have fresh air.

Leo slumped next to me as the bus peeled off again. He looked at me, amazing how an emotionless gaze could look so much like censure.

"I'm sorry." I said, trying not to snap at him.

It wasn't his fault Mrs. Dorris made me get hungry or something. I didn't actually want to eat her, at least I don't think so. It was just her body made me think of food.

Dammit...that's cutting the line a little too thin Xon.

Leo shrugged and closed his eyes as if he was going to sleep, a sign of submission that he wasn't going to try and argue with me. It wasn't the first time Leo had closed his eyes as if to say, *I'm not mad, I'm not doing anything, I'm completely defenseless.* So I let him be and looked out of the window.

The bus stayed quiet the rest of the ride and even when other students got on and tried to be loud, it got quiet again after they were told what happened. Once the bus got to school, everyone trampled off like gazelle fleeing from a cheetah, even Mrs. Dorris waddled her ample body down the steps to go report me.

Leo got off second to last with me behind him. Most of the front lawn was empty, like the news that Xon Reeves was an aggressive werewolf who threatened his bus driver had already spread and no one wanted to be around me.

"Hey, hey! Morning, Leo, Xon!" Connor had a wide smile on his face as he reached us but then his nose twitched and he stared at us. "What...what's that smell? I've never, you guys didn't smell like that last time I saw you. What gives?"

"It's us." I said, hoping I could explain this better and Connor would understand. "We're Packmates now. Like a real Pack."

Connor's dark brown eyes went wide. "Whoa, really? Sweet! How can I join? How did you do it? I mean, Javier is from a Pack but us Wildebeasts aren't a true Pack, not like his Pack in Spain."

It was my eyes to go wide next. "The Wildebeasts?"

"Yeah, that's what we call ourselves." Connor took my hand and sniffed along my wrist and forearm, examining the Pack scent. "Like wildebeest but pronounced like wild beast. The Wildebeast Pack but like I said, we aren't a real Pack. And Shane's not really an Alpha but he is the leader because he's the strongest after the Dominion."

I clarified, "That being Mr. Forrest."

"Yup," said Connor, now rubbing my hand on his cheek, like he was trying to spread my Pack scent to him but I was sure it wasn't that simple. "Basically Mr. Forrest is the leader over all the shifters in Lakeside Village. If shifters have a problem between themselves, then they go to him. But he's so mean and so angry all the time no one really wants to bother him so everyone does their best to stay in line. I heard his other form is an Ursine, so massive that he'll eat whoever gets in his way when he's in his animal form. So nobody wants to cross him out of fear they'll get eaten."

Now that last bit I could believe. I had felt some of his strength and saw how his face distorted when his beast peeked out. Not to mention my wolf had been instinctively frightened of him even though I hadn't known what Mr. Forrest was; my wolf knew he wasn't to be messed with, old, bald and grumpy or not.

"What's an Ursine?" I asked even though I was a little scared to know.

"Humans would say a were-bear," said Connor, shrugging as he let me go. His cheek smelled like me then the scent faded away as the wind blew. He puffed up his cheeks and placed his hands on his hips. "Well, that didn't work."

The late bell rang, we had been so busy talking I missed the first warning bell. Connor rushed away while Leo and I headed to American Literature.

Ms. Cannon sighed heavily at the sight of us walking in late. "Really? Again? I ought to send you both to the main office for a tardy slip."

I winced at the idea of getting a fourth detention, which would automatically get me suspended. As if Mom wasn't mad enough at me already, failing in school right at the start of my junior year would really set her off.

Ms. Cannon looked pitying and her scent was a mix of worry and sadness to make it smoky and muddy.

She sighed but then smiled. "Alright, sit down. And when the week starts again on Monday, let's start fresh, okay Xon? Don't drag Leo down with you either, okay?"

I grinned, thanked her and sat down.

Greg, the kid on my left side, muttered to the kid on his other side. "Why're those two always together? Maybe Xon swings for the other team."

If Greg thought I couldn't hear him, he was an idiot because even if I was a human being I would have heard. Plus, I could smell his smugness, like tart citrus and the scent of his belief in his words, like mint. He was gossiping right next to me and as I heard the other kid agree, I contemplated killing the both of them.

Leo nudged me with his foot across the aisle, we caught eyes and he shook his head at me. His face may have revealed no emotion but his scent was the faint piss of nervousness and wet ash of disapproval. He heard Greg and he knew what I was feeling and he knew what I was thinking and he was telling me it was a bad idea.

I looked at my work as Ms. Cannon started class but I couldn't hear what she was saying. Instead, I mentally consulted what I knew about the bible and times of trouble.

God, hear me out and please listen because I'm literally at the end of my rope. You say in James 1:2-4 that I should see trouble as joy because in testing my faith I'll get patience and wisdom and You'll give me peace or something like that. I remember this because Dad quoted it at me all the time when I was younger and I'd get frustrated whenever something didn't go my way and he'd tell me to be patient because my faith was getting tested.

Well God, my faith is tested but I don't feel any patience or wisdom or anything!

"Stop growling please Xon, it's disrupting class. Do it again and I'll report it as being vocally threatening," said Ms. Cannon as she walked by my desk.

I swallowed back the next grumble, I didn't even realize I had started to growl. Greg was pale and on the edge of his seat again.

Ms. Cannon tapped my desk. "And you're on the wrong page of the book. Try and pay attention, alright? Continuing on, Mark Twain, real name Samuel Clemens. His works *The Adventures of Tom Sawyer* and *The Adventures of Huckleberry Finn* are considered to be what's known as The Great American Novel genre..."

I tried to listen and take notes. The first period passed by without any more provocation then Leo walked me to Mrs. Ellis' class for Algebra II. I knew he came just in case Shane showed up but today it was Connor and Sky in the hallway.

Connor spoke in a high piping tone, "Wait until you smell it Sky, you'll really like it! I can't wait to smell like it too!"

Sky had a doubtful expression on her face, mimicked by the dank and cold scent coming from her. As we got close I watched her nostrils flare and her eyes went heavy-lidded for a moment, like she smelled something wonderful and savored it.

"You see?" Connor latched his arms around my waist and buried his face into my stomach, wriggling into me as he inhaled deeply.

"Connor!" I laughed as he both tickled and embarrassed me.

I pulled him off and playfully swat his head, he ducked and grinned at me. Yet even with his wide smile and bright eyes, I smelled the wet mud on him, like his skin was imbued forever with the scent of sadness. It was strange and upsetting but I didn't know how to ask him. With what happened when I pushed Leo's buttons, I didn't want to hurt Connor by being too nosy too.

Some students watched us, they all had on little twisted smirks and leering eyes. I glared at them, my lip lifted as fangs grew. They paled and scampered off.

One said, "Xon becoming a wolf turned him into a real nutcase. Did you hear that he visually threatened his bus driver?"

The other responded, "And now he flashed his fangs at us! He's got mad problems."

Sky shook her head at me as I stared after them with my fists clenched. "Let it go Xon. Its only with shifters they use terms like *visually* threatening or *vocally* threatening. If we glare or growl or anything that can be remotely animalistic, they'll report it. After enough reports, then it goes to the head shifter of our Village. And if you get the Dominion after you, that's not good at all."

"I've heard." I again remembered how frightening Mr. Forrest had become once he let his beast peek out. "So an Ursine is a bear shifter, right?"

Sky nodded. "The largest land predator shifter we've got and they're the only natural predators of werewolves, who are normally considered the top predator and in charge. See, the Ursine Way, that is, their rulebook, is to eat what they kill. So let's say you are in the forest when Mr. Forrest is there and you piss him off while you're both in shifter form, well, he'll kill you and eat you. The Ursine eat everything that they kill, so there'd be nothing left. That's why he's the Dominion, he's the biggest predator in this town."

She shrugged. "Technically Carter should be Dominion because he's a werewolf but he said no, then it would be Shane but Shane is still a little too young to be in charge of the entire shifter population in Lakeside Village. So Mr. Forrest it is."

"Who's Carter?" I asked even as the late bell rang.

Immediately, like a switch, Connor's peachy skin turned a yellowish color, drastically paling in just seconds. His scent, already stained with the wet mud of sadness, now mixed with the sickly sweet of disgust, revolting like a spoiled fruit drink. His face, the smile I had always seen on him even when he had a black eye, just slipped off and left his mouth a straight line.

Still, he answered.

"My father."

Then he turned and left, leaving behind a gaseous stench cloud that made my stomach turn, even Leo put his hand over his nose.

Mrs. Ellis came to the door, looking upset. "Please come inside Xon, and you two, go to the office and get a tardy slip before you go to class late. Xon, come in now."

I had more questions to ask but Sky walked away, saying, "Come on Leo."

I followed Mrs. Ellis into class as the other two left.

Aydan and Regan were both hovering at the small trash bin next to the door where the pencil sharper sat on a ledge, the pencils slack in their hands. They were both watching me with a look like I was an animal that had escaped the zoo, their scents overwhelming with the sour milk scent of unease, twisted with the thick smoky scent of worry.

I met their gaze with the bright glowing glare of a furious wolf.

With pissy scents to match, they spouted together like frightened children. "Mrs. Ellis, Jaxon is visually threatening us!"

Mrs. Ellis sighed and said in a firm tone, "Twins, go sit down. You too Xon."

Aydan and Regan went to the back and I took my seat at the front. I twisted the straps of my book bag in the same manner of wringing a neck then I got out my books.

If I have to hear visually threatening or vocally threatening one more time, I really will go wolf shit on everyone who even glances at me!

Even as I thought it, I thought of a scripture Dad would tell Mom whenever she gets worked up into a rage. Dad had a scripture for everything and I always admired how he'd turn to the Bible for any situation. It was me who didn't read it like I should and now everything is going to hell. I heard the verse in Dad's voice, telling Mom to calm down after she had given me a beating.

"Proverbs 15:18, a hot-tempered person stirs up conflict, but the one who is patient calms a quarrel. You know the verse Kyra, so just take a breath and relax before you go too far."

I groaned and covered my face with both hands.

Dad, God, I'm trying, I don't want to go too far but honestly, if someone else treats me like I'm nothing but a dangerous animal, I'll really lose it!

I took my hands down and paid attention before I started growling again and get reported for another vocal threat. I didn't know how many threats had to be reported before the Dominion would talk to me but I knew I had tallied up a good few. I had growled at Greg, growled at Melody, glared at Mrs. Dorris, glared at the twins and if those students in the hall told someone that I had *flashed fangs* at them, then there was another report. If all of those reports also gave me another detention, I'm suspended. Who gets suspended in the first week of school? Mom would throw a fit, beat me then not want to look at me. She was mad enough that I was a werewolf but add in a delinquent student and she might disown me.

Class went without another hitch as I strove to really pay attention and get my work done. The bell rang and it was time for lunch. When I left, Connor and Leo were waiting for me. I hugged them both, Leo around his neck and Connor around his waist, pulling them tight to me. I had to because I was so grateful for them, for accepting me at a time when everyone else either feared me or was bullying me or even both. These two were my pals, my fellow wolves.

A. E. Costello 97

I closed my eyes and focused on the scents of the two in my arms. Leo, wolf, thick heady forest, male, personal scent of lemons, sunshine and on top was the Pack scent, home, familiar, bond. Connor, young wolf, softer and wispier forest, male, personal scent of cinnamon, clover and wet mud. He didn't have the Pack scent but I would give it to him. We had to do something that would reinforce a bond between our wolves, meaning we should probably go hunting. It was Friday, I was sure I could make something work. The late bell rang, so I let go of Connor and Leo, who had let me hug them without fighting or protesting. We headed to lunch without needing to say anything and in the comfortable silence, I thought about Connor.

I wondered about Connor's stained scent and then of course his disastrous reaction to the name "Carter" who he said was his father. I loved my father and I can't imagine what he could do to make me smell like disgust at just the sound of his name. Did Carter do something to Connor that has made him permanently smell sad? What event could do something like that? I kind of wanted to know, because I cared but at the same time it felt like a morbid curiosity and I didn't actually want to know. I *did* hope whatever it was had stopped and Connor wasn't actually being mistreated at home. First I had Leo who had lost everything he loved until he became emotionally broken, and now Connor.

I reached the large bowl-like cafeteria and stood at the top of the large stairs that lead down into it. I could see my former friends already getting their table and looked away as I headed down the stairs. This time I shrugged and decided to get chili-cheese dogs and fries. I ignored the smell, it was just to get me through the day and I'll make sure to eat all of that meat at home for dinner tonight.

We all got our food and went back to sit where we normally sat. I hadn't even blessed over it when Daewon came over, looking worried.

"Hey Xon," he said, rubbing the back of his neck. "Listen...you've been kind of avoiding me...and I see that you've got new friends now but I want you to know I still consider you my best friend. I don't care that you're a werewolf, and I don't feel the way the Summers do, I know you're not a demon. Besides, it's not like you asked to be a werewolf, right?"

I nodded and managed a smile for him. "I definitely didn't ask for it. It's true I'm not a demon but I'm also still learning how to deal with this. This is Leo and Connor." I inclined my chin to each one. "They're really helping me out."

Daewon dipped his head at them. "Yo."

Leo said nothing and Connor raised one hand in return.

I said, "I'm doing okay I guess, but its true I don't really want to be around the other guys. It's not like they want to be my friends anymore."

Daewon shrugged. "Forget them. Honestly they're scared of you, but maybe they'll come around. My food's getting cold, but I'll see you later, alright?"

I nodded and he jogged away back to the table.

Connor said, in a sort of dour tone, "If I had a choice, I would *not* be a wolf right now."

Like a switch, his scent morphed into the throat-clogging suffocating scent of despair, along with the dank lifelessness smell of depression and then rushed in was the drenching piss scent of fear. His dark brown eyes fell into blackened misery as his skin soured yellow.

I stared at him, shocked at this dramatic reversal of Connor's chipper character. I had only seen it once before, when Sky said the name Carter.

Connor's father.

I asked, "Did Carter Change you into a werewolf? Your dad I mean."

Connor looked at his tray and said nothing but his fists curled into tight shaking balls, white fur slipped out of the knobby knuckles. This was clearly a bad button to press, especially because I didn't want Connor to Change right here in the cafeteria.

Trying to take it back, I said, "I didn't mean to upset you."

He nodded, still silent and his emotions were giving off such a stench, I stood up.

"I'm going to the bathroom. Be back."

Leo nodded and Connor didn't move.

I winced and went up to the bathroom across from the stairs.

Really classy Xon. You already knew there was something up between Connor and his father, then you just go and ask like that. I'm lucky he didn't attack me or something.

I opened the door and *bam*, the smell slammed me right in my sensitive nose, fecal matter, piss, bacteria, vomit, dirt, skin and hair. Coughing, I ignored it and came in.

Just standing away from the urinal was Shane Armstrong, and he sneered the second he saw me enter the bathroom. "So it's the weak little pup. You need to watch yourself, boy. Remember your place."

I looked around, we were the only ones in the bathroom.

Hmm, Leo's not here to stop me. Open Season.

I grabbed Shane's collar and shoved him against the wall. The tiles cracked around his body. My hand tightened on his collar, I dug my knuckles into the thickness of his throat.

Shane slammed his arm on my forearm, knocking me off his neck. He tackled me around the waist. I twisted while grasping the back of his shirt and heaved, so with his own momentum sent us tumbling to the ground. I was on top, my knees dug into Shane's abdomen and I pulled back my fist, my other hand latched around Shane's throat.

His eyes widened seconds before a thick heavy odor suffocated my nostrils, a hard hand clasped onto my shoulder and squeezed until I thought my bone was going to snap like a toothpick.

"Let him go boy."

I dropped Shane instantly, taking my other hand to my shoulder and trying to get Mr. Forrest's hand off me. His grip was like a steel clamp, I couldn't get him off even as I struggled. Shane laid still on the floor, his eyes frozen in place, like he was in shock.

"You, get out of here." Mr. Forrest pointed at Shane and jabbed his thumb at the door. "Git on now. I'll talk to you later."

Shane got to his feet and brushed himself off. He glared at me with vivid olive eyes but walked out of the bathroom without another word.

"Let me go man!" Tears burst in my eyes at Mr. Forrest's tight grip, my shoulder was getting crushed.

Mr. Forrest let me go with a push, I tumbled forward and hit the floor, scraping my knees.

"You fool." He spoke in a low harsh tone. "Picking fights in a public area, humans everywhere. I heard several reports about you and I thought you'd clean up your act but you really are a dumb kid."

I glared up at him. "I'm not dumb and I'm not a kid either." I got to my feet, rubbing the throbbing ache in my shoulder. "Shane's been the one picking fights all week, I finally got my chance to get back at him, that's all."

"And if you had crushed his trachea?" Mr. Forrest countered, his beady black eyes staring me down. "What if your need for dominance got so great you Changed forms in front of him? Did you think about that first?"

I looked at the floor, my head down. "No sir."

"Yeah, exactly, didn't think so. I understand there's a power struggle happening between you and Armstrong, however if you had seriously hurt him it wouldn't just fuck up your life but the life of every other shifter around. The world doesn't revolve around you Reeves, you have to think about more besides yourself but about your fellow wolves and the rest of us shifters, understand?"

I nodded again, staring at the floor as I smelled my ashamed scent, like bitterness and sour.

"Yes sir."

"Good. You're lucky I smelled your anger walking past the hallway and I put a stop to this behavior. Two wolves fighting in the bathroom would have brought about more trouble than you're worth. Now get outta here. Now!" He grabbed me and shoved me toward the door.

I left with a roar behind me. "AND STAY OUT OF TROUBLE!"

Leo looked up at me curiously when I came down to the table again, I had been gone for way too long just for a bathroom break. Connor was eagerly picking up crumbs from his empty tray, like what I had said before had never happened.

Leo's nostrils twitched as I sat next to him and he leaned into my shirt, not so discreetly sniffing me.

"Dude." I protested, using my elbow to back him off. "The smell is Mr. Forrest."

I hurriedly ate, even as my veins still tingled and sparked, my wolf growled quietly, my shoulders rocked back and rolled forward, I was tense down my spine. I had a hint of my own strength. Shane was taller than me, more muscled, he must have weighed just a little over two hundred pounds. I could have killed him, crushed his throat.

Even as there was a surge of excitement, a rush down my chest, igniting that hot hard coal in my stomach, I knew I couldn't do that. I'd never kill Shane, I've never wanted to really hurt anyone. I knew I couldn't put all the blame on the wolf, Shane really did make me mad enough to *want* to kill him but it was the wolf who gave me the power, the fangs and claws and the strength to make it possible.

Leo placed a hand on my shoulder, the bell had rung and I was still sitting down. I stood up and got my book bag.

Connor said, "Xon, you're really growing up."

He said it with a smile but his scent fluctuated from his sad wet mud smell to a quick dash of piss, fear and the smoky smog of worry.

I smiled at him. "Connor, I'd never be like Shane. I'd never hit you or knock you around just because I can. With this right here." I grasped my bicep, it filled my hand, my fingers pressed against the firm mound. "And with this." I held out my hand and clenched it into a fist, watching how my knuckles cracked, the veins raised over my wrist and the short flex of tension. "I'll use these to protect, not to harm."

Connor's eyes widened and he gazed at me like he had never seen me before, his scent morphed, intermixing with the sadness there was a new scent. It was fluffy like cotton but tense, a little tight with sweetness and lemon. Hope. Connor smelled hopeful.

Leo bumped his head against mine, and pressed his nose to my ear. If we had been in a wolf form, it would have been a soft nuzzle but we were humans; so it was more like he was knocking his skull on mine and putting his soft damp flesh in my ear and everyone was staring.

I swiped for Leo, he ducked and I said, "You'd better quit it!"

My voice was warning but I wasn't really angry at him. I pulled Connor into a hug, then with my hand on Leo's neck, pulled him in close.

I said softly into our huddle, "Thanks you guys."

"You're too heavy." Connor gasped, wiggling his head against my chest, his hands pressing against my abdomen. "And you're smothering me!"

I let him go with a laugh then pushed Leo's face away. "Let's go to class then. Things are gonna change around here."

Leo's eyes just slightly widened but his smell exploded with a burst of tingling orange and jolting citrus. Happiness and excitement.

The late bell rang as they both walked me to U.S. History. I didn't need them to but with this new sense…the feeling of resolve and the understanding of the strength I had and what I should be using it for, I let them.

I waved them on at the door, saying, "I'll see you guys after school, at the park. I have detention first though." My voice was clear and firm, I looked them both in the eyes.

Connor's smile quivered, his scent sad, anxious, hopeful, excited, scared, he was feeling so much that all the scents combined, making him just smell funny, weird. Too much going on. Leo gave me a nod then they both walked away.

"Let's go Xon," said Mr. Malone. "Class is waiting on you."

I came in and took my seat by the window. Mr. Malone started class and I paid attention the best I could, which helped class go by easier. When the bell rang, I headed straight to Ms. Hughes' class for Psychology without any incidents in the hallway.

I went and got into my seat. Melody was already inside. My seat is in the middle of the room, with Melody's at the front by the window just two seats in front of mine. This gave me a perfect view to admire the curve of her neck and the adorable golden curls at her temples. My chest tightened as a crumpled and weak scent rose from my own body, the smell of emotional pain. She thought I was a demon, and broke up with me for something that I had no control over.

I stared at my desk and did slow calming breaths. If I started growling at her then I'd get into trouble. I closed my eyes and covered my face with my hands, inhaling just my scent.

This isn't fair! I didn't ask to be changed into a werewolf! I was attacked, I was nearly killed! What's demonic about me? I'm losing my friends, I've lost my girl. I'm losing everything!

I slammed my hands on my desk and broke the wood like it was toilet paper, shattering it into pieces and the legs fell to the ground with a clatter. A few people screamed, everyone stared at me, Melody's eyes were wide and shocked.

Ms. Hughes, pale and shaking, said softly, "You have to go to the office Xon for destroying property. And because it was done in a violent manner, I'll need to report it as an act of aggression. I'll write the slip."

I nodded and got my book bag then waited by the door for Ms. Hughes to write out the notice. I didn't think anything or look at anything, I couldn't even pray right now. Melody's huge blue eyes looked at me both imploring and shameful, like she knew exactly why I had broken my desk. I looked away from her.

Ms. Hughes handed me the slip and her mouth opened to talk. I stalked out and I barely managed not to slam the door behind me.

At the office, I handed the receptionist Mrs. Mitchells my slip. She read it and sighed heavily even as she handed it back. Without saying anything to me, she dialed someone on the phone.

When it picked up, she said, "Principal Hamilton, I have Xon here with a report from Ms. Hughes. Aggressive behavior and destruction of property."

On the line, Principal Hamilton said, "Send him in."

Mrs. Mitchells tilted her head to me, so I went to the principal's office on my own. The door was parted, so I gently knocked and then came in.

Principal Hamilton gestured to the seat in front of her desk, she was taking out a file. I could see *Jaxon Reeves* written on it from the doorway.

I sighed, placed the new slip on her desk and sat down.

I said, "I didn't attack anyone or do anything aggressive. I broke my desk, I didn't even mean to! I didn't know my own strength."

"That's not the point." She said, looking through my file and tucked the newest slip inside. "Do you want to know how many reports I've received about you Jaxon Reeves over the past *three* days since school has started. Do you?"

I actually didn't but I had a feeling that wasn't the answer she wanted to hear.

She started talking without waiting for a response. "August 6th, you were reported by Ms. Cannon for visually threatening another student and you also had to be seen by Ms. Sher for escaping class. Then August 7th, Mr. Malone reported you for animalistic behavior in class, whining noises and kicking the floor like a puppy. Ms. Cannon reported that you escaped her class and had to be brought back in by another student. Two incidents reported by Mr. Dorman that you attacked Shane Armstrong in a violent manner and had to be held back. Ms. Hughes reported that you escaped class and you also visually and vocally threatened her. And now today, August 8th, first off your bus driver Mrs. Dorris had to come in and report you visually threatened her in addition to the fact you damaged the bus door. Ms. Cannon reports that you were vocally threatening in class. Then I had two students report that in the hallway you were visually threatening and showed your fangs. Mrs. Ellis reported that you visually threatened two students in class. And once again, Ms. Hughes reported that you were growling and vocally threatened another student, namely Melody Summers. And now, just now, you've been reported by Ms. Hughes for aggressive behavior and destruction of property."

She sighed, closed the folder and looked me in the eyes. "In three days Jaxon, just *three days*, that's *twelve* reports. Maybe you don't know, but it takes ten reports of a shifter's misbehavior before they are suspended and sent to an alternative school. That is troubling Jaxon, plus your three detentions, in just three days."

I had no idea my teachers were actually reporting me. They always said *otherwise I'll report* or *I can report* but they never said they actually were reporting, I thought they were letting me know that they could have if they wanted to. But the most bewildering part was that Principal Hamilton didn't know that I had attacked Shane in the bathroom and it was Mr. Forrest who broke it up. Does that mean that Mr. Forrest purposely didn't tell the principal about it? If he had done it, that would have given me ten reports and thus alternative school. So was he helping me out by not saying anything? It was nice of him but didn't help because just now I had raked up twelve reports.

Alternative school. Just great. Mom is mad enough as it is...she'll lose it entirely now. And what about Dad? I...I broke my word to him. Again.

I said, "Please Principal Hamilton, just give me another chance. I promise I won't threaten anyone again. You've got to understand my position, Shane is-"

"I do know what the shifter school atmosphere is currently Jaxon and that doesn't change the fact you are and have been continually breaking rules." She cut me off. "I tried to be lenient with you because I know you are newly Changed but now that you've become destructive I can't let this go on. The alternative school is in a different county entirely and its run by shifters for shifters. They'll teach you proper shifter behavior and they'll decide how long you should stay. I will say a week, so you will stay for that long but if they decide you should be kept longer, then longer you will stay. If you continue to be aggressive, then they'll have to report it to the government and the government will then decide if you should be entered into a correctional facility. Do you understand this process Jaxon?"

I stared at her, my stomach sinking somewhere below my knees. "Please, Principal Hamilton, don't do this."

She looked down at her desk and picked up her phone. "I need to call your parents here so that they can sign the appropriate paperwork agreeing for you to be sent to alternative school. If they refuse, then you will be indefinitely suspended from this school. Please sit there quietly."

Everything in me wanted to protest but it was clear she wasn't listening to me. So I sat there as she called my father and did my best to not start whining or whimpering or anything inhuman which would only make my problems worse.

My father came on the line. "This is Grant Reeves, to whom am I speaking?"

"Mrs. Lisa Hamilton, Principal of Lakeside Village Comprehensive High School." She introduced herself formally. "I'm in my office with your son Jaxon Reeves and I've assigned him to alternative school. So I need you to come in and sign the acceptance paperwork then take him home for the day. When he returns to school on Monday, there will be a ride waiting to take him to the alternative school. He's suspended from our school for a week while he goes to alternative school."

Dad was silent for a few seconds but I could almost smell the anger rising through the phone.

He said, "Understood. I'll be there."

Then he hung up.

For Dad to be that rude, he was furious. I sighed and covered my face again but even the smell of my own scent didn't help. My eyes pricked and I swallowed hard but the whimper came out of my throat, a low mumbling sound like a wolf that just got kicked.

Principal Hamilton said, "Please stop that. You can cry if you need to but please don't make that sound."

My teeth gritted.

So I can cry because crying is a human thing but if I whimper, which is a wolf sound, that's not allowed. So shifters can come to school but only if they act as human as possible. If they act in anyway inhuman then they get reported. Enough reports and a shifter is kicked out of school to be trained by other shifters on how to act human. And if the shifter still doesn't act human, then off into a correctional facility, where shifters go and they never come back.

I cried now and I couldn't stop it. It just wasn't fair. I didn't have any scriptures for this, I didn't know what Dad would say and I didn't know what to say to God. Why would He do something like this? Set me up for failure? Why bother to send Leo and Connor to help me if it wouldn't matter anyway?

Principal Hamilton handed me a box of tissues and I plucked some out to dry my face. I heard the strident voice of none other than Kyra Melissa Reeves, my mother. Looks like Dad called her but I wished he hadn't done that.

"No Grant, no! Don't tell me to calm down! This is such bullshit! Not my son! He doesn't get suspended, he doesn't go to alternative school!" Her voice grew louder as did the clicking of her heels and I could hear Dad's heavy treads as well.

Principal Hamilton stood up but didn't get to speak when the door slammed open. Stalking in was my mother. Her cheeks were flushed and sweat on her forehead, her fists clenched. I didn't need to see that to tell my mother was in full-on rage mode. Her scent was extremely hot, so hot it burned my nose and my heart rate ramped up. Rage just might not cover how upset my mother was.

"Suspension?" Her shout shook the rafters. "*And* alternative school? Jaxon William Reeves, I don't care what's going on with you but I'm not taking it anymore!"

She stalked over to me, her hand swung back, I steadied myself for the blow then Dad caught Mom's arm and brought it down. Principal Hamilton was staring at us like we were insane.

Dad said calmly, "Kyra, remember where we are. Try not to completely lose it in public. Principal Hamilton." He looked the other woman. "We're going to take Xon home now and get this sorted out. Please, is alternative school really necessary? He's been a werewolf for barely a week and these first three days of school are just rough. He shouldn't be kicked out so quickly, it hasn't been enough time. He can still be suspended for a week but not alternative school. If he stays home and we keep him calm, alternative school won't be necessary."

Principal Hamilton held up a finger. "One week suspension then one week probation. If he gets in one more fight or his teachers report him or give him detention, he's finished here for this semester. He'll go to alternative school and can come back second semester. Here." She gave Dad a printout. "This is the list of the reports. Maybe when you talk to him you can use this to address these issues."

"Jaxon." She looked at me with firm eyes. "Get yourself straightened out, understand? Come back to us, be that good student you've always been. Okay? You can return to school on August 15th. Friday to Friday. We clear?"

I nodded. Mom grabbed my arm, trying to drag me out of the seat. Not only was she too small and weak, I was a werewolf now. My dense bones were entirely too heavy for her. Even Dad who was taller and more muscled than me might not be able to move me.

I stood up and Mom stormed out of the office. I went after her and Dad walked the rear. There were two cars parked at the curb, Mom's Nissan Maxima and Dad's Ford Ranger.

Mom snapped, "Take him Grant! Otherwise I'll try to beat him and drive at the same time!"

Dad opened the door to his truck and I got in, by the time I was belting my seatbelt Mom was already squealing away from the curb. Dad buckled up and drove away.

He picked up his radio and said, "Kyra, slow down honey."

They had installed two way radios in their cars, something about it being safer than using cell phones while driving.

Mom didn't respond but her brake lights flickered as she did as told. We got home and Mom was out of the car and powering up the porch steps before Dad could put us in park.

He sighed heavy, saying, "She's beyond pissed Jaxon and there's only so much I can do. Be respectful, alright?"

I nodded and got out. Mom was in the entryway, pacing like a caged tiger.

She snarled at me, "Get in the living room and sit quietly!"

"Yes ma'am." I said, following directions.

The door closed behind Dad and there was no sound besides breathing, meaning they were either mouthing to each other or using some sort of body language. Then they came into the living room and stood in front of me where I sat on the couch.

Mom had a calmer expression but the hot spiciness of her smell revealed she was definitely still angry. Dad's face was lined and his wet muddy scent overwhelmingly sad.

I couldn't look into his face so I stared at my feet. I wanted to say *I'm sorry* but I knew that was the exact wrong thing to say.

So I said, "I'll do better...I really will. Its so hard to explain, what its like, having a wolf."

Mom's teeth snapped together. "A wolf Xon? What does that even mean exactly? You aren't a wolf, you are my son and my son doesn't get reports like aggressive behavior, destroying property and threatening students and faculty!" The paper crunched in her hand. "And don't you dare sit there with that pouty expression and blame it on something as infantile as a wolf!"

I looked up at her and everything I've been wanting to say came tumbling out all at once.

"Mom, it's not infantile, it's real and its happening. My other side, the wolf side, he's like an entire being on his own. He has his own wishes, his own thoughts and his own urges and it directly impacts me. If he gets pissed, I'm pissed. If he's hungry, I'm hungry. And sometimes I can't control him. Yes Mom, I'm not the person to be aggressive and threaten people but my wolf is an animal and that's what animals do."

A. E. Costello 111

"When someone is bullying me or pissing me off, the wolf wants to make them back down, so he growls or he flashes his fangs or he glares, that's how it works. Plus, the fact that I'm a lot stronger than I used to be, so when I hit the door in an attempt to get Mrs. Dorris to stop, I accidently broke it. In class, I hit the desk with both hands and I'm so strong that I broke it but my intention wasn't to break the desk, I was just frustrated."

My voice raised. "Now I've made new friends who are helping me out. What I need is my parents to understand me and all you do is reject the fact that I'm a werewolf!"

"You are not a werewolf!" Mom screamed at me, loud enough to make my eardrums ring. Her eyes were full of tears. "You are my son, Jaxon William Reeves, my baby boy I gave birth to! You aren't some wild animal, you aren't a wolf! You are my son, that's all you are! That's all I need you to be!"

I stood up but Dad pointed at me to sit back down.

I ignored him, looking my mother in the eyes. "I'm your son Mom. And I'm a wolf. I'm learning to deal with that. Now you need to deal with it too. I'm going out."

I walked out and neither of them called out to me. As I closed the door, tears ran hot down my face and this time I had no tissues to wipe them away.

4

I went to the one place I knew I would find people like me, people who would understand.

I went to the Lakeside Village Community Park.

Like I hoped, the Wildebeasts Pack besides Shane were lounging around on the playground equipment. Leo saw me coming first, loping up to meet me as I came down the steps. His fingers brushed the wetness on my cheeks, cocking his head to the side like a curious puppy.

I tried to smile but it fell without fully forming. "I'm okay, really. I had a bad day, that's all."

Connor came over next, his dark brown eyes wide and understanding. "We heard you got suspended. What did you do this time? It's only three days, even I haven't gotten suspended yet. And I'm a freshman!"

I sighed and said, "I'm just having a hard time, alright? Can't you let it go?"

"That's not good enough," said Sky, arms crossed and her hazel-gold eyes focused on me. "You don't get it Xon, what one shifter does effects everyone else. If you get humans thinking that werewolves are dangerous before you know it we won't be allowed to go to school with humans. You really want to be segregated like that? Human only schools and shifter only schools? Separate but equal doesn't work, history has already told us that."

I bared my fangs at her. "So now its all my fault? You want to blame everything on me? It's not my fault dammit! Not to mention some other shit is going down so you talking to me about segregation is not helping anything!"

Sky's eyes flickered to wolf silver as she took a short step forward, her eyes boring straight into mine. My hackles rose from my shoulders, and I stared her down right back.

Javier walked to stand in front of her, putting his hands up between us. "Amigos, please, stop. Infighting doesn't help. Xon is upset and we should be comforting him, not aggravating his condition."

Connor sighed and said in a low dull tone, "Shane is here. And he looks pissed."

Just as he said it, I smelled the hot spiciness of anger from behind me. I barely turned around in time when Shane's arm slammed into my throat and he shoved me into the side of the hill. He leaned into me, his knee slid between my legs and pinned my thigh down, his enraged face an inch from mine.

"Tell me why Forrest pulled me out of class this afternoon to complain about you, huh? He told me I was fucking up and needed to put you in place."

Shane didn't waste any time, his fist smashed into my stomach. My organs crumpled like my knees and I bent over, gasping out blood. His knee thudded into my chin, my teeth clicked together and pain radiated through my gums. I fell over backwards but then rolled to the side when his foot tried to stomp for my face. Using the hill, I pulled myself up and stumbled away.

"Don't run from me!"

Shane covered that ground with one bound, his hand tried to grab my throat. I knocked it to the side and landed a punch on his lip.

Shane touched his lip, it was busted with a few drops of blood staining his chin. He looked at me with fiery olive eyes, the gold wolf spark in his pupils bright enough to block out the sunlight.

His voice came out ruined with a growl. "So you wanna fight me pretty boy? You wanna fuck around with me?"

I shook my head, breathing so heavy and deep I was getting dizzy as oxygen flooded my system. My wolf was in full-on defense mode. Large sharp fangs in my mouth, my fingers buckled with ebony machete-style claws.

"No." I struggled to speak with twisted wolf vocal cords, my voice more a growl than human speech. "I want you to keep your hands off me."

Shane's head ducked down and he spread out his legs, his shoulders hunched. I could almost see his wolf etched around the edges of his body, readying to lunge.

"I'll put my hands wherever I want them on you. I'm the one in charge·here and you'd better follow the rules. You can't keep calling attention to yourself and getting reports all the time. That doesn't just get you in trouble but you'll get the rest of us in trouble too. I'll beat the living shit out of you until you get that straight. Forrest isn't going to kill me because of you!"

Shane charged and I tried to dodge but he was too fast. He grabbed me by the shoulders and tackled me to the ground, straddling my chest. I kicked up and bucked but he was too heavy. His thick knuckles would have pounded my face but Sky's hand caught Shane's fist, like a small kitten paw trying to hold back a lion. Yet she stopped him, veins crawling over the underside of her wrist.

Sky stood over me, her feet on either side of my head. Her eyes glinting silver with her wolf, she spoke firm and clear. "That's enough Shane. He gets the point."

Shane stood up but placed his foot on my chest, pinning me down. He pressed his weight on my chest, my ribs bent inwards but didn't break, not yet. He jerked his hand out of hers, flashing fangs as his lips pulled back in a warning snarl.

"I don't think he does Sky and it's not up to you. If he really got the point, he'd know better than to hit me back."

Sky's upper lip trembled as it rolled upwards, baring her fangs in defiance. The slim white curvatures were smaller than the ones in mine and Shane's mouth but they were just as deadly sharp.

She's defending me. Here I am, taller and more muscled than her but she's come to face off Shane to help me out. I need to do better than this.

Sky spoke. "No one likes being beat up Shane, of course he'd try and fight back! It's called self-defense! He knows, he's been suspended so he'll get his act together and he'll be fine from now on. So stop hitting him, your point is made. Its enough."

Shane stared Sky down, his hackles raised out of his shoulders, his blond hair darkened into tawny as the silk texture turned thick and coarse, fur tumbled across his skull.

He spoke in a growl. "You aren't in charge Sky and you don't tell me when my point is made. I say when its enough."

And with that, Shane kicked me in the face. My head whammed on the gravel, lights blinked on and off. Blood spurted from my nose and the back of my head cracked. Shane's foot drew back, his sneaker dripping red and struck again.

I rolled my head to the side and his foot collided into the gravel, particles exploded and sharp dust hit me in the eye. I grabbed Shane by the knee and heaved him off balance, pulling him to the ground then used my legs as a spring and forcefully rolled us over, me on top. It didn't last, Shane threw me off him with one hand. I cleared several feet and crashed to the ground, my arms cushioned my face. My nose made popping sounds as it healed and the fracture at the back of my skull crunched as it melded back into place.

"Come here you fucking bitch!" Shane's hand grasped my ankle and squeezed. His hold was like a child holding a newborn kitten too tightly, breaking bones effortlessly, my ankle crushed.

"Stop it already!" Sky's voice raised high. "He's had enough!"

I kicked out with my other foot as hard as I could. I hit air. Shane dodged and dragged me towards him with his demolishing hold on what was now just a sack of skin with powder on the inside. I screamed.

His fist slammed across my face, my jaw bone clacked out of place, blood tunneled down my throat, choking me. I covered my face with my arms but Shane yanked them to the side and his knee dropped hard on my face. My nose broke as did the surrounding bones, shattered into pieces, and several teeth rattled from my mouth in a flood of blood. My vision blacked out as my eyes were crushed back into my sockets.

This time I didn't get up and I laid still as Shane stood up, victorious.

"There," he said heavily. "I'd say you learned your lesson. Get your shit together Xon, or I'll kill you. As for the rest of you, keep yourselves in line as well. What I did to Xon was nothing, I'll do even worst to the rest of you."

With that, he walked away.

"Christ, look at Xon's face!" Connor yelped. "He looks awful. His face is all messed up."

"Let's heal Xon," said Sky. "Javier, you first."

Javier laid down on top of me, powering heat onto my face. Then others got on top of Javier, until my entire body was covered with Pack, all sending heat. The warmth seeped into me, and I lost consciousness for a moment.

When I woke up, I was underneath several bodies and so hot I was pouring with sweat, so much sweat that the grass around me was soaked in it. I was healed, my bones back in place and repaired, but I was sore, sore like I had been run over by a steamroller. Sure, my body was no longer injured but the memory of the fight remained.

How could I call it a fight? I got one little hit on Shane's lip but that was all. He had thoroughly trashed me.

My wolf was limp in his cave, so far back into the darkness I barely felt him. He was hurt, bruised, even though his physical body was safe inside me, spiritually Shane's whooping had cut him deep. We weren't as "grown up" as we thought we were and we certainly weren't ready to take on the leader. We had overstepped boundaries and paid for it.

I whispered so quietly I barely heard my voice, "Hey...I'm awake."

The person on top of me was Javier, he shifted and said, "Amigos, Xon is conscious and speaking. Connor, you may get up."

Connor said with a squished voice, "I think Leo fell asleep, he's too heavy. Sky, make him get up."

Sky said, "He's overheated. I'll move him to the side."

There was a thump and some weight lifted then Javier stood up and I opened my eyes. I was on the grass, up on the hill behind the playground, surrounded by trees and tucked inside a group of bushes. There was only enough room for me to lay out with everyone piled on top of me. Now Leo was sprawled over the bush, I could only see his legs and his arms awkwardly bent. Connor sat on a bush, panting and his ears were red. Javier jumped up to sit on a wide low-hanging branch. Sky sat behind me, leaning against a tree and this time my head was in her lap, her thighs cushioning my cheeks.

I quickly jerked up into a sitting position. I looked down and my shirt and pants were splattered with heavy doses of blood, and because I had been sweating, my clothes were clinging to me and I smelled…bad. Blood, violence, fear, stunk of sweat and disappointment and loss of face. I didn't want to smell it anymore. I covered my face, pulling my knees up and hid there. But it didn't comfort me because my jeans were sticky and wet, even worse, I smelled Shane on them, thick, heady, dominant. I wanted to rip my clothes off, I wanted to take a shower, a bath, dive into the ocean and swim away.

Sky's hand touched my lower back. "You don't have to cry or be ashamed Xon. Shane is like that, he uses his fist to explain things. He doesn't want you to cause anymore trouble, that's all."

"Yeah, yeah, I get it." My voice was low and quiet and I hated the pathetic sound of it.

Connor spoke next. "Shane beats on me all the time Xon, it's not a big deal."

"It is too a big deal!" I lifted my face, angry all over again. "He's the leader, right? If he's supposed to be in charge of this Pack, then he shouldn't be beating on us like this. He beat me until I was knocked out, and for what? How is that supposed to help?"

"Fear Xon," said Javier with a small shrug. "If you are afraid of him the way he is afraid of Mr. Forrest, then everything will stay stable. It is true what everyone says, if humans start to think that shifters are too dangerous to be in school with other humans, life will get a lot more difficult. Shane wants to make sure you understand that. And Shane being Shane, he makes it clear with pain. This way you know your place."

That last bit irked me enough that hard coal in my gut burned with life again.

Know my place? As in underneath him, as in lesser, inferior. I did not take taekwondo to get my ass beat like that. Dad used to box, he took me in the ring with him, he'd thrash me too but always taught me how to block, how to counter. Shane tore into me like I'm some pansy. No. No way. And not again.

Leo sat up without warning, bush leaves sticking out in his curly hair like green ornaments, white drool covered his lips and chin, dirt smeared over his cheeks. He made such a sight that we all laughed, the sound warmed in my chest and my stomach. Leo brushed at his face but his arm smeared the mess around, making me laugh even harder. The laughter healed, flushing away the bad feelings the fight had left in me.

Connor took it upon himself to try and clean Leo's face by picking at the stains.

Sky tapped my shoulder, so I turned around to face her. She sat behind me leaning against a bush, her legs still held open so her feet were on either side of my knees. She smiled at me and her lips were a smooth cinnamon brown and framed small pretty white teeth, her hazel-gold eyes twinkled like stars. Then she crossed her arms and her expression became serious, her mouth firmer.

She said, "Shane is the oldest and strongest werewolf in this village after Carter Hawkins. Carter refused to be Dominion, so as you know, Mr. Forrest took the position but at school he expects Shane to keep the other shifters in line. Shane does his job by beating up any shifter who acts out of turn, he uses his strength to frighten everyone into behaving."

She shook her head then said, "You're new Xon and you've racked up over ten reports in three days. Yeah, so to keep you straight and also as an example to the rest of us, he beat you senseless. If you don't like it, too bad because no one else can stand up to him. Leo is weak. Connor is too young. I'm not strong enough physically and Javier can't either. So if you don't want Shane after you again then don't fuck up again."

Her speech made sense but I didn't like it. Shane was only two inches taller than me and we were similar enough in musculature; I had about twenty pounds on him. If we had been both human, using my skills in taekwondo and boxing, I would have been the one whooping him. Yet we were wolves and it was different.

Shane was in charge, he was the top wolf and mine was brand new. The beating would have been over earlier but then I hit Shane back. Then the fight turned into one for Shane to prove who was in charge. A servant doesn't strike his master. True, we weren't in a master/slave relationship but the fact was Shane was leader and I'm the follower. Hitting him was like my wolf forgetting his place. Like Javier said, Shane beat me to put me back in my place.

My wolf, even as defeated as he was, he bared his fangs at the idea. That hard coal that had been in me from the start grew heavier and hotter.

So I'm just supposed to accept this? Dad didn't raise me to be a follower of anyone but Jesus Christ. I'm no punk either, Dad didn't send me to taekwondo and take me into the ring with him so I can get knocked around. I told him I wouldn't get in another fight and that I wouldn't let myself get hurt. Now look at me.

Sky said, "Listen, I need to talk to you, so let's make a time to meet up."

My eyes widened. "Meet up? Just me and you?"

Sky nodded. "Yes. Are you free tomorrow?"

She really does want to meet with me, but without everyone else.

I glanced at Leo, Connor and Javier to see how they felt about this, but none of them looked upset at all.

I said to Sky, "Y-yeah, I'm pretty sure I'm free."

"Then tomorrow, at one pm, Ridgeback Mall."

"Alright."

I looked down at my clothes, I was slick covered in blood. Another outfit ruined. It was dark outside, I didn't know what time it was but it was well after when my parents would want me to be home.

I sighed and said, "I've got to go home. It's really late, my parents have probably lost their minds worrying about me."

Sky placed her small hot hand on my face and scratched some coated blood off my nose. "You've got to get cleaned up Xon. We definitely can't let your parents see you like this then they really would lose their minds."

Javier said, "He can come to my house to use the shower."

Connor, finished with cleaning Leo's face, turned to me. "He'll need new clothes. Those are ruined." He rubbed his dirty hands on his jeans. "I think Carter has clothes that'll fit. You can borrow them, I'm sure he won't mind. He's tall and buff like Xon, so it'll be fine."

Even though I couldn't smell anything but myself, as the others' nostrils flared or flexed, I was sure Connor's scent had warped like the other times when Carter's name was mentioned. Another thing, Connor called his father by his name and not *dad* or *father*. I wouldn't dare call Dad by his name, like Jackson or Grant, so much disrespect right there. So Connor both disrespects this Carter and is disgusted by him. Plus, Connor's personal scent is stained with sadness and he shrugs off getting beaten on by Shane.

I asked, "How were you Changed Connor?"

He looked at me. "Do you want the clothes or not?" His eyes were like stone but I could see the flinch in his wolf spark.

I said in a soft voice, "Relax Connor, okay? Yes, I'd appreciate the clothes. Jeans and a shirt is fine."

With the plan set, we next had to figure out how to get me to Javier's house without the entire village seeing me covered in blood. I looked down at myself to check, now that my sweat had dried, my clothes were wrinkled and clasped tight to my body. Large splotches and splatters of blood decorated the cloth, along with gravel, dirt and grass. I really did look like I had been in a vicious street-brawl and came out on the losing end.

Leo took off his shirt and draped it over my shoulders. It wouldn't fit over my head because his shoulders weren't nearly as broad as mine but it was long enough to hide my chest. Leo stood behind me to hide my back while Sky walked in front of me, using her body to hide my legs. Connor left to steal his father's clothes.

We walked as quickly as we could to get to Javier's house. There were people driving on the street and some walking but no one stopped us to make small talk. I wondered if it was because they knew all of us were wolves or if because we were moving so fast they could tell we were in a rush. With the speed walking, we got across town in under twenty minutes and arrived at Javier's place.

Javier's house was a mansion tucked into the high hills in the opposite direction of the park and school. There was a gate at the sidewalk and a long winding driveway, with tall trees blocking the view of the house. The gate was open and Javier led us up the way. According to Sky's jealous recitation, Javier's parents had bought it for him specifically when he came to America.

"We are very wealthy." Javier shrugged as he let us in. "Xon, there is a big shower in the basement, so just head down there. Leo, you are covered in dirt and your hair is a bird nest. So you also might want to wash up."

Leo's mouth did a quick pull like he was going to frown but managed not to. I didn't think Leo made the conscious decision not to frown because his eyes did crinkle slightly at the corners as well. I knew he didn't like the idea but his brokenness on the inside forbid him from making expressions, forbid him from speaking. I knew his vocal cords were still working and hadn't been ruined during the

Change because he snores. I wondered what it would take to fix the broken thing, to stop the trauma from continuing to keep him from simple things, like laughing and talking.

I handed Leo's shirt back to him.

"Thanks."

Javier showed us the basement and Sky came down with us.

She said, "I've never been down here before."

The basement wasn't like mine, with a TV, couch and my gaming systems. It had a stone floor with several dips with drains at the center. The ceiling was covered in sprinklers while one side of the wall held multiple showerheads, the opposite side was equipped with deep tubs, in the far corner was a hot tub and the opposite corner a pool. Then there were a group of lockers stacked in the corner. There was a series of shelves holding towels and soaps. All the way across from where we stood at the bottom of the stair was another door, it was ajar revealing large wooden steps going up. I had no doubt they led outside. This basement was equipped purely to wash off large amounts of people after getting dirty...after a Change, running wild in the forest. There were no stalls, no curtains. It was a wide open space.

Sky's eyes went wide. "Well, I guess I better go back upstairs uh, let you guys...do your business."

At her pause, I looked over at her. Sky stepped back and blushed, her skin was dark so her cheeks turned a ruby purple. Her footsteps made soft pads on the steps as she fled.

Leo unbuckled his belt and tossed his shirt towards the towel rack. Leo then popped his top button and pulled the zipper down. He must have felt my gaze because he looked up and stared at me, his brows slightly raised.

"Oh, sorry."

I turned my back on him and gripped the bottom of my shirt to pull it over my head, it stuck to my skin. I yanked and the cloth tore in my hands like it was wet copy paper. I dropped the two halves on the floor. I grasped the waistband of my jeans and pulled in opposite directions, tearing it open, then jerked down the legs. I stepped out of the ruined clothes and tore away my briefs too. A showerhead gushed out water, Leo was already getting started.

I walked over and took a showerhead two down from him, switched the handle and hot goodness poured down my body. The water was like liquid heat. The water felt like a liquid version of the same heat my wolf had. As the water licked and slicked down my skin, the soreness seeped away. I stuck my face under the spray, the blood flowed off my skin. My nose and jaw felt smooth, soft. I rolled my shoulders and bent my spine, the water slipped over me, a soft luscious touch that wiped all pain and aches away.

"Xon, Leo!" Sky called from upstairs. "Come on already, Connor's back!"

I didn't want to leave the water but I turned off the spray and stood there, letting the droplets make their way down, crossing every contour and hard lanes of my body. Leo pressed a towel against my face, I took it and buried my face into it then dried off. Leo was putting his clothes back on, they were dirty but his body was clean now.

I hooked the towel around my waist and went upstairs, Leo behind me. Upstairs in the large living room, Javier had placed a chair with a pile of clothes on top. On the carpeted floor, Sky messed with Connor, tickling him and playfully fluffing his hair, while he wiggled and giggled. It reminded me of a puppy twisting and wagging his tail when getting his belly rubbed.

Javier wasn't there but I smelled food cooking, my stomach roared.

Sky turned around at the sound and her eyes focused on me, dashing from my chest, my arms, my legs and every other place between. I walked toward her as a thick sugary smell gushed from Sky's body. My nose was flushed clean now and my wolf labeled that new scent. Desire.

Attraction. Lust. After being beaten up by Shane, this was a nice stroke to my ego.

I couldn't help it, my lips tilted to the side, curving upwards.

"Hey." I said, my voice lowered, coming from a place in my chest. "My face is up here."

Connor burst into laughter. Javier made a shrieking high-pitched giggle. Leo's scent burst citrus.

Sky's fists clenched, her eyes paled from hazel-gold to silver. She spoke in a growled voice, "Oh, okay, so you think you're hot Xon? Think you're sexy or something? Is that it?"

"Nah." My smile was full-fledged and I couldn't take my eyes off her flushed face. "I'm just saying, you're looking everywhere but my face. Just making a comment."

Connor bent over onto his knees, gasping like his lungs were squeezed too tight to take a breath. Leo crumbled onto the floor, not making a sound but I had never smelled his scent this amused. Javier cackled again, like a hyena.

Sky stalked around me, heading for the door. "Fuck all of you, I'm outta here."

I caught her wrist, she yanked against me but I pulled her towards me. She kicked and my other hand knocked her ankle away, then grabbed her other wrist, reining her to me.

She bared fangs and snarled, "You let me go right now or I'll hurt you where it won't grow back!"

I let her go, she dropped to the floor then got back up and ran out of the house like we were chasing her. I watched her go, watched her butt hump up with each movement of her thighs, how her hips swung from side to side. Sky didn't close the door behind her, leaving us roaring with laughter. Leo crawled to the couch and stuffed his face into the pillows, his shoulders jerking in that uncontrollable way of someone unable to breathe, or rather that thing keeping him from making sounds was strangling him so he wouldn't laugh.

I dropped the towel and got dressed, no one was looking at me. Connor's face was hidden in his legs as he made short pig snorts, choking on air. Javier was cooking something amazing in the kitchen, the scents so good I inhaled deep and my mouth watered. My wolf howled and a small whimper bubbled from my lips.

Javier gestured me to a large dining table with setting for at least twelve. The table was carved out of hardy oak and the six legs were sculpted with snarling wolf faces.

"Come and eat Xon, you need it."

I dashed to the table and didn't sit down, didn't grab a fork. I gorged. I gobbled. Nothing was left. I didn't remember what I ate. There were no flavors on my tongue, I swallowed the food whole, no chewing.

My eyes dimmed, I weaved on my feet.

Javier chuckled and he touched the small of my back, herding me somewhere. "You ate worse than a werewolf my friend. Now you must sleep. Here, lay down."

I didn't know what the here referred to, my knees bent, my head pitched forward and I was surrounded in a dark pulsating place. I didn't know how much time had passed when I came back to my senses, though I was quickly aware of my surroundings. I was cuddled with three other guys.

I was in the center, my head laid on Connor's stomach, his skin soft and molded against my cheek and chin. Leo had his arms around my waist, his legs intertwined with mine and his head was buried against Connor's thighs and the top of my head. Javier was turned the opposite way, his head was nestled at my knees and his feet tucked against my collarbone. I realized we were sleeping on a blow up mattress, a huge one. Yet we were all taking up only the center, cuddled so close and tight together as if to make one unit, one life-force, one people. I closed my eyes and took in a long slow inhale then opened them.

Connor, he smelled like sadness, wet mud, even in his sleep, that scent was embedded in his skin with his personal scent of cinnamon and clover. Leo's personal scent of lemons and sunshine was dashed slightly burnt with irritation and a dose of the ammonia of anxiety, his arms around my waist were so tight, he was not only stronger than I knew but needier than I knew. Javier's feet were small and like dough, his toenails were shaped and cut. Yet there on his ankle was a small tattoo of a simplistic crown, a curved line with three spikes coming from it.

I laid there, curled by the wolves, with their skin, their bodies, their scents and kept Sky in my thoughts.

Javier woke up first, his wiggling toes tickled my chin. I jerked my head away, my skull thudded into Connor's stomach. He coughed deep and rolled over, tumbling his body over Leo's head and chest. Leo bucked, his arms swinging. I stood up and picked up Connor before he could get hurt by Leo's thrashing.

Connor wriggled in my grasp, yelping, "Put me down dammit! I'm not a pup, let me down!"

I lowered Connor to his feet. He didn't step away immediately, his hand on my abdomen to keep his balance while he yawned so wide his smooth face wrinkled and his mouth gaped like a whale shark. His scent remained sad underneath the scent of us.

Us, together, was a thick scent that laid on the roof of my mouth, lifting up from the pores of our skin. If Sky had stayed and slept with us she would have the scent too, this group scent, the Pack scent. When I saw her again, I'd make sure she smelled like me.

We let the silence hang for a moment, getting our brains back from the fog of that deep bonding sleep. Our smells were strong around us, the Pack scent was unique but totally ours. Like home, belonging, like sharing more than just our physical bodies but deeper into the metaphysical realms where our wolves dwelled.

I asked, "Javier...that tattoo, are you royalty?"

Javier shook his head. "No, not exactly. There's no monarchy within the shifter society but it's close enough.

The highest level of government in the shifter community is the UAC, or the United Alpha Council. There is no king and queen. My father is Rodolfo Méndez the Twenty-Eighth United Alpha."

I took this in then asked, "Who exactly are the UAC?"

Javier tilted his head at me. "The United Alpha Council is a council of one hundred and fifty Alpha wolves, the strongest of all wolves in the entire world. They're the top hierarchy, after them comes the Alphas of countries, such as the Alpha of the United States or Alpha of The Kingdom of Spain. Then comes the Alphas of Packs, and Packs have a hierarchy within themselves."

"The Wildebeasts Pack doesn't have much of a hierarchy," I muttered. "Seems like Shane is just in charge because he's the strongest."

"We're not a real Pack though," pointed out Connor. "At least not with Shane. The four of us though..." He sniffed his arm and his shoulder. "We're a Pack now."

Leo leaned in and pressed his face to Connor's lower back, smelling him. Connor dropped himself down on Leo's face, wrapping his arms around his neck while Leo kicked and struggled. I knew Leo wasn't hurt, his scent blossomed with the citrus of happiness. Javier jumped onto them, and the three roughhoused.

I stood there, watching them and I had to protect them. I knew nobody was going to stop Shane and Mr. Forrest wanted us to keep out of trouble, he didn't want to be bothered by us. That meant only one person could put Shane off his throne, out of his domineering violent place of power. Logically, it had to be me, but was I strong enough to do it?

5

It was pitch black outside, the time on the living room wall read it was past eleven. My parents would be worried sick about me. The last thing they knew I walked out around three in the afternoon after being suspended from school. I didn't have my cell phone or any ID on me. Anything could be happening to me.

I said, "I got to go home you guys, it's late. My parents are going to flip."

Javier sat on the edge of the mattress, rubbing his crusted eyes.

"I will walk you out." He said, standing up and stretching.

Carter's clothes didn't fit me perfectly. His jeans were longer than my legs and tighter at the waist, while his shirt was a little too large. They were fresh, clean, so I couldn't smell him on them. As we walked after saying goodbye to Javier, Connor's scent deepened and darkened to the fetid sickly scent of suicidal thoughts and the gagging smell of dread.

"Well," said Connor, looking at us through the fringe of green hair flopping over his forehead. "I guess this is it. See you guys tomorrow."

Even in the dark I could see the dull of his wolf spark, how his face slumped.

"Hey." I cupped my arm around Connor's shoulder then placed a hand on the back of Leo's neck. "Why don't you both come to my house? I can introduce Connor to my parents, we can eat and play video games. Mom can wash your clothes so you can wear them home. C'mon, the day doesn't have to end, right? It's the weekend!"

Connor's scent bubbled and popped, turning into the fluffy tense scent of cotton, sweet and lemon but combating it was a wet slimy mold scent. Hope and hopelessness fought within his small package.

Leo shrugged and rubbed his eyes, he wanted to go back to sleep.

Connor chewed on his lower lip and murmured, "I don't think Carter will like it…"

"You have to return his clothes to him anyway." I said, walking away and bringing the two with me. "I'll have them washed and you can bring them home tomorrow. Don't be scared, it'll be fine."

Connor's scent fluctuated again, the sweet fruity scent of pleasure versus the wet mud of sadness.

I picked him up over my shoulder and shouted to Leo, "Keep up with me!"

Then I ran, ignoring Connor bellowing for me to put him down.

Leo panted and wheezed when we trotted to a stop outside of my house. I laughed heartily while Connor pounded my back with his fists, his shoes kicked against my shirt. The same way Shane was so much stronger than me, Connor was so much weaker. He wasn't breaking my bones, it tickled more than anything.

"You asshole!" He cursed. "I'm not a fucking pup put me down right now!"

The door slammed open and Mom came rushing out, fists already raised for a beating. I quickly dropped Connor to grab her up and held her to my face, pressing kisses over her nose, forehead and cheek.

She protested, "Jaxon William Reeves you stop that! How dare you kiss and cuddle me when I'm ready to give you the ass-whooping of your life! Do you know what time it is? You promised you wouldn't disappear like that anymore and here you are! You've been gone for hours, no call, no text, nothing!"

I set her down then presented Leo and Connor to her.

Leo was using his shirt to wipe the sweat off his face while Connor glared at me and kicked me in the shins.

I laughed and said, "Mom, you've already met Leo Dawson. This is Connor Hawkins. He's a freshman but emphasis on the man. He's really been helping me during this tough time Mom, he's been at my side the whole time. Together, these two guys are my best friends."

I only didn't say *Packmates* because that was the last way to describe them to Mom, who didn't even want to hear me say wolf.

Connor stopped attempting to hurt me and stared up at me. His scent dropped, turning to the sharp onions of confusion, mixing with the fruity sweetness of hope, the tingly lemon of shock.

Mom crossed her arms tightly and looked down at him. "And is he mute too? Or deaf maybe?"

Connor frowned then smiled brightly. "No ma'am, I can talk just fine and I'm only deaf when I choose to be. Nice to meet you."

He saluted her. His scent was still sad, like that wet mud was a permanent smell but there was tingling orange smell of happiness covering him now.

Mom huffed then said, "Well, it's late, you two should be heading home."

"They're sleeping over, they have permission." I smiled.

Connor smiled too. Leo yawned, a whine-whistle that came from his nose when he closed his mouth. He leaned against me for a moment before standing straight.

Mom frowned then muttered, "Well, since you're already here then there's really no point in sending you home, especially since your parents expect you to be here. Come on then. You need to eat, shower then bed. You're lucky if I let you eat Xon."

"Yes Mom." I said obediently then shot grins to my fellow wolves as she walked into the house.

Inside Dad was sitting on the stairs, his face in his hands and his strong back bowed, his broad shoulders slumped. I crossed the entryway in one bound and knelt in front of him. I pushed my way into his arms, pressing my face into his neck and wrapped my arms around his waist, cuddling close. I didn't speak, I didn't want to, just inhaled the scent of family, of my father, of home.

Dad held me back close and his voice was choked. "I thought you weren't coming back Xon. I...I thought you had been...I thought I lost you."

I sat back and looked into his face, his smooth skin was lined at his eyes and mouth, crust on his cheeks from tears. Guilt punched me in the stomach.

I said softly, "I had some things I had to take care of and I ended up falling asleep. I'm fine. Dad, I'll *always* come home. Even if it's really late or a lot of time passes, I'll always come back. C'mon."

I stood then pulled him up with one hand.

"Whoa!" Dad stumbled and clasped his shoulder. "Jesus Christ Xon! You nearly tore my shoulder out of the socket! I'm two hundred and fifty pounds son, that's not a lightweight."

I bit my lip before I said, *you felt like air to me* and instead ushered him over to where Leo and Connor were standing awkwardly in the doorway.

I said, "Dad, you remember Leo Dawson. This little guy is Connor Hawkins. They are my best friends and they're spending the night. I know it's sudden and I didn't ask but is it okay? They already have permission from their parents."

I smiled at him.

"Are you hungry? It's late, did you eat already?" Mom walked in from the kitchen, holding a platter of pretzels, turkey sandwiches and sugar cookies.

Leo and Connor dove at her, she screamed and dropped the tray as she leapt back. They hit the floor, shoveling the food down their mouths. Loud obscene smacking, rough hurried chewing, gasping, gulping, like feral children who didn't even know how to behave. The food was gone in seconds, Leo sucked salt off his fingers while Connor ran his tongue over the tray to get any remnants.

At the twisted look on Mom's face, I quickly grabbed Connor's collar and I pinched Leo's neck. I pulled them both away.

"Quit it! Upstairs the both of you! My room is third floor on the left, first room. Go, shoo!"

They both hiked upstairs and I picked up the tray and handed it to Mom. It was picked clean, not a scrap left, even the floor looked shiny and new, as if they had scrubbed it with their hands.

Mom was a little pale and said with an awed tone, "They ate like starved untrained animals..."

As she trailed off, she looked into my eyes where my wolf spark glowed bright. She dropped the tray like it was on fire and the look on her face matched the disgusted smell coming from her body.

I'm not going to cry.

I lifted my chin. "Yes Mom. Leo and Connor are werewolves."

She whispered in a stark hoarse voice, "I want them out of my house."

"Kyra," said Dad with a firm tone. "You're not kicking out Xon's friends. They're already upstairs and they have permission from their parents to stay. It's going on twelve midnight, so don't be ridiculous."

Wrong.

Mom's brown eyes hardened into black pits. "What did you just say to me? Don't be ridiculous? They ate off the floor like some wild pigs! The last time I saw Leo he was naked in my son's bed! Now Xon is bringing home another one! I won't stand for it!" She glared at me. "Bring them down here and make them go home. Now!"

I knew outrightly telling Mom *no* would only piss her off but Leo lived in a dump and Connor had something seriously bad going on at his house. There was no way I was making them leave. So I looked at Dad to save me, to intervene. As I did, my stomach grumbled. I had eaten at Javier's but then I slept it off. I needed to eat again before I could go to bed.

Dad said, "Go ahead and eat son. Kyra, let's go have a talk in the study." She opened her mouth but Dad said with a finality to his words, "The friends stay Kyra."

Mom's mouth shut and she whirled around and stalked down the hallway. The study door slammed with a thud and crackling noises. From the sound of it the doorway hadn't been fixed from what I did to it earlier and Mom just made the damage worse.

I looked at Dad as he closed his eyes. "Dad, I'm-"

I bit my lower lip before I could say *sorry* because those aren't the words my father cared about.

"I know." He said as he turned away. "Just go ahead and eat."

I sighed as I walked through the dining room to get to the refrigerator that was right next to the doorway of the kitchen. I opened the freezer, and took out all the packages of meat my father refused me to eat earlier. The turkey wings went first, I tore open the package and with my teeth sharpened, chewed and swallowed the frozen meat like it was soft and raw. The ground beef, I couldn't wait to tear off the plastic wrap and started chewing through it, gobbling down the red chunked meat. I ate the rest of the meat, the chicken wings, the turkey legs, all of it. When it was gone, the kitchen counter was strewn with bloodied wrappers and meaty bits that didn't make it in my mouth.

"Jaxon."

I whirled around and saw my parents standing by the kitchen table. I didn't hear them come in and from how they were looking at me, they had been watching me the entire time.

I winced and looked to the floor. "I was hungry."

Dad sighed then said, "Alright, you need to eat more than normal, I understand. However, we can't have you eating out the entire stock like that, those meats would have lasted for at least two months. It's not like you have a job to pay for more groceries either. So I'll buy you a mini-fridge that you can keep stocked with your own supply of meat, rather than taking from the household supply."

I bit my lower lip then said, "The cafeteria doesn't serve enough food. I ate at Javier's but now I'm hungry again."

"Who's Javier?" Mom gestured to my clothes. "I'm guessing those are his clothes you borrowed?"

"Javier is another friend." I said, again not saying Packmate. "And no, these clothes belong to Connor's father."

Dad rubbed the back of his neck. "What happened to your own clothes Xon? Why did you have to borrow someone else's? Where are your clothes?"

"I threw them out."

Mom's eyes narrowed. "Answer the first two questions."

I didn't know an easy way to say this. Mom didn't want me fighting, she barely allowed me to take taekwondo and she never agreed with Dad letting me into the ring with him. I don't know if Dad told her about Shane but if he didn't, she would now.

I sighed and said, "They got some blood on them, that's all."

Mom's fists clenched and so did her teeth. "Who's blood Xon? Who's blood dirtied your clothes so much that you had to throw them out? Dear God, tell me you weren't fighting again with that other boy!"

"He's not just a boy." I had to come clean. "Shane is the leader of the shifters at school. Because of all the trouble I've been in, he wanted to make sure I'd keep my act right from now on. That's what happened."

Mom stumbled and sat down on the kitchen chair, clasping the side of her face with both hands.

Dad's body stiffened and he said in a cold and hard voice, "Are you telling me this Shane guy beat you up? He beat you for getting suspended? Who the fuck does he think he is? He's a student, he doesn't have any right to deal out corporal punishment!"

Dad doesn't curse unless he's beyond pissed, especially to drop the f-bomb. In fact, he only gets that angry when it comes to either myself or Mom getting hurt in someway. Now that I admitted I got beat up by another student after he's raised me to be no one's punk, he was already over the edge.

I sighed then rubbed the back of my neck. "Dad, Mom, you have to understand. This is shifter politics now. Yes, Shane is a regular student in the eyes of the humans. But in the eyes of shifters, he's actually the second-in-command at school. Mr. Forrest is the Dominion, that means he's in charge of all the shifters in Lakeside Village. However Mr. Forrest put Shane in charge of the shifters at school, meaning Shane is actually my boss. So because I've been breaking the rules, Mr. Forrest told Shane that I'm out of line. Because Shane is afraid of being eaten alive by Mr. Forrest, he beat me up to teach me a lesson and put me back in place. Do you get it? Everyone is afraid of Mr. Forrest so they keep themselves on the straight and narrow and everyone is afraid of Shane so they do the same. I'm the new wolf and I'm fucking up, so-"

Mom put her hand up so I closed my mouth. She was pale, turning her light brown skin the color of coffee with too much milk. Her body had a fine quiver through it and she smelled more than anything of the sharp piss of fear.

"Stop Xon. Just stop. I don't believe a word of this. You're telling me that-"

I cut her off. "Mom, I have never once lied to you. Everything I said is the truth. I know you don't want to hear it, you don't want to believe but Mom, I can't try and sugarcoat it anymore. I'm a werewolf, alright? I'm not human. I'm a wolf. I'm sorry but that's the truth. There are rules to the shifter community, rules that I didn't know about but I'm starting to learn. As I learn, I'll tell you what I know. All I can ask is for support and understanding. Can you do that? Can you back me up Mom?"

Mom stood up and said in a soft subdued voice, a tone I hadn't ever heard her use, "I'm going to bed."

Then she left without looking back and her scent was curiously blank, not even smelling of fear, which led me to believe she was very carefully not feeling anything.

Dad sighed and slumped on the kitchen chair. I walked over to him then sat on the floor and laid my head on his knee, not knowing what to say. Dad was quiet and motionless, then his hand touched my skull and stroked through my thickening hair.

"You look perfectly healthy."

"I got healed." I said. A shiver ran down my spine as I remembered the blessed water. "And my clothes were blood-soaked, so I had to throw them out."

"Blood-soaked? Just how badly...my God son...why didn't you fight back?" Dad sounded just as subdued as Mom but his scent was heating up with anger.

I sighed and closed my eyes. "I tried. I landed a hit. That just made him even angrier, so he whaled on me until I lost consciousness."

Dad shuddered like he had gotten bit by a horsefly but his scent was all anger. "Jaxon Reeves, you landed one hit? After taking a year of taekwondo lessons, after I showed you all I knew in the ring, and you got in one hit."

I tried to explain. "Dad, I'm well aware that if we were both humans I would have been the victor in the fight but as wolves, it's different."

"How so Xon? Did you fight in like wolf bodies? Fangs and claws instead of fists? Is that why its different?"

I shook my head. "No, we were in human form. But Dad, just because we're walking on two legs doesn't mean the wolf isn't present. The wolf is the other side of me, of us, and he's always there. His thoughts, his needs, his urges. And my wolf is brand new, he's like a pup. And I thought he was growing up, even Connor told me that I was growing up. So when I hit Shane back, it was like a kid hitting his father, or a servant hitting his master. I stepped out of my place, out of bounds. So rather than Shane beating me to teach me a lesson, he kept beating me to make a point."

"That point being he's the leader." Dad now sounded like he was thinking and his scent shifted to the frizzy fruity smell of curiosity. "But my question is, why would the principal allow some student walking around beating up other students? He's not really an authority figure."

"Yes he is Dad." I said. "He's second-in-command in the shifter community. The authority is Mr. Forrest then Shane then us shifters underneath. From what I can tell, shifters have to go by two rulebooks, what the humans say and what the shifters say. I honestly know hardly anything about the shifter laws, I keep learning about them every time I break a rule. Fact is, Shane is a boss, he's a top wolf, literally."

Yet as I said the last, my teeth clenched hard enough my jaw popped.

Dad's fingers gently crushed the overgrown sponge on my scalp. "You don't sound like you're ready to accept that."

I spoke very low, as if telling a secret. "I don't want to accept it Dad. In all honesty, I hate it…I want to be leader."

It wasn't until I said it that I realized that was like declaring war. I had thought it back in Javier's house, at least I had acknowledged the fact that the only person who was in any position to take Shane's place was me, in theory. But saying it outloud, telling my father, this made it real. This made it solid.

I lifted my eyes up to meet Dad's deep dark eyes, eyes like my own.

He said, "This is the second time he's beaten you. What do I always say about fighting opponents stronger or better than you?"

We spoke together. "Fight smarter, not harder."

Dad smiled and I hugged him around his waist, glad we were on the same page.

I said into his abdomen, "He's not just stronger than me Dad, he's wickedly fast. He dodges me any time I try to hit back, in fact I only got that first hit in because I surprised him, hell, I surprised myself. After that, after he realized I was putting up a fight, he seriously tore into me. I didn't have the time to think of using my taekwondo skills or the boxing moves you taught me. Sky tried to intervene and save me but-"

"Who's Sky?"

I suddenly smiled but I smothered it and said as coolly as possible, "She's the only female wolf at the school."

Dad groaned, loud and heavy. "Xon, honestly? You just got out of a bad break up with Melody, and now you're already looking at another woman?"

I sat back to look at him. "Dad, I'm not looking at Sky. I'm just saying, she's a girl werewolf, that's all. I made plans to meet her at Ridgeback Mall this Saturday at one pm. If we carpool, I can meet her while you buy a mini-fridge."

Dad sighed then said, "Alright, it's late Xon."

He patted his thighs, so I stood up and he did too. "Go to bed and we'll figure this all out in the morning."

He glanced at me. "Keep your clothes on tonight, alright?"

I nodded and gave him another hug. "Goodnight Dad."

"Goodnight Xon." He waved me off then said to himself, "Now I've got to clean this up too."

I took my shoes off at the door and loped up the stairs, taking them six at a time. In my room, there were clothes all over the floor and Leo and Connor were both under the covers in my bed, curled up in the middle. Leo looked like the yang symbol and Connor was yin, wrapped up together.

I took off my clothes and scooted my way in between, pulling the covers over us. They both latched onto me and we went to sleep, close, tight and together.

6

At some point Mom must have come in and taken the clothes because when I woke up, Carter's, Leo's and Connor's clothes were laundered and neatly folded on my desk. I sat up, having to pull Leo's and Connor's arms off from my neck and chest. Connor also had his leg slung over my waist, while Leo had his legs tangled in mine, like a spider web.

I tossed the covers off, they both started to shiver. I got out of the bed and pulled the covers over their waists. Leo was taller, so Connor's neck was covered too.

I said, "Guys, wake up. I have somewhere to be today, so you can't stay all day."

"No." Connor murmured, pulling the cover over his head. "Five, no, fifteen more minutes."

Leo didn't move or respond.

I said, "I'm taking a shower. When I come out, you two better be out of bed."

In response I got snores.

I took my shower and touched the top of my head, my fingers delved into the soft sponge of curly hair. I couldn't remember the last time I shaved my head and it was showing. I plugged in my clippers and got to work. It was close but I never went bald like Dad. I did figure once I was his age I'd go clean though.

I came out of the bathroom and got dressed. Leo and Connor were sprawled in the bed and the covers kicked to the floor. I left the room and went downstairs. Mom was cooking breakfast. Not to mention, she had been furious last night. Now she was acting like everything was fine.

"Mom?"

"Your company will be hungry," she said, flipping pancakes on the griddle. "After what I saw last night, I can only assume they don't get much at home?"

"I think so with Leo." I said. I had known he was skinny before but I saw that skinniness was etched over his entire body. He was like a skeleton with flesh pulled over his bones. "As for Connor, I don't know."

Mom nodded and didn't speak.

There was a loud shout from upstairs and a thud. Then Dad's voice boomed, "JAXON REEVES GET YOUR ASS UP HERE NOW!"

Dad shouting? Bad. I ran up the stairs. Dad was picking himself up off the floor in the doorway of my bedroom. Leo was awake and standing up, naked as he could be. He turned his back and began to pull his jeans on. Connor jolted up in bed then with a sound like a squeak toy that had been stepped on, dove under the covers and fell over the side of the bed where we couldn't see him, hiding himself.

Dad whirled onto me, his scent attacked me with so much I couldn't figure it out. He grabbed my collar and twisted his fists.

He said hotly, "Jaxon William Reeves, you tell me why those boys are naked in your bed right now."

My eyes averted to the ceiling. "We were just sleeping."

I looked away because I was ashamed of his thoughts. Unfortunately, I did that when I was lying.

Dad let me go and stood back, his scent changed to shock and confusion, a mix of lemon and onions, his eyes shaken.

"Son..." He rolled his lips into his mouth and looked away.

Trying not to be angry or show him my fangs, I said as calmly as I could, "I'm straight Dad, always have been and always will be. We're like brothers, that's all. Packmates, remember?"

Dad's eyes widened. "Xon, I've had close friends who I've felt like brothers with but never in my age did we *ever* sleep naked together. I may have shared a mattress or a couch or the floor but clothes were on. And I came in to check on you, you three were tightly wrapped together like a snake mating ball. Add to that you were all naked...what in God's name am I supposed to think?"

My teeth snapped together. "You're supposed to believe me Dad!" My voice raised, he stepped back, his brows twisting up high. "If I say something, you're supposed to believe it! I said I'm straight so I'm fucking straight, period!"

"Um, Mr. Reeves?"

Connor peeked out of the doorway, he had gotten dressed and Leo was hovering to the side. His face was still blank but I was sure he was feeling awkward as hell. I couldn't smell him because I could only smell my hot angered scent.

"Xon is telling the truth. We really are just friends, close friends, Packmates just like Xon said. I know being naked seems weird and it's freaking you out, but...we didn't do nothing!" His face got red and suddenly little Connor was angry, furious. "You really think I'd touch them like that, do you?"

His skin mottled purple, sweat beaded over his upper lip, his scent burned up with rage so hot and powerful that I could smell him instead of myself and he was breathing with deep hard heaves of his tiny chest. "I'd *never* do something like that, ever! If they even pretend to try me I'd rip their throats out!"

"Connor!" I shouted and he gasped, staring at me.

I said, "Connor, that's enough. Go downstairs and get breakfast, it's pancakes. Leo, go with him please."

Connor didn't say another word but stiffly walked between me and Dad and took the stairs one step at a time. His entire body was held tight, like he had turned into a walking statue. Leo slid between us and his hand gently brushed my waist as he followed Connor.

I sighed as Dad's eyes tracked from my waist to follow Leo, he had seen it.

"Dad, c'mere." I walked into my bedroom and closed the door behind us. Dad slumped onto my desk chair, clasping his face and sighed with a loud hoarse exhale like a wounded buffalo.

I waited but he didn't speak. I sat down on the floor in front of him and said, "Dad, we're wolves in human skin."

Dad jerked up and stared at me. I looked at my toes.

"It's hard to explain but think of Leo and Connor as wolves, and me as a wolf too. And we're a group and in the group, there's a leader. The leader takes care of the other wolves and in return, the other wolves treat the leader with kindness and respect. To keep the good feelings and the mutual respect and the tenderness strong and healthy, the wolves have to spend time together and be together in a happy safe environment. We slept together in the same bed so closely because that's how wolves would sleep, together, hugging, comforting. We were only naked because we want to feel our skin, to feel fur, to feel connected. With clothes it's like being cut off from each other. There's nothing sexual about it, it's comforting. That's it, simply put."

Dad was quiet then said, "If you're such a strong...wolf then why do you get beat up by this Shane guy? I know you explained it a little bit last night, but it sounds like you've completely mapped out what makes a good leader. So why not just explain to Shane you're a better leader and have him step down?"

"Shane is an asshole." I said. "He's vicious, he beats on Connor just because he's smaller and weaker. He's a bastard to Leo who's mute and can't or won't defend himself. Shane gets his rocks off by abusing and causing pain and violence. At first, I was so frightened of him I let him hit me, I didn't even think of fighting back. But as time went on, we...my wolf and I, we got sick of it. We didn't want Shane to keep hitting us or biting us or knocking us around. And before I knew it, last night when Shane was beating on me, I hit him back, I landed one punch. I didn't win that fight but I realized…I realized I don't *have* to be beat up, I don't *have* to let Shane win all the time. When I talked to you, I decided that maybe I could be leader. Maybe if I fight hard enough, I can convince Shane to step down. I don't want Shane to hit me or Connor or anyone else anymore. I want to be in charge now."

Dad gazed at me, his eyes both soft and sad at the same time, his scent combating the citrusy of pride and wet mold of hopelessness.

"Dad." I said. "Shane isn't going to kill me. My friends won't let him; Sky always stops him before he goes too far. I have to keep trying, keep growing up, keep defying him. Eventually though." I leaned back on my arms, turning my face towards the ceiling. "One day I can't let them hold him back. One fight is going to be serious, no holds-barred."

"Xon."

I turned my head to see him.

Dad was looking at his hands, they were trembling and he balled them up into shaking fists. "You say that you won't die, that you'll always come home but you're telling me about getting into fights and needing to be healed. Now you two are basically going to have a fight to the death. Really? Xon, can't you just talk it over? What about having elections? I mean, if you're saying everyone wants you to be the leader instead of Shane, why not vote him out of office?"

I didn't laugh at him because it made sense only in the human mind. The wolf mind knew better.

I said, "Because in the wolf world, it's not about who likes who more or who leads better or who is smarter. It's about this Dad."

I held out my arm then clenched my hand into a fist. My knuckles cracked like a whip. Veins pulsed up from the crook of my elbow, coursed down my forearm and buckled at my wrist. My nails darkened to black and began to sharpen, elongate.

I heard light footsteps and quickly shook my hand and put it behind my back as Mom opened the door. She placed her hands on her hips. "Xon! You've got me playing the hostess to your friends and those two are some hungry little scavengers, they won't stop eating. I really do think they don't get to eat besides school lunch. Maybe you should bring them home more often?"

I still didn't know what had caused my mother's abrupt about-face. Last night she wanted to kick them out simply for being what they were, now she's talking about bringing them home again. Whatever it was, I wasn't going to press.

I smiled and stood up. "Sure thing Mom. I'll see them out."

I left the room without looking at Dad's face, I didn't want to see it. Dad was a peaceful man and promoted no violence, not unless it was self-defense. I wasn't talking about self-defense, I was talking about purposely engaging in a fight to cause pain and bring myself power. It was the exact type of thing Dad left behind in his old life and did his best to raise me so I would be the opposite.

Downstairs Connor and Leo had their shoes on, waiting at the door.

"Let's go Packmates."

I shoved my feet into my sneakers and headed out. They followed me.

Connor said, "I'm sorry I yelled at your father Xon. I just...I just lost it."

"It's okay." I said. "Didn't you see me yelling at him too? No one likes to be told that they're gay when they're not, especially by someone they care about."

Connor didn't say a word. His scent flushed with the hot scent of rage, the fetidness of dread, rotten sickly thoughts like suicide, the piss of fear and his wet mud scent of sadness grew heavier and danker.

I stopped and looked at him. "Connor? If there's something that you need to talk about, you know I'm here, right?"

Connor's head was low, his chin brushing his chest.

He muttered, "I'm fine. Just ignore my scent, okay?"

I reached out and cupped his chin, bringing his head up. His dark brown eyes shined with tears that hadn't fallen. He looked away, not speaking or moving. I folded him in my arms, just holding him close, letting him smell me and feel me, understand without words. Leo came to Connor's back and hugged us both, a group hug, wolves comforting wolves. Connor's hands gripped tight on my back, squeezing small fists of my shirt. He broke into sobs, huge shuddering tears that rocked his whole body. I held him tighter.

I didn't know what it was that caused Connor's scent to darken, his mood shift when he mentioned his father, I didn't have a clue what was happening at home. All I knew was that I could be here and let him cry on me for as long as he needed to.

Eventually, Connor pulled back and Leo stepped away to let us go. Connor used his arm to rub at his sopping face and gave me a watery smile. "Thanks Xon. I should go now; it's not like I can hide out here forever. Besides, you said you have somewhere to go, right?"

I nodded then said, "If you ever need to hide out again, you know where I'm at."

Connor stared at me then said, "I want to put my hope in you Xon…but Shane is really strong. He's like a second-generation Carter. I keep thinking that once Shane is a little bit older, he could take on Carter too. You aren't at Shane's level."

I didn't really like being told I wasn't good enough and my wolf's hackles raised, but facts were facts.

I said, "Next time Connor I'll put my skills into good use. I know taekwondo and Dad taught me plenty of his boxing moves. Hey, you two have a good safe day." I stepped back with a wave. "But I need to get back to the house, Dad and I are going to Mountain Ridge."

"Carter works there," said Connor. "The city isn't too shifter friendly. I mean, they act like they are but there's a lot of racism towards shifters too."

My brows went up. "Racism?"

Connor shrugged a shoulder. "Politically correct term for being a dick to shifters. It's considered that shifters are another race of human being, so being shitty towards them is being racist. Besides, speciesism is really more for animals. Come on Leo." Connor swung away. "Let's go meet up with the others."

Leo nodded but hesitated. He came into my arms and hugged me. His arms were thin twigs and while I could feel some strength, he couldn't break my ribs. Sky was right when she said Leo was weak, though I wondered if he was weak simply because of how thin he was, or if he was weak on the inside, where his wolf was. I hugged him back then waved him off to catch up to Connor who hadn't waited for him.

Leo walked away, looked back at me with a blank gaze that seemed a lot like longing, then he went after Connor.

I went back to my house where Dad was putting on his shoes.

He said, "It's already twelve. Hurry up and eat then let's go."

I went to the kitchen where Mom had made more pancakes. I took a fork, stabbed the pile and shoved as many pancakes as I could into my mouth, which was the entire stack. My jaw stretched, elongating into the maw of my wolf to make room. I was glad Mom wasn't there to see me do something so obviously inhuman. Whatever pep-talk she had put herself through would most definitely snap.

Done eating, I went to take another shower and redress, this time with a new pair of black jeans, so they didn't have white stress marks or tears. I wore a black t-shirt with a red jacket over it. I put my wallet and my cell phone in my jeans pocket. I picked up the stud earring Mom had bought me for Christmas one year and shouted as it burned me. I dropped it, staring at the small burn mark on my finger and thumb from where I had picked it up. A small hiss of steam wafted up from the injury.

I looked at the earring, two carat diamond set in a silver base.

Silver.

I didn't dare touch it again, so instead I put on a gold chain that Dad had gotten me for my birthday when I entered high school.

I put on my black Converse weapons and I was ready.

When I got downstairs, Dad was leaning on the door, ankles crossed and his thumb flipping across the screen of his Android. He looked up as I came down and his brows arched, a smile flitted over his mouth but he dropped it when I glared.

"Sorry." He said as we were going outside. "You're the one who spruced up like it's a date. I thought you were just talking." His scent of amusement, orangey citrus collided with a pissy ammonia scent, apprehension.

"We are just talking." I swallowed back the urge to growl at him. "And stop laughing at me, would you?"

He laughed, a deep echo that rumbled from his stomach. "I wasn't laughing."

"Well now you are!"

We got in the car and Dad pulled off. Mom was standing in the doorway. He gave her a hand wave as he drove off.

"I'll stop." He said but his grin was full on his face now, his white teeth etched on his dark skin.

I slumped against the seat, crossing my arms. "Look, it's not a big deal. We're just going to talk."

Dad nodded. The ride was done in silence. To get into Mountain Ridge, there was a bridge to cross over from Lakeside Village into the city, the Wandering Bridge as it was built over the Wandering River. Lakeside Village was a small town and Mountain Ridge was a pretty large city.

All the entertainment was in the city, such as the mall, clubs, shopping, movies. Most of the good work was in the city, Dad worked in construction and Mom was a receptionist for some fancy office building.

"Alright, we're here." Dad parked in a spot outside of Ridgeback Mall and glanced at me. "Go meet up, have a talk then we'll get the fridge."

I nodded. "See ya in like twenty or so."

I hopped out and closed the door. I loped up the lane.

Sky stood by the movie posters, her arms crossed over her abdomen, and her foot braced against the brick while she leaned her shoulders against the wall. Her hair was in braids again, in some style I didn't know but it looked very regal, pinned up around her head like a crown. She wore a white camisole top with a short denim jacket, and low-riding hip hugging blue jeans that only accentuated her curvy figure. Her hazel eyes turned to see me and her wolf spark flickered gold as her gaze went over my arms, chest and down my body before looking at my face. A thick sugary smell gushed from her, and it mixed in with the scent I had already labeled as her personal one, roses and honey. The combination was enough to put me on an olfactory sugar high.

I said, "Hey Sky. So...what is it you wanted to tell me?"

Sky looked me directly in the eyes, all sweet smells gone. "This Pack you're making with us Xon...you have to protect them. You can't say you want to be leader and then not back it up. They trust you already, are following you, Leo needs you in ways I'm not sure any of us can fully understand. I won't let you throw that away Xon, let you get their hopes up then let Shane continue to defeat you."

I let out a short breath, she had already come to the same conclusion I had, and probably earlier than I had. I kept my gaze on hers.

I said, "You think I don't know that? I always do my best Sky."

Her full red lip pulled up to bare a sliver of shiny white fangs before she said, "Then your best needs to be good enough Xon. I want you to know that how you're doing this, making the Pack scent with Leo, Connor and Javier, that's an ability that only Alphas can do."

My head lifted in shock. "An Alpha ability? You mean there's things that leaders can do that other wolves can't?"

Sky's head turned to the side for a moment before she faced me again. "Leader isn't even an official status in the wolf world Xon. We're calling Shane leader because that's the only word that can be given to him. He's not an Alpha, he hasn't made Pack with us. Connor was the one who named us the Wildebeast Pack, which you should know isn't a correct name for a Pack. With you Xon, we would be the Reeves Pack or the Lakeside Village Pack."

I ran my tongue over my mouth, then rubbed my hand down my face and jaw.

I asked, "How do you know all of this? I mean, if you were Changed like me, how come you know all of these things about Packs and shifter society, and I know nothing?"

"I was Changed when I was twelve years old at a summer camp," she said, shocking me. "I got angry with another girl so I bit her arm hard enough to draw blood. Her name is Alyse and I didn't know she was a werewolf until it was too late. We've stayed in touch and she's like my mentor. Anything I know about werewolf society and world, I learned it from her."

I nodded then said, "Tell me more about what you meant about Alpha abilities."

She said, "Alphas, real Alphas Xon, nothing like Shane, they can do things that like you said, normal wolves, regular Packmembers, can't do. Gathering our trust, making a natural Pack scent, you really are becoming our Alpha Xon and we need you to protect us from Shane, to be a true Alpha in both body and name."

I opened my mouth to say something when-

"Jaxon Reeves!"

Right as I heard the call, I smelled the thick heady smell of an adult werewolf. I whirled around and standing there was a tall muscled white man with piercing gray eyes that bored into mine, so hotly like he wanted my face to explode or melt away. His scent was strong, the vivid burn of hatred and the hot harshness of violence. I knew his name was Wyatt and I didn't know his last name but I had only met him once before. Just a few weeks prior when I had been Changed into a wolf. In California. I was two thousand miles away from the sidewalk where I lost my humanity.

So what the hell is he doing here…?

He held up his hand and coaxed his finger at me, gesturing me to come here.

Dear God, what's going on? The last time I saw this guy I heard him shouting that I should be killed and I don't deserve to live, that it was all my fault. No one ever explained to me what he was talking about, I come back to Lakeside Village as a wolf, and now I'm in Mountain Ridge and here he is. So how in the world is he here?

Sky stood up next to me, and placed her hand warningly on my side.

Her voice lowered with the soft growl of a wolf. "Who is this guy?"

"He's from the Pack in California," I said just as lowly, staring at him. "I don't even know what he's doing here."

Wyatt snapped. "Jaxon Reeves!"

"I'll be back," I said to Sky. "Wait here."

Sky definitely made this worried whine low from her stomach but nodded and stood back.

I sighed and went to Wyatt. His hand lashed out, grabbed my collar and shoved me against the wall, indenting the brick surface behind my back and shoulders.

Ow! Shit!

He looked at me with gray eyes tinged bright wolf green and a feral grin, baring sharp teeth.

"Well, look who's come into the city without permission." He lifted up his other hand and grew thick ebony claws, the dagger tips glinted in the sunlight. "I'm going to gut you for this."

His intense green eyes were gleeful and anticipating, the wolf spark in the pupils burning like a bonfire.

Fuck, this guy really hates me! And he's serious! I swear I didn't do anything to him! Dear God, please don't let this crazy guy kill me!

"Wait, wait, what are you talking about!" I wrapped my arms around my stomach to protect it. "I don't even know what you're doing here! Don't you live in California?"

Wyatt's fanged grin only widened, but the pleasure in his eyes was at the idea of hurting me and nothing else. "The Stone Pack has moved here to Mountain Ridge and claimed this city as territory. That means any wolf coming onto our turf is breaking the Law and as such, is punishable by death."

This guy hates me, that much is clear! And I think he's a little psychotic!

"That's enough Wyatt."

We both looked up and it was another guy from the Stone Pack, Mikhail, also tall and hulked with muscle. He had buzz cut black hair and his scent was mighty, thick, dark and heavy, a full grown wolf.

I know Wyatt said they just moved here, but why? Maybe the scandal of having some poor country boy getting ripped to shreds in broad daylight. But if that's the case, what happened to Rocky, the wolf who tried to kill me in the first place? And why did they move here to Georgia?

Mikhail stepped forward. "You know it's my job to administer punishments. I'm the Enforcer, not you."

"The hell it isn't." Wyatt didn't back down or let me go. "I'm a Scout, I can kill him for being on our territory."

"He is seventeen." Mikhail spoke in a patient reminding tone. "We do not kill pups. Now let him go and you can leave. I'll handle this."

Wyatt's hand only tightened, his knuckles digging into my throat. The scent of his rage seared my nostrils, this wolf had some serious hatred for me and I did not know why.

"You know how I feel about him; he shouldn't even be alive. I'll take care of this problem, right here and now."

Why does he say I shouldn't be alive? And why does he hate me? I need some answers but I'd also not like to get gutted by this guy!

Mikhail's face didn't change. "I won't repeat myself Wyatt. Don't forget your place. I gave you a direct command."

Wyatt's lips twisted but he dropped my collar, my feet touched the ground and I let out a sigh of relief. Wyatt landed a sucker punch into my stomach, I crumpled to the ground, coughing up blood. Pain radiated from the central hit, I coughed up more blood. Wyatt huffed disdainfully and cursed at me in another language before jogging off without looking back.

"OK, stand up Xon." Mikhail gripped me around my arms and stood me up then held me steady as I stumbled. He brushed me off then crossed his arms, staring at me sternly. "Now what Wyatt said is true, this is Stone Pack territory now. That said, you need our permission to enter the city and if granted, you need to have a gift. Do you understand?"

I wiped blood off my lip then looked down to my shoes. Mikhail grasped my chin and forced my head upwards, my neck tensed like it was going to snap. Mikhail's eyes were no longer black but amber orange and the gold spark in his eyes was burning bright.

I averted my gaze but said, "Okay, okay, I get it."

Mikhail let me go and stood back. I crumpled and held my jaw, it pulsed where his fingers had indented the skin. He didn't speak.

I asked, "Can you tell me what Wyatt's problem is? Why did he try to kill me? Why does he keep saying I shouldn't be alive?"

"No." He said after a minute. "This is a matter I must take to my Alpha. Now, I get that you didn't ask permission, fine. I can handle that but it had better not happen again now that you know. So, you've got a gift, don't you? A gift can't be a cheap trinket, but something usually either expensive or something with a lot of meaning attached to it, emotional or sentimental value. So give me something to accept as a gift."

I jerked my head up, staring at him. Mikhail's brows were slightly furrowed, his eyes warning.

"Okay, okay." I pulled off my gold chain. "There, you can have this. It's real gold and my father gave it to me for my birthday, it means a lot, see? Here, honestly, you can take it."

Mikhail picked it up out of my hand and examined it.

"Fine."

He took out a small black cloth bag from his pocket and put the chain inside, then pulled the drawstring shut and put it back in his pocket.

"Gift accepted. Hey." He pointed at me sternly as I sighed in relief again, this time I was safe for real. "You can't come into the city without permission, understand? Call up the Alpha, tell him when you want to come here and ask if it's okay. If he tells you no, then it's no. If he says yes, then you can come but only as long as he says you can and make sure you have a gift. You're a wolf now Xon and you have to go by the rules, by the Laws that everyone else has to follow. It was true Wyatt could kill you the next time you come here without permission but this time I saved you. Got that?"

I nodded quickly. "Yes, I got it."

"Good." He gave me the Alpha of the Stone Pack's cell phone number, then said, "I'm sure Wyatt has run off to tell Antonius about our little intruder, so go while you can.

Also, relay this message to the rest of the shifters, including that miss wolf back there."

He walked away and as soon as he was gone, Sky jogged up to stand next to me.

"What was that about?" She asked through a heavy breath, her eyes wide all around.

I could smell her emotions, hot spiciness of anger, faint pissy smell of nervousness and the thick smoky scent of worry.

"Apparently the Pack in California has moved here," I said, rubbing my hand underneath my nose. "That big white guy, Wyatt, wanted to kill me for being on their territory. And the other big guy, the black one, protected me, in exchange for payment."

Sky nodded then sighed. "Alright. Then we all have to be careful coming up to Mountain Ridge."

I nodded with a sigh as the hot brush of summer wind battered my face. I exhaled then smiled.

"Can't seem to really catch a break," I said.

A beep from the sidewalk showed me that Dad had just pulled up.

I turned to Sky. "Listen, I gotta go. Do you want a ride back to Lakeside?"

Sky shook her head. "My parents will pick me up once I text them. Be careful on your way back."

"Yeah," I said. "You too."

I waved and jogged up to my Dad's car, getting inside and buckling in.

Dad's brows arched and he gave me a nice smile, one that suddenly made him look young enough to be my brother instead of my father.

He said, "Is that her? She's a fox."

"Dad! Don't be creepy." I complained. "And to be more correct, she's a wolf."

"Right..." His smile faded as he stared at me. "Is that blood on your shirt? And your pants?"

"Agh."

A. E. Costello 155

I didn't have to look down because I could smell it. When Wyatt punched me, I coughed up plenty of blood from my damaged organs. I could still smell him on my shirt, aggressive, rough, older. He smelled like bloodlust and hatred, raw tingling and vivid burning.

Dad stared at me. "Was it Shane? Did Shane come after you again?" His hands crunched into fists on the steering wheel. "I swear Xon, if you let this brat hit you one more time, I really will lose it."

"It wasn't Shane." I said with a sigh. "It was someone else."

Dad aimed the car to a parking deck, leaning over to put money into the meter before entering. "Who else then? Why are you always getting into fights? I don't get it."

"It wasn't a fight." I said, not sure how to explain this. "A real Pack has moved into the city, and the strangest thing is, it's the Pack from California."

Dad said nothing as he found a parking spot, then he turned off the car.

"So you're telling me that the same Pack who Changed you into a wolf in the first place is now living here in Mountain Ridge?"

I nodded. "Crazy as it sounds, yes. And one of the wolves found me at the mall and hit me for being on their territory."

I didn't tell him Wyatt wanted to rip my guts out and kill me, that wouldn't go over well.

Dad sighed and placed his head on the steering wheel, his broad shoulders suddenly seemed small and weak.

"I don't like it Xon, I don't like the feeling of you being…a pushover."

Now I didn't like that either.

"Dad, really? I'm not a pushover, he sucker punched me, I didn't see it coming. Besides, it won't happen again. Let's go, okay?"

Dad sighed and nodded as we got out. The smell of the city hit me like a sock to the nose. The sidewalks smelled like spit, tracked dirt, and all the combined smells of the unclean meat scent of humans. I covered my nose with both hands and wavered, my eyes rolled in my head.

Dad clutched my arm and said, "Hold on son." He hustled me inside, saying, "It should be cleaner inside the store."

The automatic doors swooshed open and fresh air bathed my senses. The store smelled like air conditioning and squeaky clean floors. I lowered my hands and sighed heavily.

Dad looked at me with his brows raised high. "Are you okay? You looked so sick outside."

"It was the smell." I explained. "I can smell everything Dad, hair, clothes, and even emotions."

Dad crossed his arms. "Emotions Xon? How can you smell emotions?"

"Fear smells like piss." I said. "Hope smells sweet. Happiness like oranges. Every emotion has a scent attached to it and if the emotions are similar, the scents are familiar. So sadness smells like wet mud, and hopelessness smells like wet mold. You get it?"

Dad rubbed his chin. "Alright, I think I am getting it. So basically no one can ever lie to you, because you'll smell it?"

I nodded. "Exactly."

A salesperson walked up to us, smiling. "Is there anything I can help you gentlemen with?" Her voice was accented and throaty.

Right away, I didn't smell that basic meaty smell humans had. She wasn't human but I didn't know the scent, I didn't know what type of shifter she was. She was short and had curvy hips. Curly, thick black hair, steamy brown eyes and full red lips, her skin clear and tawny. Her eyes lit up at the sight of me and from her slow warm smile, she liked what she saw.

Dad pinched my side warningly while giving a nice smile to the girl. "We're looking for a mini-freezer, dorm room size."

"Right this way." Her name tag read Yara. She set off at a slow easy pace, swishing her hips back and forth.

While Yara showed off mini-fridges and freezers, I tried to smell her discreetly and log what her scent was. It was definitely foreign, heady, so humid and thick. Jungle? No, rainforest.

Dad whispered, "Xon, what are you doing?"

That's when I realized I was standing directly behind Yara, leaning down into the soft pungent spot at the base of her neck. Even though I just wanted to smell her, I was acting like a real creep.

Yara turned around and smiled at me. Her smile stretched from ear to ear and her teeth lengthened into serrated edges that lined all the way down her throat, curving backwards like machetes. Her eyes were completely round, molted muddy red with black peeking through. Her tawny skin changed to olive green with black blotches.

Dad paled and stumbled backwards. "What the fuck? What are you?"

"I am an Ophidian, specifically a were-anaconda." She hissed. Far from her rich tone earlier, now her voice was slick and silky. Shivers raced up my spine. "Does that help?" Her tongue slid out, blackened, and forked, slipping at the air. "I can taste you wolf boy."

I stepped back and said as calmly as I could. "S-sorry. I was trying to figure out what you were, I didn't mean to be rude."

Yara's snake smile receded, her full lips plumped, white square teeth slid from her gums and her eyes shifted back into chocolate pools, her skin color warmed back into golden tanned, her tongue pink. Just like that, all signs of her being a shifter was gone, besides for her smell. Her smell was thriving with the exotic flower scent of a rainforest. Ophidian. Anaconda.

I knew there were other types of shifters, Mr. Forrest, Jarrod, Jayanti Sher the guidance counselor, but this was the first time Dad had seen it. I looked at him, his normal ebony skin was drained a ghoulish aubergine, his eyes strained red in the whites. He looked like he had seen a ghost and it accosted him.

I held his arm steady and looked at her. "We want a mini-fridge alright?"

She smiled, cocked her head to the side and continued with her sales job as if she hadn't just scared the living shit out of my father, and me for that fact. Dad stayed quiet and withdrawn for several minutes but as Yara brought up prices, he snapped out of it and paid attention. The mini-freezer was paid for and it was decided to box it up and take it to the car.

While we were waiting, Dad said, "Xon. What she did, can you do that?"

I said, "I've had fangs in my mouth and my eyes turn wolf yellow when I'm still human, so I guess so. I've seen Shane do the same and grow fur on his head, I've even seen his hackles rise out of his neck. So yeah, I can do it."

Dad said nothing in reply then a worker came up with the box on a trolley, so I pushed it to the Ford Ranger and loaded it up. The box felt like nothing, as if holding a carton of air or tissues. Dad paled as I lifted the box with no effort and put it in the back.

The worker, who had a sharp musty smell like he was some sort of dog, suddenly whispered, "Shit, here comes Wyatt. You'd better get out of here pup."

I barely managed to register what he said as he fled with the trolley. I turned around as the vivid burning scent of hatred rushed into my nose. Wyatt was just a few cars down, advancing straight towards me with quick pumps of his legs. His eyes were the wild green of his wolf. This guy, he wasn't coming at me to say hello.

Dad jumped in front of me, arms spread wide like to barricade me with his own body. Wyatt didn't stop, fangs gnarling his mouth so I grabbed Dad and pinned him to the ground before Wyatt killed him. Mikhail came from around the truck with blinding speed and knocked Wyatt in the chest with the flat of his hand.

Wyatt stumbled backwards and glared at him. "He's on our territory! I have every right to kill him for breaking our Law!"

Mikhail said in a calm tone, "Xon gave a gift for his right to be here so he's not under punishment. And like I told you before, we don't kill pups."

"Oh yeah?" Wyatt's green eyes billowed with gold flame in the pupils as he looked at me. I could see fur rippling under his skin, his hands strapped with ebony machetes, his hackles raised out of his neck like fleshy lumps. He was an older wolf just seconds from leaping on me and tearing me apart. "We don't kill pups, is that right? I say we do Mikhail, its already been proven we kill pups."

Mikhail moved to stand in front of me, blocking Wyatt's vision. "Get back to scouting Wyatt and be gone from here. That's an order as Enforcer of the Stone Pack. I enforce the rules, not you. Remember your place. Leave."

Wyatt snarled something, I couldn't tell because his tone was slicked with saliva and crowded with fangs. His throat must be twisted with wolf vocal cords because his voice was gruff, more growl than words. He whirled and ran off, blending into the busy streets.

"Get off me Xon!" The muffled shout made me realize I was still pinning my father down, I had one hand on his collar, the other on his lower back as I knelt over him in a protective stance. He couldn't move an inch.

"Sorry Dad." I helped him up and brushed him off but he slapped my hands away.

"What in God's name just happened?" He shouted. "One second I see this crazy ass fool running up on us, then you throw me to the ground and I hear something about killing and who's this bastard?"

He pointed at Mikhail who was still standing there.

Mikhail cracked his neck, it sounded like a wine bottle snapping open.

"The name is Mikhail. I am the Enforcer of the Stone Pack, the wolf Pack who lives here. And I just saved your son's life." He said, again cool and relaxed.

In fact, I think Mikhail's personality was similar to my fathers, always calm until something drove him over the edge. I just really hoped I wasn't around when Mikhail's strict personality broke.

Dad breathed heavy then said, "Who was that guy? Why did he attack us?"

Mikhail sighed then shook his head. "His name is Wyatt and he's holding a grudge, that's all I can say. However, what I will say is that Xon needs to not come back into Mountain Ridge. It's too dangerous."

Dad snapped back. "Well I'd say so if he's got wild ass white men trying to jump him when his back is turned! And don't you dare tell me that's all you can say, I demand an explanation of why my son's life is in danger! He was born in this city and now you tell me he can't come back? Who the fuck do you think you are? Huh, are you the mayor? Are you a police chief? Where do you get your authority?"

Mikhail's smooth face didn't budge. "I've said what I can say on Wyatt's reasoning. I get my authority from the Alpha of the Stone Pack. Now, as I've said, it is in Xon's better interest to not return here."

Dad shouted, "I want to meet this so-called Alpha! Who does he think he is that he can just order my son to not come to this city without permission? He's not a mayor! He's not a governor! Call him up, let me talk to him!"

Dad was not backing down; I hadn't seen him go off on somebody like this in a long time. Well, he's been losing his cool a lot lately since I've turned a wolf, but he's fully aware this guy he's yelling at is a werewolf, right?

A. E. Costello 161

Mikhail sighed again and glanced at me, his scent was the burnt dryness of irritation and I could tell he wanted me to get Dad off his back. I placed my hand on Dad's shoulder but he shrugged me off and didn't look at me, glaring at Mikhail.

He snapped again. "You heard what I said? I said let me talk to your Alpha, your boss or whoever's got fucking maniacs running around trying to kill my son! I won't accept some pansy ass answer about holding a grudge, a grudge against my son for what? I've never seen that man in my life and you're here trying to tell me that Xon can't come into the city because its dangerous? Dangerous because of that fucking white guy? I don't think so, I don't accept that. So come clean, let me talk to your boss, now."

That last now was blunt and cold, like Dad was two seconds from hauling off and punching Mikhail in the face. Dad's muscles actually rivaled Mikhail's and Dad was all riled up like he was ready to start swinging.

"Dad." I said, trying to sound gentle as to not get him even more worked up. "Remember when I told you there's human rules and shifter rules? It's like that. A human being may not be able to tell me to stay out of the city but as a wolf, the wolves in this city are-"

Dad put his hand up, my mouth shut. "Don't try and talk me down Xon, do I look like I'm in the mood? I want answers right now. And I don't care if you're some big bad wolf Mikhail, I will fuck your ass sideways."

What...did...my...father...just...say?

I knew Dad was seriously pissed right now, his scent was hot and spicy with anger but he was starting to sound a little gangster now. That was not the face Dad wanted to show to the world, not anymore.

"Dad." I said it more firmly. "Please, stop. Look, I have the Alpha's number, I'll call him and let you speak to him, okay? Let's go home, alright? You're overheating Dad, seriously. Rein it in Dad, relax."

Dad breathed out hard from his flared nostrils, his chin went up and for a moment, I could imagine him as some king, or a prince who was deciding on whether or not to chop off some enemy's head. That said if the enemy was a person who can transform into a wolf and eat him alive. I knew Dad was tough, but to be tough enough to get into a screaming match with a man who could punch right through Dad's chest like he was made of papier-mâché, I couldn't have more respect and pride for him.

Mikhail dipped his head. "Then I'll take my leave. Xon, if you want to come to the city, get permission from Toni. Have a gift on arrival and watch your back."

"Wait." I said as he turned to leave. "How did you get here so fast? I mean, how did Wyatt even know where I was?"

Mikhail sighed for a third time and his sharply cut jaw tightened for a moment, a flex in the strong cheek muscle. "Wyatt was scouting you the entire time and I kept an eye on him and you just in case. Once you turned your back to him, Wyatt came after you. Xon."

He closed his eyes for a moment and touched his forehead then looked at me with the intense orange eyes of his wolf. "You think and act human, you even move like a human. If you had been paying attention, using all of your senses, you would have known that both me and Wyatt were watching you. You would have never turned your back on him and you would have never lowered your guard. I know you're new but shed that humanness that's still sticking to you like glue. Peel it off, let your wolf out. We're wolves Xon, not humans. The were in werewolf simply means man as in man-shaped, not as in human man. Understand what you are Xon and accept it. Get in the car and go home. I'll wait."

I nodded and looked at Dad, who had lost all of his heat. His scent was the wet mold of hopelessness and his face was drained, lines etched onto his skin like he had aged.

Without another word, he took out the key and got into the front seat.

"Thanks Mikhail." I gave him a two-fingered wave and got in the truck.

Mikhail moved so Dad could back out and Dad did so, not speaking, his face crumpled up like a soft ball that had been punctured, beaten and tired.

I didn't know what to say and because he wasn't talking, I said nothing as he drove us back into Lakeside Village. We got home and Dad pulled into the garage.

He suddenly said, "I don't care what that shifter said Xon, you are still my son and you always will be."

I nodded and said, "Dad, whether I'm wolf or human, I am your son. Fur or skin, nails or claws, it doesn't change that for me."

Dad cleared his throat and sniffed but didn't cry or hug me, he unlocked the door, saying, "Get that freezer upstairs and set it up, I'll go buy some meat."

I followed his lead and got out, hefted the freezer into my arms and entered the house through the side-door. I could hear music playing upstairs, so Mom was home. I took the freezer to my room and unpacked it, then read the directions on setting it up. I plugged it in next to my desk so this way I can eat and do homework at the same time.

My door was knocked on and I turned around as Mom came in. She saw the freezer and her face flickered, whatever emotion she felt she damped it down so quick her scent didn't even change.

Instead, she smiled and said, "You guys were gone for a while, are you hungry?"

I said, "Mom, I need to talk to you."

She bit her lower lip then said in a low quiet voice, "Xon, I had to do a lot of prayer and meditation before I can be the way I am now. If you start telling me things… I'll lose my composure again."

"I know and I get it but I have to be real with you." Her eyes narrowed so I said, "I mean I have to be completely honest. I don't want to not say something and if things get a little crazy you won't understand."

Mom ran her tongue through the inside of her bottom lip, a movement she made when she was thinking about her response. Mom would go off the handle pretty quickly but at least she was staying calm.

She said, "What kind of crazy are we talking about Xon?"

I paused then said it, "Like a white guy named Wyatt trying to kill me type of crazy."

She blinked then went and sat on my bed. She clasped her hands together and breathed for a few moments.

She said, "Wyatt isn't the name of that boy, right?"

I shook my head. "No, that's Shane. Shane is white but he's a student at my school. Wyatt is an adult and he lives in the city. The Stone Pack has moved in and its their territory. Wyatt hates my guts and doesn't seem to want me to be alive. He kept repeating that I don't deserve to live or I shouldn't be alive. Mikhail told me he's holding a grudge but he won't tell me or Dad what that grudge is."

Mom rubbed the bridge of her nose then massaged her forehead. "I've heard the name Stone before…I know it. But what do you mean by Pack? You mean like a bunch of werewolves who live together? Like a community?"

I didn't know how to explain it. "I don't know a lot about it structurally but I know what it takes to actually make Pack with someone else, to create a bond that goes beyond our human skin into the spiritual realm where the wolf lives."

I knew I had gone too far when Mom's jaw clenched so hard the bone popped. She stood up abruptly like she had been jerked to her feet. Her back was straighter than Mr. Malone's and her fists clenched.

"I do not want to hear anymore." She spoke in a stilted tone with each word artificially tumbling out. She had changed from my mother into a robot. "I am going back to my room. I will see you at lunch. Goodbye Xon."

A. E. Costello 165

She walked in a stiff manner towards the door.

"Mom, I'm sorry."

She had already closed the door on me, it slammed so loud I knew she had been barely reigning in her anger. Her scent clouded in my room, burning hot with spices. I turned on the fan and slumped onto my bean bag. Mom was trying but I had to be more sensitive to her needs. She wanted me to be human, to just be her son. Any time I mentioned having a wolf she couldn't accept it. I didn't know why Mom seemed to hate werewolves or hate shifters, I was sure she encountered them in the city. Not to mention, she recognized the name Stone even though I didn't know it, besides from being in California when I met the Pack after Rocky tore my guts out.

I shuddered, I could still remember the pain. Wyatt had wanted to gut me.

I don't know why that guy hates me so much but what Mikhail said was right, I didn't know Wyatt was following me or that he had been coming up at my back. It was the stock worker who warned me, then Mikhail jumped out to save me. He said I'm wearing my human skin like its glue and I need to pull it off, to accept what I am.

I closed my eyes and curled into a ball. For the first time in a while, I prayed and tried to connect with God.

Dear God. Sometimes I think good things are happening, like making a Pack with Leo, Javier and Connor but now Wyatt wants to kill me and my mother seriously can't stand me.

What about Connor? He's going through something really bad and I want to help him. I'm not strong enough to beat Shane but I have to try. I think I like Sky but she got pissed when I called her out on being attracted to me.

Now the Stone Pack has moved into the city and its too dangerous to be there. My father is either getting really angry or depressed. I'm at a loss. What should I do? Sometimes I feel like You're answering my prayers, other times I can't tell if I'm even Your child anymore. I guess I need a sign or something. In Jesus name, Amen.

My door opened and I looked up to see Dad carrying several grocery bags. I could smell meat from here and I jumped up.

Dad stepped back, eyes wide. "Slow down son. You look like you're about to tackle me."

I stopped moving because I actually had been about to dive onto the meat. He came in and began to load up the freezer. I stole a package from him and unwrapped it. Ground chuck, yummy. I used my claws to scrape open the plastic wrap then took a bite out of it with sharp fangs and gnawed.

Dad watched me with several slow shakes of his head as he took a seat on my computer chair. "I don't think I can get used to you eating raw meat like its candy Xon."

I couldn't answer, my mouth full but I nodded and shrugged at the same time.

Dad cleaned up the bags and said, "Xon, what did Mikhail mean by having a gift on arrival? And where's your chain?"

I winced, swallowed then said, "Well, apparently in order to enter the Stone Pack's territory, I need to first get permission from the Alpha and then I need to give them a gift, like payment. I had to give my chain to Mikhail."

Dad's face purpled. "That chain was my gift to you and you gave it away?"

I sat on my bed and looked at my shoes. "Dad, it wasn't like I wanted to give it away but I had to. I had gotten onto their territory without permission, Wyatt wanted to kill me then but Mikhail showed up and made him leave. That's when Wyatt hit me and I coughed up some blood. So Mikhail told me I had to give him a gift so I could stay in the city. Wyatt wasn't supposed to come at me again but because the guy seriously hates me, he did. I'm lucky Mikhail was there to save me."

Dad sighed and cupped his head in his hands. "So he extorted you. If you didn't give him money or a gift, then he'd let you get killed."

"It sounds bad when you put it like that. But it's a Law, their Law. And as a wolf, I have to follow it."

Dad nodded and stood up. "I don't like it but if it means you'll be safe, then fine. Mom is making lunch, so wash up and be ready. Try and keep the wolf talk to a minimum, alright?"

I agreed, remembering how robotic Mom became earlier.

I asked, "Dad, why does Mom hate shifters?"

Dad rubbed his eyebrow and said, "She's had her history, that's all. I'll see you at lunch."

With that vague answer, he left and closed the door.

First Mikhail talking about holding grudges and now Dad talking about history. What's so hard with people giving straight answers?

I did as told, including changing my bloodied shirt, then went downstairs for lunch. It was about three pm and Mom had made grilled cheese sandwiches and French fries. Luckily because of the meat I just ate I didn't feel ravenous. I sat down at the table.

It was quiet at first, then Mom said, "I don't want to hear about what happened in the city. Let's just have a regular lunch, okay?"

I said okay and Dad said the same.

Lunch was regular like Mom said, the small talk kept to a minimum and nothing too exciting or extreme brought up. I helped Mom clean up then decided to head for the park and maybe meet up with the other Wildebeasts.

"I'm going out." I said.

Mom stared at me. Her voice was low. "Don't get in a fight Xon. I saw there was blood on your shirt but I didn't want to ask. Please…" Her eyes watered. "Don't get hurt Xon."

"I won't." I hugged her but didn't squeeze, not wanting to hurt her by being too strong. "I'll be back, promise."

"Not too late." she said as I pulled away. "Be home in time for dinner. That's eight o'clock at the latest Xon."

"I got it." I smiled. "See ya then."

Mom watched me go with saddened eyes, her scent matched it and I almost didn't feel right leaving her but I wanted to be around wolves, I wanted to be with my Pack. Maybe Mom would understand one day. Dad waved me off from his place at the table, he wasn't done eating. I put my shoes on at the door and first went to the playground but no one was there, so I went to the local park instead.

Shane was at the basketball court, playing with other teens. His blond hair wasn't even damp with sweat despite the blazing heat of August in Georgia. His white t-shirt strained against his muscles. He loped up and down the court like he was strolling yet the other kids scrambled to keep up with him.

"Hey Xon, over here!"

At Connor's shout, I looked over. The Wildebeasts Pack were under a tree tucked up on a hill overlooking the courts. Javier was perched on a tree branch, Leo was laying on the ground like he was sleeping, Sky leaned against the trunk and Connor was sitting down cross-legged.

I trotted over and Connor hugged me around my waist from his position. His scent was brushed with the thick heady scent of Shane and some blood stained his shirt and pants.

My fists clenched. "What did-"

Sky spoke over me. "Does it matter Xon? What can you do about it?"

I looked at her, her eyes were hazel-gold with just a hint of silver around the edges, her wolf peeking through. She was challenging me, trying to get a response out of me. I remembered what we had talked about at the mall.

I lifted my chin. "I'll tell Shane he needs to stop knocking around my Packmates."

When I said *my Packmates*, my voice roughened, like the word was mine to be said and no one else, possessive.

Sky's eyes widened then her brows arched. "Well, go ahead. Tell him."

Again, I smelled Shane behind me and turned around quickly.

Why didn't I hear him coming behind me? He's snuck up on me before. It's like I'm completely oblivious to my own surroundings but it'll get me killed if I don't start paying attention.

Shane stood several feet back, he had stopped moving once I turned around. His blue eyes were tinged olive and when he smiled, his teeth were too sharp to be human.

His voice roughened already, he said, "Xon? You had something to say to me?"

I wasn't scared of him, but as my wolf's fur bristled and he bared his fangs, my lips pulled back to show my sharpening teeth.

I said, "I don't want you to hit Connor anymore, or any of us."

Shane blinked and his smile slowly slid into a sneer. "Oh yeah? Well Xon, seeing as you aren't the leader, you don't get to tell me what I can and cannot do. Now you can just shut up or I'll see to it that you won't speak again, got it?"

My wolf lowered his head with his ears pulled back and snarled, the sound echoed from my mouth. Shane walloped me across the face, hard enough I stumbled to the ground, blood spurting from my broken nose. I got back up. Shane grasped my chin and neck, his hands felt like vice grips. He leaned into my face with his eyes glowing olive.

"You want to say something else pretty boy? Huh? You want to be leader? You can't even stand in front of me."

His knee came up to hit me in the stomach and I used my leg to block it while my hands snatched his hands off me. Shane jumped on me and we grappled at first before he wrapped his arm around my neck and his fists landed blows on my stomach and side, busting my organs and breaking bones with each hit.

No fucking way. I told Mom no fighting, I told my father I wasn't a pushover. I know shit, I won't let this end like this!

I gnawed Shane's arm around my neck, tearing through his muscles and tendons until hot bitter blood seeped down into my mouth. I jerked my knees up into his diaphragm, my other hand I slashed for his face. Shane blocked his face with his free hand, my claws tore through his palm. He cursed and twisted his arm around my neck like he was trying to break it. I floundered and thrashed so wildly he had to let me go. Then we both stood up, staring each other down.

My shirt was ripped, blood spreading out over the fabric. My organs throbbed as they melded back together, my ribs snapped into place. Shane's arm was clear, he wiped the blood over his jeans revealing no wound, his hand healed.

He said, "You really want to fight me pretty boy? I won't go easy on you like I have."

Shit, this is him going easy? No dammit! I know taekwondo, I know boxing! There's no reason for me to get whaled on like I'm some punk.

I lifted my chin and thought about what Dad said. "Well, we don't have to fight. Why not back down? Everyone else would rather I be leader as it is, so accept it and step down."

Shane's olive eyes deepened to a dark jade green as his scent enhanced with the vivid hotness of rage. "You really think I'll let some pretty ass boy like you take over? I've been the leader here since sixteen and now you show up and you think you can take my place? Oh no, I need to remind you just who I am and what place you're in."

I growled. "Whatever place I'm in, its not underneath you Shane."

Shane tackled me, driving me to the ground and crushed my ribs like they were dry noodles. Blood gushed from my mouth, I couldn't breathe as the shattered bones punctured my lungs. Shane's fist drew back, his knees pinned my

A. E. Costello 171

arms down to the ground and his knuckles plowed into my eyes. Pain ricocheted from my broken sockets to the back of my skull, and blood ran in rivulets down my temples, pooling in my ears. Blinded, I laid still and limp.

I lost...again.

Shane cursed something and said in a voice slick with fangs, "There, you little bitch! You want to say something else, huh?"

With that, he stomped on my abdomen, then kicked me in the face, unhinging my jawbone.

"Stop it!" Sky screamed in a voice like an enraged she-wolf, mixed in with Connor's higher-pitched howl, and I could only listen to the two charge at Shane.

No! Don't attack him! If I can't lay a hand on him, what do you two think you can do? I gotta get up...I can't let them fight by themselves!

I struggled to sit up, my bones crunching as I bent over. I ran my arm over my face, trying to clear up all the blood caking over my eyes, and used another hand to shove my jaw back into place. I was healing, but accelerated healing didn't turn off my pain sensors. My entire face burned like an electric live wire seared against my nerve endings.

"Get off of me!"

Shane roared, quickly following was two loud thuds of Connor and Sky tossed off him. The next second, another kick landed against my temple, my eardrum exploded in a gush of blood. My head snapped from the side of my neck, sound cutting off then popping back.

Someone leapt over me, quickly following was the hard thud of a strong hit, then Shane made a grunting sound of pain. He cursed and landed on his knees, then rolled into a ball.

"Nice nut shot Leo," said Connor with a pained chuckle, then two pairs of hands grabbed me underneath my armpits, heaving but failing to lift me to my feet. "Get up Xon, we need to get outta here! Shane'll just get back up once he heals!"

More hands grasped my body, and with their help, I got to my feet and blindly followed them. White light sparked in my vision as shooting pain in my sockets began to ease. Sirens wailed in the distance, someone must have called the police about a fight.

"Let him down here," instructed Sky in a breathless voice.

I coughed a few times as my body was dropped onto the ground.

Connor gasped out, "Damn, you're like a thousand pounds Xon!"

"Shane is leaving," said Javier as the sirens neared. "It appears someone has notified the police. Let me heal you Xon."

Javier laid his upper body over my face, directing his heat into my wounds, then the others crowded close to add their heat. I laid on the grass with bodies piled on top of me like before and as I shifted, they moved. I sat up and rubbed at the dried blood caking my face. The sky was still bright but it was summer, it could easily be eight o'clock and I'm pass curfew.

Connor looked at me with dark brown eyes. "You tried really hard Xon."

"And failed." I said, my voice was tiny and subdued, I sounded like I was five years old and I hated it.

Leo laid his head on my shoulder and breathed out slowly, eyes closed. I could understand that he still trusted me and preferred me, but how when I can't protect myself?

Javier said, "Leo saved you my friend."

He was sitting on a branch in a tree. The clearing we were in was surrounded by trees and thick bushes, with just enough open grass for us to fit in together comfortably.

My eyes widened. "What?"

Sky nodded, arms crossed over her stomach. "Shane was still whaling on you even though you had given in. When Connor and I tried to stop him, he flung us off and kept going. Leo kicked Shane in his balls, as hard as he could.

Shane stopped and crumbled into a ball. We knew he would get up once he was healed, so we picked you up and went over here. Shane got up and ran just as the police came and got a crew to clean up the blood. You must be growing up."

I stared at her. "Yeah, growing up? He thrashed me just like last time."

"Xon." Connor stated in a firm voice. "You fought him this time, don't you see? You even made him bleed and you held your ground. Then you healed faster. You are growing up, really."

"I didn't win." I said with just a touch of heat to my tone, starting to get irritated. "I didn't even show him any of my moves."

"God Xon, it's like you're being stupid on purpose." Sky snapped, showing fangs. "You are showing him moves, even if you clearly don't realize it. Moves like the fact you've won all of our loyalty even though you've been a wolf barely two weeks. Moves that you are willing to stand up and fight him, moves that you don't stop until he has to actually knock you down, and keep you down. None of us fight back Shane, got it? He can hit us a few times and we're good, we're finished. You don't stop Xon, you keep coming back. When he was beating you, he smelled like fear. Do you get it now?"

Stunned, I nodded. "Yeah...I get it."

Connor rubbed at his cheek, which had no bruise but I figured that was where Shane had hit him. "Well, next time will be better Xon, you'll get him next time."

I looked at him, kind of touched. "You told me I'm not at Shane's level."

Connor gave me a small smile. "Yeah but you get stronger each time you come around him."

I didn't see it but I let out a long breath and put my arm around Leo's shoulders, he hadn't moved from resting against me.

I asked, "So how many times does it take for him to knock me out before I knock him out? That's how I become leader, right?"

"You say leader like it is an official position," said Javier. "But Shane is not an Alpha, he is a de facto leader. Mr. Forrest expects Shane to keep the rest of the shifters from bothering him, that is all. We are not even a real Pack, a Pack will not have a nonsensical name like Wildebeasts, but either the name of the Alpha or the name of their territory. If this was a real Pack, we would be the Lakeside Village Pack for instance."

I said, "But we are a Pack."

I touched Leo's chin and tucked his head backwards against me so I could put my nose in the groove of his neck and shoulder. I smelled that scent we had created, the deep bond between our wolves, it was real, thick, like home and belonging. Leo didn't fight my hold or my touch, just laid against me.

Connor moved forward and I scented him under his chin and at the base of his ears, he had that scent too. Connor leaned against me on my other side, so I put my arm around his waist. I was cuddling two guys like they were girlfriends but it was like holding my brothers, my friends, my Packmates.

Javier swung his legs and hopped to the ground then scooted to sit in front of me. He held out his wrist. I inhaled his scent. His base scent of male and werewolf, his personal scent warm with honeysuckle and wood chips, then his Pack scent, flavorful and spicy, it made my throat itch.

Javier smiled and took his arm back. "That is the scent of the Méndez Pack, the Pack of my family back in Spain. The smell you have made with Connor and Leo, that is a Pack scent as well. If you want to be an Alpha, you must create that smell with all of us."

Sky crossed her arms over her stomach. "It's not that easy Javier, because he still has to beat Shane in a fight. Shane won't accept Xon making Pack with us then trying to ignore him." She looked at me. "You'll have to make Pack with Shane too."

I didn't know what to do with that, how could I turn Shane willing to look to me as a leader, as an Alpha? I sighed then nudged Connor and Leo who were both leaning on me.

I said with another sigh, "I need to get home. My parents are probably worried about me."

Connor stood up but Leo held onto my arm tighter. I stood up anyway, bringing him to his feet. His arms hooked around mine, squeezing. Leo wasn't strong but he didn't need to be strong to indicate that he had no intention of letting me go.

I looked into his face, his green eyes were fixated on mine with a raw desperation, like if he looked away he would no longer exist. I glanced at Connor who stood close to my side, he had one hand on my waist and while he was looking at the grass, I could smell his scent morphing into depression again.

"Alright then." I said. "You guys can come to my house again. It's a Saturday night, it should be fine. This time Javier and Sky, you should come and meet my family."

Javier looked excited, his scent jolted like electricity. "Yes, I am willing very much. It was not fair that Leo and Connor have been. I want to go too as well."

"Sky?" I looked at her next.

Sky gently pressed at her regal braids with two hands. "I'll come but I'm not spending the night."

I wouldn't mind having Sky sleep in my bed, in fact, I'd really like that a lot but my parents wouldn't allow it.

I nodded and smiled. "That's fine Sky, come and hang out with us for a while. Come you guys."

"Xon your clothes are ruined." Javier pointed it out as I started to walk away, Leo still clasping onto me like a limpet.

I looked down, my jeans and shirt were browned with dried blood, and wrinkled with thick clumps of it, the stains would never come out.

"I'll have to come clean." I said, still walking. Connor had his hand gripping my pocket and I put my free arm around his shoulders. "I can't sneak around or try and lie. You guys will back me up, right?"

Lakeside Village was mostly empty as we walked to my house, everyone would head to the city to get any type of nightlife entertainment. The sky was purplish blue, white stars tinkling into view. Then hanging heavy in the center was the Moon, with only a small dark sliver.

"It'll be full tomorrow." Sky pointed out as my breath caught, I stumbled while staring at it. "Your first full Moon, right Xon?"

I nodded and struggled to take my eyes off its silver brilliance. The wolf on the inside was ready to answer its call, ready to roll back my human skin and bask in it.

I said, "I feel like its talking to me, to the wolf."

"It'll be a lot more intense tomorrow," said Connor, his eyes also on the Moon, his dark brown eyes shining. "Your human skin is like too many covers during summer, all you'll want is to rip it off. It's terrible."

"I go to the forest." Javier shrugged as we neared my house. "The forest truly comes alive when the Moon Goddess heightens it with her rays."

I arrived at my house and knocked on the door but asked, "Moon Goddess?"

This was a first, I hadn't heard anything about some goddess. Besides, I was Christian, there was only one God. Even as I thought it, a small sliver of doubt clutched me. How I had been wondering if I counted as God's child anymore, how I thought He wasn't answering my prayers. Was it because there was someone else in charge of me now, someone else I should be praying and worshiping to?

The door opened and my father at first smiled then it died as he took in my clothes. He covered his mouth but I smelled his sickness in his throat.

"I'm fine Dad." I said. "I'm completely healed, my clothes got a little dirty, that's all."

Dad stared at me with eyes darkening. "A little dirty? Son, you're covered in blood. Who was it this time? Wyatt?"

"Shane." I said, gritting my teeth that I had lost again.

Dad sighed then looked around at everyone else. "I know Leo and Connor, but…"

His eyes landed on Sky and brightened as his scent flooded with both joy and relief.

"This is Javier Méndez." I said, using my chin to point to him. "He's the one letting me rest up, he's also an amazing Healer. And she is Skylark Cloud, she's really helpful too and doesn't let me mope or feel sorry for myself."

Javier inclined his head to my father. "Señor Reeves, it is nice to meet you."

"Call me Sky please." Sky smiled. "Only my parents call me Skylark."

"Come in," said Dad, backing up. "Xon, please, get rid of those clothes and you need to shower as well. Everyone else, it's almost dinner time, so you are welcome to eat with us. Xon, hurry upstairs before Kyra sees you."

I nodded and headed up, still with Leo clinging to my arm like he would never let me go. Everyone else followed me, talking amongst themselves.

In my bedroom, I sat Leo on the bed, then grasped at his fingers. "You have to let me go Leo, I need to use the bathroom and change my clothes."

Leo stared at me with green eyes like dark empty pools, he looked at me like I was light and he was in darkness.

I glanced at the others for help. Sky came forward and knelt by Leo, she first put her hand over his eyes and he jolted all over, like he was about to fight or didn't know how to react.

"Let him go Leo." Her lips were close to his ear and her other hand ran up and down Leo's chest, a soothing calming stroke. "He's not going anywhere, he'll be right back. Hold onto me, I'm here. Let Xon go."

Connor came next and touched Leo's hands, gently forcing his fingers in between my arm and Leo's grasp.

He said, "I'm here too Leo, you can hold me. It'll be okay, Xon will be back."

With the two working together, Leo slowly released me, then Sky and Connor both hugged him. Leo held onto them like he was a frightened child and they were the heroes to protect him.

I got clothes from my closet and went into the bathroom to shower and redress. I could hear laughter from my bedroom, so I was sure everyone was fine. When I was ready, I came back out and saw Leo, Connor and Javier were on my bed roughhousing. Connor and Javier were tickling and nuzzling Leo while he squirmed and made motions like to escape but they wouldn't let him, giving him their scents and their affection. His eyes weren't so dark and desperate anymore, and his scent was fruity with happier emotions.

Sky was sitting on my desk, watching and laughing, warm golden notes leaving her throat.

I walked over to her and said, "Thanks for being here Sky."

She looked up at me and smiled, her face brightening like a sun breaking through clouds. "I want us to be a Pack too Xon. You may not understand it but you're doing amazing. You have to keep getting stronger and believe in yourself, in your wolf."

I thought about the hard hot coal that's been burning in my gut from the beginning while looking into Sky's smiling face. My fingers touched her cheek then slid up to curl in the small baby fine hairs at the side of her ear. Sky's eyes widened and she went still, even her breathing stopped. I drew my fingers down to her chin and lifted her head back just enough so my nose could fit at the base of her neck and I inhaled her scent.

Her base scent, the thick heady smell of the forest. Then her scent of being female, sweet and musky. Her personal scent, roses and honey. Her emotions rose up, the sugary rush of arousal mixed with the faint ammonia of anxiety.

I said low, moving to her ear, "You know I'm not going to hurt you, right?"

Sky placed her hands on my waist and her nails dug in. "I'm not worried about being hurt by you. Your father is staring at us."

I jerked back and whirled around. My bedroom door was open and Dad was standing in the doorway. I couldn't smell him from this distance because all I could smell was Sky, but the turmoil in his eyes and how his face was tightened, I could get an idea.

I stepped back from Sky and put my hands behind my back. "I wasn't doing anything."

"It was enough," said Dad, but his voice was strange, a mix of deepness and wavering, like he was trying to be stern and laugh at the same time. "Dinner is ready, so you guys should wash up and come downstairs. Xon, keep your hands to yourself, understand?"

I nodded and swallowed hard. I tried to ignore the burning in my cheeks, the burning in my gut. My wolf was antsy, fur raised from his neck down to his tail. Sky's scent was full in my nose, the feel of her soft cheek tingling my fingers.

The wolves on the bed were upright and at attention, it seemed like it had been only me who didn't notice my father come in. Again, I had no idea he had been standing there, I didn't smell him or sense movement. If he had been Wyatt, I'd been stabbed and sliced in the back by now.

After I got everyone to wash their hands, I led the way downstairs where the dining room table had been set.

Mom stood at the entryway from the dining room to the kitchen. Her eyes immediately went to Sky and lit up like fireworks.

"X-Xon?"

Her voice wobbled as her scent gave off the tingling lemons of shock that I had brought a girl home.

I said, "This is Skylark Cloud, call her Sky. She's a good friend of mine. And this is Javier Méndez, he's the one who helped me out last time."

Mom nodded, smiling wider. "Well, everyone please sit down. Grant will lead us in prayer."

I glanced at Javier to see if he'd mind praying to God, and made a mental note to ask him about the Moon goddess went I got the chance. He peacefully smiled at me as we all took seats. I ended up with Connor and Leo next to me, Mom and Dad at either end of the table, then Sky and Javier on the other side. Before Dad could begin the prayer, I had a stab of guilt that someone was missing. Even though I didn't like Shane, in fact I was starting to hate him, Sky was right. I couldn't make a Pack with everyone and exclude Shane. He was an asshole, but he was still a wolf, and he was one of us.

I said it outloud, "I think someone else deserves to be here."

Connor shook his head, dark brown eyes full of warning. Leo also shook his head. Javier smiled with a nod.

Sky said also with a smile, "I'll give you his number."

"Who?" My parents both asked.

"Shane Armstrong." I said, looking Mom then Dad in the eyes.

Dad said, "Will he behave himself Xon?"

I had to answer truthfully. "To be honest, I'm not sure. But he deserves to be here."

Mom put her hand up. "Wait, I'm missing something. Is this the same Shane who's been beating you senseless Xon?"

I didn't like her word choice but I said, "It's the same Shane, yes."

Mom crossed her arms. "Then why do you think he should be here? What do you mean *deserves* to be here?"

I bit my lower lip and I wanted to explain but I didn't want to chase Mom away from the dinner table either.

Mom's eyes narrowed into slices. "You had better not be thinking of a lie Xon."

"Everyone at this table is a werewolf Mom." I said it clear cut. "And I want all of us to be a Pack, to be a community together like you said. So that means Shane should be here. Eating together, spending time together, playing and sleeping, that's how to make a Pack. That's why."

Mom's honey gold skin paled on her face and she glanced into Javier's and then Sky's eyes. When both of their wolf sparks flickered in their pupils, she pushed away from the table.

"Mom!" I didn't mean to shout but my voice raised.

"I'm not hungry." she said, dropping her napkin in her plate. "I'll be down later to clean up."

Dad stood up. "Kyra Melissa Reeves, sit back down."

His voice was the most commanding I had ever heard him take with my mother. If anyone was to wear the pants in my house, it was Mom. It wasn't that Dad was a pushover, but Mom was the one to naturally take charge. Now he was putting his foot down.

Mom stared at him and I froze. The last thing I wanted was for my parents to fight, I didn't care we had company over.

No matter what, don't let my parents hurt each other.

Dad said, "You can't ignore it Kyra, you can't act like this isn't happening. Xon is a werewolf, yes he is." He said as Mom's mouth moved like she was going to say something back. "And because of that, all of his new friends are werewolves too. Sit down and eat Kyra. You've never run away from your problems before, don't start now. *Proverbs 3:5-6. Trust in the Lord with all your heart, and do not lean on your own understanding. In all your ways acknowledge Him, and He will make straight your paths.* So sit down Kyra and let God handle this."

Mom slowly sat down and put her napkin to the side, scooted back in and stared at her plate like it would tell her what to do.

Sky quietly gave me Shane's number, which I put into my phone as a new contact then I called it.

A woman with a clear crisp no-nonsense voice answered. "Yes, this is Shane Armstrong's cellular phone, who may I ask is calling?"

I blinked several times then said, "This is Jaxon Reeves. I'm calling to invite Shane over for dinner. May I ask who it is I'm speaking to?"

The woman was quiet for a moment then said, "I am Patricia Armstrong, this is Shane's mother. I do not recognize your name and as such I don't feel it's appropriate for my son to visit your home."

"Mother! Dammit, give me my phone!" Shane's voice blasted from the distance with loud stomping as he got closer.

"Shane Michael Armstrong you stop that right this instant!" Patricia's voice was cold and strict, like a leather belt getting snapped warningly. "A strange boy has called wanting to invite you to dinner and I'm politely refusing in your place."

"How dare you do that? Who's calling? What invite? Give me my phone dammit!"

Even to his mother Shane was rude, abrasive and potty-mouthed.

Patricia said coolly, "He introduced himself as Jaxon Reeves. God, you never used to talk to me like that. You act more like an animal than a human these days, for the past few years you've completely changed."

Shane was quiet.

Then he said, "Mother, if he has invited me to dinner then I should go."

This was the first time I had heard Shane speak with a low normal voice, for once not growling or shouting or even cursing.

Patricia responded, "I asked you to tell me who this boy is and I won't repeat myself."

Dad was staring at me and tapped his wrist, everyone else was watching me too. Connor's fingers reached for the platters of food, I brought his hand down while Connor licked the line of drool ebbing over his lower lip. Leo had his eyes on the turkey wings that were directly across from him, his body was suspiciously still, like it was taking everything in him not to leap for it. If I didn't let dinner start, they would riot.

I spoke, "Shane, we're going to eat now but I'll make sure there is food left for you. Come when you can, alright?"

I gave my address then hung up. I knew Shane would be able to hear me no problem and if he came, he came. If he didn't, then he didn't. It was out of my hands now.

I put my phone in my pocket and said, "Alright, let's eat."

"HOLD IT!" Mom's voice could have exploded the roof off as Connor and Leo reached for the food with panting mouths and wide eyes.

I had to grab Leo's wrist before he could pick up the steaming hot turkey wings bare-handed, while at the same time I snatched Connor's collar and pulled him back before he could start shoveling food down his throat.

"We give thanks before we eat." She said, chin lifted and voice steady. Just the fact she spoke made me feel a little bit better, that she was trying.

Connor said, "Thank you Mrs. Reeves."

He tried to eat but I pulled him back again.

I said, "You can lead the prayer Dad."

Dad stood, his dark eyes looking over everyone.

"Take hands and bow your heads."

Javier and Sky did as told, while Connor and Leo looked like they didn't want to take their eyes off the food.

"Dear Heavenly Father, we come to you with great thanks. Thank You for this food that you have blessed us with, and bless the hands of my lovely wife who made it. We also want to thank you for the guests we have at our table today, Sky, Javier, Connor and Leo, who have all befriended my only child. We pray that as we eat this food to nourish our bodies, You continue to guide us in doing your spiritual will. In Jesus Name, Amen."

Prayer over, we began to eat. Connor and Leo chowed like they were starved, Javier and Sky both ate with much more class. Sky chewed with her mouth closed and drank after every bite, the movements of her mouth and throat slow and meaningful. Javier ate so perfectly, it was almost like he thought everyone was staring at him. With each bite he gently patted at his mouth, he kept his elbows off the table, his fork sat quietly on the plate between bites, he didn't clink his silverware and when he drank he didn't slurp or gulp loudly.

"Well, then." Mom looked at Sky. "Tell me about yourself."

Her tone made it sound more like *tell me everything about you or else.*

Sky smiled. "Well, my name is Skylark Cloud. I'm five-feet-three. I like to play basketball in my spare time and read books when I get the chance. My parents are married and I have two younger siblings, Falcon and Raven. Anything else?"

Mom frowned. "What I really want to know is your intentions towards my son. He's a good kid with a future ahead of him and he doesn't need any unfaithful girls getting in the way."

"I'm not Melody." Sky said plainly, her hazel eyes darkened just a shade.

Mom's head lifted a notch, her shoulders steadied then she nodded, her lips pursed and she turned back to her food without saying anything else.

Then she said, "What do your parents do?"

I caught eyes with Dad, he looked relieved and gave me a smile.

Mom and Sky talked, while Dad and I looked on. Javier, Leo and Connor busied themselves with eating.

The door was knocked on with heavy loud thuds. I stood up and went into the entryway to open it. Shane stood there, wearing black slacks, a dark red button up shirt with a black leather waist-length jacket. His hair was combed back and his shirt collar popped.

"Come in." I said, unable to stop my scent letting off waves of surprise and shock, tart smells of lemon. "There's food left for you."

"Yeah." Shane said gruffly, he smelled embarrassed and irritated, a mix of heated prickles and burnt dryness. "Thanks for the invite."

When Shane stepped in, Dad shifted to the side so he could see him. The movement was vaguely wolfish, stalking, taking in everything.

Shane's brows raised and he took a discreet sniff but Dad was human, no doubt.

"Dad, this is Shane." I said.

Dad met Shane's eyes. He held out his hand.

Shane took it and said, "Mr. Reeves."

"Grant is fine," said Dad, he turned Shane's hand over and revealed the scarring across Shane's knuckles. Shane took his hand back, a flush on his cheeks.

Dad said, "Come and eat Shane."

Mom and Sky were taking care of the empty dishes. Connor was gnawing on his turkey wing.

Javier and Leo struggled over the last corn muffin when Shane stepped over and snatched it out of their hands. He shoved it into his mouth.

He said around chewing and swallowing, "Last one is mine."

While they stared at him, Shane sat down and made a plate of what was left but he kept eating before putting the food on his plate, so he was basically eating with his fingers.

Dad crossed his arms. "So you don't get enough to eat either Shane?" His eyes trailed over the hunch of Shane's shoulders, the contours of his arms. "You look healthy to me."

"I'm always hungry," said Shane, his teeth tearing up a piece of turkey wing. "Comes with the territory."

His wolf spark billowed bright enough to overlap his pupils, giving his blue eyes a hellish glow.

Dad paused.

He said, "Try and tone it down around my wife. She prefers not to know."

"Not to know what?"

Mom stepped out of the kitchen, drying her hands on a towel, her eyes sharp as a tack and pinning Dad to the wall.

Shane answered like it was nothing. "That Xon and I aren't really friends." He looked at me with deep blue eyes. "We're archenemies."

Mom blinked then placed her hands on her hips. "So! You're the boy who's been having my son come home covered in blood?"

Shane slid his greasy finger into his mouth and sucked, his lashes lowered then he said in a low voice, "That's not all your son gets covered in, if you know what I mean."

I crossed into the dining room with one move but it was Dad who had grabbed my fist before it could land in Shane's face. Mom's high scream echoed throughout the room. Shane hadn't moved, his olive-tinged eyes piercing right into mine.

He said in a soft voice, "Going to beat me up now Xon? Make me bleed? Break my nose? Is that how you treat your...Pack?"

A. E. Costello 187

Dad was gripping my first very tightly but it didn't hurt, his strength was like a little stuffed bear paw. It wasn't him who stopped me from hitting Shane but from the knowledge that if I wouldn't hit Leo or Connor, Javier or Sky, then I shouldn't hit Shane either.

"Jaxon William Reeves!" Mom's voice was crisp and shaking. "What in God's name was that just now?"

"Nothing," said Dad, his eyes on Shane. "Shane should be leaving now."

Shane stood up, his tongue slid over his teeth and sucked with a high sharp sound.

"Alright Mr. Reeves, I'm gone. Xon." He looked in my eyes. "See you later. Maybe sooner than you think."

He walked by me, his shoulder bumped into mine and he left.

Dad said, "Xon, to the study please. Kyra, please, stay with the company." He said when she started to turn to come with us.

Mom nodded. Her eyes on me looked like raw pools. She knew I was fighting, I came home with bloodied clothes or without my clothes but she never saw me actually try to attack someone before. Tonight, just then, a little part of her had changed, had died. And it was my fault.

Sky watched me solemnly as I followed Dad. Leo and Connor also had scraped distressed eyes and their scents flushed with fear and anxiety.

Javier murmured, "Be calm."

I gave them reassuring smiles but avoided looking my mother in the face. In the study, Dad closed the door and turned on me, leaning against it. His eyes stared at the floor, his hands were knuckled. His scent was morphed into so much it was like a thick heavy blob around him.

"Are you and Leo a couple?"

He looked at me with stark serious eyes, no jokes, waiting for an answer.

My jaw clenched but Dad kept talking. "Xon, I've seen the way he looks at you. He's always touching you and yeah, he was naked in your bed."

I snapped, "Connor is the same way!"

Dad flicked his hand dismissively. "You're not interested in Connor and he's not like that for you, he's like an eager little brother, that much is clear. Not Leo, not even close."

Dad's gaze looked directly in my eyes, my wolf lifted his lip. Dad's eyes widened.

He said softly, "Just tell me the truth."

"I *have* been telling you the truth." My voice rumbled from my chest, my gums itched as fangs threatened to break free. "He was helping me out a whole lot in the beginning but now it's me helping him. He's attached, that's all. We're close, he needs me, he watches me, he trusts me and follows me. There's nothing sexual about it, alright? I like Sky, got it?"

Brows furrowed, Dad asked, "Then why did Shane say that if it wasn't true? He insinuated something that really made me feel uncomfortable."

I stared at him. "Really? Shane said that to be an asshole, that's what he is, what he does. He was testing my patience."

I stalked to the side, met the wall then turned, met the desk, turned again, the window. I paced taking those steps, my hands buckled with contorted knuckles, claws sliding out of the tips of my fingers.

"He knew I was going to want to hit him but he also knew if I hit him then it meant I would have to hit the others too. My whole...my whole *campaign* for being leader is that I'm not violent, that I'll never use my fists and let my strength do the talking. They follow me because they trust me not to hurt them, to get rough, to spill blood. Shane is the exact opposite so he said that purposely to enrage me, to make me go back on my promises. If I hit Shane and he'll be a Packmember, then it means I should hit the rest of them and they should hit each other. If the leader, who will be me, sets a stance that violence is the norm then it'll *be* the norm. Shane rules like that but I don't want to, I want a peaceful Pack. He's...he's pushing my limits."

Dad leaned his shoulders on the wall and laid his arms over his stomach, fingers laced. He watched me pace with a smooth expression.

He said, "If Shane is still the current leader, why didn't he hit you, why did he walk out?"

I sighed and cupped the back of my head, my fingers dug in just enough for pain to scatter across my skull, to keep me grounded.

I said, "Because Shane's not an idiot. If he picked a fight with me in my own house in front of my parents, he's asking for human attention. Mom would have called the police if he seriously hurt me. Shifters aren't supposed to get in a lot of trouble with the law, it looks bad on everyone else."

There was a knock on the door.

Mom said from behind it, "Grant, Xon, Sky is ready to leave."

Dad moved away from the door and I opened it. I slid past Mom without meeting her eyes, I wasn't ready just yet. Sky was at the door, adjusting her shirt over her stomach, it was pouching out from all the food she had eaten.

I held Sky's hand, felt the strength running in her slim long fingers as she held me back. "Let me walk you home."

"I don't think so." She smiled up at me, eyes glinting. "I don't want my parents to see you and jump to conclusions."

I had to grin. "Maybe that's a conclusion I want them to have."

I brought her hand to my mouth and lightly kissed it before letting go.

Sky placed her hand on my jaw, feeling my skin. "I'll see you later Xon."

She leaned up and pecked my chin before leaving.

I watched her disappear into the night as the spot where her lips had graced heated.

Leo leaned against me, running his chin over my ear and neck. I placed my head on the top of his head, letting my fingers run through his springy hair. He didn't have to speak, I knew he didn't want to leave.

"You should go." I said, looking into his stark green eyes. "Get a change of clothes, okay? I don't know if my parents will let you stay all weekend so just clothes for tomorrow."

Leo nodded and I waved him on. I closed the door and turned around to see Connor laying on the dining room floor, sleeping with his chewed up turkey wing on his neck. Javier was in the kitchen with Mom, they were having a pleasant chat over the dishes. Mom was dual-natured to me, one moment she doesn't want my friends around for simply being werewolves, the next she can be cordial and polite. It was like she couldn't figure out what her stance was, discriminatory or tolerant.

Dad stood to the side, watching.

He said quietly, "I get it now."

My brows raised. "What?"

"Leo." He said, looking at me. "He's like a puppy who's been neglected, starved, abandoned. Now he's found a new owner who's kind and gentle. Leo wants to stay around you all the time, he's like co-dependent. If he was...regular then I'd say he seriously needs counseling. But watching how he just...*nuzzled* you like..."

Dad covered his mouth and nodded, looking away for a moment. "Yeah, I get it."

I let out a sigh of relief. "Thanks Dad." I looked at him. "No more questioning my sexuality?"

Dad nodded then looked at Connor. "Guess you're going to wake him up and send him home too?"

I paused then said softly, "There is something going on at Connor's house that makes him hate being home. I brought them both home last time because Leo wanted to stay with me and while Connor was going to leave, it was all over him that he dreaded the idea. Connor…he's sad all the time Dad. He'll smile and laugh and play but on the inside the kid is in despair. I don't know why but I have to help him."

I went to Connor, knelt, brushed away the bone and lifted him into my arms. He rolled into me, arms looped around my neck and he buried his head into the crook of my neck and shoulder. He inhaled deeply and his body relaxed. He sunk deeper into a safe calm sleep. I looked at Dad, he was staring at me with eyes both impressed and vaguely shocked. His scent matched, the citrusy tingling scent of pride melding with the lemon of shock.

"What is it?"

Dad tossed a look over his shoulder, Mom had turned on the radio onto a Spanish reggaeton station, still talking with Javier.

He looked at me, saying, "It's like…" He bit his lip hard, his eyes turned to the floor and his scent fluctuated but he said, "It's like becoming a wolf has turned you into a man or is starting to make you grow up. You're taking on responsibilities of leadership, you're dealing with things that you shouldn't at only seventeen years old. You have subjects, followers. Leo and Connor truly depend on you in ways that I'd normally say is dangerous and co-dependent. You have a girl who you can really trust. Javier is a good…guy, wolf?"

Dad looked confused and looked over again. The music had been turned up a little loud, loud enough to drown out our quiet conversation.

Dad continued but even more hushed, "And Shane really *is* an asshole, I wanted to deck him myself."

Dad looked at me. "You've got to win Xon, he hates you, I can see it, he goaded you into hitting him, it's all over him. Son, you need to get in the ring with me."

I shook my head. "Dad, I'd kill you by mistake. One punch and I'll break ribs, bust organs. It's not a good idea.

Right now." I shifted Connor in my arms, he murmured and snuggled deeper into me. "I need to get my wolves in bed."

Mom walked in from the kitchen, music off. Javier was behind her. Mom's left brow went higher than her right, her hands planted on her hips.

"Why are you carrying Connor like he's a baby? He's fifteen. Put him down."

I said, "He's sleeping, I'm gonna take him upstairs to bed."

Mom moved so she was blocking the stairs and she said, "I think he can go home now."

The door was knocked on, quiet, hesitant. Javier answered it. Leo slouched in, clutching a duffel bag to his chest. His eyes were wide and he looked frightened, his scent matched. Brushed on his clothes was a raw thick scent, heated and rough. Shane.

I couldn't say, *did Shane hurt you,* not with Mom there.

I said, "Leo brought clothes, so just one more sleepover? Javier." I looked at him. "Do you want to stay too?"

Javier's mouth opened, closed, he bit his lip hard then he glanced at Mom who's face was hardening into stone.

He looked at me, saying, "It is best I go Xon. I can not intrude on the good graces of your parents."

Dad said, "If Leo and Connor got to stay, you should be able to stay too. It's only fair." His eyes flicked to me for a moment then he turned to Mom who was glaring at him.

He said, "Kyra, honey, these boys have been working with Xon for this past month, pulling him back from the brink. Look at Xon, he looks great. I don't know how but they're helping him get through it. A sleepover isn't so bad, is it?"

Mom crossed her arms snugly over her chest and her eyes went from the snoozing Connor, to Leo who quickly stared at the floor, Javier who also averted his eyes then to Dad before landing on me. I made a gentle smile and cocked my head innocently to the side.

Mom's face twitched then she smiled and gave a small laugh.

"You aren't fooling me boy." She chuckled. "However." She looked at us with a firmer expression. "Clothes stay on. Javier, something of Xon's from when he was younger might fit you, if you're not going home to get clothes."

Javier's face lit up like he had a light bulb behind his skin, he nodded eagerly and said, "Yes, of course, clothes on, as requested."

Mom moved from the stairwell and we went up.

I said over my shoulder, "I'll be back to say goodnight."

"Uh huh." Mom puffed then she said, "Grant, dear, we need to talk." Her voice was strict and determined.

I could hear Dad gulp from the second floor landing.

In my room, I laid Connor on the bed, he was fully dressed but his shirt and some of his pants were smeared and flecked with food, even his mouth and cheeks were still greasy. I was not letting him under my covers like that.

Leo placed his duffel bag on the floor, then went to Connor and grasped the hem of his shirt, tugging it.

Connor woke up like a shot, his eyes flared so wide his whites were visible all around. His mouth opened wide in a vicious scream, his teeth sharp and fanged. He jerked upright and bit Leo on the shoulder, hard. His teeth crunched into bone, blood spurted.

Javier shouted in Spanish, and he grasped the back of Connor's neck and twisted, trying to shake Connor off. I ran forward and grabbed Leo by the neck to keep him from struggling and used my other hand to try and force Connor's grip off him.

Connor tore his mouth away, his hands shoved Javier and Leo hard. Javier stumbled back and let go of Connor's neck, while Leo sagged in my arms, his hands clasped over his wound, gushing blood.

My wolf whimpered and whined. Leo's pained scent flooded my system, it smelled horrid despite the thrust of excitement that came with seeing blood. That sensation faded away as Leo's feet twisted and kicked, his head pressed against my shoulder and his body jerked in paroxysms of pain.

There were hurried footsteps coming from the hallway. Javier damn near flew to the door, he closed it and locked it. Then he knelt by me. Leo's eyes were screwed shut with tears flowing down his face. Connor jumped off the bed and ran into the bathroom, slamming it closed but I could still hear him screaming.

Javier pushed Leo's hands away, baring the ragged wound. His collarbone had snapped, the white sticks shattered and sticking out of the ruined skin. Leo gasped and tried to cover it again but Javier placed his hands down instead. Javier closed his eyes.

He muttered, "Heal, take my heat and heal."

I wrapped one arm around Leo's forehead and kept him close against me, my other hand gripped him over his heart, feeling the race, the thudding.

I closed my eyes and whispered, "Heal, heal, heal."

The heat started like igniting flame deep in my gut and billowed out, upwards then flowed over my arms and powered into Leo. Javier's heat, it was deep, thick, and slow, building up in Leo's body, focusing on his wound. My heat swam around Javier's and rushed deeper into Leo's body. It was healing other things, Leo's skin smoothed out, his organs swelled and pumped, his veins vibrated.

Leo sucked in a harsh breath and slumped against me, his head tilted to the side.

Javier lowered his hands. "He's out now Xon. All the heat inside of him is working, he'll sleep until it's over."

There was loud knocking on the door.

Mom's voice came through high and shrill. "Xon! Xon! What is going on in there?" The doorknob rattled and she pounded on the door. "And why in God's name is this door locked? You know better than that Xon! Open this door right now! Right this instant!"

A. E. Costello 195

Javier looked at me, eyes wide.

Leo's shirt was drenched in blood, Connor was growing muffled in the bathroom.

I called, "One minute Mom!"

I lifted Leo onto my bed, and Javier helped me rip the shirt off him. I folded it up into a tight ball and shoved it underneath my bed to be secretly disposed of later.

Mom shouted, "Not one minute and not one second, now, immediately! Open this door right now!"

I stood and stopped, my shirt was bloody. I pulled it off and shoved it into my closet. I opened the door just as Javier sat on top of the bloodstain on my bed.

Mom stalked in, staring around, her eyes scoured my room then she saw my bare chest and Javier sitting on the bed. The bed was rumpled and Connor was missing while Leo was also topless and sprawled on top of the covers.

Dad was behind her and he also saw everything. His face twisted, he covered his mouth with both hands but it didn't hide the struggle in his eyes. He had decided that I wasn't gay but the scene looked bad, really bad.

Mom hissed like a viper, "And what in God's name is going on in here?"

I didn't say anything, what could I say? How could I fix this? I didn't want to tell her that Connor nearly tore off Leo's head, she would flip out and make everyone leave.

Javier said quietly, "Connor had a nightmare Señora Reeves. That is the reason why he was screaming. He ran into the bathroom to calm down. Leo and Xon are not wearing shirts because they were getting ready for bed. That is all, that is it."

Mom looked at me, her eyes still dragon fierce. "And Xon? Is that true?"

I nodded and swallowed hard before getting out in a hoarse voice, "It's true. Leo was trying to help Connor take his shirt off for bed but Connor started screaming. We backed off and Connor ran into the bathroom. You came in before we could do anything else."

Mom looked over the floor and the furniture. "Then why did it take you so long to answer? And where is your shirt Xon? And where is Leo's shirt?"

I had no answer. Javier didn't speak either.

Dad placed a hand on Mom's shoulder when she took a step forward, almost like she was ready to get violent.

He said, "Kyra, these are boys, okay? Let me talk to them, man to man."

Mom looked at me dead in the eyes. She brushed Dad's hand off and stalked out without another word.

Dad closed the door and said, "Why did you have to hide the shirts?"

"They were bloody Señor Reeves," said Javier while I was still struggling to get my tongue unstuck from the roof of my mouth. "When Connor woke up, he bit Leo very badly on the shoulder. There was a lot of blood, too much to try and explain away."

Dad nodded and clasped his hands over the back of his head, he closed his eyes and let out a long sigh.

He asked, "Is Leo okay?"

I went to him and placed my fingers on his pulse. It was racing, pressed up against my fingers, and his body was hot, steaming hot. His eyelashes laid on his cheeks, his mouth parted and he was breathing deep and slow. His shoulder was a mess of blood and twisted scarring but even as I watched it was beginning to stitch together. Mom hadn't been able to see Leo's wound from her vantage in the room, if she had, shit would have really hit the fan.

I said, "He's fine Dad, he's healing."

After a few hesitant knocks from the inside, the bathroom door creaked open. Connor's head peeked out, only his hair and his eyes, he saw Dad and ducked back inside. The door closed.

I said, "Dad, we gotta talk to Connor. Can you give us a minute?"

"I'll say goodnight." He said. "Try and keep the screaming to a minimum, okay? You gave Kyra a heart-attack." He shrugged and looked at us. "I'll tell her to stay out of your room in the morning, just in case."

I knew what he wasn't saying.

I said, "I appreciate it."

"I'll see you in the morning."

Dad turned and headed towards the door.

"Goodnight."

"Goodnight Señor Reeves."

Once Dad closed the door behind him, Connor slunk out of the bathroom. He had cleaned his face but there was a large splat of blood on his shirt. His eyes were full of tears and he collapsed to the floor on his hands and knees. He crawled over to me, head bowed.

"I'm sorry, I'm sorry, I'm sorry." He repeated in a desperate mantra until he was at my feet and he placed his face on the floor, his hands clasped onto my ankles. "Please forgive me Xon, I didn't mean to do it. He scared me, I reacted. I'm so, so sorry."

I knelt down and pulled Connor up. He wouldn't meet my eyes, tears soaked his entire face. He shivered all over, his scent desperate, frightened, regretful, a dirty mix of dankness, piss and thick mud. I pressed a kiss to his forehead, he froze.

I lowered my mouth to his ear. "It's okay Connor. I understand. You don't have to grovel, I won't hurt you. Come."

I hugged him close to me and I wanted to croon to him, but I didn't know how in this form. I had done it for Leo when we were both wolves but never as a human. Javier knelt behind Connor and hugged me, which snuggled Connor between us. He closed his eyes as he placed his head on Connor's back.

Javier said, "The croon is most successful in wolf form but it can be done in human form. Focus on Connor's pain, his crying, his weak body and think soothe, think relax, think calm. Breathe deep, slow, steady. You should start to croon."

I nodded and laid my head on Connor's head, tucking his face into my neck and shoulder. I closed my eyes and inhaled deeply. I took in Connor's desperate scent, his wet skin on my skin, how his small body shivered in my hold. I didn't want him to be so scared, so upset. He had a nightmare, it happens, I understand. My wolf padded up close to me and curled around me, running his fur against my skin. My chest firmed, coughed then began to vibrate. The sound came from not within my body but deeper, invisible, the wolf.

Connor's body relaxed and melted against mine, his lips moved against my chest. "I thought…I thought…I was so scared."

"It's okay Connor." I rubbed my chin against the crown of his head, he cuddled deeper into my arms, Javier pressed closer. "We understand."

I yawned suddenly, my jaw cracked and there was a quick ache of pain, remembering Shane dislocating it. Connor shuddered into sleep, his body slipped onto mine and his head went lax, a long shaky breath left his lips and he was unconscious.

I asked, "Will he wake up if we try to undress him?"

Javier shook his head, his hand gently stroked Connor's fluffy green hair. "No, I think not. He is in a deep sleep while his heart and soul are soothed. The attentions of the physical body should not intrude."

There was a soft grunt from the bed then a ragged cough.

I looked over. Leo was trying to sit up, using his good arm to push himself upward. Javier helped Leo.

Though he said, "Move slowly my friend, you should still rest."

Leo's shoulder was scarred, ropy thick folds of skin had build up on his shoulder and there was some blood that dripped down his chest. Javier leaned in and licked the blood off, then passed his tongue over the wound several times. Leo didn't move to stop him, his eyes heavy-lidded like he was in a daze.

"He needs water," said Javier, his finger gently rubbed some of the saliva onto the scars. "The heat has done what it could and saliva isn't enough. Water should help now."

I stood up, Connor limp in my arms. "Does he need a shower or bath?"

I remembered how amazing the water felt when I took my shower at Javier's place.

"Leo can not stand up for a shower," said Javier. "The heat is still heavy in him, it has made him weak and drowsy. I do not even know why he is awake."

Javier wrapped his arms around Leo's waist and picked him up. Leo folded over, slumped onto his back. I laid Connor on the bed and quickly took his shirt off, then his jeans, putting him under the covers in his briefs.

Javier stood up but Leo was way too tall. Leo's head was nearly touching the ground, his arms bent up against Javier's back and his legs were still on the ground. Javier wasn't trembling with the effort to carry him; Leo was a featherweight but the balance was off.

"I'll take him." I said, coming over and slinging Leo over my shoulder. "The bathroom's over there, can you run the tub?"

Javier nodded and went in. Leo's fingers weakly gripped my waistband, he shifted like he was trying to get up.

"Stay still Leo." I said, walking towards the sound of running water.

In the bathroom, Javier had run the tub with hot water, steam billowing from the tap. I put Leo down but his feet slipped on the floor and he leaned his weight on me, not holding himself up. I held him with one arm around his chest, my other hand went to his pants. Javier helped and we stripped Leo and got him in the bathtub.

Leo's eyes flared and he dragged in a deep breath as his shoulder was submerged in water. His face contorted for a moment then he relaxed. His eyes closed and his head slid underneath the surface. I reached in, cupped his chin and gently lifted his head up so his nostrils were free. He breathed in and out, laying still.

I said, "How come it's taking Leo so long to heal? It was just a bite to the shoulder."

Javier said in a soft voice, "Leo is a very physically weak wolf. He is very thin, too thin. His body does not generate enough heat to heal himself properly. While our heat together does heal, it is too foreign in his body, he was rejecting the process. The water will do the rest."

I nodded. Leo's hand came out of the water to clasp my wrist, he struggled against me as some water dribbled out of his mouth. I got my arm underneath his shoulders and lifted him out. His shoulder was smooth, healed.

I heaved him out of the tub like he was a toddler and set him on his feet. Leo wobbled and his hands clasped my shoulders for balance. Javier got a towel and wrapped it around Leo's waist. Leo let me go to grab it. He looked vaguely embarrassed, his eyes widened, his face dark red.

"Let's go Javier." I said. "Leo, I'll get your bag. Javier, bed?"

He nodded, saying wearily, "Yes, very much so."

I brought Leo his bag and closed the door. Javier had taken off his clothes but left his briefs. Leo came out of the bathroom. He wore a baggy pair of shorts, the waistband was pulled tight around his thin waist.

I tilted my chin towards the bed where Javier was getting in, but Leo went to me instead. He hugged me and pressed his face into my neck, though he had to bend his knees to do it. I hugged him back and stood away as my hands touched his skin, which had plumped out, like fat had been added. His body shape was still thin, but I couldn't see his ribs, his collarbone wasn't as prominent. He looked like he had gained about five pounds, evenly smoothed out.

Leo touched my face and my shoulders, stepping close again. I took his hand and his shoulder.

I said, "Go ahead and get in the bed. I'm coming."

Leo hesitated but when he looked in my eyes, he flinched and quickly did as told. I got undressed and put on pajama bottoms, then got in bed. Like bees to honey, everyone gravitated over to me. It was uncomfortable, the clothes were scratchy, and denied the touch of skin. I squirmed. Leo twisted and pulled at his shorts.

Javier reached over to stop him. "Señora Reeves requested we keep our clothes on. We cannot."

I asked, trying not to writhe like a child. "It is so uncomfortable, like my skin is going to itch off."

Javier said, "Wolves need the touch of wolves, of fur, of skin, to feel connected. Clothes are denying us that."

I rolled over, grabbed my cell phone from the bedside table and texted Dad.

Xon: Keep Mom out of the bedroom in the morning. Please.

I kicked my shorts off, Leo took his off and Javier didn't hesitate to do the same. Connor was deep asleep and curled up in a ball. Leo snuggled to my back, rubbing his face into the back of my neck, his arms wrapped around my waist and he slid his legs in between mine, plastering his entire body to mine. Javier grabbed Connor and tucked him close to me. Connor's head nuzzled under my chin. I moved my arms so they were over Connor's shoulder and the other underneath my head. I looked at Javier who wasn't able to touch me.

He smiled and said, "I'm alright. Connor is very warm."

He placed his head on Connor's shoulder and his eyes closed.

Leo snored behind me in low gruff sounds and Connor whimpered in a soft wavering tone. I stroked his shoulder and he quieted, his hands gripped my chest even as his body relaxed. Javier had his arm over Connor's waist so his fingers brushed my abs. His legs slid between Connor's thighs so his toes were braced against my knee. I shifted so Javier's toes were on my thigh and closed my eyes.

I wanted Sky to be here but I knew my parents wouldn't allow that, and definitely Sky's parents wouldn't.

For a moment, I thought about Leah. The she-wolf who started it all. If the Stone Pack had moved here, then that meant Leah was naturally here as well. I hadn't seen her yet and I didn't know if I wanted to. It was her fault, everything that happened in California to this moment right here, it all came from her.

Yet just as I thought that, my wolf's heart made a leap. It was small but real. An excited anticipatory leap. While my human mind wanted nothing to do with Leah, the wolf was interested. It really was like having two sides, conflicting minds and emotions.

Leo jerked against me, making a strangled sound in his throat. I hushed him, moving my hand from underneath my head and placed it on his head, running my fingers through his springy hair. Leo murmured and nestled into the touch, his hands spread out and tickled my abs. Connor's hands were braced over my chest, his fingers held tightly like I was a teddy bear and he was afraid to let go.

I closed my eyes again and went to a place that was soft and green, where fur greeted fur and the scents were warm and familiar.

7

August 10th
Sunday

I woke up at the slam of my bedroom door. In the air was the lingering scent of my mother's perfume clashing with the hotness of her rage. I couldn't sit up but the covers had been kicked to the floor. I was naked with three other naked guys, Connor's briefs hung off his ankles. I had no doubt Mom had come in and immediately left. She was definitely pissed.

There was a text on my phone, I could see the blue notification light blinking. I took my hand off Leo's hair and reached, clasped it and brought it to my face.

Dad: I tried.

I sighed and tossed the phone back onto the bedside table then checked the time on my radio clock. It was past twelve, Mom didn't let me sleep in that late even on weekends. She must have come in intending to wake us up, saw us naked and left.

I sighed, knowing I was in trouble now. I pulled upwards, dragging my body through the tight clutches of Connor and Leo, even Javier had slung his arm over Connor's neck so his fingers brushed the tips of my collarbone. They all made whining sounds and clutched to me, snuggling closer. I sat up, and leaned my head on the headboard, sighing again.

Leo woke up and tilted his head back to look up at me. His eyes were swelling green pools of emptiness, an empty hole demanding to be filled and desperately wanting me, demanding me to fill him. Leo was broken on the inside, brokenhearted. When he lost his family, when his humanity was taken from him, the experience tore his heart out, it took his ability to speak and make facial expressions with him. Yet lately Leo's been making more sounds, his face was contorting and twisting more often. With me, he was slowly starting to heal.

Connor's head brushed against my neck and chin, then he rolled his head backwards onto my shoulder. He looked up too, his gaze connected with mine. His brown eyes were damaged, muddy, crusted with an internal sadness. Even his wolf spark was diminished, a quiet flickering ember. The wet mud of sadness was embedded in his skin. As our eyes connected the tingling orange of happiness bubbled over him, though it couldn't drown his sadness.

Javier shifted and leaned over Connor, his head pressed onto Connor's neck. Connor wriggled then put his hand underneath Javier's chin and pushed up gently. Javier's head lolled back and his eyes blinked open, meeting mine. His eyes were a darker brown than Connor's, deep like melted chocolate and they were soft, warm, open. He was whole, complete but he appreciated and needed my guidance, to follow. He wasn't a leader and never would be.

I looked down at them, taking in their desperate, needy, wanting eyes. Our Pack scent from sleeping and bonding together wafted thick and pungent over our bodies. I knew I had to defeat Shane. I wasn't full of bloodlust, I didn't necessarily want to kill him but if I didn't beat him, if I didn't become Alpha, he'd destroy these gentle wolves, he'd break them into smaller pieces until there was nothing left.

I kissed Leo's forehead, his skin prickled with goosebumps and he settled heavier against me. Connor's toes flexed and his legs tensed as he leaned up and let me kiss his forehead. Javier dodged my kiss and instead went for my neck, he gently kissed it.

Javier whispered, "No matter who is in charge, I will always acknowledge you as my Alpha."

The door was knocked on, Dad's voice said, "Are you guys awake? I hear whispering."

Javier grasped the covers from the floor and covered us up to Connor's shoulder, which left it around Leo's waist. I was sitting up so my chest was out and Javier wiggled so he wasn't completely submerged.

"Come in." I called.

Dad slid in and closed the door behind him then leaned on it. His eyes flitted over the abandoned shorts on the floor and how we were covering up our lower halves.

Connor asked softly, "Are you angry Mr. Reeves?"

Dad said after a minute, "Not angry...Kyra, Xon's

mother is. Xon...I don't know what you can say. She's decided you must be bisexual."

I didn't know how to respond to that, because I was aware that my mother was trying to make human-based reasons for why I behaved how I did with the other male members of the Pack. I knew those reasons were false. We needed the skin-ship to feel safe and secure with each other, and there wasn't a damn thing sexual about it.

Even right now, Leo's hand was on my abs, but he was trying to go lower so Dad couldn't see. It was going to get weird in half a second.

I grabbed his hand and said softly, "No Leo, relax."

Leo nodded and his hand went limp in my hold. I placed it higher up on my chest and looked at Dad who was staring.

Javier said, "Leo is very needy Mr. Reeves."

"I know," said Dad quietly. "You guys need to get dressed as soon as possible. The only reason Kyra isn't screaming and kicking you out is because you are naked. She's...yeah." He shook his head.

Connor asked, "Did something happen?"

"It's fine," said Dad nearly before Connor had finished talking. "Boys, get dressed, okay? Take showers if you need to, dress and I'll convince Kyra that it's only right to make lunch. Then you'll have to go home."

Connor's scent flooded with despair and dread, throat-clogging suffocation and a nauseating fetid scent. Because we were so close together and under covers, it was like being trapped with it. Leo was the first to kick away and cover his nose, then Javier hopped out.

Dad whirled around and left. Connor pulled the covers around him and wrapped himself into a ball, not even his hair was out.

"Javier, you first." I said. "Leo, you're basically clean already, so clothes on."

Javier said, "Shall I put my clothes from yesterday back on?"

I nodded. "Gonna have to I guess, sorry."

Javier nodded and walked into the bathroom, while Leo was going through his duffel bag. I tapped Connor's protective ball.

He sniffled. "I don't want to, I don't want to."

"Why?" I pressed on the ball, feeling his shoulder. "What's going on at home?"

"Nothing. I just don't want to go back. I want to stay with you."

His *nothing* sounded like it really meant *everything*.

I said, "Let me go to your house Connor and I'll stop it."

Connor tossed the blanket off him and ran to his clothes, jerking them on while saying, "No, no and NO! Definitely not, you can't, no way! Carter would kill you."

I asked, "What did Carter do about letting me borrow his clothes?"

"He threw them out," said Connor, buckling his pants. "He said he didn't want them anymore, said the smell would never come out."

I looked at Leo and Connor. "Does my scent smell bad to you?"

Leo shook his head and laid down on the bed, rolled himself over it like a puppy, indulging in the smells.

Connor said, through shrugging on his shirt, "I love…um I like the scent. Sky loves it, of course she does, she's attracted to you."

A twisted smile came on my face, definitely perverted but I couldn't stop it.

"Yeah, well, there's a lot of me to be attracted to."

I placed one hand on my cobblestone abs, remembering how she stared.

Leo snorted and scooted over to me, his face nudged into my thigh.

The door was knocked on, Dad said, "I hear water running, you almost ready? Lunch is ready."

I answered. "Leo and Connor are."

I used my hand on Leo's face to roll him the opposite way from me, his hands clasped around my arm then his teeth nibbled onto my wrist, he was really playful this morning. I laughed and then grasped him underneath his chin, pressing a little too tightly. Leo stopped biting me and laid his arms down. I let him go as Javier was coming out of the bathroom, he was dry and naked but he quickly put his clothes on. Now it was me who was naked and needed a shower.

I said, "You guys go and eat, alright? I'll be down."

When no one moved, I paused then said, "Guys, I don't like having to keep saying everything twice. I'll be down after I'm showered and dressed, I'll make sure to come see you before you leave. So go ahead downstairs."

Javier opened the door and gestured to Leo and Connor. "Come on, come on."

Leo sat up and glanced at me then walked away and Connor followed, tossing a quick look back. I closed the door behind them and got ready.

Downstairs, Mom had made cheeseburgers and French fries, a lot of them. I counted twenty burgers sitting on a platter while Leo and Connor were still eating off their plates, Javier was helping himself to the bowl of French fries.

I sat down and began to eat, carefully not looking at Mom in the face. She was sitting on the couch with a book. She didn't say anything either but I could smell that she was upset, like prickling fire and heavy exhaust. She was going to scream the house down once my company was gone.

Dad came to the table with two jugs of juice balanced in one arm, his other hand was holding a stack of four cups. I was about to get up to help but Dad said, "You eat son, you need your strength."

Mom's mouth buckled into a snarl then smooth out, she turned her head to her book, her foot swung impatiently up and down. Yeah, she was pent up.

I ate quietly and kept my eyes away from Mom, even when my hairs raised because she was looking at me.

Connor had a lump of ketchup on his cheek while he was busy chewing. He was holding two fistfuls of fries, unable to wipe it off. Leo noticed and leaned over, his tongue slipped between his lips.

"Leo no!" I said it sharply and he jerked back, giving me wide eyes.

Javier stood, walked around the table and wiped Connor's face with a napkin.

"Thanks," said Connor, not looking up from his plate.

Leo was staring at the floor, his shoulders slumped, he wasn't even eating anymore. His scent had morphed into the dank lifelessness of depression. Maybe he didn't get why I yelled at him but I couldn't explain it, not with Mom staring over at us.

Dad placed a hand on Leo's shoulder, Leo looked up at him, he stopped breathing.

"It's okay kid." He said quietly. "Keep eating, you're thin enough already."

Leo's lashes fluttered and his scent burst with the electric lemon of surprise. He went back to eating and Dad tossed me a smile, I smiled back and I wondered exactly what I would have done if Dad had rejected me the way Mom did. I needed his support in ways I hadn't before when I was a regular human. Dad said becoming a wolf was turning me into a man. Well, becoming a wolf was also turning me into a better son and Dad into a better father.

Imagine if he was a wolf too. That would be even better.

Dad walked away to be with Mom at the couch. Mom got up and walked away into the office, Dad followed and the door closed behind them.

I shook my head, standing up to pour the drinks. Leo leaned his head on my thigh, I gently patted his cheek.

I said, "What you were about to do was inhuman Leo and it would have been hell trying to explain it away. That's why I yelled. I wasn't mad at you, okay?"

Leo nodded and rubbed his chin on my wrist as I slid the drink over to him. I tousled his hair. I poured drinks for Connor and Javier, they both nuzzled me in thanks. The table was overrun with loud gulping as we all drank.

The food was gone but Mom and Dad were still in the office. If I concentrated I would be able to hear what they were saying but I didn't want to know.

I said, "I'll walk you guys home."

"Not me," said Connor. "I'll go by myself."

"I'll walk you to your block." I said. "Shane could still be around. Leo." I looked at him. "Did he hurt you last night? I smelled him on your clothes and you looked frightened."

Leo shook his head and shrugged. I could assume that meant Shane hadn't hurt him but Leo couldn't tell me exactly what happened.

I called, "Bye Mom, Dad. Walking my friends home, be back soon."

Shoes on, we all left without waiting for replies.

Javier said, "Tonight is the full Moon." He looked at me and his deep brown eyes shifted to orange, the eye color of his wolf. "It is your first Xon and the call of the Moon is undeniable. I will be in the forest with everyone else, will you come?"

I bit my lower lip. "Our church service meets in the evening."

Connor shook his head, making a loud *tsk* sound with his teeth. "Right now the Sun is in control, the hot rays is like a leash keeping our wolves back. Once the Sun is gone and the Moon takes the sky, you'll go wolf Xon. Not even God can hold back a wolf's Change on the full Moon."

I didn't like that last part at all.

I asked, "Javier, what's this Moon goddess?"

Little g. There's only one God.

Javier, his eyes still wolf orange, said, "She is the Mother of all wolves, the Great She-Wolf."

My back crawled at his intense animalistic stare, his words that brought my monotheistic beliefs into question, teachings that I've been raised in since as long as I could remember.

I looked away as we arrived at Leo's house. The house was ramshackle with its shutters broken and hanging off, paint had peeled or been completely stripped away. The grass was overgrown and his roof needed patching.

Leo waved at us and after giving me a hug, went inside.

Connor took my hand and laced our fingers.

I smiled at him and kept walking.

I asked, "Javier, are you last?"

"Yes." He said. "But Connor can come with, I don't mind."

So we walked to Javier's house in comfortable silence.

"I will go up on my own." Javier said, stopping by the gate that barred the lane to his house. "I will see you later tonight, in the forest. Bye Xon, Connor."

He kissed his fingers at us and went up, he didn't lock the gate behind him.

The trees quickly hid Javier from view.

Connor said, "My house next."

He said it like it meant nothing but his scent was drenched with dread and horror, fetid and rotten.

I didn't want him to run away so I held a little tighter on his hand as we walked.

I said, "Connor…I wish you'd let me help."

Connor didn't respond.

I said, "It's not healthy to be so depressed all the time."

"I'm fine. I've been fine and I'll continue to be fine."

His nails poked holes into my skin but I didn't bleed, not yet.

"I know. You are very strong Connor, you're handling it the best you can."

Connor looked up at me. "You really mean that?"

His brown eyes had darkened to black, it was like looking into a well, deep, dark and flooded. He was drowning on the inside, screaming for help but his pride wouldn't let him accept the hand I was offering.

I nodded.

Connor pulled me to a stop, saying, "This is my block. You can't come to my house Xon, Carter would."

He shook his head.

I said, "I can take care of myself Connor."

"No." He dropped my hand and stepped away. "Shane has handed your ass to you several times and he's *nothing* compared to Carter. If Shane is like a wave, Carter is a tsunami. Get it? I'll see you tonight."

Connor hugged me hard, his face buried into my chest and he took in a deep inhale, then he turned and ran like a green-haired flash. I took note of the house he went to.

I don't know what Carter is like, clearly Connor doesn't even acknowledge him as his father if he's calling him by his first name. However Connor is in too much pain at his house, I don't know if it's a type of physical abuse or maybe just mental, emotional. Connor must be right that Carter is much stronger than Shane. My work is cut out for me. I gotta beat the living daylights out of Shane. After that...I need to find out what Carter is about and make him stop whatever he's doing before he hurts Connor too much and does irreversible damage.

I went back home and the house was quiet.

"Mom? Dad?"

At the lack of reply, I ran to the office. The door was open and my parents were inside, both standing and not saying a word. The room was stuffed with a multitude of scents, of clashing emotions. My nose burned, I couldn't sort them out or tell which emotion belonged to who. One thing I did know was that my parents had been arguing while I was gone.

I swallowed hard then said, "I can't go to church tonight."

Dad didn't get to move before Mom whirled on me.

"Oh I don't think so Jaxon! You are *not* missing church so you can go hang out with your little friends! This is *my* house and in this house, we will serve the Lord!"

I do serve God but does God serve me? Does He still listen to me? Or is there someone else I'm supposed to be giving worship to?

I said, "Tonight is a full Moon. I…I won't be able to go to service."

Mom's face purpled. "And what do you mean by that? What does the Moon have to do with anything? It's a stupid rock in space, how does it effect you doing as a good Christian son does and going to church with your family?"

I glanced at Dad, wanting his help. Dad didn't meet my eyes, he was looking at the floor. His arms were crossed with tension wiring his muscles.

He spoke carefully. "Kyra…the Moon has…some sort of pull over werewolves, I think everyone knows that much. He won't be in a human body to come to church."

Mom's body jerked like she had gotten slapped and her eyes glistened with tears. She lifted her chin.

"Move from the door Jaxon. I'm going upstairs."

I didn't move.

"Mom, please, I just want you to understand."

"Oh I understand." Her voice was soft and silky, she even smiled. However the overwhelming hot scent of rage was flooding so much from her pores that it was all I could smell. My heartbeat jacked up several notches. "I understand that you are not my son. You are some wild animal wearing the skin of my son. You aren't human, you aren't the baby boy I gave birth to. I don't know what you are besides some filthy inhuman beast. Now move away from the door."

"Kyra." My father whispered hoarsely.

I didn't look at him and I could no longer look at my mother. Instead, I turned and I left the house entirely.

"Son! Jaxon, come back!"

A. E. Costello 213

My father called for me but I didn't look back and I didn't respond. I kept walking. I breathed through my nose, hot tears ran down my cheeks to drip off my chin. I walked to the forest and didn't Change forms. My sneakers crunched over fallen leaves and dead sticks. Over my head the birds chirruped and squirrels raced from branch to branch.

I didn't have any scriptures to speak to me, I didn't even know who I should turn to right now. I fell to my knees right then and covered my face. My shoulders shook with each ragged sob torn from my chest. I cried like Dad, with my whole body.

"What are you doing?"

I whipped around, my heart pumping. The woman standing there was short, slender with raggedy black hair. Her eyes were the most unique things about her, the left eye was brown but the right eye was blue. Her wolf scent was full and heady, her femaleness was deep warmth and musky. I had met her only once before and not under the best of circumstances.

I asked as clearly as I could while using my arm to rub away the wetness on my face, "Brenda, what are you doing here? Doesn't the Stone Pack live in Mountain Ridge?"

Brenda was the top female in the Stone Pack, and for some reason she leaned on the tree closest to me.

She said, "A crying wolf is never a good sight. What's the matter?"

I cleared my throat and shrugged, using my shirt to dry off my arm. "Nothing."

Now I sound like the nothing that means everything.

Brenda's brows lowered but she said, "You really didn't know I was walking up behind you, did you? You're more human than anything else."

I closed my eyes for a moment and said, "I wish that was true more than anything else."

"Well its not." Brenda snapped back, her voice suddenly heated and irritated, her scent burnt and dry to match.

"Once a wolf, always a wolf. And seeing a wolf with no clue as to his surroundings is really sickening. Get up Xon, you need a lesson."

I sighed but got to my feet. "A lesson in what?"

She moved to stand in front of me. "Attack me."

My brows went up. "What? You mean, like punch you?"

Brenda didn't say anything, just stood there waiting.

I didn't really want to attack a woman but I also knew I needed to learn how to fight and anything to take my mind off my problems was welcome. So I dove at Brenda, intending to tackle her. She sidestepped, grabbed my collar and flung me into the tree. I crashed face first into it, hard enough to break my nose. I stumbled backwards, blinking away the sharp ache. My nose popped back into place, blood gushing down to my mouth.

"You're predictable," said Brenda from behind me. Her hand grasped my shoulder and spun me around to face her. The strength in her hand was like she could have easily snapped my shoulder with one hand. I had felt Sky's strength but it didn't come close to Brenda. "I knew you were going to do that, just like any other wolf would have known. You are acting like a human with a werewolf's strength. Stop being human and think like a wolf. Be silent, be quick and be intelligent."

I used my shirt to clean my face. As my vision Changed to being like a high-powered microscope, I knew they were that of my wolf. Brenda smiled and her teeth were sharp at the tips, not yet fangs. Her eyes were still human.

"Don't talk so much." She said, shifting to the side and I moved in the opposite direction, circling each other without turning our backs. "Don't break eye contact unless you are submitting. Don't just watch me with your eyes, hear the change in my body as I prepare to attack. Hear my heartbeat quickening, see the bunching in my muscles as I tense up to move, use all your senses. If not, you're dead in a real fight."

Brenda took a sudden breath and I moved to block as she rushed me. She was stronger than she looked, her blows at my face had me stumbling back, I couldn't fend her off. She kicked my knee, I bent down with a gasp of pain as it jerked out of joint. She kicked my opposite knee, I fell down, my hands going to my leg as the knee twisted out of socket. Her hand lashed out and backhanded me across my face, the blow was like I had been hit with an iron skillet. I plowed face first onto the ground, the searing pain told me that I had broken my nose again. My knees snapped back into place.

"You are still a pup." She tsked, sitting down next to me. "And you need more practice."

"You're faster and stronger than I expected."

I sat up, my nose ached but then eased. I wiped at the blood from a cut on my cheekbone. It had already healed, but there was a scar on my face where she had slapped me. I touched the mark and felt along it with my fingers, stunned. No matter how many times I had gotten hurt, I always healed smooth, my wounds gone as if they never were.

I scarred? How did she get me to scar?

"It will heal within a few days." Brenda told me as my scent tingled with the lemon of shock.

"But why?" I asked. "Shane has torn me up and after I healed I wasn't scarred at all."

Brenda's brow went up. "Shane is your age, yes?"

"A year older, he's eighteen." I said. "What does age have to do with it?"

"Not much." she said. "However the reason why you scarred isn't because of age, it's because I am a dominant wolf. I have a commanding power you could say, over wolves weaker than myself, despite their age, gender or status. One of those perks is that being hit by me can leave a mark, which will heal eventually. While the dominant ability is usually passed down a bloodline, it can also be earned. I have earned it."

I nodded. I touched the scar again, it ran from the side before my ear down my cheek before my nose or lips.

"Isn't there a way to heal it faster?"

"No," said Brenda. "The mark is a sign of my dominance over you, like a burn. Fire is the one thing that can kill a werewolf, next to being beheaded."

I had heard of that, but I wasn't sure.

"So what if we get our hearts ripped out? What then?"

She said, "If you manage to Change into a wolf in time, the heart will grow back but it's unlikely due to blood loss, you'll lose consciousness and die."

Brenda sighed and shook her head. "Listen, what I'm saying is you are too human Jaxon Reeves. You still think and act like a human when you aren't one. You talk and move like a human, I can barely smell the wolf scent on you."

Brenda stood up like she was on a string, quick, straight and inhuman. She smirked at me and grasped my wrist, lifting me up like I weighed nothing.

"Use your senses." She told me. "I saw you Changed your eyes, good, but you don't need wolf eyes to focus. Use your ears, your nose, I was able to sneak up on you, that's just down right unnatural for a werewolf. Feel vibrations with your feet, sense with your aura, feel everything about you and those around you. Be a wolf, not human."

I spoke up, quickly before she could leave. "Can you teach me to be a wolf?"

Brenda's brow arched. "Oh yeah? Why are you asking?"

I told her about Shane and the fact I want to beat him in a fight to be leader.

Brenda was quiet for a few moments then said, "I see. Well, I'll pass the message onto Toni and it'll be up to him if he'll let anyone from his Pack train you to fight. After all, this is technically your problem."

I smiled a little. "Not technically, it is. Shane's knocked me on my ass more times than I want to count. Still, I can't let him continue on as leader. He's abusive, he's cruel and he doesn't deserve to be in charge."

Brenda tilted her head to the side, her two-colored eyes staring at me as if to see into me, to see something that wasn't visible on the outside. "And yet you believe you deserve to? You're a brand new wolf Xon, so new you still act and move like a human being. Yet you want to usurp the current leader. Why? Don't answer." She said just as I opened my mouth. "Figure it out first, on the inside, where your wolf is and let him answer. I'll talk to Toni."

She walked away, then looked at me over her shoulder. "Also, you shouldn't wander off alone Xon. You don't know how to sense your surroundings, so its best to have someone with you."

With that, she left the clearing. I didn't hear anything, as if she had disappeared.

I let out a breath and looked around. One tree had shattered broken bark with blood splashed on it, as well as some blood smeared on the grass. There was blood on my shirt and now I had a scar on my face.

I thought back to how fast Brenda moved and how strong. I looked at my pants which were ripped and I was bruised where she had kicked me, my knees faintly ached.

I remembered the first time I met Brenda back in California. I had gotten the feeling she could probably beat me up if she wanted to, something about her aura, she felt like strength, powerful. Now I know its dominance and I've experienced just how strong she is. Also, like Mikhail said earlier, she told me I act too human, that I don't act like a wolf. Now if I want to defeat Shane, I really need to.

Yet as I thought that, I remembered what my mother told me. Should I try and be more wolf, to accept who I am now, or try and be more human to please Mom?

With that balancing in my head, I began the walk out of the forest. I froze at a scent that wafted up from the bushes a few feet back from where I had been crying. The thick heady scent of a wolf, the musky scent of maleness, and the burning heat of hatred and violence.

Wyatt.

Wyatt had been standing right there, just one lunge reach away from me. Close to his scent I smelled Brenda, then while Brenda came out to talk to me, Wyatt's scent went in the opposite direction.

Did Brenda save my life? How long had Wyatt been stalking me before Brenda showed up? How did Brenda even know where I was? How did Wyatt find out where I was? Why did he track me down? Why did Mikhail said he was holding a grudge against me because far as I know, I've never done a thing to that guy. Did he seriously come after me and nearly kill me right here if it wasn't for Brenda?

I trudged out of the forest and decided to go back home. I had to talk to Mom and come clean about a lot of things that were going on. She may hate me for being what I am, but we're family and I'm her only child. Unless she wants to have a new baby and replace me when she's forty years old and kick me out, then there's nothing I can do. But if she has some love for me left in her heart then I have to try.

I got home and tried the doorknob, it opened. The house was quiet besides sniffling from the office and soft murmuring voices. I headed over and stopped in my tracks before I could knock on the door.

"I can't take the fighting, what if he gets hurt?" I smelled the tangy salt of Mom crying. "I can't bear it if he gets killed Grant. Not when he's our third try."

What…?

Dad hushed her as they embraced but my mind was frozen.

What did she just say?

"It'll be okay Kyra," whispered Dad. "Jaxon isn't going to die, not by a long shot. He's very strong, physically and emotionally. He's just hit a rough patch, that's all and he'll come through it, all of us will. I know he's our third try but he's here to stay, we won't lose him like the other two."

Third try? Third try at what? Third? I'm a third? So there were two before me. Two WHAT before me?

My back clenched tight, my eyes burned with tears, my heart stopped beating then ramped up. I couldn't breathe, my skin drenched in freezing sweat.

No, no, they would have told me, my parents don't keep secrets, they don't lie to me, they wouldn't, never. I don't believe it. They're lying. I'm not the third. It's just me, just Jaxon. I'm their only child, it's always only been me, just me, just Jaxon, no one else. The third? I can't be the third...because that means...my siblings...older...they died.

My head snapped back as my throat contorted into the cords of the wolf. A howl of despair broke out of the muzzle twisting its way out of my face. I buckled over as my spine bent, fur sprouted out of my skin. Another howl ripped out of my gut. Claws burst out of my stretching fingers. My shoes split open as my feet burst into paws.

"JAXON?!"

The office door blasted open but I ran.

Hunched over, my body mutating, I ran down the other hall from the opposite side of the kitchen and out of the side-door. My clothes shredded off me, I Changed into the wolf and fled.

I ran blindly, crashing into garbage cans, stumbling over potholes and scraped against parked cars. If people saw me, I couldn't see with my blurred teary eyes, couldn't hear their shouts over the roaring in my ears. I ran out of the village, through the field and galloped senselessly in the forest. I flattened bushes, collided into trees only to shake off the pain. I charged wildly as if I was being chased. I knew what was chasing me.

Demons.

Lies.

Secrets.

I'm the third.

The third child. Two were before me, older siblings I've never met. My parents never told me, they let me believe I was the only one. It makes sense now. That's what they only cared about, me, I was always the most important. That's why Mom gets so upset over little things, she cares so much that she can't take anything going wrong with me, I have to be perfect. That's why she hates that I'm a werewolf. As a werewolf, I'm an imperfect being, not human, not wolf, but someone in between.

I stumbled as my front paws pedaled on air and I backed up, gasping. I stood on the edge of a gorge, a drop that not even I might be able to survive. I didn't know how deep in the forest I was. Yet I stood there, breathing hard. My demons piled onto my back and my hunches sat from the weight. My head tilted back and a mournful howl lifted up into the air from my throat. I mourned my siblings, the lie of my life, the loss of my humanity. Everything had changed. Nothing would be the same. Mom hated me for being a werewolf. Wyatt kept coming after me to kill me, I couldn't beat Shane in a fight, and now I had two older siblings who died that I knew nothing about. I had nothing.

My howl slowly died away, I couldn't keep it up any longer. I slumped down onto the ground, panting.

Answering howls went up but I could tell they were regular wolves howling back because it sounded different from mine. My howl was deeper, hoarser and more melodious, as if my wolf was singing without words. The animal wolves were higher-pitched and wavering, fading in and out.

As the animal wolves quieted, another howl went up. Male, loud, abrasive and I could *understand* it. The howl did not translate into words but I understood that he was coming to me. High-pitched and stuttering, a younger wolf howled that he was coming too. After him came a third howl, sweet and throaty, a female.

It was the Wildebeast Pack, Sky, Javier and Connor. They had heard my cry and were heading my way.

A. E. Costello 221

I stood at the sounds of paws and turned around. One wolf broke out of the trees and stood there.

The wolf was shorter in the leg than me and heftier, fat in the body. He had dark brown fur with golden color on his face and chest, his eyes were dark orange, they were soft and warm, motherly.

He tilted his head to the side with a soft whine. *[Your howl was one of the saddest I have ever been witness to hear. I am very sorry for your loss.]*

His voice in my head was Spanish in accent and he spoke without contractions. I recognized the voice and those orange eyes. It was Javier. This was his wolf form.

A she-wolf came to his side, longer in the leg, a slim lean-hipped body and fur blacker than night with a deep purple sheen. Sitting between her slender muzzle were striking silver eyes.

Sky.

Stumbling up to her side was a much smaller bright white wolf. He would barely come to my shins if he stood next to me; he had large ears and bright red eyes. On the top of his head between his ears was a mop of green fur.

Connor.

Panting and pulling up the rear was a light brown and black wolf with long skinny limbs and a scrubby tail, his ribbed sides heaving in and out, green eyes wide all around, was Leo.

Tears pillowed in my eyes, turning the wolves in front of me into waving blurry lines.

[Guys...]

I collapsed to the ground, my legs unable to hold the weight on my back, my mind. In seconds I was covered with wolves. Leo began licking my face over my eyes and muzzle, Connor rubbed against my ruff and dug his nose underneath my chin, Javier plopped down next to me and leaned on my side, laying his head over my neck and nuzzling into me. Sky took my other side and her head laid over my leg. I immediately felt the difference in her fur compared to the others, it was silkier, smoother, not as coarse and fluffy as the males.

Leo and Connor laid down in front of me, snuggling so my head had to lay in between their heads on each shoulder, their heads tucked under my chin against my chest. Snuggled together like this, I smelled the Pack scent thickening over us, rising into the air and coating us in a blanket made out of warmth, friendliness and companionship.

Javier's chest and throat rumbled against me, then with a throaty purr-like sound, he began to croon. The melodic soothing thrum sunk into my ears then past it, deeper, like it was inside of me, brushing away my headache, my tears and my fears. It was more relaxing than being in a hot tub because hot tubs don't enter your body, go into your soul and stroke the problems, the issues. The sound caressed the deepest most painful parts of me.

My body relaxed and the shuddering of my shoulders slowed.

And with that, I slid into a soft gentle sleep. When I woke up, it was still light out so I knew I hadn't slept long. I was in human form, as was everyone else around me.

Leo and Connor were sleep in front of me and curled close to my chest and shoulders. My head was on Connor's stomach, Leo's head on Connor's upper chest. Connor's feet were dug into my underarm, Leo had his arms over my neck. Javier and Sky were both draped over my back. Sky's head rested at the base of my neck, her hand laid on my head. Javier was closer to the end of my back, his arms over my thighs.

We were all naked, warm and comfortable, I wanted to lay like this forever, with my Pack. However nature called, and I really had to go.

I wiggled my arm out from underneath Connor's back, my other arm was around Leo's shoulders. I slowly raised up, lowering Sky's arm from my head and tugging at Leo's arms around my neck. Leo instinctively tightened and I choked. I quickly grabbed him at his jaw and tightened my hold. His eyes fluttered open, dazed green then he blinked it away.

"Let me go Leo." I said, my voice stern and a bit hoarse.

He didn't, he held onto me like a child scared of monsters under the bed. His green eyes stared into mine with his wolf spark flickering at the center, not willing to let me go, never willing to let me go.

I reached inside of myself for some patience, but was met with this power in my wolf, something not tangible but real. It filled into my being then I brought it up out of my mouth.

"Leo, let go of me."

My voice, strong, deep, a growl to it that hadn't been there before. Leo's arms flopped down and he hit Connor on the chest and face.

Connor yelped and rolled to the side. I sat up. Javier flumped to the ground, though I caught Sky and slid her over into my arms before she could fall. Her eyes opened and saw me.

She said, "Feeling any better?"

I nodded and slid my hand up into her hair, the braids long gone. Her sable hair now pooled into her lap, hiding a place that I know I shouldn't have been thinking about. I could smell her, a warm musky scent that I just wanted to sink myself into. My scent flushed sugary and Sky pushed away from me. I had the idea to hold on, to jerk her back into my arms but I let her go.

I stood, saying, "I'll be back."

I looked over them. Sky had her hands over her face. Connor was playfully biting Leo on his arms and neck while Leo squirmed in protest. Javier sat up, rubbing at his face.

I did my business in a bush and came back, sitting down crossed-legged and placed my hands in my laps for Sky's sake. The other three made no moves to cover themselves. Javier had joined in playing with Leo and Connor, they looked like puppies roughhousing and didn't seem to care that Sky was sitting there naked. She pulled her hair over her shoulders to keep herself covered. I should be grateful for that but I kind of wished that Sky had short hair.

Sky looked at me. "What happened Xon? When you howled, it was like a song, an extremely sad song. I couldn't understand perfectly in words as if you were speaking, but there was pain and loneliness, and the overall sense of loss, like everything had gone wrong. Are you okay now? Think you can talk about it?"

I sighed and looked to the ground, but said it.

"I'm the third try for my parents, they never told me."

Sky asked, "The third try? As in the third child?"

I nodded. "The first two died, I don't know how or when, but they never said anything. I always thought I was the only child, the only son. Instead I'm the third youngest."

"I'm really sorry." She said in a soft hushed voice. "Maybe the idea was too painful to talk about, or maybe they didn't want to hurt you by saying anything."

I nodded but didn't want to think about the fact my parents had kept such a huge secret. I still hadn't completely gotten over what my mother said to me. I know I'm not a wild beast masquerading as her son, I am her son. I needed a chance to talk to her, prove to her that even with a wolf on the inside I'm still human, I know I am.

Javier said, "If you need to cry again Xon, it is okay."

I looked up and saw the wolves all looking at me, watching me with this look in their eyes, a look of both worry and discontent, like they were unhappy about something. I rubbed at the crusts on my eyes and sat up straighter, squaring my shoulders. If I was to be a leader, I couldn't act weak and mopy all the time.

"I'm okay." I said, giving Connor and Leo a smile, they were the ones who seemed the most upset at my behavior. Connor's dark brown eyes were turbulent, while Leo wouldn't stop staring at me. "You guys don't have to worry. I'll talk it over with my parents and figure it out."

Javier looked to the sky where the Sun was still holding reign. "I was in the forest already when I heard your howl, and the others showed up soon after. However, it will only make sense to stay here now as when the Moon rises, our human skins will crumble. The Moon Goddess will shine her rays and bring our wolves to the surface."

I swallowed but said, "Javier, I've never heard of a Moon goddess. I'm Christian so...I believe there is only one God."

Javier looked at me, a gentle smile came to his lips. "Any wolf can believe whatever they want Xon, there are Hindu werewolves, Muslim werewolves, it really does not matter. No one is saying you must worship her but she is real. She's the wolf deity who watches over wolfkind, she is like our mother. The same way God is the father, she is the mother."

I shook my head back and forth firmly. "No, no. The bible doesn't say-"

"Well it wouldn't say." Javier interrupted. "We have our own book that details the History of the Wolf. The bible is for humans."

My fists clenched and Javier paled, so I immediately unclenched them, saying, "Don't worry, I won't ever hurt you Javier. I'm getting a little upset, that's all."

Javier smiled. "I understand but you really should not fret so much. No one is saying you must worship her, it is a choice Xon, everyone can choose."

"It's not about choosing to worship." I said. "Its about the fact there actually being something else to worship. There are no other gods *but* God."

Javier actually shrugged. "Again, that is a choice to believe in. My family is Catholic and gives thanks to the Moon Goddess. You can decide what to believe in Xon."

"Let's drop this subject." Sky interceded as my eyes narrowed. "You're only upsetting him Javier. Okay, so we're in the forest now, what are we going to do?"

"Go back to sleep," said Connor through a yawn, his jaw dropping and his tongue curled up. "Wait until sundown. Then we can do something."

Leo nodded and laid down, nuzzling his head onto his arms. Connor laid with him and buried his face into Leo's stomach, Leo's head pressed against his back.

Sky smiled and came over to them, rubbing their heads and shoulders in stroking motherly motions. Javier laid down behind Leo, curling up around Leo's legs. Sky started to stroke him too and it wasn't long before they were all sleeping just that quickly.

Sky turned to me and said, "I know what Javier said really shook you up, so come and lay down, you can pray about it."

She laid down next to Connor, laying her head on his thigh. I didn't pause and scooted in next to Sky, my arm went around her waist and tugged her closer to me. Sky's hand touched my abs and pressed in firmly, her nails pricked me sharply. Her hazel-gold eyes flashed a warning silver.

"I won't do anything." I said, my voice low and hushed. Her smell filled my nose, wolf, female, like roses and honey, my Packmate.

"See that you don't." She spoke in a rumbling tone, near a growl but not yet.

I smiled and moved my hand from her waist to her upper back, felt along her spine, the soft skin covering her bones.

"If I do, I give you permission to bite me. Wherever you want."

Sky's breath caught and her eyes drifted over my hard pecs and down my solid abs before she looked away and closed her eyes.

She muttered, "I won't. I won't touch you anywhere."

Even as she said that, her hand was still touching my abs. Her skin was supple but the strength in her hand told me if she punched me, it would hurt. She may not be as strong as Brenda, but she was stronger than the three males behind her and I didn't want to incite Sky into enough rage to attack me. We were Packmates and there should be no violence between us.

I stroked my hand up her spine to between her shoulders. Her skin was baby soft and covered by a thin fuzzy pelt, like downy. Sky's hand moved from my abs to curl her arm around my neck and tugged me closer to her.

She said, "Quit it, go to sleep."

"Yes ma'am."

I relaxed my arm back around her waist. I inhaled Sky's scent again, roses and honey. My body reacted to her smell, her body heat, her arm over my neck, saluting the attention and pulling up tight to my abs. Sky was sleeping. The thick smell of heady sugar gushing from my pores went unnoticed as well. I took in my full of her face. Her skin was creamy reddish brown, her closed eyes curved like almonds, a straight nose above a wide full mouth.

I lowered my head to press a kiss to the crook of her elbow, closed my eyes and slept again. When my eyes opened from this nap, the sky was painted purple and red with the beginnings of the sunset, bright white dots of the stars pinpricked the eternal fabric. The sun boiled orange as it sunk below the trees.

The rest of the Pack woke up, shifting and murmuring. We all moved to our hands and knees, heads ducked down towards our chests, bodies limber and pliable.

The full Moon took its rightful place on the night sky. Even with my eyes closed unable to see it, I felt it like clicking in the last piece of a 2000 piece jigsaw puzzle, like being freezing cold then having a dryer-hot comforter wrapped about me. My human skin folded back like rolling up a piece of wet paper, it slumped over me and my wolf stood up, shaking its fur back.

I opened my eyes and lifted my head, looking over the multicolored Pack rustling in front of me. Sky with her midnight black coat, Connor who was snow white with a topping of neon green, Leo's coat was light brown with black, and Javier's pelt was dark brown and tawny.

The forest at night with Moonlight drifting over it was more alive than when I traveled it during the day. My wolf senses brought everything into hyper-reality, bringing me deeper into nature than I could have imagined. The leaves on the branches glittered with the water pulsing in their veins, my sharp ears listened to the soft swishing as the water rushed through. Bugs crunched their way through the leaves, taking their substance. Birds swooped and ate the bugs with sharp jerks of their beaks. Larger predators ate the birds, and scavengers ate anything left over. It all went around, the forest had its own cycle of life. Now I was here and I would fit in, I would add onto the cycle and keep it stable.

My stomach's grumbling was quickly echoed by four other stomachs.

[Let's hunt].

I lowered my head to the ground, all I could smell was us so I moved away, searching for a new scent.

Connor leapt onto my back and neck, he nipped my ears with sharp pricks of his teeth.

[Hunt? Really? You mean like eat something alive?]

I shook him off me, dumping him onto his back. I placed my paw on his chest to pin him down as he thrashed. His tail waved like a fuzzy maraca. My paw was silver gray with thick claws. Connor was so small it spanned the width of his chest. I moved away, fearful of hurting him by mistake.

[Yes, Leo and I have hunted before.]

Connor flipped to his feet and dashed in a circle, his large bat-like ears wide on his head, his tail still flapping in circles.

[What did you eat? What will we eat? How do we hunt?]

A. E. Costello 229

[Calm down Connor, please. You're giving me a migraine just looking at you.] Sky sat back and her tongue lolled out of her mouth in a smile; her silver eyes gazed on him with a fondness like a mother for her child. *[Xon has done it before, so he'll show us. Go on Xon, show us how to hunt.]*

I turned to Javier first, who was laying down on his side, he looked like a lumpy rug with stumpy feet.

[Haven't you hunted before Javier, back in Spain? Shouldn't you be in the lead?]

Javier shook his head, his dark orange eyes tame and gentle.

[I am not the Head Hunter; I have never led the Pack in a hunt. You are our leader Xon, you show us what to do.]

He rolled to his feet and shook himself from his head to his tail, his body jiggled like furry Jell-O.

[We will follow you.]

Everyone seemed to be in agreement, so I headed off into the forest. I disregarded faint and light scents that came from small animals like mice and squirrels. I needed a thick strong odor, something from an animal with fat and meat, large enough to share with five hungry wolves.

The Pack fell into line behind me. We moved as one single line, paws silently indented the grass that sprung back up, leaving no mention of our passing. We breathed in time with the wind, our fur slid against bark and brush with no hindrance, our bright eyes blended in with the natural light of the forest, keeping our presence a secret. This place accepted the wolf, accepted the Pack, we were meant to be here.

My nostrils flared wide at a strong odorous whiff. As I walked, there were signs of foraging, upturned roots of plants and bushes stripped of berries. My ears flicked at the sounds of grunting and low snorting.

My nose poked through the bushes. The large mammal was easily as tall as a toddler and weighed well over two hundred pounds. It's head was down while it tore up roots from the base of a berry bush. It had large sharp tusks jutting from its saliva-dripping mouth. My mouth watered and my stomach tightened with the need to be filled.

[Okay, there it is.]

[What is it?]

The Pack came to my side, also judging the animal eating a few steps away. It didn't hear or smell us, its back towards us and it was making such loud grunting sounds it was probably drowning us out as it was.

[A feral pig or a wild boar.] Javier's voice spoke in our heads. [We have to be careful, wild boars will attack if threatened. If aimed right, those tusks can rip out our intestines. Our best bet is to kill it before it can defend itself.]

[Look.] I glanced at Connor. [You should sit this one out buddy.]

Connor's fur on his ruff and down his back raised, he puffed out his chest. [What do you mean I sit out? I want to hunt!]

[I know but do you see those tusks? That boar could easily kill you-]

I was cut off by a very loud deep grunting sound, coming from out of the bushes. The wild boar had seen us, its heavy head lowered to the ground, nose wrinkled back. It growled again, the sound was like a broken garbage disposal, grinding and guttural. It jerked its head up and down, mimicking slashing with its tusks. A warning.

I glanced at my Pack members if they wanted to fight or not. Connor nodded eagerly, Sky's silver eyes burned gold in the pupils, Javier tilted his head to the side and Leo waited calmly for my decision.

The wild boar snorted, dug at the ground with its hooves and trotted off, flicking its tail derisively. I didn't like that. Here we were, a Pack of five grown healthy wolves and we can't take down one wild boar?

Leo knew my thoughts even if I hadn't vocalized them, he leapt through the bushes and was gone, after the boar.

A. E. Costello 231

We followed as a group then I overtook him in speed. The boar hadn't gone far and when it realized we were after it, it turned around and charged aggressively, head ducked low with the sharp tusks leading the way.

I had a plan, I would stay in the front and dodge, distracting the boar while everyone else would attack from the back and sides, staying out of the way of the tusks. I didn't speak it, there wasn't time for that, but the plan was in my mind and it echoed in the minds of my Packmates. Leo and Connor went to the right, Javier and Sky to the left. The boar was focused on me and I feinted from side to side as it tried to gore me. Leo and Connor bit at its back legs and bottom, Javier and Sky tore on its sides.

The boar groaned and collapsed. I got my teeth into the bared throat and delivered the fatal bite. We began to eat, tearing and gulping at it like we've done it a million times before. The boar's meat was fatty and melted in my hot mouth. Steam rose up wispy white from the spilled guts. It was perfect how easy it was for the five of us to feed together like this, not much scrambling over getting a good spot to feast, and the air was more companionable than anything else.

The boar was nothing but bones that Connor and Sky were chewing over, Javier was already sleeping again while Leo pushed at my face and bit my ear.

Play fighting was a great idea, good way to relax and unwind from the horrors of what I had learned earlier. Now I could just put all of that humanness to the side and indulge in being a wolf.

Leo was decidedly more jumpy today, dodging my every swipe and bite then dashing in quick to attack me. I finally got my teeth into his scruff, the thin flap of loose skin at the back of his neck and shook him around. He yelped in defeat and I let him go, using a paw to shove him onto the ground. He laid there limply like he was hurt, whining.

[Leo? Was I too rough?]

I leaned in. He bit my muzzle, twisting his head down and planted my face into the dirt.

[*Leo! You liar!*]

I jumped up, shaking the mud and leaves off my face then darted after Leo fleeing through the undergrowth. I chased him around in circles then he ran back into the small clearing where both Connor and Javier were sleep. Leo flopped down onto the ground with his body held low, submissive. I still gnawed on his ears in punishment, then I laid down too.

Somehow, this feels so natural to me. I didn't just accept my new life as a werewolf, I kicked up an amazing fuss, I've cried, I've been sick, I've bled. Now I have a Pack, people who are like me and can understand my struggles. If I could go back to being a plain human again, and not have Leo or Connor or Javier, and definitely Sky, I'm not to sure I'd want to...

Once Leo was sleep, Sky sat up. Her ghost-like silver eyes met mine. She tilted her head to the side and disappeared into the black forest.

A hot coal burst into life in my gut, not the same one like before. This one didn't hurt and boiled lower, tightening my haunches. Swallowing, I followed after her.

Sky melded in with the night, the deep purple sheen to her coat camouflaging her movements. She sat down next to a tree, her ears pricked forward and her eyes focused on mine. Somehow, with her sitting with her back so straight, her paws together, she looked regal and ancient at the same time, like a wolf queen.

I sat in front of her and placed my paw next to hers. Mine was easily triple the size of hers, my paw was like a truck wheel to her dinner plate sized paw. Her claws were slimmer yet longer than mine. Her legs were slender and curved with sleek muscle. I bet she would be faster than me in a race and wondered if when she got older if she could take on Brenda.

Sky faced me. *[What you did just then, projecting a plan in our heads, that's something only a real Alpha can do Xon.]*

I lowered my head a little. *[Something you learned from Alyse?]*

Sky's eyes bored into mine, like she was trying to read out of my skull, or maybe read directly from my soul. *[What I'm saying is that you've made a Pack with us. As an Alpha, you have to protect your Pack. Those boys back there all trust you to take care of them, lead them.]*

A high-pitched call came from the clearing, Connor. He wanted to know where we were and sounded close to tears.

Sky stood up and looked over her shoulder at me. *[I have put my trust in you too Xon. Don't screw this up.]*

Her tail flipped over my nose as she trotted away, making this thrumming calming noise in her throat to Connor.

I followed, flexing my nostrils at the soft silky brush. Sky laid next to Connor, he rested his head against her chest and quieted down. The Pack all laid in a circle, everyone trying to touch everyone else. I walked around them, nuzzling and licking here and there, spreading my scent, the Pack scent, thick and warm over everyone. The Moon was close over the trees, and as I looked at it, I sensed it.

Like being watched, watched the way parents come into your room to check on you while you sleep, watched like how mothers watch their children on playgrounds to make sure they aren't playing too rough, watched the way a father does as he teaches his son to ride a bike to make sure he won't hurt when he crashes. It was a gentle loving watch and I wanted to howl, to call to it, sing to it, praise to it.

Instead, I laid down next to Sky and rested my head over her back, closing my eyes. I prayed in images, feelings, sounds. I knew more than anything that I had to protect my Pack.

The wild wake-up calls of birds brought me to my senses. I woke up once again in the forest naked on the ground with four other people, three guys and a girl. The girl was plastered against me, every part of her body aligned with mine. I closed my eyes tightly, enjoying the naked damp skin, the touch of round plump softness. I knew there was nothing that could come next, that I couldn't go any further, no matter how tight and hard it would be.

So I sat up slowly and lowered Sky to the ground next to me, gently brushing her hair over her shoulder. Her eyes opened, the hazel-gold hazy then blinked into clarity. She sat up and placed her hands on her lap then looked at me right in the eyes.

8

August 11ᵗʰ
Monday

I put my hands up.

"I did nothing nor saw anything."

Sky's eyes narrowed then she looked up at the sky. The sun had only just broken the tree tops, the hot rays made my skin bristle.

She said, "We're not late to school yet but I definitely need to get home. My parents know it was a full Moon last night but they always worry when I stay out all night."

I bit my lower lip, saying, "I don't know if I can go home."

Sky's slim brows arched. "Yes you can Xon and you will go. You'll talk to your parents about what happened then you'll hug and forgive each other. You can't run away each time something bothers you then all you'll know how to do is run away. You can't be an Alpha and be weak-willed."

My teeth showed. "Don't call me weak-willed."

My voice had that harsh growl to it that it had only taken once before, that power in my wolf leaking out.

Sky's eyes went wide then she smiled. "Then don't do weak-willed things. Connor, Leo, Javier, I know you're awake, so stop laying there and let's go."

I looked past her, they were all awake and eyes open, but not sitting up or moving, lounging on the grass and leaves. We all smelled strongly, like Pack, like outdoors, like sweat and a shared meal, a shared bed. It was a thick pungent smell that I wanted to roll in, bask in, never wash off. I was also well-aware that Shane wasn't here, and if I was to make Pack with him and truly be an Alpha, this was the sort of situation he needed to join in with.

"Let's go guys." I said.

I leaned over and rustled Connor's green hair, then rubbed the back of Leo's ribbed neck. Javier made a warbling whining noise, so I stroked the underside of his chin to his neck. He wiggled and gave me a happy smile.

I smiled back and rolled onto my hands and knees. The Moon still had a hold on me, my human skin folded back, melted off me and my wolf was there, strong and able-bodied.

My Pack were all Changing, and it looked as effortless as it felt. The human skin peeled off, revealing the wolf body right underneath it.

My own words came back to me so clearly as if I was saying it again in my ear.

Dad, we're wolves in human skin.

Words of Brenda and Mikhail, telling me that I acted too human, that I didn't act like a wolf, I understood what they meant. Then my mother's words came back to me, that I was a wild beast and not her son. So how? How could I bridge my humanness and wolfness together so that I could be an Alpha of a Pack and still be the only child of my family?

Sky nudged my face with a low rumble, everyone was waiting and I realized they expected me to lead them out of the forest. I hadn't ever been this way before but wolves had homing instincts. So I licked her muzzle, from the tip of her nose to the base before her eyes. She jerked back and bared her fangs at me in warning. I was tempted to lick her again but I held back and turned away, leading the way out of the clearing.

We walked in comfortable silence, fur brushing against fur, breathing as one equal group. Again my mind went to Shane, and I wondered how he spent his full Moon. It had been an amazing experience, joining my Pack with nature and understanding the importance of spending time with Pack.

In the field that spreads out before the forest in between the outskirts of town there were several piles of clothing. I watched my Pack Change forms and get dressed, however I had no clothes to wear and had to get back to my house in wolf form.

Javier looked at me, his eyes and scent full of worry. "It is really not a good idea to walk around humans in your wolf form, in fact, most Packs will kill a wolf who comes out in their fur."

I knew telepathy in wolf form didn't transfer into human form so I dipped my head in acknowledgement. I traveled the side streets that I knew would lead me all the way home. I moved quickly and didn't show myself to anybody. At home, the door I had run out of was open, claw marks scraping over the floor.

I stopped short.

Why would my parents leave the door open?

Swallowing hard, I stepped inside. The office door was wide open and the house was silent. I flexed my nostrils, sniffing carefully. I smelled the emotions from last night, as if it was stained into the walls, the floor. Anguish, pain, fear, sorrow, it was all over the place. Sharp furrows were scrabbled on the wood floor. I placed my paw on one, my claws fit into the grooves.

I didn't hear anything as I walked down the hallway and into the living room. My clothes and shoes were gone but Mom had been right there, did she see me Change or had Dad somehow shielded her eyes?

I looked around, a few pictures were off the mantel and on the floor but the glass wasn't broken. The couch had some tears in the leather and a scratch on the wooden leg. It was pushed away from the wall. It seemed like my parents had left everything in the same condition as it was when I left.

I left the living room and a quick poke of my head into the kitchen showed it was empty. I didn't smell any food remnants, my parents hadn't eaten. The dining room was also unoccupied. I went down the hall toward the front door, the house alarm wasn't on.

My heart picked up speed, where were my parents and what had happened after I ran away? I looked up the stairway, I didn't hear anything. My spine clenched as I slowly padded up the stairs. My wolf form was as large as an overweight pony yet made no sound as my pads and fur cushioned my movements. The first floor was quiet and I went up to the second, nothing. Even more frightened for my parents, I charged up to the third floor. Dad jumped back, dropping the baseball bat in his hands.

"Dear God." He whispered, staring at me. As a wolf, my head was level with his chest, proving just how massive my wolf form was.

"Jaxon?" he asked weakly, his voice thin.

I nodded and pressed my face to his chest with a long sigh, glad that he was okay. I could hear Dad's heart pounding, his blood rushing in his veins, his stomach sloshing and his lungs inhaling. Sure, I could smell his human unclean meat smell but I didn't care, he smelled like my father and he was alive.

Dad carefully patted my head between my ears and sunk his fingers into my fur.

"You're so real." He murmured quietly, massaging up to my ear and it flicked on contact. He stepped back from me, looking sad. "How can I believe my son is inside of there?"

[It is me.] I thought to him but he couldn't hear me, just put his hand over his eyes, taking in a deep controlled breath but I could smell him getting ready to cry.

"Grant?"

Dad reacted quick, he grabbed the scruff of my neck and pulled me toward my room. I went into my room and he closed the door behind me after locking it.

"Sorry Kyra, I thought I heard something in the hallway."

"I heard talking. Oh God is Jaxon back?!" My doorknob was grabbed and tried to twist but it was locked. "The door is locked! Get the key Grant!"

Dad said, "I know what happened yesterday was very stressful but-"

"Stressful Grant?" Mom sounded quietly distraught and enraged. "He heard what I said, didn't he? That's why he ran away and ripped off his clothes, he hates us now."

"No Kyra, no." Dad hugged her tight. "Jaxon could never hate us, he loves us so much. He ran because he didn't want to hurt us. Imagine the hurtful things he could have said or done, he didn't want to cause us pain so he ran before he could."

"But why tear off his clothes?" Mom sniffled. "Does that mean he ran out in public completely naked? He's probably been arrested for indecent exposure. I don't know why they haven't called us yet. We should go to the police station and ask about him."

"Jaxon will be home soon. Let's eat something before we both collapse. Come on, it'll be okay."

Dad led Mom down the stairs.

I went into my bathroom and hunkered to the floor. I closed my eyes and thought of my human face, my human body.

Come back, come back. Change back.

My skin burned as the fur shrugged back inside. My bones snapped and broke, disconnecting then rejoining, like taking them apart then putting them back together in different places. My face shriveled as my muzzle shrunk, my ears slid into place at the sides of my head. My back bent outwards, my hips clicked then I stood as human being.

I took a quick shower, I smelled like fur and forest. I brushed my teeth and got dressed. When I left my room, it was silent. I didn't hear anything, or smelled any cooked food.

I quietly dashed down the stairs and stood in the hallway.

"Mom?" I called, worry tightened my spine. "Dad?"

There was no answer at first until a soft moan came from the living room. I rushed over and saw my parents lying down together on the sofa. Mom looked smaller than usual, Dad looked thinner than before. They were asleep but it was more like they had just crashed; both had baggy eyes, hair undone, strained lines at their mouths.

I did this. I caused this pain. Everything had changed once I became a werewolf.

I sat down in front of the couch and laid my head back, touching Mom's stomach and Dad's hand over it. I closed my eyes and breathed them in. Both of them had that veneer of the human unclean meant scent, but they smelled mostly like my parents, a warm deep scent, like home. If I had been blinded and deaf, I would know they were my parents because of their smell.

I didn't want to cause my parents any more pain, but they had caused me pain too. Why hadn't they told me about the two others before me, that I'm their third try? I'm seventeen, isn't that old enough for them to come clean about it? What was their plan now that I knew? Had they intended on never telling me, ever?

I touched Dad's hand and rested my head on Mom's stomach. I closed my eyes as I fell asleep.

"Xon...Xon wake up...Xon...wake up son."

A gentle shaking of my shoulder and the continuous voice intruding eventually had me open my eyes and see my parents kneeling in front of me.

Mom hugged me tight, her grasp around my neck strangled me. She sat back and held my face, looking into my eyes.

"Xon, I'm so sorry, okay? I know we upset you and that's why you ran away from home, but please, don't torture us anymore. We love you and never wanted to hurt you. We're sorry, really, we are."

I placed my hands over hers and offered a small strained smile.

"I love you too Mom."

I looked at Dad. "And you too Dad. I just got so upset, I couldn't control myself and I ran away. Please."

I lowered Mom's hands and looked at the both of them.

"Tell me the truth." I swallowed hard and forced down that deep pain. "Am I really the third try?"

They winced.

Dad nodded and said, "We had a very hard time conceiving Jaxon. We were told at first that we couldn't have children at all, but we worked at it. Yes, we lost our first two children, neither made it through the first trimester. Kyra wanted to give up, I did too, we were both heartbroken and didn't want to deal with another death, but somehow."

Dad smiled at me. "You were a miracle; you came out of nowhere. The doctors said you were very healthy and if Kyra took care of herself, you would make it. And you did. Nine pounds and ten ounces, you were strong and you've always been strong."

Mom added in. "We didn't tell you Xon because we wanted to keep it in the past. Our first two, we never met them Xon, never named them or even knew their genders. I don't want to say that means they were insignificant or we didn't love them, but they are gone. It's you, only you who is here now. You are who is important and you are who we care about. Forgive us and let's move on, okay?"

My parents looked at me imploringly and after a few tense moments, I nodded. They sighed heavily and then group hugged me. I hugged them back and they both yelped in pain.

I pulled back, watching as they both rubbed their ribs.

I winced. "Sorry."

"You had a grip like a sumo-wrestler." Mom whined. "Felt like you were going to squish my insides out of my mouth."

My eyes widened. "Was it that bad?"

Dad half-grinned at me. "You've have to learn your own strength son. That did hurt. Come on." He stood up and patted my knee. "When was the last time you ate?"

I didn't want to tell my mother that I had gone hunting in the forest and had eaten a wild boar.

I nodded and said, "I ate. Did you guys eat?"

Mom gave me a solemn look. She had dark eye bags, her brown skin pale, tension lines at her mouth. "How could I eat? I thought horrible things had happened to you. I thought you were running around town butt-naked. I thought I had finally driven you insane." Tears filled her eyes. "I'm too hard on you, I know. I demand too much; I nag too much. I know it's all my fault."

"Stop it Mom, please." I embraced her and slightly tensed my arms. "I'm fine, I just had a small breakdown. I'll be fine from now on. Let's go eat, okay?"

I led her into the kitchen where Dad had already started to cook something. My stomach clenched up tight, like I punched myself. It made a monstrous rumble, the wolf in me howling for food. I may have eaten in the forest but that was last night and I had Changed forms, I needed to eat again.

I slumped down on a seat, groaning. "I'm so hungry!"

"Go do homework." My mother instructed. "You're suspended for a week so you might as well catch up on all the work you've been skipping out on."

I agreed and bounded upstairs. After homework and eating breakfast with my family, both my parents decided to go ahead and call out for work, to spend the day with me instead. We settled down in the basement to watch a movie. I ended up falling asleep again, wanting to bask in the moment. When my alarm went off, the alarm that meant I should be home working on schoolwork, I woke up.

"School's out," said my father, patting at my shoulder for me to get up. "Think your friends are waiting for you?"

"Definitely." I said, clenching my fists.

I've got to face Shane.

Mom looked into my face and said, "You have to promise me you won't get in another fight Xon."

I bit my lower lip and looked at her. "Honestly Mom, that's one promise I can't keep. I know you raised me not to be violent and I really don't like violence either but Shane has to go down. The only way I can bring him down is by proving that I'm stronger than he is. That means we have to fight."

Mom's jaw tightened. "But you keep coming home without your clothes and covered in blood! If he's stronger than you, then why can't you accept it? Just accept it and if you listen to him he won't feel the need to hit you!"

I shook my head and barely managed not to suck my teeth, she hated that. "Mom, it's not that easy. Shane doesn't need a reason to hit anyone, he likes violence and he likes causing pain. You can just look at him sideways and he'll knock his fist in your face. No, I can't let him do it anymore. A Pack is supposed to protect each other, that's the kind of Pack I want to lead. Not one that beats and dominants and frightens each other."

A. E. Costello 243

Mom stared at me like she had never seen me before, but when Dad placed his hand on her shoulder, she nodded and looked away.

I said, my voice low and soft, "I'll be back Mom. That's the one promise I can keep. Every day, no matter what happens, I'll come home."

Mom sniffled and I encased her in my arms, kissing her forehead.

She whispered, "I just don't want to lose you."

"You won't lose me. I'll be back, always." I stepped back as Dad hugged her. "I have to go now."

Dad looked me in the eyes, his face hardened. "Come back Xon. I understand if you have to go fight and get bloody, I accept it. But you had better come back."

I saluted him. "I'll be back, no matter what."

I ran upstairs, got my shoes on and headed to the park. While I walked, I called up Javier.

"Xon!" Javier shouted as soon as the call picked up.

He spluttered something in Spanish before gasping, "Shane is on a rampage, I cannot stop him. I tried and he, well."

Spanish again, definitely cursing. His voice came back in heavily accented English.

"Sky tried and he hurt her, ah."

More Spanish curses.

He yelped. "But Connor."

Spanish.

"I not strong, I drag him. Come, help. Madre de Dios! Come quickly!"

I shoved my phone into my pocket and ran. I ran like wind had picked up around my ankles and spurred me faster. The park spread out before me and I smelled it before I found my Pack. I smelled the bitterness of blood, the stinging rush of bloodlust, the hot harshness of violence and more, worry, fear, confusion, pain.

I stopped short, staring and taking in the scene, frozen.

Shane had Leo by his arm, twisted up behind his neck, while Shane's other fist landed punches to Leo's chest, stomach and back, breaking bones and spilling blood with each blow. Connor and Javier I didn't see. There was blood in a long wide streak pulled away from the open area into the bushes. Sky was crumpled on the ground, clutching her face as blood gushed between her fingers, drenching down her arm and hair.

After taking it all in, I took a step forward. Shane looked up and tossed Leo away like he was a sack of garbage. Leo hit the ground and laid there limply. If he was unconscious or simply too hurt to move, I didn't know.

Sky looked up at me with one eye. A shaky smile came over her face. Even with her scent thick with blood and pain, the happy citrus flushed from her pores.

"Xon, you're here."

Shane grinned at me, his teeth sharp like machetes. "There you are. You caught me beating your sickening scent off my Packmates."

His voice was deep and rough, his wolf talking from his chest.

"They're not your Packmates."

My eyes burned as they shifted to wolf. Blood drenched Shane's hands, splattered on his chest. The smell of my Packmates pain hurt my nose, like razors slashing my senses.

My voice roughened as I talked, vocal cords twisting with the wolf's growl. "That scent is our Pack smell. I was going to give you that smell Shane, I was going to accept you into our Pack. But you know what, I've changed my mind. Instead, I'll beat the shit out of you. I'll rip your throat out, I like that a lot better."

Shane's hackles rose out of his shoulders, his eyes burning wolf olive. "Oh yeah pretty boy? Well, come on and try it."

I dashed forward and rammed my shoulder into Shane's chest, the crack of his ribs in my ear was like a shotgun going off. Shane stumbled back with a look of stunned pain on his face. He shook it off and snatched for my neck with hands strapped with claws. I dodged to the side, then pushed off with my right leg and slammed my left heel into Shane's mouth as hard as I could. His jawbone popped out of place and blood gushed from his mouth. Shane clasped his broken jaw as he snapped it back into place like a Lego piece.

He said with bloody teeth, "What was that just now?"

"I practiced taekwondo for a year."

I moved my body into the back stance with my knees bent. My arms I held at the ready.

Shane laughed and spat a wad of bloody saliva on the ground. "You look fucking ridiculous. You really think because you know some fancy shit moves you'll be able to beat me? You aren't Neo, you aren't the One. What you are is a fucking prick who thinks he's more grown than he actually is. Now I'm going to kill you, here and now."

I beckoned him with my hand. "Come try me bitch."

Shane dashed forward, claws braced. I blocked with my arms, which stopped him from scooping my guts out but my arms got slashed into ribbons. Gritting my teeth against the pain, I foot-swiped him to the ground. He put his arms out to catch his fall and landed hard on his back. Straddling his chest, I grasped his head with both hands, lifted it then slammed him down on the ground. The back of his skull shattered like throwing rocks into glass windows. Shane's eyelids fluttered closed and his body slumped. He wasn't dead but I had knocked him unconscious.

I looked at his bare neck. My wolf howled for me to take the shot.

It would be so easy. I could kill him, right here, right now.

"Xon!"

I turned around at Sky's high cry as the whirls of sirens blared. Sky struggled to her feet, her jean leg torn off, blood trailing down her calf and knee. Her shirt was ripped across her abdomen, blood seeping from a row of claw marks. She held her hand over one side of her face, blood still pouring between her fingers.

She said, "We have to get out of here. Before the police come and before Shane gets back up."

I said, "Can you help Leo? I need to get Connor and Javier. Go to my house, I'll catch up with you there."

She nodded, breathing heavy. "Hurry."

She clasped Leo around his arm with her free hand and hefted him up. He put his arm around her waist and they both limped away.

I followed the trail of blood. A flicker ran through my head, a thought, a hush, a whisper. I turned and focused on it. It came again, louder, a direction. I followed it into the trees. The scent of blood grew thicker. The flicker was throbbing, a beat, pulling me forward. There they were, tucked in a large hole dug down underneath the roots of a tree that had lifted up off the ground. I couldn't see Connor completely because Javier was laying on top of him.

I knelt as Javier lifted his head. The only mark he had on him I could see was a lump on his forehead, like Shane had punched him, a warning hit to stay out of the way. The blood on his clothes was not his. He looked at me with starving brown eyes like black pits in his face.

He said in a shaky voice, "Connor is hurt real bad. I have healed him as much as I can. He needs help Xon. Please, help us."

"Come out." I said. "I'll take Connor to my house, Sky and Leo are already there."

Javier crawled out and I pulled Connor's limp body into my arms. His skin was cold and his head lolled backwards, his neck was bloody but Shane hadn't torn it out, just scratched it deep enough to cause it to bleed like he had.

His eyes watered, his voice ruined with tears, Javier whispered, "How will we get to your house looking like this? I am covered in blood, Connor looks near death and you are barely dressed. What are we going to do?"

"Be calm Javier."

I walked away. He quickly came to my heels, his hand clasped onto my waistband, it was shaking, damp with both blood and sweat.

I broke through the trees and saw Shane standing up just as the police pulled into the parking lot. He turned and looked straight at me, blood streaking down his forehead and his neck.

He shouted. "You didn't win Xon! You're running away, just like the punk ass you are. I've beaten your disgusting scent off my Packmates and then I'll make them smell like me. Go ahead and run, just know you didn't win. I'm still in charge and I'll kill you before I let you take my place."

He ran off, his bloodied blond hair flashing into the distance.

Javier clutched my waistband tighter as police swarmed the park, talking to each other and on their radios. Other people were showing up, wanting to know what was going on.

Javier whimpered. "What are we going to do? There are police everywhere."

"Okay." I said, an idea formulating. "We're going to take the long way to my house Javier, the back way."

Javier stared up at me with wet eyes, his voice shook. "The b-back way? I do not understand."

"You don't have to, just follow me. Stay quiet Javier and don't look around, keep with me."

I walked the opposite direction from the crowd and from my house. Javier did as told and breathed very slowly and carefully, making as little noise as he could. His shoes didn't slap against the pavement as he walked on his toes. We followed the park down then crossed the street once the lights had faded, now we were in Downtown Lakeside, this is where all the restaurants and shopping stores were. I slid us in between the *Benny's Pizza Parlor* and the bookstore.

Now we were in the back alleyways. This was the way I had to get home from the forest in wolf form.

I whispered, "Stick to me Javier."

I started to run but I had to move slowly so Javier could keep up. The same way Leo was so thin he didn't have much heat, Javier was overweight so he couldn't move as fast as I could, tall and muscular and fit. Even if as a species we were faster and stronger than human beings, the same laws of nature applied.

The concrete alleyway ended and spilled out into someone's backyard, the lights were out, no one was home. Pass that backyard, there were the country roads that winded and twisted around homes and a few public buildings. I cut straight through them all, I could smell whiffs from when I had been here last in my wolf form. I got my leg over the gate to enter my backyard and Javier dashed in front of me to get the side door opened.

I called out, "Dad! We're here, where are you?"

"Upstairs, guest bathroom." Dad called back, his voice was loud but trembling, uncomfortable.

I went up, Javier kicked off his shoes as he followed. In the guest bathroom, Sky's ruined clothes laid in a heap on the floor and she was in the bathtub full of hot water. Leo had one hand underneath her chin to keep her head up and his other hand was under the water, I couldn't tell what he was doing. Dad was using a washcloth to press water to Sky's face. My stomach pitched at the mass of scars that contorted her pretty face. It looked like Shane had tried to tear her face off her skull, the twisted scars raised like burns.

Dad had covered up his entire body, long pants with boots and the socks pulled up. He wore a long-sleeved turtleneck and gloves. He even had a skull cap for his head and a cleaning mask over his mouth and nose. The only skin that showed was his eyes. There was no way he'd get infected by werewolf blood this protected.

Dad looked up at me, his eyes wide and spaced far apart, I could see the whites all around.

He said shakily, "She's healing Xon. I can't see it if I stare but each time I look back, it's better. The water...it's like magic."

"I know." I said as I went straight to the shower stall.

Javier helped me get Connor's clothes off without asking and turned on the removable showerhead. I took it down and began to spray him down with warm water, Javier used his hands to spread the water around, wiping the blood away.

Connor was crisscrossed with scars like Shane had used him to sharpen his claws. There was a row from nipple to nipple, then two streaks down to his belly button then five rakes across those. Connor had vicious clawing on his forearms, defensive hits from trying to protect himself. His thighs and legs had bite marks and chunks pulled out leaving indents and dips in his skin that had sealed over. Javier's heat had closed all of his wounds but hadn't put him totally back together.

It was sadistic, Shane had known exactly what he was doing.

I called out, "How's she doing Dad? Connor needs a bath, stat."

"Uh." Dad made a sound like he was swallowing something hard and blocky, his voice came out choked. "I think she's okay, the water is too dirty for me to see anything. Her face gets better each time I blink."

I looked at Javier. "Can you go and see if it's okay for her to come out?"

Javier nodded and left my sight, then Dad was scrambling over to my side. He turned so we were back to back and his head rested against my mine. He was breathing heavy and I could hear his closed lashes fluttering against his cheeks.

I said, "You're doing amazing Dad."

"I feel like a farm boy trying to do open-heart surgery." He said in a shaking weak voice.

He coughed and said a little clearer in his normal low tone. "I'm so out of my element son. Everything in me wanted to call an ambulance, get her to a doctor but Leo moved like he knew what to do, and to him, that was stripping her naked and putting her in a tub of water. Now, I knew you guys needed water to heal, I know you did it with Leo but I didn't want to see your girl naked. And come on, she's bleeding, she's unconscious, she's covered in open wounds. It didn't seem right."

I let him talk, he needed to say it. I held Connor against my chest and activated my heat, pouring it into him. His body was like a cold empty well, freezing and lifeless. He was alive, heaving in short strangled breaths. His heart chugging along like a determined train but he wasn't waking up. There were wounds on his back against my arm. He must have turned to run and Shane didn't stop, kept attacking him.

Dad continued, "While I ran the tub, Leo was holding Sky against him, skin to skin. She was out cold but his face, he was straining to do something even though he wasn't doing anything but holding her, sweat was popping out on his face and I could hear him making this noise, this grunting and sighing noise. I couldn't tell why."

Dad shook his head. "Then he suddenly gave up, he gasped then pulled her toward the tub and put her in. I wanted to put the water on lukewarm but he turned it up as hot as it goes then pushed her all the way down. Before I could yell that he was going to drown her, he held her head so her nostrils were above water. His other hand was scooping and spreading the water over the wounds, and it was like the water was smoothing over the blood and when it washed away, it was better."

"Each time I blinked and the water was running over, her wounds were healing. So I got a washcloth to wipe away the blood on her face. I almost threw up, Leo actually pushed my head into the toilet bowl but I got a hold of myself. Her eye was punctured Xon, like a deflated white balloon and was sliding off her face. Leo didn't even react, he pulled it off and it fell in the water."

Dad's shoulders shuddered with the memory. I would have felt sick even though I knew that it would grow back, every injury I had gotten healed like new.

Dad kept talking, "Then I did throw up, in the bowl and had to go brush my teeth. When I came back, he had her head under water completely and I swear to you Xon I thought he was trying to drown her. I was right about to tackle him when he lifted her up and she breathed, water ran down her mouth and she was gasping like a fish but her face was clean and her eye was back, I could tell even though her eyes were closed. Her eyelid wasn't right, it was hanging off center, drooping and Leo was about to pull it off. I covered my face, waited until it fell in the water then I got the washcloth again and covered her with it, squeezing water over it. I lifted it up after a minute and her eyelid was there, like it had always been there."

He let out a heavy shaky sigh. "I know you get into fights with Shane, you come home covered in blood or without your clothes but you don't ever even have any scars and a part in me, this small part that always screams bullshit when you talk about wolf things, I didn't believe it. But right now, after watching Sky's eye just heal like that, I believed. Every time I think well, he's got to be making it up or this is all just a bad dream, something happens right before my eyes and I gotta think no Grant, he's not lying and I'm not dreaming, it's real."

There was a loud splash and a small commotion.

Sky's voice ran out, "Jaxon!"

"I'm here." I called, unable to run to her, not holding Connor and not with Dad at my back. "I'm right here."

Javier was speaking in Spanish, soft and soothing things but Sky was still splashing, struggling to get out of the tub.

Dad stood up and he got a towel off the rack, he came over, saying, "Sky, please darling, cover up."

"W-what…Mr. Reeves? Why…why are you here?" Her voice was breathy, tired and confused. I couldn't smell her, I couldn't smell much of anything. My sense of smell had been singed.

"I'm helping." He said it with an awkward chuckle. "And please, cover yourself up."

"Oh, right." She also sounded embarrassed and it was enough to make me laugh just a little bit. "Jaxon?"

Her feet padded onto the ground and Dad lead her to me. She limply laid herself across my back and nuzzled her face into my neck, her arms went around my shoulders. I managed to kiss her forehead and her ear.

She whispered, "I'm okay now, right? I'm safe."

"Yeah." I said, resting my head on top of hers. "I'm right here. Can you tell me what happened? Why did Shane attack you guys?"

"I'm too tired to talk." She said, her voice growing faint. "But I want to sleep with you Xon, I need to."

"I have to help Connor." I said. "Did you fight Shane, is that what you did?"

"I had to stop him." She yawned but it was more like an exhale, her breath whooshed out of her. She cuddled closer to me but the towel was wrapped around her breasts down to her waist. She couldn't feel my skin and couldn't get comfortable enough to sleep without it. "He didn't go for me or for Javier, he tore onto Connor without waiting, without warning. Javier held me back at first, saying it was too dangerous so I punched him as hard as I could in the head. He fell down so I jumped between Shane and Connor. Shane just got me out of the way and when I came back he nearly tore my leg off. When I came back again, he slashed me in my face."

"Then he went back to Connor who was trying to run, attacked him at his back. Then Leo tried to get involved, so Shane threw Connor away, grabbed Leo and started beating him up. I knew I couldn't stop him, Javier couldn't stop him, I had to find you, had to get you to help but I was afraid if I left Shane would kill them. Then you showed up, like you knew. Leo and I started to walk to your house but I passed out by the time we got to the door, next thing I know I'm waking up in the tub. I don't even know what happened. I'm sorry Xon, I'm sorry I couldn't protect our Pack."

"You did everything you could Sky." I said, listening as the others drained and cleaned the tub.

Dad muttered, "Get the skin out, get the skin out. God no, don't show me, throw it away. God, just God."

Dad wasn't squeamish far as I knew and he had done things in the past that he refused to tell me. And it wasn't every day he had to watch a girl's eye fall out of her skull then grow back.

Javier said, "Alpha, the tub is ready."

"Dad." I said. "Could you put Sky in bed?"

"No!" She protested in a suddenly strong intense voice, her hands held onto my shoulders. "I'm not leaving you."

I said, "Okay, okay. Dad." I looked up at him standing over us. "Take Connor from me, get him in the tub, please."

He nodded and he didn't even protest that Connor was naked. He knelt and carried Connor over to the tub. I think he had gotten desensitized to naked bodies, just the way I had. Dad was a wolf on the outside but human on the inside. Everything he did, he was involved in, had to do with werewolf business, the only thing he was missing was the wolf itself. Again I got the urge, the thought of Changing him. If he was a wolf too, this would be so much easier. Just as I thought it, I dashed it away.

Being a werewolf was not easy. At first, I wanted to die before I accepted it, I couldn't accept it. Then I got help and I made friends who pulled me through. In some ways, it would be easier to Change Dad, make him a wolf in body as well as knowledge. But then I had to think about Mom.

How would it affect her that her husband and son were wolves and she was a human being? I didn't want Mom to become a wolf, she was fine who she was, she deserved to stay human, Dad deserved to stay human.

Sky wasn't sleep on my back, she was hanging on and her lashes flicked against my shoulder each time she blinked. She probably didn't have any strength left to talk, her body weight was completely on mine, her legs were like noodles.

There was a loud splash from the tub and Connor spewed water.

Dad shouted, "He's alive!"

That made me laugh and I stood. I moved so I caught Sky before she could flop onto the floor. I lifted her up into my arms. Connor shook water from his eyes and he was healed, there was some reddish pink on his chest and arms but after we all slept together, it would be gone. Leo wasn't wearing a shirt and his pants were drenched in water. He was still bruised, large mottled eggplant-colored marks over his chest and back. Javier was naked, even his briefs were gone and he was in the tub with Connor, I could only guess that he was adding more heat to him along with the water. Poor Dad, he was looking at me right above my forehead, Sky's towel had slipped down around her waist. He was surrounded by nakedness and couldn't do anything about it.

"Come." I said to my Packmates. "Let's get in the bed."

Javier and Leo helped Connor get out of the tub. His legs wobbled and he teetered like he had just gotten off a wild rollercoaster. Dad followed us out of the bathroom and he without asking pulled down the top sheet and then him and Javier unrolled the covers. I laid Sky down first and took off the towel, tossing it away and then undid my pants.

Dad stared at me. "Xon! She's a woman!"

"I know." I said even as I pulled them down then my boxers with it.

I already knew that any type of clothing was hindering and uncomfortable when sleeping with my Pack. Dad's face built up with anger but I couldn't smell it, my nose still burnt out. As my Packmates clambered onto the bed, all naked and waiting for me, Dad stepped back and this was where his humanness was combating him. I was about to get in a bed with a bunch of other naked teenagers, to him, this was completely wrong.

I was naked at the side of the bed, they were all in and watching me, staring at me and I could feel it, a tug, a pulse, a pull. And this time, I tapped into the collective thought, the Pack, they spoke to me. They wanted my skin, my hug, my touch, my kiss, because I would heal them. I would soothe the fear that was drenched in their minds, their bodies were aching, desperate and I would relieve them. I would chase away the nightmares, I would bring their pain onto myself and release it, fling it away and it would be gone. Everything about me would enhance them, heal them and they needed me.

I brought all of that I heard, felt from them, breathed in through me, it showed on my face as I looked at Dad and willed him to understand. Dad's eyes wrinkled at the sides and he stepped back, his mouth weakened then firmed.

He turned away, and said, "Keep it platonic Xon. I'm locking the door behind me. Don't let any of them come out here naked. Send me a text when you need clothes, I'm aware none of them have any now."

I nodded.

Dad locked the door then closed it.

"Alpha."

They all said it together and I turned to look at them. All of their eyes were like bruised sores in their faces, their bodies wounded, aching, needing attention, hands reached out. I got on the bed at the foot end and crawled over, I pressed my face to the hands and kissed them, they caressed my face, felt down my neck and rubbed over my skull.

I came closer and felt Connor under me first, his arms went around my neck and I kissed his forehead, his cheeks and his chin, his thighs pressed against my waist, I smelled the fear dart through him and I let him go, rolling over.

I accepted Leo in my arms, snuggled his face and his neck, ran my hand over his chest and stomach, he hugged me close. I let him go and turned over at a brush of soft hot hands down my back.

Sky slipped against me and I kissed her neck, up the slender column and brushed over that side of her face. The skin was smooth, clear and I licked over her eyelid, it was soft, new and fresh. Her hands spread over my pectorals and under my arms, clasping over my back. She cuddled closer, her breasts flushed against my chest, soft and warm mounds of flesh, alive. Her heartbeat behind them, her breathing was deep and slow, healthy. I hugged her tight, nestling my chin into her thick cloud of hair.

There was a desperate pleading whine behind her, someone hadn't gotten my attention. Javier. I kissed Sky's forehead and she willingly pulled back as Javier gently climbed over her.

I opened my arms and he fell into them, he wasn't very heavy. His body felt like dough, large, cumbersome and pliable. I hugged him close and he peppered my face with eager thankful kisses, nuzzling his face over my jaw and into my neck, licking now and then. My hands played over his soft lumpy back then squeezed the extra folds on his sides. He wiggled and made a protesting squeal, so I stopped and hugged him.

Then Connor and Leo were at my back, pulling forward and Sky moved over Javier to take her place at my side. There was shifting and murmuring as everyone got comfortable so everyone could have a least a hand or foot touching my skin, then as our Pack scent throbbed and melded over our bodies, connecting us, we closed our eyes and slept.

9

August 12th
Tuesday

When I opened my eyes, the sun was peering through the windows behind the bed and heating up my body. This meant I had slept all day yesterday and it was tomorrow. My Pack slept on top of me, arms, legs, torsos, hands and feet, everyone trying to touch as much as my skin as they could. I turned my head to see the radio clock on the bedside table, blinking that it was ten in the morning. Well, my Packmates were all late for school. I doubted they would be going at all.

My wolf howled inside of me just as my stomach ripped with a massive ache, my head pounded. When was the last time I had eaten? Oh yes, breakfast yesterday. I hadn't had lunch or dinner, and combined with fighting with Shane, all the heat I had given over to others, I had no nutrition left for myself. I had to eat, pronto.

The Pack laid heavy on my body, Sky was directly on top of me, her breasts and stomach flush with mine. Her lower body had been twisted over because it was Connor on top of my groin and thighs. He was upside down, his feet tucked into Sky's side. His arms wrapped around my upper thighs, his head laying in between. Leo, like always, wound his legs in between my legs, his arms grasped my waist. Javier had taken over my calves and feet, his head touched Connor's head, my toes pressed into his stomach and upper thighs as he curled around me.

I wasn't uncomfortable at all though I realized I should be. I wasn't even overheated with all the body heat and the sun. I was perfectly warm, I didn't want to even get out of bed. But my wolf gnashed and shoved against me, my stomach heaved with pain again. No, I had to eat and I knew my Pack would be starving once they woke up as well, especially Leo, Connor and Sky who needed nourishment from being injured.

I slowly sat up, using my hands to gently roll Sky and Leo off my chest and neck. I leaned back against the headboard and crossed my arms underneath my head, waiting for them to wake up. I knew they would soon because when I wake up and I move, it resonates in them and they react to it. I noticed it the last time I slept with the guys together. Once I woke up, Leo, Connor then Javier woke up and they all watched me, waiting for what I would do.

Sky wiggled closer and her head buried into my chest, then she lifted up. Her eyes looked into mine, blearily hazel-gold, woozy. She rubbed them and looked around, then gasped and her hands covered her breasts.

I said softly, "Relax, okay? We aren't going to do anything to you."

Her head bowed and her hair fell forward, which she combed over her shoulders. The hair was long enough and thick enough to hide her breasts completely.

She said shakily, "It's not them I'm worried about, they don't desire me."

A small smile ticked my lips and I said, "I didn't do anything to you last night, why would I suddenly molest you now? I told you before I wouldn't pressure you or force you, I meant it. If you kiss me, I'll kiss you back but once you say stop I'll stop."

Sky nodded then said, "Your father said keep it platonic. So even though I really want a good morning kiss I won't chance his anger."

I said, "He purposely locked the door when he left. If you want a good morning kiss, I'll give it to you. And that's it, I promise."

Sky bit her lip, her heart skipped, then she scooted closer to me. My arm went around her shoulders, my other hand touched her chin. She gasped softly and I gently pushed her head back, just a little too far so her neck tensed. Her eyes were dazed and her scent flushed with heated sugar. I lowered my head and placed my lips on hers.

I lifted up and whispered, "Good morning Sky."

Her trembling hands laid on my jaw, she looked at me with the luxurious eyes of a she-wolf wanting more. She didn't have to say it, I kissed her again, deeper. My tongue didn't ask for permission, I slipped inside and licked the roof of her mouth. Sky shuddered and her arms wrapped around my neck, she pressed closer. My hand left her chin to cup her neck, then played down to her collarbone. My palm burned, itched, I wanted to go lower.

"Just a little." She panted before kissing me again.

I slid past the protection of her hair and gently let one breast fill my palm. My fingers widened and explored the sweet tenderness of the flesh. My fingers pulled close and I gently pressed her nipple together.

"Whoa Xon, too much!"

It wasn't Sky who said it, she had moaned but then covered her mouth at Connor's voice, breaking our kiss.

I looked over, the three other members of our Pack were sitting up and were completely aware of what we were doing. Connor was gaping at us, while Javier was covering his lap and staring down at it. Leo had been watching but his eyes were simple green dots on his face and his expression blank, he wasn't covering his lap. Connor was definitely embarrassed but had his hands in his lap like Javier. Sky covered her face with both hands and turned to the side, huddling into her body. I couldn't detect their scents, too full of my own and the Pack scent, of sleeping together in the warm sun.

"Sorry guys." I said, rubbing the back of my head. "You're right Connor, I did go too far." My scent was heavily aroused and my reaction prominent, pointing upwards towards my collarbone, brushing against my abs. "Do you forgive me?"

Leo nodded and so did Javier.

Connor averted his eyes and mumbled, "And I'm guessing every time Sky sleeps with us I'm supposed to be treated to that?"

Sky flinched and pulled her legs to her chest and placed her face onto her knees, her arms tightened around her ankles. Her hair billowed downwards to hide her even more. She was pulling away from us, making her own place where she was accepted and wanted.

Now I was pissed and I turned my glare onto Connor, he gasped but I spoke anyway. "Don't humiliate Sky, understand? Yes, I went too far and I've apologized. Because it bothers you, next time I won't do that. You're making her feel bad Connor and that's not right. We're a family, we're a Pack and when we're in the same bed, we're all equal, we're all welcome. You treat her like she's not allowed to be here and she won't want to come back and that's not right. Make her feel better Connor, bring her back to us."

Connor paled but then he nodded, and crawled over to her, needing to move over Javier's outstretched legs, who curled them into himself Indian-style. Connor rubbed his head over Sky's head and whispered, "I'm sorry Sky, I didn't mean to say those things, for them to come out like that. I'm okay with morning kisses." He dotted a kiss on Sky's shoulder then her upper back, her skin rippled. "I just don't want to see you two make out. A kiss is fine but don't go too far, okay? I'm sorry that I hurt you." He leaned heavily against her legs, until she had to break her arms away and lifted her head. He snuggled against her and she hugged him, he gave her a sweet smile with doe eyes. "Do you forgive me?"

Sky nodded and pecked him between his eyes, he whimpered and kissed her nose. She kissed his forehead then he kissed her cheek until they were collapsing into giggles. Leo padded over to me and nudged his head underneath my chin, he didn't make a sound but rubbed his shoulder into my chest, asking for affection. I wrapped my arm around his neck and pressed my fingers to the hinge of his jaw and cheek until his mouth parted and I tickled him like that. Leo wriggled and his tongue lolled out of his mouth. Life jumped into his eyes, and his scent shuddered with amusement, orange and tingling.

Javier protested at being left out again and jumped onto Leo's chest, who's eyes bugged. He gasped for air then his arms swung out, he grasped Javier by the neck and pushed him backwards on to the bed. This time Leo was on top and he bit Javier on his ear then gnawed on his cheekbone, which was protected by Javier's plump skin. Javier giggled and his fingers dug into Leo's undersides, tickling him.

I laid back and watched my Pack interact, romping and playing with each other, acting like puppies.

The door was loudly knocked on and Dad's voice broke though, "Xon? What's going on in there? Are you awake? Let me in."

The doorknob rattled. His voice was suspicious and annoyed, uh oh.

I pulled on my abandoned jeans and unlocked the door, stepping back as it opened. Dad's eyes first scanned me, seeing I had bottoms on then he turned to look at the bed. Sky was sitting up with a pillow pressed to her chest and another pillow over her lap. Connor was laying on his stomach, chin propped up on his hands with a wide-eyed smile. Leo and Javier had pulled sections of the cover to hide their lower bodies. Everyone had on innocent expressions, besides Leo who looked wiped clean like nothing was happening.

Dad's eyes narrowed but there was nothing to suggest we had been doing anything out of order. He sniffed several times not even being discreet. Though Sky and I kissed, we hadn't gone far enough to leave any type of odor. Sky's face purpled. Connor pushed his face into the mattress, not enough to hide his embarrassed giggle.

"Dad!" I stared at him. "Really? Could you not, honestly!"

Dad crossed his arms and leaned on the doorjamb. "Fine, sorry, I had to check. If you're anything like me when I was your age then I know not to trust you."

I blushed, flames burning on my cheeks and Sky made a strangled sound from the bed.

I glared at him. "You're really pushing it Dad."

Dad's eyes twinkled and he smiled before saying. "I had to go to Goodwill while you slept and buy clothes that looked about your sizes. Here."

He bent down and picked up a large cardboard box from the floor beside the door and handed it to me. Balanced on top were fresh towels.

"Shower, dress then come eat. I know you guys will be starving so I've been cooking while you were sleeping to make sure there would be enough."

Now that the door was open, I could smell the food. I stepped forward, pressing against Dad. His eyes widened and then he pressed back against me. The cardboard box thudded into my chest and I blinked a few times.

He said, "Don't go wolf on me Xon, just do as I said."

"Yes Dad."

He closed the door.

I turned and saw my Pack was leaving the bed, inching toward the door.

"You heard him." I said, dropping the box on the floor. "We have to get dressed first. Connor and Leo, in the shower. Sky and Javier, you can take the tub."

"I want to shower with you."

They all said besides Leo, they were all looking at me.

I said, "This isn't Javier's basement, there's not enough room for all of us to shower together and I'm not going to take five showers one after another. So I'll shower by myself and you guys double up."

Connor's eyes watered. "But…what if you stay in the shower and we take turns?"

"Yeah," said Sky, nodding. "That's a good idea."

Javier said, "That would work."

Leo stared at me with that intense emptiness, as if he looked away he would die right then.

I let out a short sigh but nodded. "Okay. I'm taking one shower, a fifteen minute shower and you each get five minutes. So make sure you're getting clean then you get dressed and we'll all go downstairs together."

"First!" Speaking together besides Leo, everyone raised their hands in the air.

"Youngest to oldest." I said. "So Connor, then Javier, Leo and lastly Sky."

Sky pouted. "Ladies first."

"No way," said Connor. "You'll start making out again and take ten minutes long. Sky definitely goes last."

"The richest should go first," said Javier then yelped as everyone pounced on him, biting and pulling on his hair.

I dropped my pants and went into the bathroom with the towels. I ran the water and got inside, calling, "Fifteen minutes, starts now."

There was scuffling from the bedroom and two minutes passed. Connor was slipping into the shower. I handed him a soaped washcloth and he began to bathe but he was shivering and kept his head down.

"Connor." I said quietly. "You know I'm not going to hurt you, right?"

Connor nodded jerkily, his green hair was plastered against his skull, like he had seaweed growing from his head.

I wanted to touch him, comfort him, but he might run if I did.

Instead I asked, "Have I ever hurt you Connor?"

"No." His voice was weak and soft, almost drowned out by the thundering water on the tiles. "Not even once."

I chanced it and placed my hand on his head, stroking my fingers across the slick hair covering his skull. Connor turned and pushed his face into my abs, breaking down into tears.

He gasped between speaking, "He attacked me, jumped on me and I thought he was trying to kill me. I screamed for you and that made him even more enraged, he bit my legs, he tore pieces off me and I tried to run, he slashed up my back and I thought it was all over, that I was dead. I thought my life had always been shit, I had Carter at night, Shane during the day and all I've wanted was nothingness. I've tried to slit my wrists but it healed right away. I tried to hang myself but I didn't die, I just hung there not breathing and I passed out. I thought I died but when I woke up, Carter had cut me down and I began to breathe again, once the pressure was off it was like I hadn't hung myself in the first place. I've drowned myself in the toilet but when I slid out the water ejected from my lungs and I started breathing again. Nothing works, nothing kills me. Then Shane was going to kill me, he was trying to kill me but this time, for the first time, I didn't want to die because I had you, I had my Alpha who was going to protect me and care for me but I was going to die!"

I held Connor tight around his shoulders and knelt down, pressing my face against his and nuzzled his face with a low croon. The shower stall opened. Sky slid in, hugging Connor from his back and he slumped against us, held between us and a power grew. It rose up from the depths of my wolf and seeped into Connor who moaned softly. Sky's wolf's power seeped from her body and met mine, they twirled around each other, greeting and then made one and spread out through Connor, comforting and healing him.

Connor's head fell back onto Sky's shoulder and she kissed his forehead and neck. I leaned over him and ran my lips down his nose and chin, then pecked down his jaw.

Connor's eyes fluttered open and he smiled up at us, his brown eyes were warm and deep like chocolate, his skin peachy gold and he was breathing easy, happily.

He said softly, "Thanks my Alphas."

My eyes widened but Sky said, "Connor...we're not even mated. And I didn't protect you, I ran."

"You ran to get help." His arms went up and around to hold her face, he slicked her hair behind her ears and stared up at her with the eyes of a child looking at his mother, deep, loving, protected. "And you tried, I saw you throw yourself in between us. Javier didn't do that, he never could and Leo wouldn't do that. But you did. You took blows that Shane was directing at me, you bled for me. And Xon is with you, you are with Xon. He is my Alpha and you are the Alpha queen. I trust you to protect me and hug me and care for me. Or are you rejecting me?"

Sky kissed his eyes closed and ran her nose down his nose, saying in a thrumming tone, "I'd never reject you Connor. Thank you, thank you so much."

At footsteps, I looked up to see Leo and Javier hovering outside the stall, they wanted to come in too but couldn't with all of us in here.

I said, "Sky, Connor, you'll have to get out and we'll switch with Leo and Javier."

Connor pouted but they left. Leo slid in and he hugged me for a moment but then picked up Connor's abandoned wash cloth and began to bathe. Javier didn't come in, there wouldn't be enough room for the three of us. Leo bathed and paused to run his hand over my face or nestle his head into my neck and shoulder. I caressed him back and kissed his chin, keeping him calm and understanding I was right here.

Javier said quietly, "You made me last again Alpha."

I said, "You were second in the plan but it just didn't turn out that way. You can sit next to me while we eat, okay?"

He nodded but even with the hot water cleansing my nose I could smell he was upset. Leo was clean so I ushered him out and Javier stepped in, his head held low. I took the washcloth and ran it over his shoulders, then brushed the two mounds of his pecs and made sure to get under the folds. Javier yelped and jerked back then covered his flesh with both hands.

"X-Xon! Now that is too much even for a wolf!"

I laughed and handed him the cloth. "Then stop pouting and bathe before I wash somewhere even more embarrassing."

Javier blushed and I watched as the red bloomed over his entire body, turning his pale gold skin a shade of cherry all over him.

Javier protested in a high shrill tone, "Stop staring at me Xon!" He turned his back and kept bathing, squealing, "You are not supposed to stare!"

I laughed again, even louder. "You're a guy like me and you know I'm not attracted."

Javier growled, "I am telling Sky on you."

That really made me laugh but I finished bathing and we both got out after rinsing. We dried off. Dad had included my clothes in the box. Dressed, I ushered them downstairs. The kitchen counters were covered in pots, pans and baking sheets of food, the kitchen table didn't have any settings but was covered with platters and bowls and plates of food.

"Go eat." He said, he was standing at the stove cooking something and there was what looked like a chicken baking in the oven.

My Pack didn't ask twice, they rushed past me and dove onto the food. My wolf howled for me to charge and eat. Instead I went to my father and I hugged him close, I nuzzled my face into his ear.

I said, "Thank you so much for everything."

Dad patted my back.

My stomach bellowed, pain clawed at my insides.

He laughed and stepped back, saying, "Eat Xon, before your Packmates eat everything."

I ate, I devoured and didn't take note of what I was eating. I didn't use a fork or a knife and if I drank I chugged it straight from the jug. My Packmates didn't use any class or finesse, they bit and snatched and gorged. Connor was the first to stumble back from scooping out a platter of sweet creamed corn, he plopped onto his butt then curled up and snored. Sky was slurping down a jug of orange juice, some of it was sliding down the corners of her mouth but she didn't miss a beat until the jug was empty, then dropped it, waddled over to Connor and laid down with him right there on the kitchen floor, knocked out sleep.

Javier and Leo were still eating and didn't look like they were ready to stop but I was finished, my wolf curling up to sleep. I went to Connor and Sky and lifted them each against a shoulder as if they were toddlers. Dad was gaping at me because even though he was strong, carrying two nearly full-grown teenagers each in one arm was too much. I walked them over to the living room and gently laid them on the carpeted floor, watching as they cuddled to each other.

There was a large thud that shook the room. I turned to see Javier sprawled on the kitchen floor, mouth agape as he slept, body limp. I picked him up and placed him on the living room floor, rolling him so he was against Sky and he snuggled against her.

Leo was moving around the kitchen, steadfastly eating all crumbs or leftovers that were either on the floor, the counters or still in the containers. Dad moved to the side, watching Leo's single-minded determination to make sure no food got left behind.

Once the kitchen was picked clean, Leo lumbered over to the living room and I had to stop him from taking his clothes off. He laid down at Sky's feet and tucked his face against the crook of her knees, her feet against his chest and they were all sleeping.

Dad came to my side and watched them. They were breathing deep and heavy, their stomachs all pouched out and bodies relaxed. His mouth opened then closed, he rubbed the back of his head not saying anything.

I said, "I have to protect them Dad. I have to..."

I paused then said, "I'm going to have to kill Shane."

Dad jerked and stared at me, his breath caught.

He shook his head. "No son, no. That's not the way."

"Did you not see what he did?" My voice raised, sharpened and I jabbed a finger at the sleeping wolves, they didn't even flinch. "You saw, you were there. He ripped at Connor's body like he was a plaything, he hurt my mate, he hurt Leo. He did it to get at me, to hurt me he hurt them. I can't let him get away with it, he's got to pay."

"Jaxon listen to yourself!" Dad snapped back though his scent was weak, frightened. "I understand the best I can, I was there, you're right, I did see and I did what I could to help but son, killing him is *murder*, don't you understand? And once you kill someone, once you watch the life leave their eyes and the last breath disappears, it's finished, it's done. The dead don't come back Xon, you can't bring the dead back and say sorry, sorry that I did it!"

His voice rose until he was shouting at me and his tears flooded down his cheeks. "And I will not stand by and let you do that, let that type of thing stain your memory, get life blood on your hands that'll never wash off. It doesn't go away Xon, you won't kill him and walk away and act like nothing happened. It'll be there, it'll always be there and they won't let you forget, they don't forget what you did. So yes, yes, Shane has hurt your people and you're furious and he has to pay, fine. Beat the shit out of him, break his bones, blind him, deafen him, cause him pain that'll make him *wish* for death but don't you dare kill him Xon, don't you dare take his life from him because no one has the right to do that, no one gets to decide who lives and who dies. Tell me you're listening, tell me you understand!"

I stared at Dad and said softly, "I understand Dad...I won't kill him." My fists clenched. "But I will make him understand if he ever touches them again, it'll be me he's answering to."

Dad nodded and sniffed, using his arm to dry his face. "That's better son, that's much better."

I paused then asked, "Do you still see their faces?"

Dad's body stiffened and his face was in his arm but he nodded, his voice shook and was squeezed thin.

"Yes...every night when I sleep. On anniversaries, I don't sleep and all day I see it playing over my eyes. If I see someone who looks like them or someone who used to be with the crew or I go by that place where it happened or I remember where the body is, I think I'll just end it."

"Your mother." He ran his hand down his face and turned his back but I placed my hand on him and made him look at me. His eyes were strained red, wrinkles pulled at his mouth and creased his forehead, he looked like he had aged ten years.

"She knows." He said in a choked voice. "I told her and she knows but she didn't tell, she could have. I told her everything like she was a police officer who had gotten me to confess. What I did, where, when, how, all of it. She could walk into the station, tell them what I said and I'd be in jail by sundown. But she didn't, she comforted me, held me and."

He suddenly laid his head on my neck and was crying again, not able to say another word. I held him close and only lightly squeezed so I wasn't hurting him, just letting him know I was there. Tears birthed in my eyes as I realized Dad really was right, I couldn't kill Shane. He was goading me to try, he wanted me to try to kill him because he wanted to kill me but a fate worse than death for Shane was to learn that I was better, I was stronger and he had to listen to me, had to be dominated by me. He wouldn't accept it until my wolf cleaned his wolf's clock, until I had destroyed him in every way possible without taking his life.

After a few minutes, Dad pulled back and I got him a cloth to clean his sopping face. He used it then shuddered several times before standing up straight and adjusted his shirt, coughed and cleared his throat. I could smell his guilt and embarrassment and shame, sour mud, heated prickliness and sickly humidness. He had completely broken down in front of his son, when he was supposed to be the strong man, the leader.

I said, "Dad, it's okay. It's not like I'm going to hold it against you or see you as lesser than me. You're amazing, awe-inspiring. I'll always look up to you, period."

I looked outside, the sun was going down.

I asked, "Where is Mom? Why wasn't she here when I got back last night?"

Dad rubbed his hand over his scalp, it made scratchy noises, he was due for a shave. "She had gone out with a few of her girlfriends but when Sky and Leo showed up beat up, I called her and told her not to come home for a little while. She was furious but she agreed. So I'll call her to come back after this is finished up. I'm exhausted Xon, I hardly slept last night. I kept seeing eyeballs falling out of skulls, skin coming together like glue, and blood, more blood than I've wanted to see in my lifetime."

He laid down on the couch on his back and laid his arm over his eyes, letting out a long slow breath. I took down the throw quilt from the armchair and placed it over him. I looked at him, my father, laying in sleep and down over at my Packmates curled on the floor together. My stomach tightened into a knot and that hard burning coal rose up and steamed in my throat. If there was anything important I had ever done in my life, it was protecting my family. My cell phone rang from upstairs. The cell stopped ringing but then started again just as I reached it.

I answered it without looking at the caller id.

"Jaxon Reeves."

"How is everyone?" The voice was low and threaded with amusement.

I barely stopped my hand from clenching, it would have broken my phone.

"Shane."

"That's me." He sniggered but then cut it off, saying more clearly, "I know they're all at your house. No one's home at theirs, well, Sky's parents are worried little bugs and they promised me to tell them if I saw their angel. Her siblings are ugly, glared at me like they know something."

I spoke, my voice harsh and heated, "I know why you're doing this Shane and don't act like I don't."

"Oh yeah? Try me."

I paused for a second then said, "You're trying to scare me off, get me to decide you're too strong and I shouldn't dare fight you, make me fear dying and submit before we actually fight for real. Because it's *you* who's scared to fight me. You know there's a real chance you'll lose; you know I'm just as dominant as you are now. I'm not the little frightened pup I was when we first met. The last time we clashed, I won and you know it. You're afraid Shane and be afraid, be *real* afraid because next time I see you, I'm not gonna hold back. I'm gonna tear into you until you'll wish you were dead, got it?"

Shane's side of the call made a sharp crushing sound, like crunching ice, grinding his fangs together then he spoke in a rough voice, "Alright then Xon. You keep saying fight for real like this whole time its been fake or not serious. Fine. You want a real fight? Wolf form, tonight, at the field. I'm sick of wasting time punching you around because you don't get it. When I rip your throat out with my fangs, then I'll be in charge. Let's make it midnight."

"Deal."

I hung up before he could say anything else. There was knocking on the door downstairs, then the bell rang. I didn't want whoever it was to wake up my Pack so I went down and opened it, putting my phone in my pocket. Of all people, Wyatt was standing there. He had his back to the door and he was texting, I could read it.

Wyatt: Toni, why me? Why dammit!

I cleared my throat and Wyatt whirled around, shoved the phone into his pocket and glared at me with the intense green eyes of his wolf. The look seethed with malice and hatred, the scent of it rose off his skin, sharp and peppery, vivid and burning.

He asked gruffly, "Are you alone?"

"No." I said, keeping my eyes locked on his. "My father and my Pack are here. They're sleeping, so keep it down. In fact, let's talk outside."

I stepped forward and Wyatt didn't move, so now our chests were touching and the tips of our noses centimeters apart. I stepped forward again, our hips brushed and Wyatt stumbled backwards off the steps, breathing hard and his lips pulled back, baring fangs. I closed the door behind me and leaned on it, crossing my arms loosely over my chest and watched him calmly.

Wyatt's hackles rose up from his shoulders, his eyes glowed gold as the wolf spark ignited. Black curved claws leapt out of his fingernail beds.

I said, "You came for a reason, so say it then go."

Wyatt snarled, "You can't talk to me anyway you want to! You're nothing but a Rogue, a stupid pup!"

I snarled back. That power slammed up from the inside, from the wolf.

My voice boomed out, "I'm the Alpha of Lakeside Village! You're on *my* territory and unless you have a gift to offer, you can get the fuck out of here before I kill you!"

Wyatt jerked back and blood spurted on his face, a small rip had appeared in his cheek as if I had nipped him. He clasped the wound and stared at me like I had grown two heads. He went into his pocket and flung something at my face, I caught it. It was a platinum Rolex, easily worth more money than I've ever owned in my life.

I looked at Wyatt who was glaring at me, breathing hard and the blood was still running down his cheek.

I said, "What is this?"

Wyatt's teeth gritted but he spat, "It's a freely given gift and should you accept it, I will follow your rules as such until you give my leave."

I blinked then said, "Gift accepted." I put it in my pocket. Then I said, "Why are you here Wyatt? What do you want?"

His fists clenched, muscles strained against his skin and I could see his wolf pressing against him, fur flittered under his skin, the wolf stared at me behind his eyes and all he wanted was to jump onto me, kill me. The only thing keeping him from doing it was because his Alpha had forbidden him to and I had just accepted his gift. In any other situation, such as when I was wandering alone in the forest, he'd end my life.

I pulled my upper lip back, and my fangs slid down, touching my bottom lip. "I'll ask you again Wyatt then I'm ordering you off my territory. What do you want and why are you here?"

Wyatt rolled his head and cracked his neck then relaxed his shoulders, he looked at me with his human gray eyes, intense and stormy but his wolf was sliding backwards, retreating.

He said, "The police cleaned up a shit ton of blood in the park yesterday. Do you know how dangerous it is for shifter blood to be left laying around like that?"

I winced. "I know but Leo, Connor and Sky got badly hurt. I had to get them home to heal them, there was nothing I could do."

Wyatt grinned but it wasn't friendly, it was more of a grimace that stretched his face and bared his sharp teeth, his hackles raised again and his fists buckled.

He spoke like the words were being wrenched out of him. "Oh Great Moon, I want to rip your throat out so bad, I want to tear your intestines out and I want to break your legs off and beat your head in with it until I don't have to look at your stupid face anymore."

The vitriol and shake of his voice, how he glared at me with the hungry demented eyes of his wolf. I wanted to ask him why, but I remembered how Leo reacted when I poked that part of him. If I pressed that button in Wyatt, he'd snap and kill me straight out.

I said, "I understand, alright? So what are you saying? What did you want me to do? It was Shane who attacked the Pack, he's the one who hurt them and left the blood everywhere."

Wyatt bit his lower lip and his teeth went straight through, puncturing his lip and blood sprinkled out. He licked his lip and it healed but the cut on his cheek hadn't even scabbed over, bleeding little trickles at a time. It really was a small little cut, like I had lightly scratched the surface of his skin with a claw. But the fact was, I hadn't touched him. I hadn't even moved, I just yelled at him and he bled.

Wyatt ran his hand over his mouth but he didn't even wipe the blood off his face, the blood had slid down his jaw and droplets plopped onto his shirt collar.

He said, "The problem is Xon, if this is your territory, if you have a fight and there's blood fucking everywhere then you got to clean it up, shit." He glared at me, hatred turning his gray eyes into a storm. "You like acting like you're in control and you're some hotshot teen wolf with powers of an Alpha but you don't even know how to clean up after yourself. You don't even have Shane under control, you're an idiot, you're a stupid fucker who needs to be put in his place."

I said coolly, "Your message was delivered Wyatt, you can tell your Alpha that it was received and understood. Now you can kindly get your ass off my territory. Now!"

Wyatt's shoulders hunched and his thighs bunched, ready to leap on me then the door opened behind me, it was Dad, looking tired and confused. Wyatt swung around and walked away without another word. I watched him get into the car that was parked on the street, he cut a hard U-turn, burning the tires into the pavement and peeled off.

"Damn!" Dad stared after him. "What the hell is his problem?"

I said, "I have no idea Dad. He hates me, has this entire time. I can't figure it out. I asked once and I was told he's holding a grudge against me but for Christ's sake, I never did a thing to that guy. I don't know his deal, not at all."

Dad lightly popped my lip with his knuckle, saying, "Don't take the Lord's name in vain Xon, don't curse like that."

"Sorry."

I stepped in and closed the door behind us, leaning on it again. I told him about Shane's phone call and why Wyatt had came. I handed him the Rolex.

Dad's eyes bugged. "Holy shit...Xon." He stared at me. "This is a Rolex platinum Yachtmaster, this...this is well over eight thousand dollars. And he gave it to you, just like that? Just gave it away?"

I said plain and clear, "Dad, I don't give a damn about the watch." I covered my face with both hands, breathing out hard. "Yes, Shane hurt them but there was blood everywhere and I left it like that. Why didn't I think of cleaning it up? Dammit!"

"Xon, please," said Dad with an urgent lift to his voice.

I looked up at him, unable to soften the hard lines of my face, how I glared.

Dad took a step back but said, "This is all the more reason to get Shane under control. You've been saying it and you're right, he's pushing his limits, he's goading you into attacking him. Maybe he's not just trying to scare you off, maybe if he keeps making all of this mess and you're letting him get away with it, it looks bad on *you*, like you can't keep your subjects in line. Maybe Shane is supposed to be the leader but it's clear to everyone, including Shane, that *you* are the real leader."

"Those kids back there," He pointed towards the living room where snoring was still peacefully rumbling, "they have pledged allegiance to you Xon and they're getting caught in the crossfire. Sitting here feeling sorry for yourself isn't helping. It's sad and I'm sick and wish it didn't have to happen just like you. But unlike me, you have the power and way to do something about it."

He looked back at the watch in his hand then held it out to me.

"You keep it." I said, standing out the door and putting my hand on the knob. "Maybe pawn it and get the money to buy something nice for Mom or take her to dinner. We both need to find a way to apologize to her for what's been happening."

Dad rubbed his head and at the coarse sound, he said, "I have to shave. Xon." He glanced at me as he moved to the stairs. "Don't break any rules."

I half-smiled. "Dad, I won't do anything. She's sleeping anyway."

His eyes narrowed but he smiled and headed upstairs. I closed the door behind me, and stood on the front stoop.

My cell phone rang. I pulled it out, caller id said Toni.

I answered it. "Jaxon Reeves."

He said, "I saw Wyatt."

His voice was strange, it was calm and collected besides this note to it, a lilt. It wasn't fear…caution. Wary. He's never sounded liked that to me before but I had only met him once. His voice was rough and low in pitch, not deeper than Dad's. Yet as my neck hairs raised and the tips of my fingers tingled, I knew the werewolf on the other side of this phone was powerful in a way I hadn't yet understood. A power that I had just tapped into it without knowing how.

I burst into an explanation. "I didn't touch him, I didn't attack him. That cut, I-"

He cut me off. "Wyatt told me exactly what happened, so don't worry. I'm not going to come after you. Xon, do you know what it means or what it takes to hurt another wolf, to draw blood without touching? Have you done that before, ever?" His tone was steely, solid.

I sat on the stoop and pulled my knees up to my face. It was midday and the sun's rays were heating up the pavement, the cars. There was no wind and the air was thick, muggy. I used my arm to shield my eyes.

I said, "Wyatt told me I'm a hotshot teen wolf with the powers of an Alpha. What does he mean by that? Toni, there are things happening to me that I don't understand, that I can't explain."

"Tell me."

I breathed slowly and told him about when Leo wouldn't let me go and this power came up from my wolf, it was mighty and strong and when I spoke it out of my voice, Leo listened immediately when before he wasn't responding to me. I told him about being in the shower with Sky and Connor, how we melded that power together and used it to heal Connor from the inside out. Then I told my side of what happened with Wyatt, how the power built up and I slammed it out of my voice and that was when Wyatt got a cut on his cheek.

"I don't know how it works. And I don't really know how to call it, sometimes it comes on its own. I don't even know what it is."

Toni was quiet for about five minutes and I didn't interrupt or say anything else, I knew he was thinking.

Then he sighed quietly and said, "You are a dominant wolf Xon and somehow, you grew into it amazingly fast."

I said, "Brenda told me to become dominant you are either born or it's earned."

"Yes but it can also be learned." He said. "Someone can learn to be dominant by practice and meditation but it's very difficult and takes years. In your case Xon…I think you became dominant through a mixture of earning and learning. Not only that but you've developed into pure dominance."

My eyes widened and my stomach watered just a bit.

I tightened it hard and asked, "Pure dominance?"

"It's an extremely rare ability for dominant wolves." He said. "The power you felt coming out of you, it's dominance, the aura of dominance, the power of your wolf. And it can be used not only to command your voice and your eyes, but to cause pain. You could crush the power of someone else, force them to their knees, to physically submit. With Wyatt, you flung that aura out of you, you

The Other Side 278

slashed it through your voice and it cut Wyatt, it hit him and sliced him. As Brenda also told you, marks made by a dominant wolf take longer to heal. Wyatt's cut continues to bleed."

My eyes widened. "But it's been like twenty minutes already, and it was so tiny, it should have been healed."

"You're not listening Xon," said Toni, irritation tightening his voice. "I said you're not just dominant anymore; you have *pure* dominance. It's not going to heal, it's not going to stop bleeding, not so easily or quickly."

I said, "But Wyatt is more dominant than me, he-"

Toni cut me off, this time his voice was calm and to the point. "Wyatt is not a dominant wolf, not in the way you are thinking. He is simply furious every time he's around you, he's always at the brink of homicide when you are in his presence. That's the only reason you think he's dominant. Yes, he's not a weak-willed wolf or a pushover but he certainly is not Alpha material, he can lead the Scouts but nothing more than that. He is strong enough on his own but will always be a follower."

I placed my hand on my forehead, my shoulders hunched. "Are you saying I'm more dominant than Shane now? Shane keeps beating me, though last time it was me who won. The next fight will settle it, fight in wolf form at the field at midnight. Either way, I can't let Shane win Toni, I know he's older but Leo and Connor, he'll destroy them. Toni, what am I supposed to do exactly? I've never fought in wolf form before."

It was true I had play fought with Leo a few times but play fighting versus seriously trying to hurt someone else was entirely different.

"You fight Xon." He said in a tone that suggested I was somewhat stupid for asking. "What do you want from me, to give you a guidebook? In wolf form, fighting is just like in human form only with fangs and claws. You bite, you slash, you slam, it's fighting, period."

A. E. Costello 279

Toni took in a breath, held it then let it out and spoke through a sigh. "If you're that worried about it, I give you permission to come into the city, make sure you have a gift and I'll have one of my members give you a quick lesson in fighting in wolf form."

I asked, "Are you going to offer Shane this deal?"

"Why should I?" Toni responded with a question. "To make it fair? It's not about being fair, if Shane doesn't have any way of preparing himself for the fight, especially if this is his first time fighting in wolf form, that's his folly and it's not mine or your problem. You're thinking like a little kid Xon, talking about cheating and fairness. Quit it and start thinking like an Alpha. You may not officially be Alpha but you're definitely already in that position. You have a Pack to run, Packmembers to take care of. The fact is, if you lose the fight, it's over."

"Alpha of the United States Law plainly states that if an Alpha loses the fight against a challenger, he cannot be Alpha again. So unless you're prepared to be booted from your spot forever, get your ass over here and get trained. Let me be clear, if you guys were a *real* Pack and not a bunch of teenagers, I wouldn't offer you my help, something like getting prepared for a challenge is always the Alpha's responsibility and his alone; so consider yourself lucky. I'll have you trained tonight then for the fight I'll come to referee personally. Alright?"

I nodded quickly, my stomach quivering.

I asked, "What's the chance I'll die from this fight?"

"Little to none at all," said Toni without pause, my stomach calmed. "First off and most important, I'm going to be there. I won't stand there and watch as the two of you start ripping out throats, once I decide you or Shane has been injured enough and can't fight anymore, I'm ending it. So all you need to worry about is just doing your best, there's absolutely no need for either of you to die. It's about one in the afternoon, I'll see you at my house at five, be on time."

He gave me his address then he hung up.

I put the phone in my pocket and hearing some sounds from the living room, I headed there. Sky was awake with Connor and Leo's heads and arms curled into her lap. Javier was also awake, laying on the floor rubbing his pot belly, he met my eyes and smiled but didn't stand up.

I knelt in front of Sky, looking into her hazel-gold eyes. "You okay?"

"I'm fully healed." She said, touching the side of her face that Shane had done his best to destroy. The reddish brown skin was smooth and soft like creamy butter. "And I can see fine. I have been a werewolf for five years and I've never lost an eye before. The fact that it honestly grew back, well." She shrugged, a smile on her face. "It makes me wonder if I'd really go back to being human if I had the choice."

I didn't expect her to say that, and thought back to my broken ribs and fractured skull, how quickly they healed. Also the times I had been knocked unconscious but with the help of my Packmates also easily healed. If Dad got hurt on the job he could be laid up in the hospital for months but if he was a wolf, he would shake it off and be perfectly healthy in just moments.

Sky leaned back against her hands, regarding me with a cool look. "So, what's the news? You fighting Shane or what?"

I told her about his phone call and the one I had with Toni.

Javier sat up straight in a quick sudden lift of his upper body, his eyes focused on me. "You cut this Wyatt with just the power of your voice?"

I nodded, asking, "So you know about it Javier?"

"Most of the males in my family are all purely dominant." He admitted as his cheeks paled. "My uncles and my father, some older cousins. I have seen them force other wolves to their face, prostrated flat to the ground with the strength of their dominance. My father has done it to me several times, it is like having the sky fall onto my back and pin me to the ground. Like my bones are all splintering, like my lungs are flat as a pancake."

He looked into my shocked face. "The aura of a wolf Xon, the power of the wolf, the dominant ability is incredible but also mysterious. In truth, I have been noticing how quickly you have grown but I did not think you would develop to this degree."

I mimicked Sky's pose, putting my arms behind me and leaning against them, my fingers curled in the carpet.

I said, "But does this mean I will be able to defeat Shane?"

"Dominance doesn't equal fighting ability," said Sky. "But if you really are getting trained by some wolves at the Stone Pack then I'm sure that'll give you an upper-hand at the least. I honestly should be getting home, my parents and siblings are probably going crazy worried about me. Then I'll come be at the fight at midnight."

We both started to gently shake Leo and Connor, saying their names and rubbing their faces and neck. Connor woke up first, his brown eyes dazed and warm, before he blinked it away and sat up. I tucked my arms underneath Leo's armpits and brought him into a sitting position, he laid limply against me at first before holding himself up. Connor licked his hand then rubbed it at his eyes, removing the crust there.

I laughed. "Connor, are you a cat or a wolf?"

He smiled as he lowered his hand, blinking. "I am a wolf, really. What are we doing now?"

"Going home. I know my parents are worried for sure," said Sky. "Shane and Xon are going to fight in wolf form at midnight tonight, so we'll see each other again in a couple hours."

Connor's peachy skin paled a sickly yellow and his eyes dimmed, he looked at his lap. His scent gushed the dank lifelessness of depression, the fetidness of despair and other sickening emotions like anxiety, hopelessness, fear and the twisted mint of knowing. It made him stink, he smelled awful because of his emotions.

I said with the touch of a growl to my voice, "Connor, tell me what's wrong."

"It's nothing." He said in a stilted automatic voice, still staring at the floor.

Sky said, "Connor, you can't possibly think that holds up, do you?"

"It doesn't matter." He got to his feet. "Nothing matters."

I got up and caught his wrist. "Connor, if you'd talk to me then I could fix it, I know it."

Connor looked me in the eyes, his brown eyes had darkened to black, already turning into cold dead pits.

He said flatly, "Xon, if you can't fight Shane and win, then there's no way you can fight Carter and live. He's nothing like Shane; if Shane is the first level boss, then Carter is the final boss. Unmatched, understand?"

This wasn't the first time Connor had used something to compare Shane and Carter and I got what he was saying. I didn't like the idea of Connor getting hurt by Shane at school then hurt by Carter at home. I remembered what he said in the shower, that he had tried to kill himself but because he was a werewolf the attempts failed.

So I said, "One day you'll trust in me enough Connor to let me help."

I looked around at everyone else. "I'll walk you guys all home, okay? Just in case Shane shows up."

Connor nodded, and everyone else got ready to go. Dad came down the stairs after I called up we were leaving. He smiled at my Pack, like a father watching his family.

Dad said, "You guys stay safe out there, alright? If stuff gets too rough, you're always welcome here, okay?"

Everyone nodded, but it was Leo who came forward to get a hug. Dad's eyes widened in shock and his scent burst with tingly lemon, but he smiled and patted Leo's back.

A. E. Costello 283

"Learn to protect yourself." He said to him when Leo stepped back. "Don't lay back and get beat up. I don't know everything about wolf politics, but with Xon in charge, you won't have to be a punching bag. Right?"

Leo nodded and while his face didn't emote, I smelled the tingling orange of happiness and hope, like fluffy sweet cotton.

"See you in a minute Dad." I said, giving a two finger wave as I led the way out.

Even though it wasn't in order of where everyone lived, we walked Javier and Leo home safe first. We all smelled Shane around the premises, just like he had told me, he had scouted out all of their houses and called me when he realized no one was at home. Just the same way Brenda told me not to wander off alone, my Packmates needed to make sure they weren't setting themselves up to be jumped by Shane.

My fists clenched at the idea, remembering Leo getting beaten, the horrible wounds on Connor and Sky.

No matter what, I have to protect my Pack.

Connor again didn't want me to take him to the door, but I did. I walked up the pathway, ignoring Connor clasping my arm and tugging on me. Sky waited at the sidewalk, keeping a lookout. I banged on the door. It didn't take but a moment for it to open and I came nose-to-nipple with the infamous Carter Hawkins.

He had two inches on the six-three Leo, taller than Shane and Dad, me included. He was only wearing a pair of jeans ripped at the knees and his pants were unzipped, hanging low on his hips. His cream-colored chest was broad and covered with a thick pelt of black hair, his belly then arrowed down to disappear below the waistband of his briefs. I dragged my eyes up to see his face.

He looked nothing like the smooth-faced Connor. Carter had a rugged roughly-cut face, a long straight nose, wedged jaw and his eyes were bright red with a circle black pupil, his wolf spark fiery gold in the black depths. His hair was black, cut and trimmed neatly, professionally. It didn't match the large pecs, the thick rippling abs and his bulky arms. I had always thought Dad was the most muscled man, then I saw Wyatt but this wolf even beat out Wyatt.

I took a step back as I breathed in deep and got his werewolf scent, dark and musky, it smelled hotter than mine, more dangerous. Adult. He also had this odorous tinge to him, raw and pungent, thick and offensive to my nose. It wasn't body odor as in like he hadn't showered, the odor was the smell of his wolf. This man's wolf smelled rotten from the inside. It was so thickly clouded around him, I couldn't break past it to get to his personal scent, in fact, I didn't want to smell him at all anymore. It was only my well-mannered upbringing that prevented me from putting my hand over my nose, I may dislike him but I wasn't going to be straight up rude to him at his own house.

Carter blinked down at me then looked over my head where Sky stood, staring. He cocked his head slightly to the side, like a curious puppy then lowered his eyes back to me. His nostrils flared and he took a delicate sniff, his brow went up then a smile curved, revealing slightly pointed teeth.

"Ah." He said, his voice was throaty, slow and amused with a thrum of a Southern accent. "You must be the Alpha."

Though unsettled at the sight of this massive wolf, I stood straighter. "So you know who I am?"

"Of course." His voice was low and his lashes were long, they lowered, shuttering his eyes but my skin itched as his gaze traveled down my body. "Connor never shuts up about you. Besides." His hand clasped my chin and he tilted my face up. "Your scent is all over him. It's disgusting."

I tossed my head away from him and realized this had to be like the third time someone said my scent was sickening or disgusting.

A. E. Costello 285

I lifted up my chin and said as firm and clear as I could, "I decided to come meet you in person. I wanted to let you know that whatever you're doing to Connor that's hurting him has to stop. Today."

Carter's red eyes narrowed into slits then he glanced at Connor hovering at my side. Connor flinched but rather than cling to me or speak up for himself, he edged around Carter and went into the house.

"Connor!" I called out and took a step forward.

Carter put his hand on my chest and pushed me back. He didn't push me hard, just enough to stumble me back two steps but his hand was an anvil or some other heavy weight. Shane was strong but this was like a kitten paw versus a lion paw, no, a goldfish compared to a great white. Connor hadn't been lying when he compared Shane and Carter. This wolf was seriously strong, and he could take out Brenda if he wanted.

Carter said, his voice sharp like knives, "Connor is my son and I'll treat him how I want. You'd better butt out little Alpha before I decide to show you who's place you belong. Now get the fuck off my property boy, you've got ten seconds."

My fists clenched and that power in my wolf rumbled, billowing up my throat. Sky clasped my arm, when she had walked up, I didn't know.

She said, "Let's go Xon, please. You don't want to get in a fight with Connor's father, not like this."

I nodded but kept my eyes on Carter as I walked backwards down the pathway. Carter smiled, his pink lips spreading upwards and baring white sharp teeth in a gruesome parody of a smile. His expression looked like he was imagining killing me while my back was turned, or maybe hurting Connor in front of me while I couldn't do anything about it. When I hit the sidewalk, off his property, he slowly closed the door then locked it.

Sky squeezed my arm as I stood there, staring. "Xon, I know that was hard to do but I've got to get home. We'll figure this out, we'll stop Carter, I promise. Just not now, we can't do anything now."

"He's hurting him." I said, my voice twisted with a growl. "The moment Connor is away from me, Carter is doing something to him. I can't let it continue."

"I know, I feel the same way." Sky tugged on my arm then started to walk away, so I came with her. "Still the fact remains Carter is Connor's father, and unless we either one, convince Carter to stop doing whatever he's doing that hurts Connor, or two, get Connor somewhere else away from Carter so that Carter can't hurt him anymore, there's really nothing we can do."

She made sense but I was sick of the can't, sick of the helplessness. So I ended up not saying anything.

Sky said, "This is my house."

We had stopped outside of a red brick house with a black roof, the lane was lined with yellow and blue flowers. There was a very small totem pole in the middle of the lawn, only about four feet tall. There was a raven, a falcon, a skylark and a wolf. The wolf was at the top and looked newer than the rest because it was a brighter wood and not as weather worn.

"Falcon did that," said Sky, shaking her head. "My parents decided the wolf was a protective spirit and let it stay."

She led me up the way then knocked on the door.

She said, "I don't bring my keys or cell phone to the forest, I'll lose them."

There was thudding footsteps then the door blasted open with an enthusiastic shout. "I got it!"

The young boy there had to be Falcon, about twelve years old. He was tall, maybe five-eleven, long-limbed with a thick black braid that swept his ankles. He stared at me with narrowed hazel-gold eyes and the first thing he looked was directly into my eyes, he grinned the moment my wolf spark flickered gold.

He said, "Falcon Cloud."

He stuck his hand out.

I took it.

"Jaxon Reeves."

I shook very gently but he winced and I quickly let him go. He shook his hand but grinned even wider.

"Nice grip," he said.

His scent was overloaded with the sharp oil of confidence and twisted mint, knowing. I glanced at Sky, she was staring Falcon down.

He grinned again and backed up, shouting over his shoulder, "Mom! Dad! Sky's got a boyfriend!"

"You little monster!"

Sky swiped for him but Falcon ducked, her hand snatched on air and he scrambled away, laughing. "Sky's got a boyfriend! Mom, Dad, Sky brought a boyfriend!"

Sky growled as she let me in and closed the door behind me.

A girl glided into the front hallway from down the hallway. She looked like a taller slimmer younger version of Sky. Her hair was straight and dropped to her hips. Her eyes were hazel-gold just like the rest of her siblings but much wider and rounder than Sky's, luminous circles in her small face.

"Sky." She sighed, her voice soft and breathy. "I was wondering when you were coming back." She turned those giant eyes on me, she smiled knowingly, her scent the soft cotton of understanding and acceptance. "And who are you Mr. Wolf?"

I winced but said, "Jaxon Reeves. And please don't call me that."

"Of course not." She bowed with a sweeping motion of her arms then clasped her hands on her stomach, looking at Sky again. "I hope you weren't being a bad girl Sky."

She said it with a sweet smile but I suddenly envisioned fangs on that small pert mouth. She was being gentle and kind but I knew there was a force on the inside not to be reckoned with. I was afraid for when she grew up, no man would be able to handle her.

Sky glared at her but said, "Xon, this is my younger sister, Raven Cloud."

Raven smiled again. "Hello Mr. Reeves."

"Xon is fine." I said, a tightening in my spine. Her huge hazel-gold eyes seemed to be staring right into me, through me, seeing everything.

Sky said sharply, "Enough Raven. You're purposely creeping him out. Stop it already."

"Yes, naturally." Raven blinked and glided away down the hall, her black hair floated behind her like a cape.

I stared then looked at Sky. "Can you explain that just now?"

Sky heaved a large breath. "She's very mystical, spacey and into spirits, being of the other world. You'll get used to her."

I asked, "How old is she? She acted like she was the older."

"She's fourteen."

Sky's parents walked from the hallway. Well, the tall one walked and a short dumpy one ran and jumped into Sky's arms.

"Skylark! You're back, you're home!"

I blinked and realized this was the man, her father. He was just under Sky's height at five-feet tall, with a thick body and his black hair came to his hips. He clasped Sky's face with his wide fat hands and kissed her nose.

"I was wondering what had happened to you!"

His voice was breathy and soft, like Raven's. His eyes were hazel-gold, the color he had passed on to all three of his children.

"Honey. Can't you see we have company?"

The tall woman was my height, six feet and she was where Falcon was getting his height from. She had astonishing white hair and white brows but her red brown skin was smooth, she was ageless. She could be between thirty to sixty. Her eyes were steel gray, and she looked right into me.

She ordered, "Name, now."

I straightened my back, held my shoulders firm. "Jaxon Reeves."

"Age?"

"Seventeen."

"Grade?"

"A junior."

"Employed?"

"No ma'am."

"Car?"

"Yes ma'am."

"Parents married?"

"Yes ma'am."

"Do they have jobs?"

Now I was starting to get annoyed but I answered politely, "Yes they do. My father is in construction and Mom is a receptionist."

Sky's mother looked down at my clothes. I managed not to look too but I knew I was wearing fresh jeans and clean sneakers. Her eyes narrowed and she looked at Sky who was trying to peel her father off her. Raven and Falcon had come back, Raven's eyes were bright while Falcon was grinning.

"Skylark." Mother Bird spoke crisply. "Where have you been? Who is this boy? How dare you bring him into my home without any warning? You never mentioned a boyfriend and I'm not happy."

"Oh stop it!" Father Bird squealed and clapped his hands together, his hazel-gold eyes bounced between us. "They look great together! He's tall and handsome and so smart-sounding! I like him. Skylark, my elegant bird, when did you meet?"

Elegant bird? I'm starting to see why she wants to be called Sky and not Skylark.

Sky said, "We met earlier this semester."

Mother Bird's eyes narrowed into slits. "The semester has barely started Skylark, it's been two weeks. Did you meet him over summer vacation?"

I opened my mouth to explain I had a girlfriend over the summer but she hissed venomously, "I am talking to my daughter."

I shut my mouth and stared up at the ceiling.

Yikes. She's worse than Mom. Lord please, don't let them meet.

Sky shook her head. "No, really, we met like last week. Besides, Xon had a girlfriend over the summer. They broke up just before school started."

Mother Bird turned those hard grey eyes on me. "So you bounce from girl to girl? Flit from relationship to relationship? Is my daughter one of many, just another notch in the bedpost?"

I spoke, "We're not officially together, first thing. Second thing, and I'm man enough to tell you this, but I am a virgin. We both are."

Father Bird gasped and his eyes went wide. He tugged on Mother Bird's stiff hands. "Come now sweetie, you can stop the hawk act."

Mother Bird breathed in and let it out slow, a shudder rolled down her shoulders, arms and her legs, just like a bird rustling her feathers. She smiled at me. Her hard gray eyes lightened to almost silver and I swear I was looking at Sky's wolf eyes.

She held out her hand. "My name is Anna." She gave me a strong firm shake. "And this is my wife Nosh." She placed her hand on the father's round shoulder.

I blinked then said, "You meant husband. In our culture, the man is the husband and the woman is the wife."

Nosh bit his chubby lower lip and looked up at Anna to speak for him, his eyes worried and hesitant, his scent matched.

Anna's smile firmed at the corners, her eyes hardened back to that harsh gray. "I never said I was apart of your culture Reeves and therefore I can call my wife whatever I want to call him."

I took a step back, if she had fangs she would have flashed them.

I said, "Yes ma...sir."

Anna tossed her shoulder-length white hair back as she laughed, a gentle soothing sound, totally at odds with her militant exterior. "You may call me ma'am, it's fine. However, Nosh would prefer to be called ma'am, don't call him sir."

Nosh wiggled uncomfortably next to Anna and muttered something under his breath but I caught it. He said *stop calling me him.*

I glanced at Sky, she gave me a weak smile and shrugged one shoulder.

Anna watched us closely then said, "Well would you like to come in Reeves? You can join us for lunch if you'd like."

"Call me Xon please." I said. "And yes, that'll be great."

Nosh and Anna stood back so Sky and I could leave the doorway. Raven wanted to speak to Sky privately but Nosh wanted to come too, so the three ladies left. Anna excused herself to start lunch, leaving me with Falcon in the living room.

Falcon grinned at me, he hadn't dropped it yet. "So, wolf guy, you're the Alpha around here, huh?"

My eyes widened and I glanced towards the kitchen. Anna was playing a radio interview loudly and Falcon was talking quietly.

I said softly, with a growl to my tone, "The name is Xon, not wolf guy or Mr. Wolf or anything like it. And yeah, I'm the Alpha so maybe you should show some respect."

Falcon lunged at me, I grasped his collar before he could hit me but he grabbed my shoulders tightly and spoke in a low hiss, "Bite me Xon, let me be like you."

"Hell no." I growled.

He was nearing six feet but my grasp on his collar lifted him up off the ground. I swung him around and dropped him on the sofa. He bounced then jumped back up with a swiftness that I hadn't expected.

Falcon stared me down. "I looked it up once I figured it out about Sky. It's not saliva, kissing or licking won't do it. It has to be blood, a bite. Sky won't do it, but you will, I know you will."

I stepped back from him, the words *you're crazy* on the tip of my tongue when Sky and Raven entered the living room, Nosh went into the kitchen.

Sky looked at me, my high shoulders, body tense and at Falcon, who quickly straightened up. Sky's eyes narrowed into slits and they flashed silver.

Raven said, "Falcon, you aren't pestering the wolfman are you?"

My fists knuckled but Falcon said, "He wants to be called Xon. And no." He looked at me, his chin lifted. "We were just making ourselves clear."

"Crystal clear Falcon." I said, striving not to growl at him.

Sky sighed heavily and moved to stand by me, I placed my arm around her shoulders so I wouldn't make a fist, my other hand I shoved into my pocket. Raven flitted over to Falcon and touched his shoulder, they both sat down on the sofa and Sky and I sat on the loveseat.

It was stingingly silent. Falcon was staring at me, his grin finally gone, while Raven gently rocked back and forth, either not aware of the awkwardness or not minding it.

Sky finally said, "Falcon, we've been over this."

He leaned forward, his lips peeling back in a very wolfish like snarl. His voice came out low and tight. "I know everything about it Sis, I've looked it up and I know its what I want."

I gritted my teeth before I said *you're insane.*

I said instead, "You're only seeing the highlights Falcon but even those are huge downturns. Super strength? Yeah, but you can't let anyone see you throwing cars with one hand or kicking holes through steel walls because its considered dangerous to society and then you'll get locked up. Super fast? True but if humans see you running so fast you're blurring that's dangerous, it raises suspicion. Super hearing, super sight but you'd better not let any human tell what you're doing. All sounds great but Falcon, you can't use any of it when you're in the public eye. Humans are tolerant of shifters but only if we act as human as possible. Once you start showing how inhumanly strong and fast you are, you'll make life a lot harder for the rest of us."

Falcon's hands clenched into fists but he closed his eyes and sucked in a deep breath in his nose and slowly let it out of his mouth. His hands relaxed as he calmed.

Hazel eyes on me, he said, "I know it, I know all of that." He looked at Sky, who's bowed head was shaking slowly from side to side. "I've seen Sky at it, I know what its like and I know I can do it. I want to do it!"

I was getting seriously pissed now with a burnt irritation scent steaming from my body. I glanced to the kitchen. They were out of sight, talking along with the loud radio. As long as we kept our voices down, there was no way to be overheard.

I faced Falcon again, my voice was hard and snarling, "Look kid, you're acting like this is some group or clique you want to join or a team or a club you're asking membership for. It's not like that, that's not how it works. Once you're a werewolf, that's it, there's no take-backs, there's no do-over's or reversals. Once a wolf, always a wolf. And if you Change then decide you can't handle it and don't want to do it, then its too fucking bad because it'll be too late. The only other option would be death, got it?"

Falcon paled under his red brown skin, mottling his skin dark grey. Sky placed a hand on my knee and I let out a long breath. I didn't mean to speak too harshly but he was being so flippant about something that's a huge deal.

Shy looked at her younger brother, speaking softly, "He's right Falcon. And I can't take the chance of that happening to you. Being a werewolf is a lot harder than it seems and a lot more goes into it than having some super abilities and a wolf form. It's a *life* change Falcon, everything completely changes and it doesn't go backwards, like he said, there's no reversals. Falcon, you're just a boy, a kid and right now you're a little obsessive. I'm positive if you keep living the way you are you'll have changed your mind."

Falcon's eyes darkened, a thundercloud formed over his face and his cheeks reddened. His scent flooded sour milk of uneasiness mixed with faint weakness of uncertainty and all of it tied up with the heat of anger.

"I am twelve years old, not two years old." His voice was stiff and firm. "I'm basically a man already and I know what I want. I told you, I've seen you Sky and I've researched it, I've made my mind."

I opened my mouth when Nosh walked in, wearing a bright red apron with pink hearts all over it. He said in his soft sweet voice, "Lunch is almost ready. If you'd all wash your hands and faces please. Xon, help me set the table."

Nosh smiled and gestured to me to come to him.

I hesitated, looking at Sky, she gave me a wide-eyed glance then stood, saying, "Falcon, Raven, you know what to do."

Falcon stormed to his feet, snapped, "I'm not hungry."

He took off into the bowels of the house.

Raven sighed and gracefully stood, saying in a voice like her father's, "I shall tame the wild falcon."

She drifted off after her younger brother.

Sky moaned and took my hand. "Mama, I'll take Xon to wash his hands and face."

Nosh pouted. "But I wanted to talk to him alone."

"Later," said Sky, tugging on me and walked away.

I followed, my mind whirling and I said, "No offense Sky, but your family is weird."

Sky laughed heartily, letting me into a medium-sized guest bathroom, it had two sinks.

She said, "Xon, I can't take offense. I've been raised with them, I know how weird we are."

I washed my hands first then saw the pile of washcloths on each side of the sink.

I said, "Do I really need to wash my face too?"

"Yup," said Sky, dampening her face with water then soaping up a cloth.

I didn't complain, just used the materials to wash my face then I joined her parents in the dining room. Falcon and Raven weren't there.

Anna's eyes narrowed into dark slits and she focused her hawk stare on Sky. "Skylark, where are your siblings?"

Sky said, "Falcon said he wasn't hungry so Raven went to talk to him. They might come back later."

Nosh pressed his fingers together. "Oh no, we can't eat without them. Skylark my elegant bird, please go bring Falcon and Raven to the table. I can't bear for them to go hungry."

Sky paused but Anna said, "Do as your mother told you Skylark, don't embarrass us in front of company."

"Yes Papa." Sky left the table, though her hand gently brushed the back of my neck as she exited the room.

Nosh turned his hazel-gold eyes on me. "Now then, tell me about yourself."

I looked at my empty plate, and hid my hands under the table in case nerves made my claws grow.

"I'm not sure what I can say." I looked up with a quick smile. "Your wi…husband already took my stats."

Anna grinned at me and it was like looking at a female older version of Falcon. "True but Nosh is interested in the internal parts of you, not your stats. Like your feelings for our oldest child."

My eyes went really wide but I looked at Nosh, who was leaning forward and his fingers curled against the wooden table.

"Uh…I like her, a whole lot, more than I've liked any other girl before. I mean." I looked at my plate again. "She's so feisty, and she's not afraid to yell at me or get angry. She doesn't let anyone push her around and she knows how to say no, she'll never let anyone get the best of her. Sky is."

I sighed and relaxed against my chair, this time looking at the ceiling. I shrugged and looked at Nosh, he was staring at me with teary eyes.

"She's mine," is what came out and I couldn't even blush because I meant it.

Anna's white brows arched. "I know my child, she wouldn't want to be claimed."

I thought about Sky being my mate, about me being the only one she would kiss, make love to. I didn't say anything because Sky was coming back with both of her siblings. Sky took her seat next to me, then Falcon and Raven across from us, while Nosh and Anna were sitting at opposite ends at the head and foot of the table.

Anna lead the prayer then everyone served themselves. The conversation was light, Anna and Nosh had been satisfied by the grilling they had done and I wasn't the sole subject of the talk. Falcon had been quiet and sullen at first but after a few minutes his grin came back and he was laughing and sharing tales about being with his friends at school. Listening to Raven talk about her mediation and how she was certain she was learning how to talk to animals, I took back that I said Sky's family was weird. She had an amazing family, Falcon who was rough and tumble, so sure and confident of himself. Raven, gentle and sweet yet also full of surety in her world. Nosh and Anna who had switched the considered normal gender roles yet both loved their children fiercely. Anna would make for a scarily powerful Alpha queen. In fact, she would be the

Alpha and Nosh would be the lesser non-dominate wolf. I had never heard of a female ruling a Pack but if it was possible, it would be Anna.

After lunch, Anna and Nosh relaxed in the living room while Sky and I cleaned up. Dishes done, I made my goodbyes to the Cloud's. Falcon shook my hand again and his eyes looked straight into mine, he didn't have to speak, I knew he hadn't given up, he hadn't changed his mind. Raven hugged me with a kiss to my chin and drifted away. Then Sky walked me to the door.

"I take it back." I said to her. "Your family isn't weird. I wish I had siblings."

I stopped abruptly, pain stabbed me in the chest. I *did* have siblings. Two, older than me, who had never been born, never named but they had existed, at one point, they had been alive.

Sky put her hand on my shoulder and said softly, "It's okay Xon, really, it's okay. You may have grown up an only child but with the rest of us now, Connor, Javier, Leo, we're your family. We're your sisters and brothers."

"Just brothers." I said, looking at her. "I can't see you as my sister. And if I did, that means there's something wrong with me."

Sky slowly smiled. "Then that means something is wrong with me too."

There was a cough from the living room, Anna. "Skylark, honey, come inside now."

Sky looked up at me. "I guess you'd better go." Her voice was soft.

I tipped Sky's chin up and placed a light kiss on her lips. "Goodnight Sky. I'll see you after school tomorrow."

Sky nodded, her golden eyes gazed at me. "See you."

I walked away and looked over my shoulder, she was still in the doorway, watching me. Sky wasn't dependent or needy or wounded like Leo and Connor, she didn't need me like that at all. But I wanted her with me, I wanted her at my side.

I waved, she waved back and I jogged home. I came inside and at the sound of sniffling, I dashed into the living room. Dad was sitting next to Mom with his arm around her shoulders. Mom sat on the couch with a tissue clenched in her shaking fist and looked at me with red-strained eyes.

She spoke, her voice hoarse, "I thought you were out fighting again. I thought you weren't coming back."

I went to Mom and knelt, I took her free hand, it was soft, damp and I placed it on my face.

I said softly against her skin, "I'll try to do better, I really will. Time got away from me, okay? I was with my friends then I went to Sky's house to meet her family. Please Mom, don't cry."

I kissed her hand then her wrist. I wrapped my arms around her waist and snuggled my head into her stomach, and kissed there.

Mom jumped and placed her hands on my face, pushing me back and her voice shook with laughter. "Xon! That's too much, get off me."

I let her go as I stood up and Dad stood up too, he put his arm around my neck. "He has a girlfriend now, he'll have to learn new ways to apologize for being such a knucklehead."

Mom stared up at me, rubbing her hand against her stomach where I kissed her. "Yes well..." She stood up and sighed slow, placing her head on my chest, her hand on Dad's chest. "You two are both grown up. Not boys."

"I haven't been a boy for a long time Kyra." Dad gently touched Mom's chin and his thumb pressed on her lower lip, she blushed and lowered her lashes. "And Xon, well." He looked at me, his dark brown eyes were deep and soft. "He's growing up too."

For a moment, we stood there then Mom backed up. "Are you hungry Xon? Did you eat?"

I nodded. "I ate at Sky's house but I'm more than willing to eat some more. Did you make lunch? Is there enough for me?"

A. E. Costello 299

"We ate already son," said Dad, his hand placed on my head, feeling the contours of my skull. "But there are leftovers, you can eat that."

I went into the fridge, took out all the pots and plastic ware, then I ate standing up at the counter, I didn't reheat anything. I cleaned my mess then found Dad in the living room, cross-legged on the floor, reading the Bible. I didn't like to interrupt him, but it was already going on four pm and I didn't want to be late to Toni's house.

I sat down in front of him and waited for him to give me his attention.

Dad spoke, his eyes still on the page. "Luke 10:27. *And he answered, "You shall love the Lord your God with all your heart and with all your soul and with all your strength and with all your mind, and your neighbor as yourself."* Xon, do you love the Lord?"

I bit my lower lip as the word *yes* didn't immediately come. I thought about this supposed Moon goddess, I thought about how sometimes I thought like God was answering my prayers and other times I felt totally abandoned.

Dad looked at me with his dark eyes. "Why no answer son? You've been in church every Sunday since you were in the womb. You are my son Xon and I love you, but in my house, we will serve the Lord. You understand?"

I nodded and said, "I do understand. Dad, I have to go into Mountain Ridge so I wanted to let you know I was leaving."

He tilted his head to the side. "Isn't Mountain Ridge where that Pack lives? You'll need a gift."

I groaned. "I totally forgot about that! And I already handed over my chain. And yes, I'm getting trained for the fight tonight, the Alpha offered."

Dad sighed and said, "Alright, I'll cover the gift. But about the fight." He stared me down, his jaw buckled. "Your mother is worried enough about you Xon."

"Dad, we spoke about this." I rubbed my forehead. "And you know what I have to do. Toni is coming to referee the fight himself, he said he won't let either of us die and that he'll stop the fight the moment he decides one of us has had enough. So don't worry."

Even as I said it, worry stiffened my jaw and I looked at the floor. Dad cupped my chin and lifted my head up so our eyes met.

"You will win Xon." He said, his hand making me nod. "Leo and Connor are dependent on you, they need you. I've never seen looks on people's faces that deep, that desperate. They watch you constantly, like if they take their eyes off you you'd disappear. They are afraid of abandonment, afraid of you leaving them. They're too young, fifteen and seventeen, such young lives, to feel like this."

I said, "Leo's past has made him like that and Shane's rough treatment hasn't helped. Connor has something really bad happening at home that he refuses to talk about. Yes, they're very needy now but I hope that I can get them better. Heal them."

Dad lowered his hand from my chin and rubbed at the back of his neck. "People like that, who are that broken, it takes therapy, lots of therapy and help before they even know there's a problem, then they have to be convinced to change their situation, change how they feel. It takes years and you aren't a therapist Xon, you aren't a licensed psychiatrist. They need professional help."

Dad was right, he made sense but at the same time, it didn't work like that, not for wolves.

I said, my face pulled down in a frown, "If they were human, then yes. But they aren't human, their minds and emotions can't be healed that way. What Leo and Connor need is a leader they can trust, someone who can calm and soothe them. They are hurting right now Dad and they need me to relax them, to feel safe and cared for. After a while, they'll feel better, be better and they won't be as needy. When I first met Leo, he didn't talk or make expressions."

I smiled. "But now he's already making more noises, he grunts, he coughs, he's making sounds and his face moves more. He's opening up. And Connor, he doesn't let himself get pushed around, he'll speak his opinion. He yelled at you too. He's not a victim…not with us."

"Talk to your mother first," said Dad after a minute of silence. "Everything I tell her is second-hand, and all she does is get upset. So get things straight with her, then you can go. She's in our room. Knock first."

"Okay." I headed upstairs to my parent's room and gently knocked on the door. "Mom? It's Xon. Can I come in?"

"Enter."

I parted the door and looked in, Mom was sitting on the bed, her head down. She was holding a photo album. I could see my baby pictures from here. I went and sat down next to her.

She spoke before I could. "Xon…your father has been trying to explain to me everything you're going through and that I should be more understanding. But its hard for me."

I looked at her, into her light brown eyes. "Because you hate shifters. You never told me why."

Mom glanced down at the pictures, breaking eye contact. "I just want you to be my son Xon. I don't want you to be a wolf, I don't want there to be any type of politics going on at school with some sort of power struggle and hierarchy. I just want my son, my baby boy."

I smiled a little. "Mom, sometimes I want that to, wish things were different. But at the same time, so much good has come from my new life, I don't want to." I looked at my hands now. "I…me and Sky…I feel something there, something I haven't felt before. Not with Melody, not with other girls I've ever had crushes on."

"I can't even be happy about that." She said, her voice growing quieter. "Sky is pretty, she's smart, she looks good with you. But when I see that spark in her eyes…I just…"

She trailed off into silence.

"Mom." I said. "You have to figure out this hatred on your own, I can't heal it. I have to go to the city for a little while, meet up with some friends. Then I have something to do at midnight, so I probably won't see you again until tomorrow morning or afternoon. I wanted to let you know now so you won't worry about me. So you don't have to cry."

Mom looked at me, but she looked at my forehead, very carefully not looking me in the eyes. "Jaxon Reeves, why are you being so secretive? What meeting? What friends? What can you possibly be doing at midnight?"

I said, "When you can look me in the eyes, I'll answer you."

Mom flinched as if I had popped her and looked away again, whispering, "Then good luck with whatever it is you're doing."

"I'll see you later."

I stood and left, lifting my chin to stop the tightness in my throat.

Dad was at the foot of the stairs by the garage door, he was holding my car keys and had a black box in his other hand.

"How'd it go?" He didn't hand over my keys.

I sighed and said, "Do you know why Mom hates shifters?"

Dad sighed and put the black box in my hand. "Here's your gift." Then he handed over the keys. "Just come back home safe. I bet I won't see you until tomorrow, right?"

I sucked my teeth but nodded as his eyes narrowed. "Sorry. And yeah, tomorrow. See ya then."

He watched me enter the garage and I flipped the switch to raise the doors. My car was a 2007 Subaru Forester, in silver. I hadn't been driving lately, not since I came back from California. I got in and pulled out. When I looked back, Mom and Dad were both in the doorway, watching me. I didn't know why the two of them were conspiring to keep the cause of Mom's hatred a secret. Secrets had done enough to us already and I've been trying to be honest and upfront from the start.

I had Toni's address, so I put it in the navigator on my phone and drove off. I played some soft rock music on the radio and focused on driving since I hadn't done it in a while. I raised my brows at the neighborhood I was entering. Toni's house was in the upper levels of Mountain Ridge, rising upward onto the mountain.

My phone told me I had arrived so I parked on the street, though there was another car parked along the sidewalk. Toni's house was five stories with a wraparound porch. There was a four car driveway and the garage doors were open, with a total of eight cars in each spot. The winding walkway curved around rosebushes and the green land was flecked with willow trees, their long crying branches reaching downwards.

I made sure I had the gift in my hand as I loped up the lane. The door opened once I came near. It was a Latina with red hair, bright blue eyes, dark gold skin; that same girl who I had been talking to when I got bit.

Leah.

My wolf stiffened at the sight of her and my hackles slowly rose. Her eyes widened and she stepped back, her scent flushed pissy ammonia, worry and anxiety. At the scent, I swallowed and shoved the bristling wolf inside of me back down. He jolted antsy inside of me, and the initial aggression he had expressed disappeared. Now that heart leap was back and he brushed closer against my chest, as if wanting to rub against Leah, spread his scent to her.

Struggling to ignore the conflict going on the inside, I said as calmly as I could, "It's been a while."

Her red lips parted in a smile but it fell when I didn't smile back. "Yeah, it has." She stepped back again and opened the door wider. "Come in Xon, take off your shoes here."

"Alright." I did so as she closed the door. "What now?"

"Come this way." She walked and I followed. "I've been hearing a lot from others, like Toni, Brenda and Wyatt. You're a new wolf, not even a full month and already challenging to be an Alpha. That's really something unusual. Even Ze'eva says there's a strange power at work."

"Who is Zay...what?" I asked.

"Ze'eva, pronounced Zay-eve-vah. She's the Pack mystic," said Leah, opening a door, revealing stairs.

We went downstairs, the temperature instantly began to get colder with each step down, we were going underground now.

Leah said, "The magic-user."

I stared at her. "Magic-user? Magic is real? Next you'll tell me the Tooth Fairy is real!"

Leah snorted, saying with a laugh, "Now you're getting silly Xon, of course the Tooth Fairy isn't real, that's a fairytale, made up by humans. Real fairies are rare by now though, I'm sure they live in places where humans can't get to them. You won't be meeting any of those any time soon."

We stepped off the stairs and down in a large open area with a dirt floor and brick walls. On one side there was a pile of cots stacked up together and a closet that was halfway open because too many things were stuffed inside of it, it looked like computers and other machines, like medical equipment actually.

Before I could ask, Leah said, "This is our Infirmary where our Healer, Dr. Will Norris, takes care of and heals sick werewolves, it's also here where pups are born. Anyway, Toni had us clear up all of this space so you can train here without anyone hearing anything or being bothered."

Rapid footsteps down the stairs shook the walls. I turned around at a thud as he jumped the last few steps. Antonius Stone walked towards me. I remembered what Toni looked like vaguely, like trying to recognize a face through a blurry photograph.

Toni was taller than my father and whipcord lean. His hair dyed electric blond, his brows stark black in contrast. His eyes were inhuman, just like how Carter had the red eyes of his wolf, Toni's eyes weren't normal. His irises were actually a darker black than his pupils, making his pupils seem gray. Add in the gold spark in his pupils and Toni definitely did not seem human. His scent though, I got the full whiff of the heavy dark must of a male werewolf but that was it. I couldn't smell, no I *didn't* smell his emotions. It was like he wasn't feeling anything at all.

With his gray slacks, white button-up shirt and his blond hair looked like it was brushed, he came off approachable and respectable. The top two buttons were undone, showing his collarbone and dip between his pectorals. The sleeves rolled over his forearms, baring a thick coating of black hair, veins roped down the limb and buckled over his hands. The knuckles were large and heavy, scarring over the back of the palms. He was like the mix of a slick professional and a lightweight prizefighter.

As he came closer to me, this cold presence vibrated around him, spreading out before him. An ocean wave, invisible but just as strong, just as inevitable, pressing against my wolf. He was a *real* Alpha, he wasn't like Shane who just happened to be older and stronger than everyone. Toni was power, he was might, he was raw strength.

I looked at his forehead, the only place where I could still face him but not meet those black impenetrable eyes.

"Hi."

"Incorrect." He said, looking me in the eyes. "The proper way of meeting an Alpha is like so. First, on your knees."

The wave roared over me, climbed onto my back and shoved. My knees crumpled under the strength and I hit the ground on both, my hands clutched the dirt floor, knuckles grinding into the surface. Tears burned in my eyes as the cold wave piled onto me, like I was trying to hold the ocean on my back.

"Now," said Toni, with only his shoes in my watery vision. "You say, greetings Alpha of the Stone Pack. Then you'd offer your gift by saying, here is a freely given gift and should you accept it, I will follow your rules as such until you give my leave. Got it?"

I couldn't nod, my neck bowed under the strength of Toni's dominance. I pushed out my shaking hand that still gripped the black jewelry box.

"Greetings Alpha of the Stone Pack." My throat squeezed out the words.

The wave lifted up, retracted and I sucked in air as my lungs inflated. I looked up at him and held up the gift.

"Here is a freely given gift and should you accept it, I will follow your rules as such until you give my leave."

Toni took the box and opened it. Glitter reflected in his irises.

"Gift is accepted." He said as he pulled the stainless silver cufflinks out of the box. "Now, you may stand."

I pushed up with my arms and stumbled to my feet. My back ached like something heavy bore down on me, and my legs wobbled as if I was standing in the surf. I arched my back but the pain didn't let up, a deep throbbing ache from my shoulder blades down my spine to the dip before my butt.

I looked at Toni who was handing off the gift to Leah. "Will I be able to do that?"

"Eventually." Toni's lips quirked like he was amused but his scent didn't change. He smelled like himself, his Pack scent, the scent of his clothes but no emotional scent. "But you're only seventeen. You may be growing fast but the idea of a seventeen year old newly Changed wolf with enough dominance to force other wolves to their knees is ridiculous."

Putting that to the side, I asked, "How come I can't smell your emotions Toni? I know you have them. Leo doesn't talk and he doesn't make facial expressions but his smell changes with emotions, everyone else I can smell their emotions. But not you. Why?"

Toni chuckled and his scent morphed, orange, tingling, amusement. He laughed but then his scent drained away until it was just him again.

I stared. "How...how did you *do* that? How can you turn your scent on and off?"

Toni smiled for a second then said, "It's called scent withholding and all it means is that I can prevent my scent from changing with my emotions if I want to. I have perfect control over my scent."

"But how?" I could smell my emotions all the time and Sky's scent betrayed her feelings for me constantly. "Can I learn to do that?"

"Eventually." He said again. "It takes a lot of practice Xon and it also comes with age. It's a learned ability so don't think you can master it anytime soon."

I remembered something that I did when I went hunting. I told him how I made a plan in my head and sent it wordlessly to my Pack, how we executed it and then ate.

Toni was quiet long enough I wondered if he was ignoring me before he suddenly spoke.

"Xon...the ability to mentally create a plan and send images to Packmates is an Alpha ability. No one but the Alpha can do this and certainly not Changed teen wolves."

My eyes widened. "But...I'm not really an Alpha, you said so. I didn't even win the fight yet, I haven't fought Shane. How is it possible?"

Toni's brows furrowed and he spoke with careful deliberation, "Your Packmates view you as the Alpha and even if Shane is technically considered the leader, you had made a Pack with the others and you gave them the Pack scent that *you* created. At this point, he's the leader in word-only and you are the Alpha in all senses of the word. However, if Shane does win the fight at midnight, the law is the law."

I nodded, swallowing hard. "Well." My chin lifted. "I'll just have to train my hardest. I won't let Shane ruin this, destroy what I've made. The Pack is mine to protect and to care for."

Toni's breath hitched, like he was going to gasp but smothered it.

Then he said, "You nearly spoke an Alpha phrase Xon, almost word for word."

My eyes widened. "An Alpha phrase?"

Toni's expression was blank as he said, "It's a traditional phrase that you need to be taught to say. Similar to how I instructed you in how to properly greet an Alpha in their territory."

I thought about Javier who came from an official Pack in Spain.

"Javier is born a wolf, so he knows all the rules and laws and traditions but I don't know them. So how could I say something that sounds like a phrase I can't possibly know?"

Toni rubbed his hand over his mouth and I watched the scars dance over his knuckles. I knew for a fact that so far every injury I had been dealt healed, even Brenda's scar on my cheek had faded. What could have Toni done that left that amount of scar tissue?

He said after a minute, "I don't know, I really don't but...you are one of a kind Xon."

I said, "Can I ask another question? It's about Shane."

Toni looked at me. "Go on."

I said, "Shane...he seems really animalistic, more so than the rest of us. He's always angry, violent, cursing. I heard him talking to the phone with his mother one time, and she mentioned that he never used to talk to her rudely or be so animalistic, that he changed a few years back. I was wondering if-"

Toni said, "I've yet to meet the little angel myself, but from what I've gathered so far, Shane is a typical example of why it's illegal to Change humans."

I steadied my shoulders and waited for his explanation.

Toni said, "This rule deals more with predator shifters than prey, however, the Law stands for all of us. The fact is, sometimes, a human who is Changed into a predator shifter, the Change causes extreme personality modifications in someone who already had certain tendencies or latent potential tendencies that...let's say are *enhanced* by becoming a predator."

The blood drained from my face. "What the hell happened to Shane?"

Toni shrugged a shoulder. "It's not like I personally know him, but with the information I've gathered, and that you've presented to me, I'd say that Shane Armstrong might have been a normal kid who had anger issues or even just a shitty personality but never had any way of acting on it. Maybe he beat up his pillows, or broke his favorite toys. Then he becomes the top predator of the shifter world, a werewolf. He's granted physical strength well beyond anything he's ever dreamed of, the natural weapons of the animal world, fangs, claws, the burning desires of a wolf and all the dominance trip a guy like him should never have. With that said, someone who's never been dangerous before is now completely dangerous. And for that reason, it's illegal to Change humans into wolves, especially without knowing what changes can take place in them. Rocky Changing you into a wolf was highly illegal."

I nodded, my tongue and mind numb while Toni checked his wristwatch, it was another Rolex, only this one was white gold and studded with diamonds.

He said, in a low mutter, "Where the hell is Wyatt? He's late on purpose."

My gut clenched as I knew who would be training me. "Toni...why does Wyatt hate me so much? Mikhail said he was holding a grudge against me but what grudge? What did I ever do to him? It's like he's wanted to kill me since the moment he saw me and I don't know why."

Toni was absolutely silent, I couldn't even hear him breathing and even though I was looking at him, his body was stiff like a statue.

Then he said as he breathed again, "I can't tell you like this. What I will say is watch your back from now on. I keep telling Wyatt to stop stalking you but he does anyway. You met Brenda in the forest the other day, right?"

I blinked and nodded, but I figured she must have told him.

I said, "Yes."

"Wyatt was there." He said. "He was about to kill you when Brenda showed herself. She had been following Wyatt, Wyatt was following you. Brenda is my Alpha queen, my second half. When she talked to you, she was making it clear that Wyatt couldn't touch you. She stayed with you until Wyatt left, then she made sure Wyatt was gone. Do you understand?"

I nodded, sweat beaded over my upper lip as I remembered discovering Wyatt's scent just a lunge away from where I stood.

"If it wasn't for Brenda...I'd be dead now."

"He was going to kill you in the woods, bury your body and never say a word. It would look like you disappeared or maybe killed yourself in secret."

Toni's scent didn't change, but with how his eyes flashed with the dark amber of his wolf, I knew he actually did feel upset about it.

I nodded then said, "Got it. Thanks Toni...I really appreciate it." Then after a minute, I asked, "Is Rocky still around? I mean, not that I want to see him or anything, but I just wondered."

Toni stilled, just like he did before. Even though he was standing right in front of me, if I had my eyes closed, I wouldn't have been able to tell. I couldn't hear him breathing, or his heart beating, even his cold dominant aura just stopped. He straightened his shoulders and his cold wave pressed against me again then receded, like it was inhaling and exhaling.

Then with a long breath, he said, "You don't have to worry about seeing Rocky."

I didn't like the secrecy but it seemed to be a trend with people to not tell me the whole story.

So I asked, "How come Carter isn't the Alpha? I mean, I was told he said no to being Dominion, but why not become the Alpha of the Pack?"

Toni whistled, a short high burst of air, then said, "Carter isn't actually Alpha material. He's more a Rogue wolf than anything, so if he actually wanted to be in any position of power, the Dominion position was his best chance."

My brows arched. "A Rogue wolf?"

Toni placed his hands on his hips. "You don't know anything about the wolf hierarchy, do you?"

"Alphas at the top."

Toni shook his head and rolled his eyes at the same time, making me frown and I barely managed not to growl at him. His eyes tilted in a small smile.

He said, "A Rogue wolf is at the bottom of the hierarchy. In fact, Carter is technically a Rogue slut, which is actually at the rock bottom of the hierarchy."

My brows went up high again. "Whoa, a Rogue slut? So he's had a lot of sex or something?"

Toni shook his head again. "No. A Rogue slut is for a unmated female who isn't in a Pack but has a child. Carter is an unmated wolf with a child and he's not in a Pack. He's a Rogue because he has no Pack and he has no loyalties, he has no respect for anyone. He's considered a slut for being unmated with a child. If you've met him, then you noticed that his eyes are the color of his wolf. Rogues' human forms tend to have wolfish qualities because of all the time they spend in wolf form. Rogues are usually much less intelligible. With all the time spent traveling in wolf form, they start to lose human speech and become more like a wild animal. Aggressive, violent, brutal. They usually also live off the map, no job, no IDs, nomads. Carter is a little different because he does work and he has a house, so while he fits the Rogue category, he also is a little like a Loner too. So Carter is a specialized case and he's handled differently than if he really was a pure Rogue."

My fists clenched as I thought about Connor and the pain his father was putting him through.

One fight at a time. I have to defeat Shane first, if I can't beat him then I can't face Carter.

I said, "So if Rogues are such bad news, what do you do with them? You say you're handling Carter differently, so what's the normal handling?"

"If they enter Pack territory, kill them." Toni shrugged a shoulder. "If they're off Pack territory but we get word they're causing trouble like raping and killing, then we kill them."

I asked, "So why haven't you killed Carter? I don't know about raping and killing, but he's hurting Connor."

Toni looked in my eyes as his cold aura flexed against me, like testing me. "Familial problems aren't my concern. Carter hasn't caused any trouble and he's not on my territory. You sure are full of questions tonight Xon."

I cracked my knuckles. "Wyatt made mention that I don't know what I'm doing, so I should start learning how to be an Alpha. Only way to do that is by asking another Alpha questions."

Toni rubbed the back of his neck, his face creased for a moment as if he was uncomfortable but his scent remained clean, emotionless. "Technically you shouldn't even be an Alpha. You're only seventeen, if you were in a real Pack with adults, you wouldn't even be allowed to speak during

Pack Meets. In human terms, it's like a five year old running for mayor. It's just not done."

I bit my lower lip for a second, not wanting to get snappish at the Stone Pack Alpha, as he could very easily take back his offer to train me.

A door opened upstairs then Toni disappeared. I did see him turn around to face the stairs but then he was gone, moving so fast that he didn't blur.

Upstairs I heard him say, "What the hell took you so long?"

I didn't hear Wyatt say anything back but there was a loud thump, clearly a punch in the head. I knew for a fact it wasn't Toni who had gotten popped. There was no talking but the basement door opened wider and I got the thick musty scent of an adult wolf, already heated and burning with hatred.

Wyatt was a white man, tall and heavily built with short thick dark brown hair, and his gray eyes stormy and intense. He didn't have a mark on him, so I could only assume Toni hadn't hit him that hard.

I asked, "Why did you volunteer?"

"The hell I volunteered." He walked past me and looked around, cracking his knuckles. "I'm the lead wolf of the Scouts for this Pack, that means I'm the biggest, the fastest, most muscled and considered the best fighter out of the entire Pack. That's why Toni chose me." He turned to see me and that psychotic grin took over his face, his irises turned to the green of his wolf. "I'm going to train you so well you'll die from it." His voice growled on the word *die*.

I couldn't help it, I took a step back from him. I immediately regretted it when his wolf green eyes leapt with satisfaction.

"Now Wyatt, be gentle with him." Toni stood at my side, his hand clasped my shoulder and squeezed in a friendly manner. "This teen wolf only has a few hours to prepare for an official challenge, we need to make sure he stays healthy enough to actually live to see the fight. Where's Will?"

"I'm here." The Asian man who came down the steps. I also remembered him vaguely, saw his face through a hazy gaze. He had tended to me after Rocky had nearly killed me.

Dr. Will Norris was average height with black hair, dark curved eyes, and pale skin. He shook my hand with a nod. "I'm the Healer for the Stone Pack, or the doctor. During and after your training, I'll heal you up the best I can so that you can keep training. So first thing, Change into your wolf forms, both of you."

I realized that meant getting naked and Leah was still standing there. While I had been engrossed with talking to Toni, I hadn't even noticed her.

"Leave Leah," said Toni with a lift of his chin towards the door. "This isn't your business."

She nodded and gave me a deep glance I couldn't read. My wolf sat up at attention, ears pricked, tail waving. I imagined beating him in the head to get him to calm down. I didn't get it. He kept *reacting* to Leah, and I didn't even like Leah!

I looked away from Leah rather than stare at her like the wolf wanted.

Then she was up the stairs and the door closed behind her.

My shoes were already off and Wyatt had already stripped down to his boxers, jeez, the guy was more muscular than me *and* Shane put together!

I lowered my head and got undressed, then went onto all fours to Change. It came quickly and I shook myself as I stood up, my head came to the chest of Dr. Norris and Toni. Standing in front of me was a giant wolf with dark gray fur and bright green eyes. My ears stood level at his chin, making his head level with the heads of those in human form. His body was so heavy with muscle, I would have thought he'd be slow but he had already said he was the fastest of the Pack.

Biggest, fastest, most muscled, and best fighter. Holy shit...

I stepped backwards, a low whine leaving my nose. I didn't want to be scared of Wyatt, I hated the idea but this wolf was gigantic and he hated me and he really actually wanted me dead. I had never fought in wolf form before and this wolf wanted nothing more than to rip me to shreds. Looking at the ebony swords slicing out of his paws, it wouldn't take too much effort for him to do that.

"Calm yourself Xon." Toni put a hand on my head and rubbed the fur between my ears. "Wyatt isn't going to hurt you, he's teaching you how to fight. Wyatt, like I said, be gentle with him. He's never had a serious fight in wolf form before, so tell him how to balance his weight, how to judge the distance between his blow and the opponent, you know what I mean. Got it?"

Wyatt nodded with a grunt from his nostrils then padded away to the open area away from the stairs, I followed to stand in front of him. He turned to face me and his eyes caught a red glow from the row of hanging lights on the ceiling, I stepped back again.

"Xon." Toni spoke with a snap of impatience. "He's not going to hurt you, relax. Pay attention."

I nodded and firmed my spine, keeping my eyes on Wyatt.

Wyatt's voice spoke into my mind. *[In an official fight there are no rules. There's no such thing as fighting dirty or cheating or foul play, we aren't humans, we don't do shit like that. All you need to do is get Shane incapacitated, there's no need to kill in this case. Make it so that he can't fight anymore, whether it's knocking him out to breaking his legs. You can bite his ears off so he can't hear, you can claw his eyes out so he can't see, whatever is necessary to win, do it. A good blood-less technique is suffocation, which you can do by covering his muzzle with your own, covering up both his nose and his mouth or by biting his throat shut but not ripping it out. You got it so far?]*

I nodded, logging all of this to memory. I had made my mind to fight and now I had to learn how.

[Got it.]

[Good.] Wyatt took several large steps back from me though his voice stayed loud in my head. *[First thing, is to learn how to block an attack. I'll charge you, a quick rush towards your face. Most wolves' natural reaction is either to freeze up in fear or run. If you do either of those in a fight, it's over. What you're going to do is block then attack in return. Ready?]*

I nodded then I was rolling over and over on the dirt ground, lights flashing in my eyes and my ribs broken, I wheezed for air and I couldn't stand up.

What the fuck...just happened?

"Wyatt!" Toni's voice was sharp. "You moved too fast for him to even see you coming!"

My chest clenched up tight, paralyzed by the unseen blow. It was true, I didn't see Wyatt move, I didn't know he had charged me until I was already on the ground. I had thought Brenda was fast...

"Get up Xon." Toni ordered. "Get up and get back into the ring. You only have these few hours before midnight, there's no time to be lazing around. You should have healed already, on your feet."

I stood up as my ribs snapped back into place, it panged then eased. I steadied myself then walked back to where I was standing before.

Wyatt's eyes were coldly amused; he had totally done that on purpose.

[Ready?]

I nodded, narrowing my eyes. I had to see him move this time. I flew backwards and crashed into the ground from a hit I never saw, again dammit, again he moved that fast. My ribs were broken, maybe crushed entirely, I couldn't breathe at all, my body twitched spasmodically.

"Wyatt! Now it's you who's playing around!" Toni shouted at him. "He'll never learn anything if you attack him like that, you're not even trying! Do this right! Xon, get up!"

My ribs made loud cracking and popping sounds as they healed, my head swam, my stomach squirmed with sickness. Hands took my ruff and heaved me onto my feet, I wobbled and had to lean on the pair of legs standing next to me, it was Toni.

"Come on Xon, shake it off, you're okay. You can't let yourself get totally laid out from one hit like that, in an official fight you'll lose if you're taking the time to lay there and wait to heal. Go on, get back in there. Go."

Toni slapped my hindquarters. I jumped then walked over. I stopped in front of Wyatt, who's muzzle was parted in a wide eager grin, his eyes glowing green.

I bared my teeth. *[I let you get those cheap shots in, but not again. Your speed won't affect me this time.]*

[Oh yeah?] Wyatt lowered his body to the ground in preparation to pounce and I loosened up my body, ready for his attack. *[I'll teach you how to fight and I'll teach you the way I learned! Real practice, with teeth and blood and sweat! Even if it kills you, you'll learn how to fight!]*

Wyatt lunged and I jumped backwards to dodge but he was right there instantly, his long legs covered the distance and his paws slammed on my head over and over. I hit the ground, dizzy.

[Get up Xon dammit!] Wyatt's teeth sunk into the scruff of my neck and jerked me to my feet, he lifted me up like I weighed nothing. *[Now fight me, don't just stand there! Attack!]*

Wyatt lunged at me again, his heavy body pushed me to into the dirt and his fangs slashed at my face, slicing up my muzzle and blood ran into my eyes from the numerous cuts on my face.

"Xon! Xon fight back! He'll take out your eyes if you don't do something! XON!"

Hearing Toni's voice at the same time a fang scraped the very corner of my eye, I reacted desperately to get this guy off me. I kicked up my legs and I jerked up my head to avoid his teeth. My jaw knocked Wyatt in the face with a clear thunk as bone hit bone and he stumbled back, rubbing at his cheek with his paw.

"Great Xon! Now get up!" Toni urged me on and I got to my feet, blinking at the dried blood sticking to my eyelashes and my nose was clogged with it.

Dr. Norris cleaned up my face with a warm washcloth but he didn't give me any type of encouragement or tips.

Wyatt shook his head. *[Let's try this again and this time actually attack me, okay Xon?]*

I growled and got ready as Wyatt pounced for me. This time I jumped forward intending to use my weight to overpower him. We collided chest first but it was me who sprawled backwards, the wind knocked out of me.

Wyatt stood over me, coldly watching me struggle to catch my breath. *[That was a good strategy to use your weight to your advantage but you're not taking into account MY weight. I'm twice your size Xon, you could never hope to overpower me with pure strength, but nice try. However, Shane is in your age range and probably closer to you in size, so that could actually work on him. Now get up.]*

I stood up, shaking myself and focused my eyes on him, I had to get this right, I was getting tossed around like a chew toy. I remembered what Brenda had told me, that I thought like a human and not like a wolf.

Wyatt began to circle me and I quickly moved so that my back wasn't toward him, circling the opposite way.

Wyatt's voice came in my head. *[You honestly suck Xon, at this rate Shane can kill you with all of his paws hogtied! You don't think at all Xon, your reactions are either so slow that I don't see them or you don't react at all, you lay there and let me attack you! Let me put it this way.]*

I nodded, perking up my ears even though he spoke in my mind.

A. E. Costello 319

[You have to be fast, agile, you have to think instantly to execute your attacks and you have to anticipate your opponent's movements. When you look at me, figure out what I'm about to do before I do it. Watch how I hold my body, listen to how I breathe, track my muscles as they flex and constrict, don't take your eyes off me, you have to pay attention. It's like your mind isn't even here, you're completely oblivious to what's happening right now.]

That is literally word for word what Brenda told me. As much as I am a werewolf, at the same time, I'm not one. And now it's time I learn how.

I thought to Wyatt. *[Then what do I do? How am I going to learn how to fight before midnight?]*

Wyatt rolled his neck and gave me a heated green-eyed look. *[I'm going to keep on attacking you Xon, I'll attack you over and over again until you finally get it, until you start thinking like a wolf. You'll learn to fight Xon or you'll die. A wolf who can't think or behave like a wolf dies like a human, got it?]*

I nodded, steadying myself.

[Are you ready?]

I lowered my head down defensively and bared my teeth.

[Bring it.]

Wyatt attacked.

We fought like vicious dogs let off our leashes, or like attack dogs in an illegal fighting ring, raised only to kill. Toni always interceded when Wyatt got too aggressive, but even with that, Wyatt broke all of my ribs, he fractured my skull, knocked out my teeth, he bit off one of my ears and attempted multiple times to stab out my eyes. Dr. Norris healed me each time my injuries grew excessive. While before I had thought Javier's heat was intense, Dr. Norris's heat felt like an inferno, one that burned through me and healed up every injury.

I didn't know how much time had passed, but Toni said, "That's good Wyatt. It's already nine, so let's switch to Brenda's training now."

I sat back on my haunches, breathing in heavy through my mouth and letting it slowly out of my nose. I had hoped to fight Brenda again. Before she kicked my butt in human form. Now she was going to be a wolf. Wyatt Changed back into a man, put on his clothes and while he said goodbye to Dr. Norris and to Toni, he left without even looking at me again.

I watched him jog up the stairs and again wondered what type of grudge he was holding against me, why he hated me so much when as far as I knew I hadn't done a thing to him.

The basement door pushed open wider then Brenda came down into the basement. She was short with choppy black hair, a lean body and her left eye was brown, her right eye was blue. Her aura, her dominance was tense around her. Far from the cold wave of Toni's dominance, hers felt like a hot sparking wire, get too close and she'd fry me alive.

Toni said, "He's got three hours to face off with an official challenge. Make a wolf out of him, no pups here tonight."

Brenda nodded then started to take off her clothes. I quickly turned my head away, swallowing back my heart that leapt into my throat. At a low growl I looked up. Brenda the wolf stood there. She had black fur like Sky, but hers leaned more towards a silver black, black with light gray highlights and not the deep purple black of Sky's coat. Her eyes were again mismatched. Her left eye was bright green and her right eye was electric yellow. Her legs were slim and her body streamlined with not an ounce of fat with tight corded muscle. Her wolf form was just like her human form, she may be physically smaller than me but without a doubt she could pound me into the ground if she wanted.

Brenda's voice brushed in my head.

[You ready to dance?]

A. E. Costello 321

I nodded and bounced a bit on my toes, my tail swiped the floor and I rotated my neck, my shoulders rolled. Brenda hunched to the ground and leaned back up then stretched her legs.

Toni placed a hand on my head, he said, "Use everything Wyatt taught you earlier and be ruthless. Don't you *dare* hold back because Brenda is a female. Brenda is not a human Xon and she doesn't bend or break easily. She's going to do her very best to show you everything she knows as a fighter and you'll do your very best to fight back. There's no holding back Xon because Shane's not going to hold back. He'll be coming after you to kill so you need to learn what it's like to fend off killing attacks and fight back. Brenda, tear him apart. Xon, fight her like you mean to kill her. She can take it and Will is here to heal the both of you. Don't fear death Xon, you won't die here. Ready?"

I nodded, letting out a slow breath and relaxed all my muscles, focusing my eyes on Brenda. Her head ducked low, her gaze directly on me. She stood still, like she was a statue but it didn't mean she was slow, it meant she was building up energy to her legs, her muscles, getting ready to attack.

Toni backed away and said, "Start."

Brenda didn't move and I didn't wait, I lunged. I hit the ground like I had jumped on air, Brenda simply wasn't there anymore. I didn't know she had moved, I didn't see her move, I didn't even see her get ready to move. I jumped up and whirled around, Brenda was across the room and watching me. I charged, keeping my eyes steady and she was gone. I skidded to a stop, twisted around and she was on the other side of the room.

My heart leapt into my throat. I thought Wyatt was fast as a wolf but Brenda...she was unreal. When we fought in human form, I was aware of how fast she was but now I knew she really had been toying with me. She was playing around while making sure Wyatt didn't kill me. Toni told her not to hold back. She wasn't. She hadn't attacked me yet but this she-wolf was the fastest creature I had ever seen.

I wrinkled my muzzle and bared my teeth. *[Stop playing around Brenda. You're fast, I get it. How is this helping me if you're not letting me land a hit?]*

Brenda responded coolly. *[I'm aware that Shane is faster than you Xon and while I am stronger than you, you had Wyatt to teach you how to fight a stronger wolf. I'm going to teach you how to fight a faster wolf. To do that, you need to pick up your speed.]*

I let out a heavy breath and paced from side to side, keeping my eyes on her. *[How then dammit? You're so fast, even if I don't blink you still disappear right in front of me. Not only that, I can't even tell when you're going to move. You don't shift your weight, you don't tense your muscles, I don't even see you changing how you breathe. You're just gone, bam, like that, like air.]*

Brenda dipped her head down. *[That's right Xon, I'm like air. You won't have ever heard this, but there's a wolf saying that goes like "wind picked up at the ankles" which is only for wolf form. It means when a wolf is running so fast, it's like the air itself is at their feet, making them faster.]*

My eyes went wide. *[Are you saying you have magic powers? You can control air?]*

Brenda snarled, her teeth flashed silver as they reflected the light. *[You idiot! Did I say magic? No! I said air, wind! It's an ability Xon, it's a learned ability that I practiced until I'm fast, I practiced until I can move so fast it's like air, I'm like air. I didn't say I could control air, listen to when I speak!]*

I growled right back. *[I am listening! How can you teach me to be so fast like air in just one night? I don't have enough time to practice that!]*

Fangs were in my face, slicing across and just like that, the world went black. I howled, blood steaming hot down my muzzle and I collapsed to the dirt, writhing. She had blinded me. Brenda ran at my face and ripped my eyes out of my head and I didn't know until it was too late.

[Get up and fight Xon.] Her voice thundered in my head. *[Shane is fast and he's smart. The first thing he'll do is make sure you can't see because most wolves who can't see can't fight. Your eyesight is a handicap Xon. Lose it and use your other senses.]*

[Why aren't I healing?] I gasped, blood running in hot rivulets staining my cheeks, a hot poker shoved into my eye sockets.

[I'm dominant, remember?] Brenda circled me, she was so close her fur brushed mine and I could hear her paw steps, hear her breathing. *[I told you that wounds made by a dominant wolf take longer to heal. Your eyes will not grow back, not so easily.]*

My heartbeat raced and jumped into my throat, my lungs seized. I couldn't help it, rage roared up my spine. *[You bitch, you blinded me!]*

[Yes, yes, we've been over that.] Her paw pressed on the back of my neck, I bared my teeth. *[Now get up Xon and fight me. Fact is, I am too fast for your eyes to follow and you hinder yourself by trying to do so. To fight a faster wolf, you need to rely on senses other than sight because sight is useless when you cannot see your opponent in the first place. Without your eyes, what do you have Xon? What other senses do you have now that you cannot see?]*

I breathed heavy then grunted. *[Hearing. My nose. Taste.]*

[Yes, and what else? There's more Xon, think.]

I swallowed and I coughed, some blood had slid out of my eye sockets down into my nasal cavity, sliding into my mouth. Brenda took her paw off my neck and vibrations radiated from the spot where it touched the floor with a soft thud.

[Touch. I can feel your movements.]

[Good Xon, good.]

Brenda walked away and the farther away she walked the fainter and lighter the vibrations became, telling me how far she was going away from me. I concentrated on my hearing, her fur rustled as she moved her legs, her breathing was slow and easy.

I snuffled, flexed my nostrils in and out, sucking down air. I could smell her, Brenda smelled like a female werewolf but not like Sky, who's scent was sweet and musky. Brenda smelled deep and warm, matured. Over that was the Stone Pack scent, which was foreign and sharp. She also had the scent of Toni on her, a very light tinge of it but I smelled him on her. What was she to him?

Brenda's voice ran through my head. *[Good Xon, good. I see you listening, see you smelling. I am going to walk and you are going to tell me where I am. Don't move yet, lay there, using your senses.]*

I nodded and pricked my ears, lifted my head and flared my nostrils. My paws I spread out on the floor, pressing my pads down.

Brenda was moving, which way, her legs brushed against her body, fur rubbed against fur, her scent was trailing as she moved, vibrations shuddered through the dirt, her claws clicking and then she stopped, was still.

[Where am I Xon? Where in the room am I?]

I swallowed hard as a lump of hardened blood sloughed down from my empty sockets, passed my nose and landed on my tongue then rolled down my throat. It was disgusting but I had to focus. Shane was probably faster as a wolf, four legs versus two and he was equipped with fangs and claws. He wanted to be in wolf form because he wanted to make it easier to kill me. He was beating the shit out of me in human form with just his fists, add stiletto bladed claws and machetes for teeth, he'd kill me with no problem. So I had to train, I had to focus.

I flexed my nostrils in and out, turning my head from side to side. I smelled Dr. Norris and Toni to the side and behind me, and heard their breathing and heartbeats. I tuned them out, pushed it away and slowly rotated my head to the other side, focusing harder. Brenda wasn't moving at all but she had to be breathing, her heart had to be beating, her blood had to be flowing. She had a scent that she couldn't cover up, I could find her, I had to try.

Without my eyes, the world was black but everything else began to heighten, enhance. My ears flicked forward. A heartbeat with a soft light thud, much lighter than the heavy blows at my back. Breathing, like a squeezed whistle through a hole, trying to make as little noise as possible, much softer and quieter than the deep heaves behind me. The scent from that direction, deep warm musk, adult, female. Not wanting to wait, I raced forward and chomped down on fur that tore out of my mouth but left a chunk in my teeth, Brenda had twisted away before I could get a good hold.

Loud clapping broke the deep silence.

"Yeah! Good job Xon! Good job!"

Toni's voice was loud and ecstatic. I focused and heard his heartbeat had picked up a few paces, his breathing was more agitated but his scent was still his, no emotions had morphed it.

Dr. Norris spoke next, "Should I heal his eyes now Brenda?"

I didn't hear Brenda say anything but I heard fur rustling, heard her legs shift.

Dr. Norris said, "Alright, carry on."

Brenda's voice was in my head. *[Okay Xon, next exercise. You can find me when I stop moving and I'm standing still, good but Shane's not going to be standing around waiting for you to attack him. So I'm going to move around, I won't run, not yet and you're going to track me. Follow me, find me, using all of your senses left available to you. Understand?]*

I nodded and licked my muzzle, tasting the blood that had dried and caked up on my fur.

[I'll make you pay for taking my eyes like that Brenda. You didn't even warn me or anything, I'll get you back for that.]

Brenda chuckled, a low soft sound in her wolf throat while a feminine human version echoed in my head.

[Then come Xon, listen to me and do your best. I walk now.]

She moved, the vibrations shuddered through the floor, her scent wafted as her legs rubbed fur against fur, I heard the rustling, listened to her breathing and how it all shifted as she walked. I stood, cocked my ears and began to walk. She was moving away from me, the sounds growing fainter, lighter, the vibrations changed course.

I followed her and picked up my pace, I wanted to bite her, shake her. Brenda moved faster and this time changed directions, the vibrations shattered as each paw touched a different spot. She walked so her legs were spaced apart, denying the frictions of fur. She was trying to disorient me, confuse me and I wasn't having it.

I focused on her heartbeat, it beat faster and her blood sped up, I could hear her breathing and I dashed forward. My jaw snapped and I clashed into her jaw. She bit down and her teeth sunk into the tenderness of my nostrils, she was trying to take my sense of smell. I slashed out with my front paw and my claws sunk into something soft and only covered by a soft down of fur. She yelped.

Toni shouted, "Brenda!"

Brenda let go of my nose and I pulled my claws back but whatever I hooked into came out with me. There was a splattering sound and the smell of blood flooded my system. Brenda made a twisted whimper of pain and her body collapsed to the ground. Someone pushed me to the side, hard enough that I stumbled.

Dr. Norris said, "Toni, relax, it's not fatal. Look, she's healing. Brenda, Change back into a human, alright. Do it, it'll speed the process."

I padded forward, my heart was beating hard but not as hard as Toni's, I could pick his out from Dr. Norris's because the doctor's was calm, cool, practiced. Toni's was thudding against his ribcage like to break out, I could smell his nervous sweat because even though his emotional scent hadn't changed, he was still withholding it, the smell of his body betrayed him.

There was soft slurping and sucking sounds then Brenda gasped and the scent of her fur faded, the musky thick scent of the wolf faded and I smelled skin, slick, bloody skin. I pressed forward and my fur brushed against hair, I nuzzled it and a hand pressed on my forehead.

Dr. Norris said, "Can I heal him now Brenda? Is the lesson over?"

It was him I was standing next to and my front paw was stepping on something, it was thick, tubular and my stomach turned.

Brenda sighed out and then her hand laid on my forehead, slid down to cover where my eyes should be and Dr. Norris covered hers, then Toni was beside me and his hand was over theirs. I didn't have eyes or eyelids, Brenda's fangs had ruined them and they had to stretch their fingers so they weren't putting them directly in my sockets.

Brenda said softly, "Heal, take my heat and heal."

Her heat ignited, like a candlewick burst into a white hot flame, I flinched.

Toni's other arm hooked around my neck and held me still, he said gruffly, "Don't move Xon. The healing is going to hurt but don't run, just stand still."

Brenda's heat crashed into my skull then Toni's joined in, his heat was like a boulder of flame, slamming into me and my knees went weak. I slid to the ground with Toni's arm holding me up like my head was just a giant basketball. Dr. Norris's heat slipped in like a twine, or a piece of rope and he tied up Brenda's and Toni's heat, roped them together and directed them, focused them. My eyes healed, no, regrew. Like my sockets were empty cups and my eyes were golf balls dropped inside, plunk, plunk and a shutter, my eyelids, slipped over them.

Dr. Norris said, "Keep your eyes closed Xon, they aren't ready to be used. Change forms but keep your eyes closed then too. You gotta let him go Toni."

The hands lowered and Toni let me down, my head laid on the floor and I let my wolf slide away. The fur slumped back into my skin, my bones popped and my muscles slid around them, my skull reformed, my muzzle dissolved and my eyes rolled around in my sockets but I didn't open them like I was told.

I laid on the cold floor, naked, there was blood on my face and on my hands. A damp cold cloth gently wiped my eyes, nose and forehead then a warm bandage tied around my head, tight enough that it kind of stung and pinched my skin.

I sat up and Toni grasped my shoulder, saying quickly, "Whoa Xon, take it easy."

"I'm fine." I said. I wanted to see but the bandage was pinning my eyelids to my face. "How is Brenda? Is she okay? Brenda, did I hurt you? What did I do?"

"Relax." Her voice was low, warm, calm. "You gutted me Xon, that's all."

I gasped and my skin went cold. "I…I what?"

I remembered Wyatt's psychotic grin, how he held up his claws and threatened me.

Brenda said, "Your claws punctured my abdomen and pulled out some of my intestine. You didn't go deep and you didn't tear or rip, you slid in and slid out. It was a clean hit and non-fatal. I'm fine and I'm proud of you."

I smelled it, the citrusy tingling scent of pride was flooding from her in spades.

She laughed, definitely seeing my dumbstruck expression. "I'm not lying Xon, I mean it. I've never seen a pup adapt, learn and react as quickly as you do. Yes, I blinded you without warning, you were wounded and you

A. E. Costello 329

cursed me but then you got over it and listened, you learned. And in the end, you defeated me."

I would have been staring at her if I could but I said, "You said it wasn't a fatal blow, you healed it like it was nothing. You could have kept fighting, right?"

"In a real fight yes Xon," said Dr. Norris, he had a strange lilt to his voice, like he was fighting off a smile. "If you two were enemies and truly fighting, Brenda could have kept fighting but even with you blind, that was your only wound and you had overcome it. A gut wound is very serious and you could have kept attacking, kept ripping and tearing. In a real battle, saying it went along these lines, Brenda was in very real danger."

My jaw dropped and Toni's hand, large, calloused, closed it. "You did good kid." He said with a raspy chuckle. "Accept it. As for now, we need baths and bed. Will, does Brenda need a night down here?"

Brenda protested. "No!"

Dr. Norris said, "It wouldn't hurt, but a long hot bath and a good night's rest will take care of it. I'll check on you in the morning Brenda and if you're having any type of stomach pain, I'll put some earth on it and you'll have to stay off your feet. Got it?"

I asked, "Earth?"

"Wolf healing technique," said Dr. Norris. "The same way water is a powerful healing agent, so is earth. Why do you think our infirmary has this earthy floor and is in the basement, underground? Same."

I reached out, my hands brushed soft tender skin, thighs and I jumped upwards, grazed over round flesh topped with warm hard stones and went higher, neck then cheeks. Brenda's hands touched mine and she squeezed.

I said, "Brenda, I didn't mean to hurt you that badly, I didn't do it on purpose."

"I know you didn't Xon." She said, lowering my hands. "Soo Bin is a worrywart. I've healed Xon, I'm a dominant wolf. Not only do my attacks take longer to heal, my own injuries heal quickly. So relax, really."

I let her put my hands back into my side and I asked, "Soo Bin? I thought his name was Will Norris."

"It is." The doctor said. "It's my American name. My Korean birth name is Kim Soo Bin. Brenda is one of the few who call me my birth name, most of the Pack stick with Will or Dr. Norris. Easier to remember, easier to pronounce. Now let's get upstairs, it's very late and some of us have work in the morning."

Arms gripped underneath mine and lifted me up like I was a puppy. My feet left the ground and I scrambled for purchase before my toes hit earth and I stood.

I growled a little. "I can walk!"

Toni's hand gripped my wrist and he clenched hard enough I flinched in pain, a small yelp left my mouth. "Yes you can walk and move but you don't know where you're going. Now you either shut up and follow me or I'll let you stay down here and sleep naked on the floor all night, got it?"

I said quietly, "Yes sir...wolf."

Toni chuckled and walked away, I could hear Dr. Norris and Brenda going upstairs. "Good, you really are a fast learner. Xon." He paused then said, "First step, lift up your foot."

I did so, my toes crunched into the ledge, I grunted and lifted up higher and stepped down. The flash of pain in my toes healed and Toni lightly tugged my wrist, I judged the distance properly and found the next step.

Toni said, "Brenda is right Xon, you learned and fought back so quickly. To be honest, I want to see you train with Wyatt just to see you pit your new moves against him."

I shook my head but stopped when my eyeballs rattled in my skull like they were loose or disconnected. Nausea rolled in my stomach.

I spoke, my voice a little thick, "He told me he's the best fighter in the Pack. He'd destroy me."

"If I'm standing there and he knows better than to kill you with me right there then he won't. He will be holding back from dealing a final blow but he will be doing his best to cause you pain. And with you not holding back at all." Toni made a soft cough. "I'm interested in seeing that."

I wasn't sure about what Toni just said. It was like he saw me and Wyatt as fighting dogs, animals to put in a ring together and watch them fight for sport. In a way, I couldn't tell if I should be flattered he thought I had a chance against his best fighter or upset he wanted to make me fight just to see what would happen.

In the end, I said nothing and Toni led me down a hallway. He stopped and took my hand, pressing it against the wall, no, a door.

"This is the bathroom." He said. "Walk two steps down this way and here is the guest bedroom. Inside there is a door that connects the two. Keep the connecting door locked, understand? If you're in the bathroom then fine but once you're in the bedroom, then lock it back. Got it?"

I nodded and Toni got me into the bathroom, he sat me on the toilet and I listened to him run the tub.

I said, "Shouldn't my eyes soak in the tub?"

"You shouldn't get the bandage wet." He answered. "Just soak in the water and bathe, the materials are right on the tub ledge. I'll put a towel on the toilet for you to use. Once you're all dry, I'll have pajamas on the sink counter you can put on. Call me if I'm not here and I'll get you in bed."

I nodded and Toni took my hand and I stood up, he shuffled me over then said, "Step over and raise your leg high Xon, don't bang your foot on the rim."

I nodded. Using his arm as a balance swung my leg over and lowered it. My foot sunk into steaming hot water and I got my other foot in. I sat down then slumped down, balancing my shoulders under. I kept my neck out, everything else submerged. The water swirled over me and simmered, stewed. I leaned my head back but a hand suddenly cupped my chin and kept my head from sliding under, close to what I did for Leo.

"Don't forget to bathe Xon," said Toni and his hand on my shoulder helped me sit up. I bathed and he wasn't there, though the towel and pajamas were right where he said they'd be once I got out. He must have been waiting in the bedroom because before I could call for him he took my arm and led me out of the bathroom.

"The bed is high." He said. "There's a stepstool to get up but I'm going to throw you on. Ready?"

I was about to protest when his hands clasped my hips, he lifted me off the ground like I was a toddler and tossed me onto the bed like a sack of potatoes. I didn't dare yell or growl at him, not when he was taking care of me like I was his own. I scrambled over the pillows and the edge of the covers. Toni helped me pull it down, I snuggled under and I was sleep before my head hit the pillows. If Toni had said anything, I didn't hear it.

I woke up to breathing over me, soft, feminine, bathing my nose and lips. I flared my nostrils, sweet musk, Stone Pack scent, and the slight stench of fear. Leah.

The bandage was still tight around my head, I had slept like the dead, hadn't even changed position.

I asked, "What time is it?"

"It's 11:35." She answered. "Toni's not here, so I'm to wake you up, get you fed, dressed, eyes healed then on your way."

I paused then said, "Well, can I get my eyes healed first, then dressed, then fed?"

My stomach growled and my wolf pressed against me, he wanted food first.

Leah sniffed, the scent of fur rose over my skin.

She said, "If you eat in bed and Will comes in, you can get those done at the same time and dress after."

"Deal." I said, sitting up.

"Be back in a tail wag." She said as she left.

I chuckled. *I haven't learned all of the official lingo or werewolf slang, but I can tell tail wag is the same as second or just a minute.*

Leah returned with a tray of food and Dr. Norris was behind her. I had mastered the skills Brenda taught me, I could smell the food, hear Leah holding it, smelled Dr. Norris and heard him walking. I realized now if I ever ended up losing my eyesight for real, I could still take care of myself. I would need to memorize where everything was, learn to recognize everyone by smell and sound but it was doable.

Leah placed the tray in my lap and asked, "Do you need me to feed you Xon?"

She sounded kind and gentle but her scent, there was a trace of sharp oil, confidence.

I said as clearly as I could without being rude, "No thanks Leah, I got it. Thank you though."

"And you'd be in the way." added in Dr. Norris before Leah could respond. "Go ahead and eat Xon, I'm taking off your bandage but don't open your eyes until I tell you to."

"Got it." I said, placing my hands in my plate. My fingers zapped, burned. Scrambled eggs, crispy bacon, juicy links, toast with butter. Even though it was nearly midnight, I had been served breakfast food. I didn't wait for a fork, I began to eat. Dr. Norris cut my bandage off. My skin sucked in air and I winced at the tightness from being so tightly compressed.

Dr. Norris laid his hand over my eyes and heat seeped in, tucked around, melding and bringing nerves together, stitching up.

He lowered his hand and said, "Open slowly and don't stare or bulge. Blink a few times, get used to the light."

I slowly raised my eyelids and everything was blurry for a moment, out of focus. I blinked and my vision cleared up, the room came into view. Leah was on the left side of the bed, leaning over to see me because I was on the right. Dr. Norris was very close, his eyes peering at me.

He held up five fingers. "How many?"

"Five."

He made three. "How many?"

"Three."

He leaned his arm as far away as he could and held up three fingers again, his pinky, his thumb and his middle finger. "And now?"

"Three." I said.

I looked at Leah. Her red hair was in curls down to her shoulders, her dark blue eyes surrounded in dark mascara and her lips painted a light pink. She was wearing a shirt with a scoop neck, revealing lightly tanned breasts. I suddenly remembered I had touched Brenda's breasts a little while earlier, had felt her nipples.

A blush roared up to my cheeks and I looked away to my plate. It was empty, picked clean.

Dr. Norris coughed and said, "I think you're seeing just fine Xon. Any pain, pricking, throbbing, numbness?"

I shook my head and looked up at him. He had blackness edged under his eyelids.

I asked, "How's Brenda? Is she feeling okay?"

I watched him as he stood up straight from leaning against the bed. I noticed now he was wearing a lab coat and a name tag pinned to his chest pocket.

Dr. Norris nodded, adjusting his watch on his wrist. "She's sleeping right now and I've placed earth over her stomach so she'll be fine. I really must go now. Leah, watch over our guest but behave yourself, clear?"

Leah rolled her eyes sharply and said with a bite, "Yeah, yeah. You're not my father or my Alpha, so don't give me orders."

Dr. Norris's dark eyes narrowed. "Leah, remember your place. I may not be high on the hierarchy but I'm still above you. Yes, I can't truly order you around nor can I punish you but I can mention to the Enforcer you're being a nuisance."

Leah growled at him, her pretty lips snarled and bared thin but sharp fangs. "Could you try to stop being a jerk in front of company? Ever thought about that?"

Dr. Norris growled back then suddenly stopped and walked away, saying over his shoulder, "Your attitude problem is what got Xon to where he is now, you ever thought about that?"

Leah went pale, draining her light gold skin to a yellowish milky shade.

I stared at her. "What did he mean by that?"

I remembered the circumstances that led to my being Changed, but what if there was even more back-story behind it that I didn't know about?

"N-nothing." She said, gathering the tray. "Your clothes are in the bathroom on the toilet, along with a toothbrush. Use it then meet me in the living room."

I reached for her but she dodged then she rushed out of the room, the tray shook dangerously and the silverware clattered but she was gone.

I got up from the bed in borrowed pajamas and realized Toni, Brenda and Dr. Norris had all seen me naked. As I realized it, I also realized I hadn't gotten embarrassed last night, in fact, I hadn't even thought about it. Not only that but no one else mentioned it either. Brenda hadn't even slapped me for touching her, Toni didn't get mad at me for touching her or make me cover myself. Everyone had behaved like being naked meant nothing.

In the bathroom, my clothes were laundered and I got dressed, put on my shoes and brushed my teeth. Back in the bedroom, I locked the connecting bathroom door just like I had been told. I went to the living room.

Leah wasn't alone but there was about twenty people in the living room and their energy, like a throb, a beating pulse surrounding them, lifting off their skin and it grew stronger with each step. They looked at me, it was all men besides Leah, a few boys my age and a little older. They were the Stone Pack and they were stronger when they were together. I was an outsider, someone in their space and I had injured one of their own. They weren't going to hurt me at the order of their Alpha but in any other situation in which I wasn't a welcome guest, I wouldn't be so lucky.

I knew these things not like in a telepathic sense as if I was reading their minds but like the information was being sent to me, like a collective thought they were letting me know as they thought together as a group. It's just like how some times I knew what my Pack was feeling, when we grouped together as a unit.

An older male wolf spoke. "I heard you gutted Brenda, even while being blind, no eyes at all. That true?"

Everyone was watching me with cold yet curiously blank expressions. Blank, empty, waiting. They didn't know what to make of me, there was nothing yet to examine. I was a tall muscular black teen wearing jeans and a t-shirt. There was nothing impressive about me.

I nodded and watched them, not moving. "It's true."

I didn't offer any details, he just wanted a confirmation. The minty scent of truth grew around my body, I wasn't lying.

A ripple ran through the Pack, like my words had tossed a stone in their collective water.

A male wolf around my age, he had to be like eighteen, grinned at me and his brown eyes shifted into a leaf-green with gold sprinkles, his wolf glaring out. He wasn't taller than me but his body was bulked with muscle like a body builder. He wasn't wider than Dad but his muscles bulged against his shirt and his traps were as thick as my fists.

He bared teeth sharpening to fangs. "I don't believe it. He's a thin scrap, can't hurt nobody. He wouldn't lay a claw on me."

My inner wolf snapped and lunged against my body. The other wolf was challenging me, right here. If I broke eye contact and looked away, I was submitting.

I can't back down, I'm an Alpha. If I look weak here, I'll be weak everywhere else.

A. E. Costello 337

My eyesight enhanced as they Changed into those of the wolf. I stared down the boy and a long low growl edged from my lips. Just a warning, if he backed down I'd leave him alone. Up to him.

The older teen ducked his head down and his wolf spark billowed, I could sense his wolf gathering up to pounce.

Leah protested, "He has to go Ethan, leave him alone."

Ethan ignored her and I didn't take my eyes off him. Ethan snapped his teeth, his face distorted with the fangs filling out his mouth, his nose had slumped into a mass of blackened flesh and his lips thinned and darkened. He was still grandstanding, trying to scare me off in front of everyone else.

My wolf lunged forward and I didn't hesitate. I crossed the room in one bound, my shoulder turned and rammed right into Ethan's diaphragm, yanking the air from him as it crumpled. He hit the ground and thrashed, his mouth gaped for air, the shock had turned his face human again and he sucked in deep then scrambled to his feet, gasping.

I met his eyes. "You had enough?"

Ethan growled but the other man said, "Stop Ethan. He won, it's over."

Ethan mumbled and backed away from me but his eyes were calm. Yet his scent, while there was anger, there was a thread of knowing, of understanding. He was angry but he knew he lost, he understood I was stronger than him.

I asked, "Can I leave now? I have somewhere to be."

The adult male laughed, clearly he was speaking for everyone else. "You get blinded, you gut our Alpha queen. So is that also true then, that a teen wolf is challenging to be an Alpha?"

I didn't like that I had to answer this guy's questions, especially when the clock on the wall read that it was 11:45, but I was a guest and I couldn't just walk out being rude.

I said, "Yeah I am."

The Stone Pack murmured amongst themselves, it was like before, like the collective thought rippled. They found me strange, different, but now that I had defeated a challenger of their own, maybe I was impressive, maybe I was something different.

The male wolf shrugged his shoulders. "Then I guess you'd better head out."

Leah went to open the door for me. I walked over, put on my shoes and Leah put a hand on my chest before I could leave. I looked down at her. The wolf leaned in close, and I did end up lowering my head just enough that my nose brushed the top of her red hair. Leah's personal scent was lemongrass and vanilla. My wolf liked the smell, but I remembered Sky's scent, roses and honey. The clash of my mind and the wolf mind made me step back from her.

A smile crept over Leah's face. She asked, "Will you come back again?"

"I don't know." I said.

Her dark blue eyes fluttered. "Maybe I'll have to come see you."

She smelled like herself, that tinge of fear that seemed like it would always be there when it came to me, and a very light brush of sugar. Not pure arousal…but interest, flirting. She liked me.

There was a loud growl and Leah was yanked away by the same adult wolf. He shoved me out of the house, I tripped and the door slammed.

I got in my car and sent a group text to Sky, Connor and Javier.

Xon: I'm on the way, picking you guys up in my car.

10

August 13ᵗʰ
Wednesday

A. E. Costello 339

My dashboard read the time was already midnight, so I sent Shane a text.

Xon: I'll be there soon.

He sent back a picture of his middle finger. The knuckles twisted and buckled, sparse tawny fur sprouting through the skin and his nail a black scythe. A text came in with it.

Shane: Bring it bitch.

I went to Leo's ramshackle house first and leaned on the horn. When Sky gave me the Pack's cell phone numbers, Leo didn't have a number. The window blinds parted, then Leo came out the front door. He looked from side to side then darted to my car. Strangely, he got in the back seat instead of next to me, but he leaned up and pressed his face against mine and nuzzled my neck. I rubbed the back of his neck and stroked his ears in greeting, then headed to Javier's place. Javier stood outside at the gate and he also got in the back seat.

"Are you all trained up?" He sounded breathless, his excited scent matched.

"Trained as I can be." I said, now heading to Connor's place. My fists clenched over the steering wheel but I stopped when it made a loud crunching sound.

Javier said, though quietly, "Maybe we should get Sky next. Just in case."

My jaw worked but I went to Sky's house. She was also waiting at the sidewalk and she hopped into the front passenger seat.

"Hey Xon." She dropped a kiss on my cheek, then leaned into the backseat to get nuzzles from Leo and Javier. "You guys feeling okay?"

"Very excited," said Javier with a small laugh. "Tonight it will all be over."

Sky nodded and looked out of the window as I steered the car towards Connor's place. "This is a nice car Xon. Why is it the first time I'm seeing you drive it?"

I shrugged as I parked outside of Connor's house. "I got it over the summer, so I guess I'm still used to walking everywhere. Dad and I split the cost, I worked at his old gym to earn the money."

Sky opened her door before I could get out and was at the front door before me. She looked at me when I opened my mouth.

"I'm here with you Xon. The last thing we need is for you to attack him. I care about Connor too, but we have priorities."

I nodded and knocked on the door, rapping with my knuckles while calling, "Hey, Connor, come out. We gotta go."

I waited for several minutes and raised my hand to knock again when the door swung open. Connor stood there, wearing jeans, a t-shirt and no shoes. He looked up at me with stark black holes for eyes. If eyes are the windows to the soul, Connor's soul was damaged and worn, desperate.

I hugged him tight, squeezing him against me and his arms looped around my waist, he gripped me back hard enough I could feel the supernatural strength that ran in his bones, his muscles. Connor was short, slender but he was a wolf, a young one who needed protecting. I inhaled deep, taking in his scent. Throat-clogging of despair, a strong rotten scent of horror, his sadness scent of wet mud was thicker than ever but running over him was a smooth fruity scent of relief with a tingling orange of happiness chasing it.

I looked up over his head nuzzling into my stomach into the house. I didn't see anyone, Carter must not be home. I stepped back and Connor didn't let me go. I knelt, grasped his thighs and lifted him up onto my chest, his legs wrapped around my waist, his arms around my neck. Connor clung to me like a desperate woman not wanting to let go of her long-lost lover. Maybe that was a bit dramatic but I had only brought him from my house for a single day

A. E. Costello 341

and already Connor was like this, reduced to a shaking traumatized wolf unable to let me go.

Sky closed the door as I carried Connor to the car. Javier opened the backseat and scooted back to let me in, I couldn't get Connor off me, his hold was too tight, too needy. I slid in and sat down with Connor on my lap, my arms around his waist with Connor's face buried into my neck. Leo crawled over Javier's lap and nudged Connor's face, sliding his tongue between us to lick Connor's cheek. Connor flinched away, a whimper came from his throat.

"Connor." I said softly, resting my hands on his shoulders, rubbing the small fragile bones. "Connor look up at me, okay? Come on, look at me."

Connor lifted his head from my neck and looked at me with red strained eyes, his face damp and so was my skin, my shirt. I gently held his face, he was pale white and his brown eyes looked like drained black wells. I placed my lips on his forehead and Leo leaned in, nuzzling Connor's face with his nose and cheek. Connor sniffled and took one arm off my waist to hug Leo around his neck.

"Are you okay?" I held his hips, my hands spanned them and could connect the fingers across his back. I knew Connor was small but had he always been this tiny or had he simply lost a lot of weight over the hours since I left him.

Connor nodded and a weak smile trembled his lips then quickly fell. "Now that you're here." He spoke in a raspy voice, like his vocal cords were worn out, strained.

Sky, who was standing next to me outside of the car, caressed Connor's temple and ear. "Are you sure? Where did Carter go?"

"He went out." Connor closed his eyes and he laid his head on my chest. "I don't care about him."

"I have to let you go now." I said. "I have to drive."

Connor nodded and we switched places so that Connor was on the seat and I got out of the car. Sky got in the passenger seat while I got back into the front. I called Toni as I started to drive. He picked up.

I spoke first. "I got my Pack and we're going to the field now."

Toni didn't say anything for a moment then said, "Alright, I'll get Will and be on my way. If I speed, I can get there in twenty minutes so when you see Shane, don't start the fight until I'm there."

I knew it wouldn't work like that, Shane and I wanted to fight now.

I said, "We'll warm up first."

Toni let out a quick shocked laugh then said, "See you when I see you."

I hung up and pulled into the field. Shane stood in the center, illuminated by the headlights. He wore blue jeans ripped at the knees, and a bright white shirt. I killed the engine and turned off the lights, we got out of the car and walked over to him. I walked in the front, with Sky at my side, the three walked behind us.

Shane grinned at me but that smile was bloodthirsty and the billowing wolf spark in his eyes was centered at me. His scent was raging hot, violence, pain, bloodlust, hatred.

"Make a circle." I told my Pack. "And don't get in the way."

Sky kissed my face first and I pulled her against my chest, my arms around her and I drank from her mouth, needing to feel it, taste it. She held my face and kissed me back just as strongly, demandingly.

"Jesus Christ give me a break!" Shane shouted. "I don't need a show, let's get started already!"

Sky stepped back, her eyes fluttered and her scent heady then she backed away, completing the circle.

I faced Shane, his hackles were raised, his head was covered in fur, eyes livid wolf olive.

I said, "Toni is on his way along with his doctor. He's going to referee the fight."

Shane bared thick fangs. "I'm not waiting. I want you dead."

I held up a calming hand. "Let's warm up first Shane."

My eyes went wolf, able to pick out the individual sweat droplets running down his forehead, peppering across his collarbone, the strain in his eyes, the tension at the corners of his mouth and his fangs widening his jaw bones.

Shane grinned, a distorted grotesque twisting of his mouth, his lips were blackened and thin, his jaw protruded outwards, stretching halfway into a muzzle.

"Alright then." His voice was deep and rough, wrenched out of a throat bulging with wolf vocal cords. "You take the first swing." He held up his hands, claws sliced out like switchblades.

I hunched over, my shoulders buckled and my hipbones pressed against my jeans, my wolf lifting up against my skin. I smiled, my fangs sliding down to touch my lower lip. I bounced on both of my toes, dashed forward, twisted with my left leg and swung my right foot up, my heel smashed into Shane's mouth and he tumbled backwards in a spray of blood.

The Pack made no noise, they didn't howl or hoot or clap because that would be distracting and rude. This was a battle of wills, of dominance, of who deserves to lead. They were to watch and be silent. Even with that, the rush, the leap of heartbeats and quickened breathing was electrifying.

Shane used the back of his hand to slowly wipe the blood away and he blinked with a set of wolf eyes in his human face, his sclera was black and his olive eyes were narrowed. His wolf was melding more into his body but he was holding back the Change. We were warming up, heating up the muscles, testing out the limits.

I backed up a few steps and lifted up my hands, spreading out my legs enough. Shane's eyes narrowed and he jumped for me, wanting to knock me onto my back but I twisted to the side in a dodge. My kick slammed out, got him in the abdomen, he bent down. I kicked again and again, crashing the hardness of my shin into his ribs and with a loud audible snap, his ribs broke.

Shane stumbled to the side, his arms around his abdomen, and threw up blood. The bones had punctured his liver, spleen and kidneys, as the broken sticks jabbed downwards into the organs below, rather than collapse inwards into his heart and lungs. I didn't kick him in a way that could kill him. I kicked him to show my strength and to cause him pain.

A black truck was driving up, no headlights and in the pitch black of a field only lighted by the stars and a very thin silver of Moonlight, I knew it was Toni.

He hopped out before the engine had fully cut off and barked, "Shane, Xon, back up off each other, now!"

I walked away from Shane and my Packmates went to me, hugging and caressing. I wasn't hurt, Shane hadn't gotten a hit in but I knew that was because in human form, I had taekwondo skills. I kicked him so he couldn't get close to my body. If Shane had gotten up close, his claws could have eviscerated me, he wouldn't have toyed with me like he did Connor, he would have torn my insides out.

Dr. Norris went to Shane who was sitting on the ground, still bent over his destroyed ribs. Dr. Norris knelt by him and talked softly to him, introducing himself and asking permission to heal him.

Connor burst out, "Hey! He's healing him! That's cheating, what the fuck! Stop it!"

Toni put his hand out in front of Connor who looked ready to jump onto Dr. Norris who was healing Shane, his hands pressed against the mottled bruises.

Toni stared down at him, "This wasn't the official fight, they were," he glanced at me then back to Connor, "just warming up. Besides, once Shane Changed forms he would have healed. Will is speeding up the process. Okay, Xon, Shane, pants off, into position."

My Pack got in one last nuzzle and caress, Sky kissed my lips then I took off my pants and bent down, ready to Change, poised. I glanced up, Shane was doing the same thing and his eyes focused on me.

"Everyone back up much further than that." Toni instructed. "In fact, go over by my truck. Now."

He snapped when there was sounds of protest. They moved grudgingly and Dr. Norris came over to stand by Toni.

"Alright." Toni faced me and Shane. "This will be a quick easy fight. No need for either of you to die. Change forms and simply try to incapacitate the other. Don't go for throat-ripping, it's not necessary. Are we ready?"

Shane stretched his legs and arms so that muscles rolled up and down his back like water slipping over a duck's feathers. Slick, strong and natural.

"Yeah, I'm ready. You ready to get your wolf ass whipped Xon?"

His head bowed as the Change took over him.

I grunted. "I'm ready to kick your ass Shane."

I closed my eyes, called to my wolf. He charged up and flung himself against my body. The Change exploded, my human skin burst open and my wolf leapt out, fully-formed and ready for battle.

Dr. Norris cursed. "Holy shit."

Toni didn't hesitate. "NOW!"

I flung myself into Shane, shoving my blocky shoulder into his chest. Shane's hoarse gasp for air sent a thrill up my spine. My teeth snatched for his face, wanting to take out an eye but Shane slumped down, my jaw clicked on air. He was underneath me now and bucked up, his head heavily slammed on my neck. Now it was my turn to feel air wrenched from me, I croaked. Shane whirled with claws strapped for my face, he raked five furrows down my muzzle. I jolted backwards, he followed with olive eyes bright, gold spark flaming in his dark pupils.

"Don't retreat Xon!" Toni's human voice blasted through air rigid with snarls, growls and heavy salivation. "You can't be an Alpha by running! Fight him, face him and fight."

Shane charged, I raised up on my hind legs and dropped onto him, his head drove into the grass. My teeth sunk into the ridge of his spine, tearing for that cluster of nerves. Shane yelped and twisted, I fell and he rolled, claws and teeth flashing, struggling until we broke apart.

This was why Shane wanted to fight in wolf form. As wolves, he had the advantage of fangs, claws and being stronger and faster than me.

We circled each other, Shane was breathing hard with blood running down his back. I had blood dripping off my muzzle, and the slices stung as they etched together. I licked the blood away, revealing healed skin.

Shane snarled and leapt at me, I dodged but he whirled around too fast and his teeth slashed into my hindquarter, tearing a chunk of fur, flesh and meat away. I yelped, my heart thudded into my mouth and I stumbled away, my leg twitching as blood rushed down.

"XON!" Toni roared at me. "Use your fucking training! Stop being a pussy and fight back!"

Shane charged again, his teeth were slick with my blood and when he pushed off with his back legs to leap, I slid underneath him. His body landed hard on my back and I heaved upwards with my shoulders, tossing him across the field. He rolled over and over, I crossed the distance and my teeth snatched onto his leg, biting down. I tore at it, my growls thunderous. I jerked my head back and forth, grinding my teeth into the bone. Shane howled in pain and he pulled his leg back toward him but I didn't let him go. I slammed my paw down on his shoulder, pinning him down. My teeth sawed through the bone, starting to amputate it.

Shane flung himself onto me with his good legs and his teeth chomped onto my ear. His bite was like a machete and he yanked backwards and took my ear with him.

Immediately that side of my head went silent, it was like half the world had been muted.

I reared back, dropping Shane's leg and fell to the ground as blood tunneled down the ruined hole, like pouring hot water directly inside my skull. I dimly heard Sky scream my name. I wagged my head fiercely, shaking the blood out.

Shane got to his feet but held the one I had viciously chewed against his chest, now he had three legs and I was missing an ear. This wasn't enough, this wasn't showing who was winning. I needed to show him I was stronger and prove to him I was the dominant one.

I dipped my head low and raised my hackles, puffed up my fur all over, making myself look large, intimidating and parted my mouth wide, showing my saliva slick with his blood sliding down my thick sharp fangs.

Shane snarled right back and snapped his teeth together. A bit of my ear was sticking against his lower lip and he tossed his head, flinging it towards my face. A challenge, an insult. I didn't stand for it, I ran forward and crashed myself directly into Shane's ruined leg, he collapsed with a shriek of pain onto his side, his body sprawled out, his head knocked back, his throat bared. I dove for it, my jaws opened wide and just like that, fists gripped in the thick fur at my shoulders and heaved me backwards.

"That's it, it's over," said Toni's voice over my head, holding me back even as I bucked against him, the rush of the battle flowing in my veins. "You won Xon, quit it, the fight is over. You won. Calm down."

I still struggled, heaving against Toni's hold, my teeth snapping and snarling, demanding to get Shane's throat.

"Dammit Xon, enough!" Toni lifted me up then slammed me into the ground, his elbow locked over my throat and began to press, cutting into my air.

I kicked at first then calmed down as his knee landed on my chest, holding me down even further. I growled at him and lifted my lip but slowed my breathing, my tail flipped up and whapped against Toni's leg.

He grinned at me and asked, "If I let you go, you promise not to try and kill him? Just nod for yes."

I nodded and he stood, letting me go.

[Alpha! Alpha!]

My Pack ran forward in a charge of wolves, their voices combined and collected in my ears. They bounced onto my body and licked me, Sky cleaned my ear wound. Dr. Norris pressed in, shooing them. His hands gently pressed onto the empty space and his heat activated, it speared like a hot rocket into my face and within in moments my new ear was flickering around, my hearing went back to normal.

I stood up on all fours and Sky rubbed her face against mine and licked my muzzle and lips, whimpering. I licked her back and nuzzled her.

[I won Sky. I won.]

[I know.] She gently nibbled on my freshly-grown ear. *[You were amazing Xon, I couldn't take my eyes off you. I want you so badly right now, I want to celebrate, I want to feel you all over.]*

She licked my mouth and slipped inside, licking Shane's blood off my teeth.

My knees buckled then I climbed onto her, my teeth connecting on her shoulder.

"Whoa, down boy!" Toni was there again and he shoved himself in between me and my attempts to mount Sky, his hand forced my head away from her. "I don't think so, you need to stop that."

I growled roughly at him but Sky crooned and licked Toni's hand then rubbed her head against his chest, her tail wagged.

Connor and Leo and Javier crowded around, whimpering and pawing against me, wanting conformation that I was okay, that I was Alpha. I gave it to them, licking foreheads and damp eyelids, growling gently, comfortingly.

Toni backed out of the circle and ran his arm across his forehead that was slick with sweat.

He laughed, "That was something else, wasn't it Will?"

"He's different," answered Dr. Norris. "Shane's leg isn't responding completely to my heat. It's healed but he's in a lot of pain."

"Xon's dominance won't let it heal completely," said Toni, hands on his hips and he stretched; leaning his back in a curve, his spine popped. "Wyatt's wound has scarred. Tiny scar but it's there."

At the sound of Shane's name and Wyatt's name, I pulled away from my Packmates and trotted over to where Shane still laid on the ground, breathing heavy. His ears flipped as I walked over and he lifted his head off the ground, his eyes focused on me before he looked down.

I stood next to him, taking in his leg. It was matted with blood but no longer ripped open and wounded. I looked back to Shane, and while he glanced up at me, he then looked down again, not holding my gaze, not being defiant.

I stepped closer to him and ran my nose down his forehead, over his eyes. He relaxed under the touch, not stopping me. I sniffed his muzzle then ran my tongue over his cheek. The Pack scent strengthened over him, my scent, my Pack. He was mine now and I was his Alpha. The Pack came close and began to lick and nuzzle Shane, rubbing their fur and bodies against him. He was their Packmate, he was family, one of them and they accepted him as their own. Not only that, but Shane nuzzled and rubbed against them back, allowing his scent to meld with theirs.

Watching this, Toni said, "Looks like Shane's aggressive wolf has been pushed back down. With having an Alpha put Shane back into place, that'll curb that type of behavior. Being aggressive doesn't equal dominant. Shane was violent, but he couldn't become an Alpha and make a Pack. When you return to your human form Xon, Shane's aggression will be calmed, and he'll turn somewhat back to normal as he was before he became a wolf. Good job."

Shane stood up and tenderly placed his leg down, he winced and stumbled then brought it back up to his chest. He was healed but like Dr. Norris said, it still hurt, ached with the remnants of my dominance on it.

Toni said, "We're leaving now. Go and hunt, go and be wild with each other. Good job Xon. Let's go Will."

I watched them leave and get in the car, then waited until I could no longer see it. Sky whimpered and her nose nudged mine. She wanted to run into the forest, they all did.

I licked her face then I took off at a sprint, the Pack leapt to be at my side, behind me, around me with me in the lead. Even Shane was able to run, though he moved tenderly on his hurt leg. The forest bloomed and flooded. The ground thundered under my paws, and my head tipped back, the howl flew from my lips and joined the stars. Sky howled next, joining with my voice. This was us, our forest, our territory and we were here.

Leo made a short bark from the back of the Pack, he was tired and hungry. I slowed down then trotted to a stop, facing my Pack. Shane flopped to the ground, panting and licked at his leg. It was healed and the blood had flaked off during the run but the pain wouldn't go away. Javier slowly walked over to him and hesitated then laid by Shane. He rustled over until his upper body was hovering over Shane's leg. Javier closed his eyes at warm brush of his heat activating, seeping into Shane's body. Shane winced, his eyes closed and ears held flat to his head. Then, as the heat worked and Shane's body relaxed, Shane gently licked Javier's forehead in thanks. Javier's tail wagged just a bit, and he looked calmer, his ears flicked.

Sky nudged me and danced around me, her teeth took sharp painful nips at my face and flank, she wanted to play. I took my eyes off Shane and indulged her, snapped at her legs then gently used my paw to push her away.

Connor joined in happily, shoving his bright white-furred body between us and wagging his tail hard, slapping against our bodies. Like this, I realized how small Connor was, especially compared to me. I knew as a wolf my head came to Toni's chest, and Sky as a wolf her head only came to my neck. Connor's ears graced my shoulder. He was only two years younger than me, he shouldn't be *that* small.

Leo snuffled over and whined, running his head against my ruff as his stomach grumbled. He was ready to eat, for a hunt.

Connor nodded eagerly and pounced on his feet. *[I'm with Leo, let's hunt! Let's eat!]*

Javier stood up from Shane who rolled to his feet and tested his paw. It ached but it wasn't as bad as before. How I knew how Shane felt, the pain in his leg with a knowledge as if it was me instead of him, it was because it was my power, my pure dominance that hurt him and left its mark, so it was still connected to me.

I looked at Sky and Javier. *[What do you guys think? Ready for a hunt?]*

Javier shook himself so his chubby body wriggled like a worm. *[I am feeling empty. I wish to fill up.]*

Sky made a husky sound deep in her throat as her laugh flittered in my ears. *[I'm ready. Shane?]*

She looked at the large golden brown wolf who was pressing his paw into the ground then lifting it up before pressing it down again, testing his leg.

Shane looked up. *[I'm hungry...I guess. I've never hunted before.]*

I turned and padded into the forest, now flexing my nostrils for scents, my ears flipped up to hear. The Pack melded into the forest, also sniffing and listening, walking softly. Shane didn't know what to do, his anxiety wafting from the nervous twitches of his body, plus the audible rumbling of his stomach. Connor was excited and snatched up the bugs he found crawling over sticks and leaves but those did nothing to ease his hunger. Leo was trembling, aching on the inside and he stared over at me rather than paying attention to finding food. Javier knew what he was doing, he paused to listen and sniffed the ground for scent trails, looked for recent defecation and effects of grazing. Sky watched the other Packmates and watched me then copied even though she didn't know exactly what she was trying to smell.

We spread out further and it was me who whiffed it, a musky stark odor and heard the crunching of hooves on leaves. I slid into a bush and waited, the wolves around also went still and silent. A deer stepped out of the darkness, he was young, a fawn who's spots were only faintly disappearing. Why he wasn't safe in a thicket with his mother, I didn't know and it didn't matter. Now my Pack would feed, the racing heartbeats of my fellow wolves, the saliva running down parted jowls and I sent them a plan. I was going to attack the deer at the front and they join in at the back and sides, but to be careful of hooves.

I leapt out and the deer froze, eyes wide. The other wolves burst from the bushes and trees and the deer took off but he ran straight into me. I lunged forward, fangs slick and he kicked out, glanced over my muzzle and thudded into my eye, crushing it inwards. Sky screamed out of a wolf's throat, wretched and gut-clenching. She shoved the deer to the side with her shoulder, bending its leg inwards. The fawn collapsed downwards while Sky went to me, her tongue bathing my wound. My eye was a crumpled mess and the blood gushed downwards.

The fawn was thrashing so wildly that my wolves couldn't get close without risking getting slammed in the face like I had. So they paced around the edges, snapping and growling. The only thing we could do was wait until the fawn tired out. Sky snuggled my face into her chest and her heat swarmed into me, condensed on my eye and charged it. My old damaged eye sloughed out of my socket, and slipped to the floor, while a new one plopped forward and I blinked, the ragged eyelid ripped off as the new fresh one rolled down.

Sky backed up and licked my face, cleaning up the dried blood. *[Are you okay?]*

I got to my feet and blinked a few times, my vision was blurred then focused. *[Yeah, I'm fine. Let me kill this deer, as Alpha it's my right.]*

Sky licked me again then moved to the side. The fawn's kicks were becoming feeble, his eyes rolled in fear and froth dripped down his mouth. I stood in front of him, my wolves were seeping around the sides, eyes glowing and fangs flashing. The fawn pushed himself to his trembling feet but his eyes were on me. He feinted from left to right as if he was going to push by me but the wolves were circling tighter, he had nowhere to go and he was looking death in the face.

I lunged forward, my head smacked his chin upwards and my teeth clenched onto his throat, he bleated desperately and I tore backwards, blood sprayed out and his body crumpled, twitching as the breath left his body.

I turned to Sky with the fold of flesh in my teeth and she licked over my muzzle then accepted the piece.

[Can we eat?]

Connor's desperate voice broke into the scene and I turned back to the kill. The four wolves were hovering along sides the body but no one was eating because I was supposed to get the first bite. Shane was staring at the blood pooling from the fawn's open throat and his body was wired tight. I stepped in, Javier and Leo parted the way. I gripped my teeth into the fawn's belly and tore it back, ripping a large hole and the smell of fresh meat blurted out, steam rose up.

I started to eat and Sky came next to me, she licked over my face then began to eat. Shane went for the neck, Leo and Connor were working on the chest on opposite sides, Javier helped himself to the flank. We ate quickly, tearing the meat and gulping it down.

I was finished, my stomach was tight and firm from fighting, from training and I didn't need much. Javier and Leo scrambled over the leftovers, Connor laid down and watched with heavy-lidded peaceful eyes, his tail gently wagged. Shane had a section of the spine in his jaws and gnawed on it.

Sky pressed her body against mine and licked me slowly across my muzzle, her silver eyes focused on my face. Then she tilted her head and walked away, paused and looked over her shoulder at me. I followed after her, focusing on Shane for a moment and thought specifically to him.

[Stay with the Pack.]

He jumped and watched me disappear into the woods after Sky.

[Got it Alpha.]

Sky walked ahead of me until I caught up with her and I made that connection just between us.

[Is everything okay Sky?]

[I wanted to be alone with you.]

She slipped onto the ground and rolled onto her back, baring her stomach and her legs held against her body, looking up at me. I stood over her, and lowered my head to lick her face, then down her neck. She pressed her paws against my body. I was twice her size, my chest broad and my body stocky with muscle, my legs long and curved. She was smaller, slender and I smelled a quick dash of fear.

I laid down next to her and placed my head on the ground between my paws, made myself look harmless.

[You know I'd never hurt you, right?]

Sky rolled so she was next to me and tucked her nose under my leg, her eyes blinked at me.

[Yes. Xon...we haven't known each other long. But already I want to be with you all the time. The feeling that you complete me is frightening. I've done things with you I never thought I would, not like this.]

I nuzzled my head towards hers, lifting my leg to place it over her shoulders and she cuddled to me.

[If it wasn't for Toni stopping me, I would have tried to take you right there, in front of everyone, as a wolf.]

Sky shuddered. *[And I wasn't trying to stop you. It felt right, normal. That scares me too.]*

I licked her muzzle and across her eyes. *[Do you want to go back to the Pack now? We should sleep together, as a unit.]*

She stood up and looked at me. *[Are you upset? I didn't take you here to do it, are you mad?]*

I crawled over to her, then rubbed my face into the silky hair of her chest. *[No, I'm not. I don't want us to lose our virginity in the forest, and I especially don't want to with the entire Pack able to hear and smell what we're doing. Let's wait.]*

Sky murmured and nuzzled me then trotted off, I followed. The Pack were sitting down or laying, waiting for us. When we stepped up, Connor, Leo and Javier rolled onto their backs, stomachs bared. I went to each, and gently gripped their throats in a light commanding hold then licked them, marking them as subordinates, as mine.

Then I came to Shane.

He laid down onto his stomach, then rolled over. I gently nipped his throat and stood back.

Sky came forward and nudged Shane's face. *[Come, rest with us. Come and sleep with the Pack.]*

Shane let her lead him to where the Pack was curling up together for the night. I followed then laid down in the center, Sky laid next to me. The other four scooted close until everyone was comfortable.

I closed my eyes and slept. When my eyes opened, it was still dark outside and I was still in wolf form, which was a first. I could only take that to mean that I hadn't slept long enough to slip from fur to skin. I sat up and saw with a jolt that it was just me and Shane laying here. The rest of the Pack was gone.

I leapt to all fours and twirled in a circle but I didn't see Sky, Leo, Javier or Connor. I dove onto Shane and gripped my teeth in the back of his neck, shaking him.

[Wake up dammit! Wake up!]

[*Ow!*] Shane pulled away and got to his feet. [*What the shit is your deal?*]

[*They're gone.*] I tossed my head to encompass the empty clearing. [*Our Pack is gone.*]

Shane's eyes widened and he turned as he looked around. [*You're right. Maybe they went hunting again. Or decided to run for a little while. Sky is with them, she can protect them. Besides, it's just us in this forest, no one to hurt us.*]

Before I could respond, a loud heavy bellow wrecked the night sky, one so deep the trees shook and startled birds flew to the skies. Seconds following it was screams of frightened trapped wolves.

Shane and I met eyes then took off. At this distance, I couldn't hear words of my Pack, just desperate feelings of fear and helplessness burst in my head, and the screams of the wolves continued.

Shane's voice exploded in my mind. [*What is that? What's going on?*]

[*The Pack's in trouble.*]

I charged my legs harder, wondering how they had run so far in such little time. I thought Connor was too young, Leo was too thin and Javier was too fat.

Then we bust out into a clearing and my stomach dropped away. My wolves were cornered against a high sheet of rock and blocking their way out was a living mountain of furry muscle. It stood tall at sixteen feet to the shoulder, the body was blocky, the legs thick with muscle and claymore-like talons equipped the huge paws.

Fear slammed into me like a wave and I trembled, my breath snatched away. Shane froze next to me and his fear clogged his throat, he wheezed.

The beast thudded around to see us. It was an enormous bear, much too big to be a regular animal, it was even larger than a full grown African elephant. The thick heady scent of it, raw and rough, it was potent and stank, my nose seared.

A. E. Costello 357

Shane's voice whispered in my head. *[Think we can take him?]*

I glanced at him, he was staring down the beast with a heart that was slowing down to deep careful beats, his breathing calm and controlled and his rage was centering down to a small intense dot. He had found something to take that rage out on.

I whispered back. *[First, let me see if I can talk him down.]*

I stepped forward and thought to the giant beast. *[Leave my Pack alone!]*

In answer, the bear roared and like a bridge reeling upwards, it reared onto its back legs, making this beast tower twenty feet high and it crashed downwards. The ground shattered, and we went flying backwards to hit the trees. The beast turned back on my Pack and I didn't think a second further, I charged and Shane was at my side. His teeth snapped onto the bear's leg while I tried to jump onto the monster bear's back but couldn't clear it and instead hung on his hindquarters. His scent was so thick it nearly knocked me out and his fur was too heavily padded, I couldn't get past it.

The beast roared and swung around but I didn't let go and neither did Shane. The bear snapped and growled but he couldn't reach all the way around to his back; Shane and I were out of his reach. Then he began to sit down and we both jumped off him, if this fifteen ton bear sat on us we'd be dead, no doubt.

[Sky, get the Pack and run!] I shouted it over our connection.

The bear was facing down me and Shane and we began to circle him. I didn't know where this giant creature had come from, I had never seen it before but I wouldn't let it hurt my Pack.

Sky's voice burst into my head. *[The Pack is too scared Xon, they won't move and Leo's passed out! They're frozen stiff, paralyzed. I can't get them to listen to me.]*

I couldn't see her behind the beast's girth and the behemoth took a heavy step forward. The short blunt muzzle pulled backwards and reveal fangs longer than my own muzzle, the eyes were small, black with red fire burning in the ebony depths. He growled, a grating gruff noise that brought my hairs raising straight.

Just like that, it clicked. The horrific scent, the unnatural fear, the eyes. I stood there shaking as I looked at Mr. Richard Forrest, the chemistry teacher at my school.

The bear stepped forward, sword-like claws crunched into the ruined earth. Shane stepped to the side and the bear's eyes tracked him, then I moved to the opposite side and it watched me. An idea sparked in my head and I sent it to Shane.

[Got it.]

He kept sidling over and I did too, the bear moved to try and watch us both but we were on both sides of him. He roared and lumbered forward then turned around, watching us. This way, we had switched sides and now I was standing in front of my Pack.

I couldn't take my eyes off the bear to look at them but I thought to Sky, *[Drag Leo to safety. The other two will follow you, trust me.]*

[I'll do it.] Through our connection, Sky's voice was firm with determination, and the strength to protect our Pack.

The bear roared and the scent of rotten fetid breath brought me to my knees before I shook it off and got back up. Sky edged behind me, her teeth in Leo's scruff as she dragged him with her. Javier and Connor tottered after her, they smelled so much of piss but not because of their fear but because they had both gone on themselves.

The bear gnashed his machete fangs and stepped forward, the ground shuddered. I backed up, following the Pack backwards and so did Shane, keeping our eyes on him. The bear thundered forward, head lowered in a charge, he wasn't going to let us get away.

[Now!]

Shane dashed, the bear's head mouth opened to bite him, I jumped up and landed on his face. He was so huge, my pony-sized body on his tank-sized face was like a flea on a windshield. He roared and jerked his head but I hung on, my teeth gritted into his forehead and my right paw slashed down. I sliced over his eyelid then down his eyeball, then to his cheek, blood spurting up in a red spray.

The great beast's teeth gnashed in pain but then he lowered his head down until his nose touched the ground, letting me to my feet. I got off him, staring up. He blinked, blood rolled down his torn eyelid and pooled in the thick fur of his cheek. He dipped his large head in an acknowledging bow. He turned and walked away with heavy ground-shaking thuds until he was gone into the dark trees.

In the aftermath of the struggle, the forest was silent.

Shane came next to me, his olive eyes wide all around. *[Did that thing...Mr. Forrest...did he just bow to you?]*

My tongue stuck to the roof of my mouth, thick and bristly but I swallowed. *[Yeah, he did. I guess...I guess I won the fight.]*

We joined the rest of the Pack, breathing heavy.

Javier pushed his face into my ruff, his eyes closed and his breath ruffled my fur. *[Ursine...their Way...Mr. Forrest lost because you drew first blood. They aren't like wolves who fight to the death. Because Ursine have such thick fur and fat skin, it takes a lot to make them bleed. So should two Ursine fight, the loser is the one who bleeds first. You won Xon...you defeated a King Ursine.]*

My stomach dropped, taking my legs with it and I sat down abruptly. The Pack crowded around me, even Shane did it.

I looked into Javier's bright orange eyes. *[King Ursine? Mr. Forrest is a King?]*

Javier shook his head, laying his chubby head over my paw. *[Not as in royalty, the Ursine have no single ruler.*

No, he is a King Ursine by blood. A male bear that is naturally large and are extremely hard to kill. And you defeated him. A newly Changed teen wolf.]

His eyes closed and he said no more, suddenly falling asleep in the middle of his speech.

Connor was also not saying anything, his head tucked into my side, his paws dug underneath my abdomen. Even in sleep, he was breathing with quick high heaves of his chest, trembles still going down his spine.

Sky nuzzled both Javier and Connor, then dragged Leo over to lay in between them. Even though Leo was taller than her in the leg, she outweighed him by at least thirty pounds. Once his nose was pressed against my fur, Leo's eyes opened in a slow weary drag. The greenish brown eyes were blackened at first, but as our eyes met, the color filtered in, life returning as fear was chased back. His pissy scent was thick but I caught the whiff of citrusy happiness clouding over him before his eyes closed and he sunk back into sleep.

Shane moved away from me to lay next to Javier as Sky came to take that place at my side. She laid her head over my back, curling up close next to me. The Pack, together, safe, as one. Our scent, that smell that labeled us more than family, more than friendship, as a unit, warm, heady, pulled over us, heated in our nose and we all slept together.

11

August 14ᵗʰ
Thursday

I woke up with a long inhale and opened my eyes. I was human this time and clearly we had slept the entire night in the forest. The sun was bright and the rays heated up my face.

Sky's face was directly next to mine, our noses touched and her breath was my breath, we shared it and our hearts beat together. Even if we hadn't gone all the way, even if our bodies hadn't been intimately connected, we knew we were one. I leaned in and gently laid my mouth on hers, her softness press against my firmer lips. Her eyes fluttered open and she sighed, then her arm slid around my neck, she cuddled closer. I kissed her again, deeper and my hand glided down her back but I didn't caress, I didn't go further.

Sky broke the kiss and whispered, "You remembered."

I nodded and pecked her chin then slowly licked along the side of her jaw, she had some dried blood there. Sky wiggled and then leaned in and licked my upper lip, gathering up crusted sweat. Lust rose up in my chest, not lust, need, desire, aching and felt it expand at my lower body, pulling up tight. The scent was stark, sugary rush and Sky's smell matched it.

Sky kissed my nose and swallowed hard then got out, "We'd better stop."

"Yeah." I sat up and looked at the sleeping Packmates. I knew they wouldn't be sleep for long, once I woke the break of my sleep would resonate in them.

Leo's eyes opened first and he shifted, Connor's head rolled off his shoulder and down his arm. Leo sat up and held Connor against his chest so the younger boy didn't hit the ground. Connor woke up and nuzzled his head into Leo's neck, his arms went around his waist and his eyelids sunk down, drowsy. Javier was cuddled against my legs with Shane against his back, their legs were entwined and their bodies one line, nothing but sweat came between them. I knew Shane wouldn't like that once he woke up and he might attack. Sky also knew and she got between Javier and Shane, rolling Shane onto his back and he snapped awake. He jolted up, his eyes wild but because Sky was next to him and none of us guys were, he calmed. He laid back with a deep heavy sigh, crossing his arms underneath his head and stared up at the bright blue sky.

"So...you won." His voice was curiously calm and flat, stating facts. "You beat the shit out of my wolf."

Despite his calm voice, his scent morphed into depression and emotional pain, dank lifelessness and crumpled weakness. He had accepted the fate but didn't like it and it hurt him.

I said after a minute, "It's not like it was easy Shane. We both struggled."

Shane's jaw clenched then relaxed, he shrugged like it meant nothing but his scent darkened, he didn't speak.

I looked at Sky for help. She met my eyes over Javier's head, he was nuzzling into her chest but it wasn't sexual at all, his scent was warm and happy, no desire. His eyes were closed and he hugged her like someone would hug their mother, wanting comfort and platonic love.

Sky looked at me. "I don't know what time it is but it's still a school day. You're suspended Xon but the rest of us aren't. We need to get home and get to school as soon as possible."

I agreed and gently shook Connor and Leo. "Come you two, Change forms."

Connor bent over, his wolf lifted through his skin like his skin was paper that rolled backwards, or a costume he was sliding off to reveal his true form.

Leo crumpled on the ground, his body twisted and contorted, jerking the bones in and out of place, the muscles coiled and wrapped, his fur burst out and his wolf was remade. Leo laid on the ground, breathing hard, eyes closed.

I Changed as well then I shook myself. I looked back at Sky, taking in her sleek form, her legs were short but streamlined, her tail was large and looked like a horse's mane, silky and full.

I walked away out of the clearing. *[Come on you guys, let's get home.]*

I led my Pack back to the field, and all of our clothes and shoes were right where we left them. After getting dressed, I drove everyone back to their house, except for Shane who decided he'd walk the same way he had gotten there.

Back at home, I got straight in the shower to wash off the scent of the forest, blood and sweat. When I came back in my room, my father was opening the door, he was on the phone. He turned his back as I got dressed but he didn't leave.

He said, "Yes, he's right here." He looked at me. "Principal Hamilton has some words to say to you Xon."

He held it out. He was smiling and his citrusy scent matched. I took it, still adjusting my pants around my waist.

I said, "Yes ma'am, Jaxon Reeves here."

"Xon." She said. "I had a talk with a certain Antonius Stone and after a lengthy conversation, I've decided to be a bit more lenient. I know your suspension is over tomorrow, but I've decided I won't keep your reports on record. A new slate."

My jaw dropped and I stared at Dad, he grinned and nodded.

I coughed then said, "Wow, well, thank you so much Principal Hamilton. I promise I'll be better, I won't get anymore reports."

"I know you'll do your very best." she said. "However, the probation still stands. If you don't clean up your act, I really will send you to alternative school. That's how it has to be."

"Yes ma'am, I understand. But, if I may ask, what did you and Toni uh I mean Mr. Stone talk about?"

I had no idea that Toni would go this far, he never even mentioned helping me out at school. I don't even remember telling him I had been suspended in the first place.

She said, "Mr. Stone is a well-known shifter who's prominent in the community. He may not have been here long but he was a force to be reckoned with in Los Angeles and he's brought that same power here. He made a sound argument. Still, I have a favor to ask of you."

"Name it."

"Connor Hawkins hasn't come to school today." she said. "I know you two are friends, so if you'd check in on him I'd appreciate it."

I checked the time, it was going on one in the afternoon. Maybe Connor hadn't had a chance to finish getting presentable to go back to school or maybe he decided to go back to sleep instead. Either way, this gave me a reason to go back to his house and find out what was going on.

"Yes I will." I said. "I'll go over right now."

"Thank you Xon. I'll see you tomorrow, don't be late and don't skip class."

"Yes ma'am, see you then. Goodbye." I ended the call and handed the phone back to Dad. "Dad, she didn't tell me what Toni said but whatever it was, it worked. I can go back to school tomorrow. Suspension is lifted but I'm still on probation."

"You'll do better now, won't you Xon?" Dad slung his arm around my neck and squeezed me against him, the muscles in his thick arm constricted.

I nodded, grinning. "I will, no doubt." Then my face hardened. "Now I have to go to Connor's house and check on him."

Dad's brows raised. "Connor? The little one?"

I nodded again. "Yeah. Principal Hamilton says he hasn't come to school and asked me to go see him." I cracked my knuckles. "So that's what I'm going to do."

Dad spoke, his voice lowered. "Son, you just got in a fight and while it's true you look great, like nothing happened, I don't want you fighting again."

"Who says I'm going to fight?" I got my shoes and tied the laces up tight. "I'm making sure Connor is alright, that's all. His father should be at work, it's a Thursday. I'll go see why Connor didn't go to school and come back, that's all."

Dad nodded and checked his watch. "Alright. Twenty minutes Xon, be back home by then. I'm here because I was waiting for you to come home. I couldn't go to work and focus when I didn't know what was happening with you."

"Where's Mom?"

"Grocery shopping. You're always hungry when you come back and you eat like a pig. Or a wolf rather." He tossed me a smile and left with me behind him. "I'll have food waiting for you, okay?"

"Got it. Thanks."

I got in my car and drove away. It was true Connor's house was in walking distance but I had missed being behind the wheel. I got to his house and parked on the street.

Oh great.

A car was parked in the driveway.

Doesn't matter. Even if Carter is home, I'll tell him Connor has to go school so whatever he's doing has to stop.

I got out and went up the lane. I raised my fist to knock on the door, but my ears made me pause; bedsprings, squeaking. Carter's voice, mocking and cruel. Connor, making sounds of pain.

What the hell?

Rather than knocking, I went around the back of the house, listening to the sounds getting louder as I got closer. At the back of the house I was at a window, the blinds were partly drawn and I could see into what was Connor's bedroom.

My brain tried to shield what I was looking at first, so I couldn't understand, but as I refused to look away, my brain processed what my eyes were focused on and cleared up, revealing the horrifying truth. My heart had stopped beating and I couldn't breathe, just stared. What Carter was doing to his own son was deep in the areas of illegal, shocking, repulsive and plain evil.

When Connor screamed at a deep thrust from his father into his behind, I couldn't watch anymore, my heart jolted back into high speed and I sucked in a hard breath of anger, I was blind with rage, everything narrowed down to white except for my eyes zeroing in on Carter.

I bust through the window, my skin and shirt sliced but I didn't feel that pain, I felt Connor's pain and it was one thing I couldn't allow to continue.

"GET AWAY FROM HIM!" My voice was pure wolf, deep and snarling.

Carter stood away from Connor, not even upset. His penis was stained red with blood and he pulled up his pants, but didn't zip them all the way up. Connor scrambled from the bed and into a corner of the bedroom, his hands over his ears while he screamed.

"Ah, the Alpha. What are you doing here?" He raised a brow, a half smile on his face.

"Doesn't matter. Connor, come here." I held out my hand to Connor, ready to take him home with me.

Carter grasped my wrist with a strength like the bones of his hand were made out of reinforced steel. "No, I don't think so Jaxon Reeves. This here is my boy and he's not going anywhere."

"Then think again you piece of shit."

Using his grip on my wrist, I yanked my arm back while slamming out my other fist to bring his face hard into the blow, then I tackled him down. We grappled and Carter threw me across the room. I hit the wall on the ceiling, indenting it then fell down onto the bed, breaking it in two pieces. Carter walked toward me with blinding speed but I flipped up and met him with both feet to his face, kicking twice as hard as I could.

Carter stumbled back, his face hideously disfigured. It had been dented inwards, blood pouring down. He shook his head and his face *popped* back into place, he wiped the blood off with a brush of his arm as I got back to my feet.

"You still wanna fight?" He asked me as we began to circle each other, slowly, wolf eyes focused on each other. "If you walk away now I won't come after you."

"Whether or not you're telling the truth," I said. The room was overflowing with the scents of sex, blood, violence, pain and fear, I couldn't smell if he was lying or not. "I'm not leaving Connor here with you, not for another second."

Carter growled, his lips pulling back to reveal fangs three times the size of my own, but I refused to be intimidated, I was taking Connor with me no matter what. I growled back, showing my own fangs, then leapt for him.

Carter twisted me so my back was against his front and his arms clamped over my neck, suffocating me. I bucked my body and while he didn't let go, he fell backwards. I kicked my legs up and rolled, my body crushing Carter to the ground. He let me go as I finished the roll. I got up and stomped for his face but he stood up with a swiftness that had me taking a step back in shock. He whirled around and slammed me across the face.

I fell to the ground with my jaw out of line and my cheekbone shattered. Carter got on top of me, pinning me on my back and doled out sledgehammer punches to my face and chest even as I hit him back with my own super strengthened fists. I wasn't going to win by strength alone, no, I needed to use my intelligence too. I needed to put Carter down in one move. I remembered a move my own father taught me when I was younger, he said to only use in life or death situations because it was very dangerous and possibly fatal. Sounded good to me.

I made the peace sign with my fingers then brought them together so they were touching each other, firmed them hard and without waiting another second, I jabbed them in Carter's throat, at the indention where the left and right collar bone meet. The blow was made to cause his pharynx to cave in and stop him from breathing.

Carter croaked hard but he wasn't out, even though my fingers had gone into his neck, blood pouring down from the wound. I did it twice more consecutively, my hand going all the way into his throat, blood coming down my arm and it was splattered on my face and chest. His skin sucked at my hand, trying to heal over it.

I tore my hand away, ripping out his throat and he slowly keeled over sideways, eyes closed and body limp. The thud of his body hitting the floor was loud in the sudden silence, Connor had stopped screaming, Carter and I weren't fighting and snarling.

Death had fallen over the room.

I stood up with a tight curse. My shirt was drenched in blood, with both mine and Carter's. I looked down at him, he was unconscious, but the raw open spot where his throat used to be was slowly coming back together, the meat rebuilding and the skin sliding over it. I wanted to rip it out again but got another idea. I used my foot to nudge down his pants then stomped the shit out the part of his body that hurt Connor so bad, until there was nothing left but blood, even the meat had been eradicated.

I picked up Connor's shirt from the floor and dressed him in it. "Come on Connor, let's go."

Connor didn't speak, he was trembling so bad he could have been in a blizzard, he was pale and his eyes emptied. I took his hand and led him out of the house. It was the afternoon; everyone was either in school or at work. All the blinds of the houses were drawn, had no one really heard that deafening fight, the pounding, the screams, the snarls?

I helped Connor in my car and I got in the front seat, peeling away and zooming toward my house. I hoped the police wouldn't pull me over for speeding, being caught speeding while covered in blood would be exactly what we don't need.

I opened the garage door with the sensor clipped onto my sunshield then drove in. I didn't want any passersby to happen to look in my car and see the blood all over the seats, the steering wheel and the gear shift.

I parked and turned off the engine then helped Connor out of the car. He moved like an old woman, each step was slow and shaky, he wobbled as if he was being hit by a strong wind. I didn't try to force him to move faster. I kept my arm around his shoulder and murmured comforting things. We finally got to the garage door entrance and I helped him up the few steps then I opened the door and let us in.

"Xon, is that you?" Dad walked in from the hallway then froze at the sight of us.

I was covered in blood, while Connor was only wearing a shirt, his thighs damp in the same liquid. Thoughts raced over Dad's face, I couldn't smell him because the scent of blood and violence was thick in my nose.

He finally asked, "Did you kill him?"

I shook my head, leading Connor forward. "No, I just beat the shit out of him. Connor needs to get cleaned off and in new clothes."

Dad nodded and said, "Can he walk upstairs? He can wash in the guest bathroom."

I held Connor around his waist and across his shoulders then picked him up.

"I'll carry him."

I walked up the stairs with Connor curled in my arms, he still shivered and his eyes closed tight, his mouth pinched together. He breathed in quick shaking gusts from his nose.

"It's okay Connor." I said, bringing him into the bathroom. "Do you want to take a shower or a bath? A hot bath will feel better, but a shower can clean you quicker."

Connor whispered, his voice croaked and dry. "Shower."

"Okay." I set him down on his feet and opened the stall door. He hobbled in and I gently took the shirt off him then turned on the water. It flushed pink around the drain.

I turned my back, saying, "Go ahead and wash. I have to shower too."

He didn't say anything so I warned, "Don't do anything Connor, don't hurt yourself. I'll be right back. Alright?"

"Alright."

I rushed back to my room.

I heard Mom running up the stairs. "Xon! Xon where are you?"

I turned around as my door burst open and Mom stared at me, her horrified eyes looking me up and down. She swallowed hard. "Jaxon, tell me what happened. Your whole upper half is drenched in blood." She put a hand over her mouth, gulping as she swallowed back vomit. "Did you kill someone? Did you kill the person who did this to him?"

Anger gripped me. I wish I had killed Carter, he deserved it. How many times did he subject Connor to his filthy intentions? I realized I hadn't answered Mom and she looked like she was about to throw up.

"I didn't." I said finally. I wanted to hug her, but not when I was all bloody like this. "I just hurt him enough that I could get Connor away."

"What happened?" asked Mom, standing up straight. Mom was a strong woman and I didn't know what Dad had told her.

I looked at Mom with a slow hard breath, my eyes narrowed and jaw held tight. "His father has been raping him. I don't know how long it's been going on exactly, but I know it's been since I met Connor earlier this semester."

Mom touched her stomach and closed her eyes, breathing in slowly.

"I have to shower, but Mom, Connor needs clothes. He has nothing."

She nodded then rushed out just as quickly as she came. I tore my clothes off, ripping them into ribbons. With Carter's and Connor's blood on them, I could never wear them again. I showered quickly but made sure to scrub as hard as I could to take away the stench of violence, blood and Carter's touch. Dressed again, I went downstairs to meet with my parents.

They were in the living room, Mom was pacing up and down while Dad sat on the couch. Neither of them were talking but the stern furrowing of their brows meant they were thinking hard.

I said, "Connor is my brother now. I won't let him go back, ever."

My parents looked up at me. Mom's face was sickened but also kind. Dad nodded and crossed his arms.

Mom looked to the floor then back at my eyes. "Xon, you have to be sure about this. Connor is traumatized, he needs professional help."

"I'm the help he needs." I said and looked at Dad. "Connor needs clothes."

"I found jeans and a shirt that'll fit him." He said. "I put them in the guest bedroom."

Mom cupped her chin and cheeks with her hands. "Grant, Xon, he'll need more than just hand-me-downs. He can have the guest bedroom as his and-"

I cut her off. "Mom...you mean it? You'll let Connor move in?"

She looked down then looked me right in the eyes. "Xon, you've said before that something bad was happening at Connor's house, I've seen the desperate look he's given you. I didn't really understand, in fact, I didn't really care, didn't *want* to care. But seeing you, seeing him, like that, I know you care, you put your life on the line to end it. Yes Xon, he can stay."

I hugged her, lightly tensing my arms so she'd feel it, feel how happy I was. "Thank you Mom. Thank you."

She grunted and patted my back. "You're welcome. Now let me go, please."

I let her go and stepped back, wincing as she wrapped her arms around her waist. "Sorry. I held back, really."

She looked at me with wide eyes. "That was holding back? My God, no wonder you managed to beat up his father."

Soft footsteps had me look up as Connor entered the living room. He wore clothes several sizes too large for him, his eyes were dark pits on his face, his golden skin washed milky white.

"Connor."

I strode over to him and hugged him close, bringing him tight against me. His arms held me back, his fists clenching in my shirt as he buried his face between my pecs, crying and smelling me at the same time. I knew my scent was comforting and I rocked him back and forth while rubbing my arms up and down, trying to spread the smell of Alpha and Pack over him. The scent of belonging, of home, of safety and comfort.

"It's okay Connor, I'm here. I'm right here. You'll never be hurt again; I swear on my life that I'll protect you." I nuzzled against the side of his face and shoulder, making sure he heard the truth in my voice, smelled the mint bursting from my body.

The doorbell rang then knocked on.

Mom said, "I'll get it. Xon, take him to sit down, calm him."

I brought Connor over to the armchair and knelt in front of him to make him sit down. He didn't let me go, he moved his arms around my neck and put his face on my scalp, his tears ran down my neck and over my ears.

Mom said, "Yes? Who are you?"

The voice that spoke matched the disgusting Rogue scent leaking from down the hallway. "The name is Carter Hawkins ma'am. You see, you have something of mine that I'd like returned to me."

I jolted up as Connor paled then my mother screamed.

Dad ran but I got there first. Carter stood in the doorway, one arm around Mom's waist with her arms pinned to her side, the other around her neck. He wasn't squeezing but I knew Mom couldn't get away, he was way too strong. He smiled at us. Only the bright red rage in his eyes and his scent told his true emotions, his face was schooled into a polite expression.

"Evening Reeves." He said like he was a gentleman caller come to visit. "Now, we have some business to take care of. That is, Jaxon here has taken something from me and I'd like him back."

Dad stepped forward. I put my arm in front of him before he got too close.

Dad said calmly even with his scent heated with anger and pissy with fear. "Let go of my wife, now."

"Of course," said Carter, dipping his head. "Give me my son and you can have her back. A trade, simple as that. My son for your wife, nice and easy."

I stared him down. "Let her go." I growled, my vocals twisting to wolf. "Now."

My head lowered as my skull grew heavier on my human neck, my ears furred and pointed, I was about to Change.

Carter smiled, baring sharp teeth. "Give me my boy and I will. A trade."

Connor came from around me, tears pouring down his face and stepped forward. I grasped his arm and pulled him back, still looking at Carter. "There's not going to be a trade Carter. You're going to get out of my house before you get hurt, got that?"

Carter said, "You know, here I come to your house all polite and friendly-like but I sure don't feel welcome. I'd like to sit down and have a glass of water, where are ya'll manners?"

Dad's body twitched like he had almost attacked him but he said, "Fine. If you let go of my wife then you can come in, sit down and we'll have a reasonable discussion about Connor's future. Let her go."

"I'll come in," said Carter, stepping over the threshold and used his foot to push the door closed.

Dad backed up towards the living room, not taking his eyes off Carter or turning his back. I did the same and kept Connor at my side, I wasn't giving him up. I swore to protect him and I would.

"Now." Carter said, standing in the living room with my mother strapped to his chest. "Give me back my son and I won't ask again."

"No." I said, still holding Connor's arm. I spoke in a deep rough tone, trying to push back the Change so I could talk. "Now let her go and leave, then I won't hurt you."

My hand buckled with thickening bones, fur sparsely growing out of my knuckles, my nails blackened. My ears and eyes stayed wolf and my claws grew, yet my head lifted up, but my shoulders grew broader. My body was confused, anger and fear brought on the Change but I was shoving it back when I didn't have that much control over it yet. I had to get Mom away from Carter before I Changed, then I could end up hurting her by mistake.

Carter laughed, amused. "You, hurt me?" He smirked. "Ripping out my throat was a nice touch, but then trying to castrate me, that made me mad." His eyes narrowed. "I'll have you know I grew back, even bigger and better than before."

He thrust his hips against Mom and she screamed, twisting to get away, tears coming down her face. Connor broke away from me to throw up in a corner, his retching made my stomach harden into a ball.

"You have one last warning to leave her alone, or you're dead." I warned him as my spine rose up and my skin burned as fur slowly pushed through the flesh.

Carter's hand twisted and bubbled, then his index finger grew a long black talon. He placed it against her cheek.

"NO!" Dad shouted but I used my arm to bring him back before he did something stupid.

Carter smiled. "It would be a shame if her pretty face got scarred, wouldn't it? Give me my boy back and there's no need for anyone to get hurt."

My voice slick with saliva as I spoke around fangs, I growled inhumanly low. "If you don't leave I'll just rip it off all over again and this time I'll make sure it doesn't grow back."

Carter's expression distorted with anger and with a flex of his clawed finger, he drew a long line across Mom's cheek, breaking her skin and her blood slid down.

Even though it was my mother's blood, blood was blood, that hot smell added with my fear and anger, the Change burst forth and I charged him on all fours. Carter tossed Mom away and met me head on, Changed into his wolf. He had white fur like Connor and his eyes were bright red as they were in human form, but he was much bigger than I was, bear sized while I was as big as an overweight pony.

This fight was nothing compared to the training with Wyatt and Brenda, and the fight with Shane might as well been a play fight in regards to fighting with Carter in wolf form. We were in my living room, not outside, so the battlefield was small and cramped, I couldn't back up or dodge, there wasn't enough room. Carter was too strong, his paw was the size of my head and knocked me down with one blow. His bite tore past my fur and skin, taking chunks out of my side and legs, eating me alive. I could hear screaming, both Mom and Connor; my growling filled my ears along with Carter's infuriated snarling.

He rammed his shoulder into my chest, I flew off my feet and hit the couch, smashing it like it was a pancake. Standing over me was a polar-bear sized white wolf.

Carter bared his bloody teeth in a low rumbling growl. *[You're a fool Jaxon Reeves. You might have beaten me once but in this form, I'm a god. You can't beat me.]*

I shakily got to my feet, blood drenching my gray fur. I didn't break eye contact, peeling my lips back to flash my fangs.

[I won't let you hurt Connor again. You'd better leave now while you still can!]

I lunged for him, my paws hooked onto his shoulders and with one slash of my fangs, I tore out Carter's eyes, digging in hard enough to break his orbital sockets, crushing them.

Carter screamed and bucked me off him, shaking his head around as blood streamed from the ruined holes in his head. I attacked again, this time I chomped onto his right ear and bit it off, while my other paw ripped the other ear into shreds.

Deaf and blinded, Carter screamed and swung his paw out blindly. He was trying to fend me off while waiting for his wounds to heal but I was in my wolf form, my dominance was in full force. His wounds wouldn't heal that easily even though I had seen how quickly he healed before, I was in a human form then. I didn't know everything how dominance worked, but being in wolf form made it stronger, as it is my wolf that gives me that power in the first place.

I dove at Carter, using the strength of my lunge to hit him around his abdomen. He was already staggering around off balance, which was the only reason I was able to knock him off his feet. He splayed out on his back and I didn't hesitate, I slashed my claws and fangs into his bared stomach. His abdomen split open and his insides tumbled out, I grabbed them in my jaws and yanked them out, scrabbling both paws in his guts. Blood gushed from the gaping wound and the scent was thick in my nose, the metallic taste spreading down my throat.

Carter flailed around and his back leg slammed into my jaw, sending me spinning across the living room floor. I got up and saw him scooping his intestines with his leg, trying to pull them back into him. His white fur was slick with blood. His scent had changed, there was this new scent I hadn't smelled before but I recognized it, the cold acrid smell of impending death of another wolf. Listening to his wheezes as he struggled to breathe, how his blood continued to rush from the gaping hole in his abdomen, I charged to end it.

With a paw, I knocked his head backwards, baring his throat. My teeth gripped in until I had clenched around his spinal cord. He jerked in vain as I snapped my jaws shut then heaved back with all of my strength. His tendons popped like a guitar string, blood rushed down my throat and with a loud crunch, I crushed his bone. The meat of his throat and neck shredded like wet paper and with a sharp twist of my head, I severed the giant wolf's head from his shoulders, then smashed it to the ground.

Breathing hard, I stepped back and watched the ruins of the white wolf shudder, melt, then ease back into a human being. Carter's torso was ruined, his ribs cracked open to the air, his insides smeared on the carpet. His head lay crumpled at my feet, the skull dented with grayish pink brain matter oozing from the fractures. A new scent oozed from him, thick, gagging, acrid, like suffocation. Death.

I sat back, cocked my head and howled in triumph, the feat of victory belting from my throat, my ears rang. The house echoed with abrupt silence as my howl faded. When it finished, my body jiggled and wobbled until the wolf form slid away and I stood up as a human being, naked, covered in blood from head to toe, healed and whole.

I looked around. The living room was destroyed, all of the furniture smashed into pieces. The carpet was ripped up from large slashes of claws, revealing the wood underneath, there was even some holes in the floor all the way through the basement ceiling. The walls were splashed with blood, fur and saliva. Several windows were broken and the wall separating the living room from the kitchen was cracked, plaster and paint dusting the floor.

My family must have managed to escape the fight because they weren't in the living room. Cocking my head, I could hear talking from upstairs.

I stepped over the ruins of Carter's body and would have gone upstairs when Connor came running down. His skin was ice-white and his eyes wide enough to show the white sclera all around. His mouth flopped as he stared at me.

Then he asked, "Is it over?"

I nodded.

My voice gravelly, I said, "It's over. Carter will never touch you again."

Connor's eyes filled with tears. "Thank you Xon."

"Where's my parents?"

"In the bedroom. Your Mom called the police, I tried to stop her but she wouldn't listen. Mr. Reeves called Toni though, so I hope he can help."

I nodded. "Alright."

I wiped at the blood on my face, from my forehead to my chin. Doing that didn't help as my hand was wet with blood.

Connor shook his head. "Nothing but a shower will clean you Xon. You really…" He walked around me and stood in the hallway, a direct shot to see what was left of Carter Hawkins. "Holy fucking shit. Xon! You did that?"

"Yeah." I tried not to sound prideful but the knowing grin Connor gave me told me I failed. "I wanted him dead Connor, what can I say?"

"Xon?" Dad called down from the top of the stairs. "Xon is everything okay?"

"It's fine Dad. Carter…I killed him Dad." I looked at the floor, that prideful feeling washed away as Dad ran down.

Standing at the hallway from the door, Carter's body was visible in the living room against the wall. Dad covered his mouth and turned his back on the sight, facing me. I was covered in blood from head to toe, healed of my injuries. Whatever Dad would have said was cut off as sirens wailed from outside.

Dad cursed. "I tried to tell Kyra not to call but-"

He was cut off by several loud knocks at the door.

Dad opened the door but parted it instead of opening it all the way. "Yes?"

"Hello. We got a phone call about a murder at this location. Can you tell me what's going on here?"

I smelled two men behind the door, humans. I also smelled the metal of their guns.

Dad coughed but said, "Uh, yes, that's true. Ah…there's a body in the living room."

A short silence then the other man said, "Let us in so we can see the body sir."

Dad glanced over his shoulder at me, wincing but stepped back and opened the door. From the doorway, Carter's ruined body could be seen straight down. Both the cops drew their guns, eyes looking everywhere.

"Jesus Christ." The first cop saw me, standing right by the stairs, wearing nothing but blood. He held the gun on me, so I put my hands up even though it had to be clear I didn't have any weapons on me.

The second cop asked Dad, "Who else is in the house?"

"Just my wife," said Dad. "She's upstairs."

That cop lowered his mouth to his radio against his shoulder, saying, "Dispatch, start more units. Be advised there is a body on the ground." He glanced at Carter's remains, he paled and swallowed but he spoke calmly, "Victim is a white male, he's not alert, not conscious, not breathing. Again, start more units at this location." Then he clipped his gun back into its holster and pulled out handcuffs. "Alright, you three, you're all being detained."

Connor's eyes watered. "You're going to arrest me? But I didn't do anything!"

"Detained," said the officer. "Hands behind your back, now."

He touched Dad's wrist and Dad put his arms back without a complaint, his face calm. The officer cuffed him, then had him sit down in the dining room. Connor got cuffs on then also had to sit down.

When it came to me, the officer was very careful not to smear the blood on himself but cuffed me as well.

"Grant? Xon?" Mom's voice came from upstairs. "Is everything okay?"

"Who's up there?" The cop trained his gun on the stairs. "Come down slow, hands up where I can see them."

Mom came down, her hands by her head.

One cop cuffed her as well, saying, "You're not under arrest, we need you detained until back up arrives and we figure out what's going on."

More sirens wailed from outside and within minutes the house was full of uniforms. I couldn't get the scents; my nose clogged with the stench of the fight. Nobody made any move to let me shower or get dressed. I sat on the end of the steps naked and bloody, with one cop watching me. Everyone else got to work, taking pictures of the living room where the fight took place and asking Mom, Dad, and Connor questions.

Eventually they took me upstairs to the guest bedroom where a crime scene technician took pictures of me while I was being watched. I didn't talk to them because they weren't asking me any questions. It was clear that I was the murderer, Carter was in pieces and I was covered in his blood. There were three witness who knew I killed him and I know it was Mom who called the police on me. I was as good as in jail.

A black man came upstairs, he showed me his badge. "I'm Investigator Charlie Davis. Can you give me your name for the record please?"

"Jaxon William Reeves."

"Alright Jaxon, this is what's about to happen. I'm going to let you put on some clothes but not to shower. After you get dressed, you're coming with me to the county jail. Jaxon, you're under arrest for murder. You have the right to remain silent and refuse to answer questions. Anything you say may be used against you in a court of law. You have the right to consult an attorney before speaking to the police and to have an attorney present during questioning now or in the future. If you cannot afford an attorney, one will be appointed for you before any questioning if you wish. If you decide to answer questions now without an attorney present, you will still have the right to stop answering at any time until you talk to an attorney. Knowing and understanding your rights as I have explained them to you, are you willing to answer my questions without an attorney present?"

I nodded, numb. Even though I knew I would probably be arrested, having this guy read me my rights made it real. They led me into my bedroom and uncuffed me only so I could get dressed. Then the cuffs went back on and I was led downstairs.

"Xon!" Dad got up from the dining room chair but he was blocked from coming to me.

I couldn't meet his eyes. He had told me not to kill, he told me that the blood doesn't wash off easy, that I wouldn't forget. But getting a glance of the coroners using separate bags to pack up Carter's body, I felt nothing but triumph. Carter would never hurt Connor again, and his death wasn't easy, he didn't die quickly. Maybe that made me a murderer but in my eyes I had rescued Connor from his pain and I'd never let him get hurt like that again.

Outside there was a TV van and a crowd gathered outside. There were shouts and gasps as I was revealed. Even with clothes on, it was just a T-shirt and jeans. My revealed arms were crusted in dried blood, my head patched and flaked with the dried liquid.

"Back, get back!" The police refused to answer questions thrown at them, and I was put in the back of a cruiser without saying a word. I kept my eyes on the floor in front of me and tried not to think too hard. I should cooperate with whatever the police wanted because I was already in enough trouble, I didn't need to make it worse.

The door opened and I was helped out. The building read the words Lakeside Village County Jail. I breathed out slowly but walked with the officers into building through a sliding door. It closed behind us then another door opened in front.

A man was standing there, his nametag said Correction Officer Tom Michaels.

He said, "Are you hurt? Have you been injured?"

He was staring at all the blood on me.

I shook my head. "It's not my blood."

Tom Michaels blinked and glanced at the other two officers, who nodded but didn't offer any information. I got searched though I had nothing on me, then they took my height, weight and I got my mug shots taken and my fingerprints recorded. After I was finished being processed, they gave me an orange jumpsuit to wear and I was finally allowed to take a shower. Watching Carter's lifeblood run down the drain, even though I was in prison, the sense of pride that I had killed him remained.

Dressed, I was put in a cell by myself. After about ten minutes, an officer came to my cell.

"Reeves, phone call."

I sat up straighter. "For me? Already?"

The officer nodded and unlocked the cell. "Let's go."

He held my arm and led me to a room where there were several phone booths, there were other people in orange jumpsuits on the phone. If I concentrated I would be able to hear all of their conversations, but instead I got on the phone that the officer directed me to.

"Jaxon Reeves."

"Hey nephew. This is Jeremiah Reeves."

The voice was unknown but similar, like Dad but gruffer, rougher, older.

"I'm your father's older brother."

My stomach dropped low in my gut and I froze.

"Well, I know you're wondering why Uncle Jerry is contacting you after so many years of silence but the fact is I heard about the trouble you've gotten yourself into. Damn Jaxon, a murder charge at seventeen? That's some serious shit."

I swallowed hard and licked my lips before saying, "I did what I had to do."

Connor won't get hurt anymore, that's all I wanted. Whatever comes next, I'll handle it.

Jeremiah chuckled, his voice coarse but smooth. "I see. You sound serious. I'm calling to let you know I won't let you waste away in prison. I'll get you out as soon as possible, alright?"

I nodded. "Okay."

A hand came over my shoulder, the same officer as before. "Time's up."

"I have to go." I said to the uncle I never knew.

"See you soon nephew."

He hung up and I put the phone back on its hook.

I was put back in my cell but I didn't wait long until Investigator Charlie Davis came. He took me into a small room that only had a table and two chairs across from each other. He had me sit down and he took the other chair.

He put down a tape recorder on the table and with his thumb clicked it on. "For the record, I'm Investigator Charlie Davis. Jaxon William Reeves is here to talk about a murder investigation. Jaxon, this conversation will be recorded, understand?"

I nodded. "Yes."

Charlie Davis put down a folder on the table, flipping through pictures of the ruined living room, lots of blood splatter, and Carter Hawkins' leftovers after I was through with him.

He sighed heavily and said, "It's been a long time since I've seen something this brutal. Not since I lived in NYC back in the day."

Charlie had iron gray hair and his dark brown eyes were just as steely. I could smell him, he was human and had a personal scent of oil and grass. His words smelled like mint, truth.

I didn't have anything to say to that and nodded silently.

He looked at me and said, "I thought I recognized your face when I saw you, but it was really your father that nailed it. Wouldn't have thought his son would have followed in his footsteps."

My eyes widened. "What?"

"Jackson "The Punisher" Reeves." He said, a wry smile twisting his mouth. "Small time hustler, drug dealer and errand boy, he did the head's dirty work. Jeremiah "Gravedigger" Reeves, the older brother and leader. Your father got arrested multiple times and did time for possession and assault with a deadly weapon. There's whispers he might of murdered for the big man but there's no proof. Ran jobs for the gang from fourteen to twenty-four. Broke off, cleaned himself up, went to college, got married and works in construction. And now here goes his son, killing too. Only this time you didn't cover it up, did you? Right in the living room of your house. I guess your father didn't tell you all the tricks of the trade now did he?"

My hands were cuffed behind my back and my fists clenched. The handcuffs weakened so I stopped before I broke them.

I said, "My father is a good man. I don't care what he did in the past, he raised me right."

Davis's thick brows arched. "You killed someone Jaxon or maybe you didn't realize it? This man." He checked the file. "Carter Hawkins. You tore him into pieces."

I opened my mouth to say *he deserved it* when the door opened, an officer stood there. "Davis, Reeves's lawyer is here."

A man I had never seen before stepped in, saying, "Nathanael Murray, Stone Industries attorney at law. Jaxon, don't say another word."

I closed my mouth tight.

Stone Industries? As in…Toni Stone? So Dad did get in contact with him.

Davis stood up. "Alright then. I'll have him taken back to his cell until his court date is set."

A. E. Costello 385

"His bond has been paid," said Murray. "He's coming home now."

Davis's brows furrowed. "No, that doesn't make sense. He's a murderer, there's no way he's been given bond."

"A certain Antonius Stone had it settled." Murray held out a piece of paper. "Read it if you'd like." He snapped his fingers. "Jaxon, with me."

I got up and went over to Murray while Davis looked down at the paper. Murray walked away so I followed him. After my handcuffs were removed, I was given new regular clothes and then taken to my father.

"Xon!" Dad hugged me tight to him, and I was careful not to hurt him when I hugged him back. "Are you alright? They didn't hurt you did they?"

"I'm fine." I said, but I looked at Murray. "What's going on? Did Toni call you?"

Murray nodded and that's when I saw the gold fleck in his pupils. "That's right, I'm his lawyer on retainer."

Dad said, "But how did you do it? Xon, he clearly." Dad paused then said, "All the evidence is plain. There's no way they would let him walk."

Murray dipped his head. "Antonius Stone has a lot of pull, let's say that. Now, shall we go?"

And just like that, I walked out of the jail with my father and the lawyer. However what Investigator Davis said had stuck with me. I knew a little about Dad's past, he had told me and raised me to not be like him but to be better than him.

Murray led the way into the parking lot when a large black SUV pulled up in front of us. The passenger side front window rolled down and if it wasn't for the fact I knew my father was standing right next to me, I would have thought I was looking at him. This man had the dark skin of my father, his features molded and handsome, a shaved clean head. There were differences. His eyes were darker, colder and there was a scar in his brow, a short white nick in his skin. His nose was crooked slightly off-center, it had been broken. He slowly smiled and revealed a silver tooth, his left canine had been replaced with a silver replica. The sight of it made my eyes prick and I stepped back.

Dad whispered, "Jerry, what are you doing here?"

Jeremiah "Gravedigger" Reeves, my father's older brother and my uncle that I had never met until now. He got out of the car and stood in front of us. He smiled again.

"I came to bail out my nephew but I see it's been taken care of." He looked at Murray then back at me. "Shame nephew, this is the first time I see you and its about something like this."

Dad stepped in front of me, blocking Jeremiah's view of me. "I never wanted you to meet him Jerry. Now go away, back to whatever drug house you came from."

"Come on Jackie." My uncle made a soft huff. "Is that anyway to talk to your dear older brother? You haven't seen me since...since my nephew was born. After that you've treated me like I'm the plague."

Dad said darkly, "You bring death everywhere you go and I want nothing to do with you."

I had never heard Dad say something like that before, and to think it was to his own brother.

Murray said, "We have some place to be, so if you'd excuse us."

He touched my back and my father's shoulder, trying to get us to move away.

Jeremiah smiled but sidestepped to stop us from leaving. "What do you know. You got a lawyer? And not just any, a high-class fancy lawyer from Stone Industries. Top-notch. But what I want to know is how my little knuckleheaded nephew could even afford a lawyer of that caliber. Jackie you don't make enough in a year to pay this man for a month's service."

My father lifted his chin. "None of your business Jeremiah. Now move, we're leaving."

Jeremiah's eyes widened. "Jeremiah? That's what it's like between us now, formal? So you want me to call you Jackson now?"

"I don't want you to call me anything because I don't want to see you ever again." Dad's knuckles cracked into fists. "Now let us pass. You go back to your life and we'll continue ours."

Jeremiah spoke softly. "I just came to help out Jackie."

"Well your help wasn't needed and never will be needed." Dad's voice was firm, final.

Jeremiah raised and lowered his shoulders. "This is a damn shame Jackie, that this is how I meet your boy. I'd prefer we all sit down and eat together, be like family."

"I don't want to be your family Jeremiah," said Dad, his voice low and warning.

Murray said, "We really need to be on our way. If there's anything else then you can take it up with me later."

He held out his card to my uncle.

Jeremiah flicked it away with his fingers and got in the car. "Alright Jackie, I see how it is. I guess I'll see you another time, hmm?"

The SUV pulled off with my father watching it go.

"Dad." I said. "You never told me you had a brother."

"Because I wish I didn't."

That was his only reply as Murray led us to his BMW.

Murray had driven Dad here but instead of taking us home, he was heading into the city.

I asked, "Where are we going?"

Dad answered. "They took your mother to Toni's house. Said something about an infirmary and their doctor wanting to look at the scratch on her face."

My heart leapt into my throat and pulsed hard. "You mean, is she, did Carter?"

"I don't know." He said it calmly even as his scent soured pissy with fear. "All I can do is pray. Jaxon." He closed his eyes and rubbed his brow. "Did you have to kill him? I got us out of the living room the moment you two began to fight. When it got so bloody and Kyra was screaming, Connor was sick, I got us all upstairs. Even two floors up I could hear it, sounded like a war going on underneath my feet. The house was shaking Xon, and the growls, the snarling, it was all so inhuman. I thought you two were killing each other."

"It was to the death." I said, looking out of the window. "It was either him or me. I fought to protect Connor, to put an end to the pain he was in. I had honor on my side, the protection of my Packmate. Carter was nothing but a disgusting foul Rogue. He deserved how he died."

"I told you before Jaxon, I told you that no one should decide who lives and dies." Dad's voice thickened like he was about to either cry or throw up.

I had nothing to say to that and just kept my eyes out of the window.

The rest of the ride was done in silence, then Murray parked outside of Toni's house. Murray got out and we followed him. Inside there were a lot of people, all Stone Pack. Their energy pulsed, throbbed and they all looked at me with billowing gold sparks in their eyes.

Dad made a short gulp in his throat and clasped my wrist tightly. The basement door opened and Dr. Will Norris stood there.

"Come." He said, disappearing back downstairs.

Dad let me go and rushed after him.

I glanced at Murray who was heading to the front door. "Thank you."

Murray nodded and quietly left.

I went downstairs. Mom sat on a cot, with Connor at a chair next to her. Her clothes were ruffled with a few drops of blood on her collar. There was a bandage on her cheek.

"Mom!"

I ran to her side and gently encased her in my arms. She wriggled so I let her go, then Dad hugged her and pressed kisses to her forehead and nose.

"Are you alright?" We both asked together.

Mom said nothing, just looked at her lap.

Dr. Norris said, "She's fine. The scratch has scabbed over but there's no sign of infection. If she was going to Change it would have happened immediately."

Dad and I both breathed out heavy in relief and we shot each other grins.

Dr. Norris got a message on his phone, glanced at it then said, "Toni is upstairs. He'd like to talk to you."

Dad held Mom's elbow and helped her stand up, she wobbled and leaned on him. I touched Connor's shoulder, he put his hand into my pocket and we all went upstairs. The living room was crowded with Stone Pack wolves, including Wyatt and Leah. Wyatt was giving me an ugly look and from across the room I couldn't smell him but the curl to his lip and the utter hatred in his eyes, I didn't need to smell him to know his emotions.

Leah broke away from her Pack and went into my arms like she belonged there, wrapping her arms around my neck and placed her face into my chest. Her lemongrass and vanilla scent rushed into my nose, along with that tinge of sugar and fear. Sky's face flashed in my mind at the same time Leah's breasts pressed against my chest. The clashing mix made me freeze in her grasp. I wanted Leah to let me go. The wolf wanted to stay in her arms. I didn't move.

Leah gasped out. "Xon! I'm so glad you're safe! To think, you fought and killed a Rogue wolf, at only seventeen and still newly Changed. That's incredible, insane!"

Even before I could react, Connor growled at her. In human form, his nose wrinkling and his lips peeling back towards his teeth could be seen as childish, if it wasn't for the sharp machete-like fangs stretching his mouth.

"Quit it Leah." A black guy stepped forward, he grasped the back of her neck and yanked her off me. It was Ethan, the wolf who I had defeated in a challenge before.

He said, "You're embarrassing your Pack. Show some restraint."

Leah showed her fangs to him but stepped away from me.

Mom and Dad were staring at her like she was insane and both of them had their fists clenched. If it wasn't for Ethan, I had a feeling they both would have forced her off me.

Toni stood straight from the wall he was leaning on, and gestured to us. "Reeves, come with me to my office."

The office was by the back of the house. The desk was oak and huge, the floors were carpeted, the entire back wall was covered in full bookshelves, books squashed into every free space. There was a plant in the corner that reached up high towards the ceiling.

He sat at the desk. There were two chairs in front of the desk, so I had Mom and Connor sit down, then Dad and I stood behind them.

Toni leaned back in his chair and crossed his arms behind his head. His platinum blond hair was growing out, peeking black roots at his forehead. He also hadn't shaved, his chin and jaw dusted with black growth.

He looked at us. "So I need to tell you what's going to happen now."

Dad stood straighter. "About Xon. He killed a man."

"He killed a wolf." Toni corrected, making both of my parents stiffen. "A Rogue wolf at that. This is shifter politics now Reeves and the humans no longer have any say. They weren't even supposed to process him as a murderer in the first place, had my people gotten there first." He glanced at my mother who gasped quietly. He continued as he looked back at us, "then that wouldn't have happened. I'll have his record cleared, it's not a problem."

Dad said, "Are you telling me that Xon isn't in any trouble?"

"He's in a little hot water, yeah." Toni shrugged one shoulder. "However nothing will happen at the moment to him, the case is being sent to the Alpha of the United States and he will decide. As of now, Xon is free to continue about his life. As for you Kyra Reeves." He looked at her again, her breath hitched. "It looks like you're free as well. Even though you were scratched you weren't infected. If you were, you'd have Changed at the scene. Looks like your cut is healing at a normal human pace as well. I'll get someone to take you home."

"What about Connor?" I placed a hand on his shoulder. "He can come with us, right?"

"He doesn't have any other family." Toni said. "So I don't have a problem with him staying with you. If you want to formally adopt him, give him the Reeves name, that's up to you guys."

He stood up and stretched his arms in front of him with his fingers laced, popping a few joints with a rough sigh.

"Anyway, that's all. I've got nothing left to say."

"Wait." I said. "Toni, can you tell me why Wyatt hates me? He gave me a real ugly look just a moment ago and I swear I haven't done a thing to him. Mikhail told me he was holding a grudge but what grudge? I've never even seen him before until he tried to kill me."

Toni rubbed the back of his neck then said, "You don't have to worry about it. I've kept Wyatt on a tight leash, he won't come after you again. Now go ahead, the car is waiting for you."

So he's not going to tell me.

Mom stared him down. "I don't think so. Xon told me a little bit about some white guy who would try to kill him. If there's a chance my son's life is in danger then I want to know."

Toni sighed and gave me an annoyed look but his scent stayed clean as he looked back at Mom. "Listen, I have Wyatt completely under my control. He won't try to kill your son, you don't have to worry about it. I wouldn't say this if I didn't believe it. Wyatt isn't allowed to go into Lakeside Village and when Xon comes here Wyatt isn't to go anywhere near him. Xon is safe from Wyatt. There's no need to worry, so go ahead and let my driver take you home."

Dad touched my shoulder and Mom's. "Let's go you two. We've overstayed our welcome, so let's go."

I left Toni's mansion with my family, Connor included. A slick black sedan quietly purred at the curb, and the door had a large stylized SI symbol on them, along with little flags on the hood.

Dad glanced at me as the driver got out and opened the back door. "Stone Industries. You made a friend in a high place Xon."

I ushered Connor in and slid in after him. Mom got in next to me then Dad. It was really roomy in the back, even though Dad and I were both two hundred pounds plus, I didn't feel squished or cramped.

Connor laid his head on my shoulder, his hand curled around mine and he gripped tightly. "Is it really over Xon? I keep feeling like I'm dreaming, like I'll open my eyes and I'll be back home, with Carter."

I placed my free hand on his head and stroked his bright green hair. "It's no dream Connor. I got rid of him for you, he'll never hurt you like that again. I won't let anyone hurt you."

Connor flicked his eyes up to meet mine then he blushed and looked down but leaned heavier against me, relaxing with a relieved sigh.

"Who was that girl Xon?" Mom spoke as the car silently pulled off from the curb.

I sighed but said, "Her name is Leah. I met her in California, before I knew the Stone Pack or anything. We were talking, I guess she was kinda putting moves on me or whatnot. Then Rocky showed up and did his best to disembowel me."

Mom made a retching sound, so I quickly said, "Sorry Mom. Anyway, I Changed right there. Now fast-forward to present day, the Stone Pack has moved here, I'm a wolf too and she still likes me. I don't know what happened to

Rocky though, I haven't seen him since and no one will tell me what happened to him."

Dad tsked as he shook his head. "So she chatted you up while you were human and now that you're a hotshot teen wolf, she's taking her second chance."

My brows rose at the heat to his tone, his spicy scent matched.

"Even if that's the case, I like Sky."

It was my turn to blush at my own blunt admission.

Connor grinned up at me. "Just wait till she hears what you did."

"Everyone should know at this point," said Dad with a short sigh. "It was all over the news Xon, there's full coverage of you being lead out of the house in handcuffs covered in blood." He touched his mouth. "What I saw, I can't believe you did that. His body... there was nothing left."

Mom retched in her throat then mumbled thickly, "Please, stop."

Dad apologized and cuddled her to his chest but she pushed against him, rejecting his hold. There was pain in his eyes but he let her go.

The rest of the ride was done in silence.

"Thanks." I said to the driver when the car stopped outside of our house. It looked abandoned. The grass was rumpled and there were sheets of paper and yellow tape on the floor, the door was closed with yellow tape crossed over it. A window was shattered.

The driver looked over his shoulder as we got out. "Alpha will send people to help with the damages tomorrow, so try and bear with it for now."

I nodded and followed my family into the house. The door closing behind us echoed loudly in the quiet house. The front walkway was dirty with muddy footprints and black smears. There were white and red markers on the floor and wall. In the living room were chalk outlines of where Carter's body used to be. All the blood had been cleaned up, though the holes in the floor, the shattered plaster, the crushed furniture were left.

The stench of death was thick in the air, the last remains of Carter's presence in this world.

Mom retched again but as she ran up the stairs I knew she wasn't able to hold back the vomit this time. Dad rushed after her.

Connor stood in the walkway, staring at the outline. His scent thickened and molded together, it was so full of different emotions that I couldn't sort them out. His expression though looked calm and straight.

He spoke in a soft distant voice. "That's the end of him."

"Yeah." I said also quiet.

Then my stomach growled and cramped with pain, I bent over a little bit. I hadn't eaten since the hunt last night and it was five o'clock right now. Connor's stomach echoed mine, he must not have eaten either.

Connor's eyes widened and he went into the kitchen. "There's food, Mr. Reeves told me he had cooked and Mrs. Reeves had gone shopping."

I came in after him as Connor opened the refrigerator. We both began to eat standing up right there. Connor ate and drank what was closest to him, I easily reached over his head and ate from the higher shelves. We didn't talk besides the chomping of chewing and the gulping of drinking. It took about five minutes, but the fridge was cleared out so we moved onto the freezer to keep eating until it was picked empty.

I stumbled back, my stomach bloated. "I'm stuffed."

Connor burped and rubbed his pouch.

"That was good." He said with a thickened voice, burping again.

I grinned and headed up the stairs. "Come on Connor. Toni's people will come clean up tomorrow, so we might as well go to bed. Mom gave you the guest bedroom, right?"

Connor and I got ready for bed even though it was only about five pm, I didn't see any real point in staying up any longer. Besides, I was allowed to go to school again and I should get my rest.

After another shower, I got into my bed and relaxed. I fell asleep for about two hours or so when I opened my eyes because I heard movement in the hall. I sat up as my door was knocked on quietly. Connor peeked in. It was dark with only light from the Moon stealing in from my window, but I could see Connor clearly. His eyes were wide and he was breathing slightly elevated, the scent of piss from fear was rolling off him almost in a visible tangible cloud.

"What's wrong Connor?" I asked, patting the side of the bed next to me to show he could sit down. "Why are you so scared?"

"I don't want to sleep by myself." He said quietly, sitting down. "Every sound I hear it's like Carter coming after me. I can't even keep my eyes closed. It's nerve-wracking."

I peeled back the covers. "Then get in, we'll see how you feel in the morning, okay?"

Connor got in with a grateful smile and wrapped himself tight against my pillow. I tucked the covers up to his shoulder and laid back down. Connor wasn't sleeping next to me, he was unmoving and quiet, but he was still awake.

I paused, then did what Mom used to do when I couldn't sleep, I put my hand on his stomach and began to rub it in slow gentle circles. Connor jumped for a second but then his body relaxed under the soft touch. In only a few minutes he snored as he breathed in through his nose.

I was glad he was sleep and closed my eyes, I rubbed him for a while longer before I fell asleep.

12

August 15ᵗʰ
Friday

"Where's Connor?" asked Mom as I entered the kitchen for breakfast the next morning. "Isn't he hungry?"

"He's sleeping." I said, washing my hands at the sink. "Very heavily asleep, I bet he'll wake up in time for dinner."

"He shouldn't sleep for that long, he'll throw off his sleep cycle." Mom frowned. "Besides, what about school?"

"I know but we should leave him." I said, urging Mom to sit down as she moved like to get up to wake him. "This is probably the first time in a long time he's been able to sleep so well. Back at home, every time he went to sleep his bastard father would sneak in and rape him. Now he can sleep without that fear."

"Oh right." Mom nodded, her eyes a little wide and her scent sickened. She looked at the kitchen table where she had the Lakeside Times newspaper. Right there on the front page was my own face, flecked in blood and blank of emotion. I looked like I wasn't feeling anything.

I asked, "What does it say?"

"It's talking about the fact you're not going to jail or being incarcerated because you are a shifter who's killed another shifter." She said, crinkling the edges of the newspaper in her hands. "If you had killed a human being, it would be a completely different ball game. However, when crimes take place between shifters, it's up to the shifter community to deal with it and humans have no say in the matter. The article says the police were wrong to arrest you in the first place and the first responders shouldn't have done anything the moment they realized it was a shifter politics, as it had nothing to do with them. The investigator who took over the case is having an inquiry for pursuing your persecution when he should have known the murder was technically none of his business. It mentions he

A. E. Costello 397

might have a grudge against your father and he's taking it out on you."

"Wow." I said it softly. "That reporter really did his research…Will Dad be okay at work?"

"He's on the phone with his supervisor now." she said, lifting her chin towards the study. "At this point, I think they want him to take a while off until the heat dies down. He shouldn't be getting fired I don't think."

I sighed out in relief, glad that my issue hadn't ruined anything for my parents. I glanced into the living room, it looked like the cover of a home design magazine. New paint, new hardwood floor, new furniture and broken windows had been replaced, we even had new curtains.

I asked, "When did they come to do this?"

"Five in the morning." she said. "They finished by seven, worked amazingly fast and very efficiently. Humans couldn't have done it that fast."

Mom stood up and tossed the newspaper into the garbage. "I saw what you two did to the refrigerator." She sighed and rubbed the back of her head. "So I had to go shopping again. Listen, I know you two get hungry but cleaning out all of our food like that will have to stop."

I winced and looked at the floor. "Sorry Mom. It won't happen again, I promise."

She huffed but waved me out of the room while she started to cook.

I went to the study and listened in, but I didn't hear Dad talking. I knocked once then peeked inside.

Dad was at the computer, elbows on the desk, holding up his head with both hands. A burnt scent of irritation wafted off his skin.

"Dad?" I crossed the room in one lunge and knelt down at his side. "Are you alright?"

"I'm fine." He said, sitting up so I got to my feet. "Jeremiah is trying to contact me again, so I'm a little upset."

I shook my head. "I'm sorry, it was my fault that he's bothering you."

Dad shrugged a shoulder like he didn't care but the wrinkles at his eyes and the tightness to his mouth told me otherwise.

"Anyway." He stood up and stretched. "I have a question for you, it's been bothering me since yesterday when everything happened."

I nodded and leaned against the desk. "Shoot."

"How was it that Carter was able to well, hold Connor down?" Dad asked me. "He's a werewolf too, right? How come he didn't fight back? Aren't werewolves ten times as strong than humans?"

"Well let's go with that." I said. "Me and you for instance. Say we're both human. As my father, you're taller, you're older, stronger and more experienced. It's pretty obvious that you can beat me up if you want to, because of those factors. Now that I'm a werewolf, and saying I'm ten times as strong, then yes, I could beat you up. Now apply that to the Hawkins. Carter was taller, older, stronger and more experienced than Connor and he was ten times stronger than Connor. Even though Connor's a werewolf, the strength applies just like it does with humans. Little kids aren't as strong as the adults and if they have no muscle, they aren't as strong as someone who *does* have muscles."

Dad nodded slowly, rubbing his chin. "So because Connor is weak physically as it is, he can't defend himself against someone bigger and stronger, even if he is a werewolf."

I nodded. "Not all werewolves are the same strength, we may have the basic ten times as strong than a human, but up-against others like us, some are stronger than others. I mean, there's the Alpha queen in Toni's Pack, named Brenda. She's beaten me up more than once and she's female, sure, but she is also older and stronger and more experienced. She's short and not as muscled as me but she outmatched me by far. Get it?"

Dad nodded. "Yeah, I do." Then he paused and said, "Kyra probably wouldn't want me to tell you this, but she was sick last night."

I stood straighter. "Sick? Like how?"

"Maybe it was nerves." He said with a dismissive wave of his hand but I caught his shoulder and made him look at me. He sighed but listed, "She was sweating but her skin was cold, so she was shivering too. Her heartbeat was racing to the point I could actually see her pulse throbbing her neck. She also complained of stomach cramps, enough that she took some pain killers."

I nodded but asked, "Isn't that a period or something?" I blushed when Dad's eyebrows raised. I stared at the floor, my ears burning. "I mean that it doesn't sound too strange, that's all."

Dad laughed and hugged me quickly. "It was nerves, like I said."

Mom called, "Xon, honey, breakfast is ready."

I darted out of the study and sat down at the table where my plate was waiting. I gobbled it down in seconds, then asked, "Can I have more please?"

Mom stared at me like I was insane then said, "I know you're hungry and I know you're a wolf now, but I'd like it if you'd eat with the manners I raised you with. That was disgusting."

I winced and said, "Sorry Mom."

My chest warmed. Mom had called me a wolf. Somehow with everything that's gone on, she's managed to accept the fact that I'm not human. I looked at the scratch on her face, it stretched from her temple across her cheek to the side of her nostril, splitting her face in half. Carter did that to prove a point, because I had mocked him. I was angered but only for a second because Carter was dead, I had killed him. He'd never hurt Connor again and he had paid for hurting my mother.

Dad came to the table and the three of us ate together. Mom got three helpings, which was a first, she didn't normally eat that much. I remembered what Dad said about her feeling sick last night.

Could Mom be pregnant? No, they said it wasn't possible. But Dad looked at me when I said she was on her period, so maybe she either doesn't have them anymore or she hasn't gotten it yet, which means she could be pregnant. But if she is, what if she loses the baby again, my sibling?

I put it away at soft footsteps and I looked up as Connor hovered at the entrance of the kitchen between the living room and the hallway. I stood up and enfolded him in a tight embrace, he hugged me back just as firmly before we stepped back.

I asked, "Are you hungry?"

He nodded quickly and I made his plate and he sat at the spot no one sat at unless we had a guest. He ate the plate in a whooping two seconds, it was like he shoved all the food in his mouth and swallowed it at once.

Mom glared at me and I flinched but then said, "Mom doesn't want us to eat like that Connor. So next time, use your fork and eat slower, okay? Manners."

Connor nodded, looking at her as I got him more food. "I'm sorry Mrs. Reeves. Um." He looked at the table but didn't eat as I set down his next plate. "Is it really okay that I live here now? I know Xon has saved my life and I don't have other family, but I'm sure I could make due somehow. I mean, if I get a job, I'll be fine, really."

Mom and Dad exchanged glances. Dad lifted his chin to Mom, she was the one who had to answer. Mom glared at him but it was good-natured as she was smiling. She tapped the table so Connor looked up and met her eyes.

"Yes you can stay." she said. "Xon has been worried about you ever since he met you and all he's wanted was to make sure you were happy. He's done everything he could to get you somewhere safe and that's here in our house. This is your home, if you'll have it."

Connor's eyes watered. He jumped up and grabbed Mom in a hug. She yelped like she had been stepped on and he jerked back.

He winced. "Sorry Mrs. Reeves."

"It's okay." She laughed in a dry hoarse voice. "I'm used to it from Xon. You guys hug with arms like steel beams."

Dad laughed and gestured to Connor back to his seat. He asked, "Are you going to school Connor? You can stay home for today if you'd like. After all, we need to find out what to do about your old house and everything inside it. I got a call earlier today from a social worker while you were sleep."

Connor gasped. "Will they take me away?"

I growled low but stopped when Mom paled.

I said instead, "We won't let them Connor. This is your home now, you're my little brother and my brother lives with me."

Connor looked up at me and smiled, a wide true smile that brought sparks to his brown eyes, his gold spark flickered like it was dancing.

I tousled his hair then said, "I'm going to go to school though, my suspension is over."

Connor said, "I wonder how everyone will treat you. The entire town knows what you did."

I shrugged. "I'll do me and they can do them."

Dad smiled. "Alright then. Go on before you miss the school bus. We'll take care of Connor's business."

I nodded, saluted him then had ten minutes to finish getting ready and get to the bus stop. I jogged down the street to the stop sign. Jarrod Fletcher and Gavin Houston were both there. Gavin had an article cut out from a newspaper in his hand, the two were leaned close as they read it together. Three guesses as to what article they were reading and the first two don't count.

"Hey guys." I said it as casually as possible as I walked up, my hands in my jeans pocket.

They both looked up. Jarrod's pale green eyes widened all around so his whites flashed, and his ghost-white skin flushed red on his cheeks. His scent, the grassy warm earth scent of him, flooded with faint ammonia of anxiety. Gavin shoved the newspaper article into his bag as if to stop me from seeing it, but I recognized my picture on it. His scent, the sour infected meat smell, heightened with the pissy scent of fear.

I looked at the both of them then said, "You don't have to worry. I have no intention of killing anyone else."

Gavin choked. "Fuck man. Why...they didn't give a motive. Why would you haul off and kill someone? I mean, I don't know you too well but you've gotten violent since you Changed into a wolf. Now straight up murder? It's like you've totally changed."

I put my hands behind my back. "I haven't gotten violent. I'm a new wolf so my control was out of whack. When I'd normally let things go I get the urge to fight instead. That's normal wolf behavior. As for killing someone, it was something that I had to do. Like I said, you don't have to worry about me killing you or anyone else. I don't need to or want to."

Gavin stepped back from me and his scent clouded with fear, it made me step back from him.

Jarrod spoke, "Is it true the wolf you killed was Connor Hawkins's father?"

I looked at him in his eyes. "It's true."

Jarrod's brows rose up into his bangs. "And is he okay with that?"

I nibbled on my lower lip. There was no way I was about to air Connor's personal business but I didn't want to lie either.

So I said, "He was there at the time and he understands."

Gavin whispered in a shaking hoarse voice, "You killed your friend's father right in front of him?" His voice hardened and slowly began to raise, until by the end he was shouting at me. "That was yesterday and now you're here about to take the bus to school like nothing happened. You got arrested, you were on the front page, you were on TV. I saw it, you were covered in blood Jaxon. And you're acting like it's a normal everyday occurrence!"

The bus heaved its way up to the curb then wheezed to a stop. The doors clanked open, it had been fixed since I broke it. I got on after the two went first. All the laughter and shouting died instantly as I stood at the front of the bus. Mrs. Dorris gaped at me like I had two heads and the only reason I didn't show her my fangs was because I didn't want to get another report then get sent to alternative school.

I looked at the rows of pale sweating faces, heard heartbeats racing top speed, breathing quick and shallow. The stench of the bus was pure piss, like everyone had gone in their pants. If they were a Pack I would be able to read their communal thoughts but they weren't, they were just humans and they all smelled like fear.

I said loud and clear, "I'm not a murderer. I'm not a man-eater. I'm here to go to school and get my education like the rest of you. So if any of you are entertaining fantasies that I'll go wolf and start killing well cancel them right now. I'm not interested in killing anyone, period. Go ahead and text all your equally frightened friends that Xon Reeves is not a serial-killing wolf hell-bent on killing everyone who ever laughed at me or talked about me behind my back. I don't care. You do you and I'll do me."

With that I took a seat at the front by the window and took out my cell phone to play a game to pass the time. The bus was silent until the next stop then eventually conversation filtered back in. Each time someone got on and saw me sitting there, they all paled and stared before hustling off to a seat. Eventually the bus rattled to a stop at the school and I hopped off. I hadn't gone far when my name was shouted.

I turned around and clasped the body that had leapt into my arms. Sky kissed me hard on the mouth then hugged me around the neck tight enough I croaked. She stood back on her feet.

She shouted. "You idiot!" She clasped my face in both hands, squeezing my cheeks together, glaring at me with the incensed silver eyes of her wolf. "I told you not to fight Carter, I told you! If you were going to his house you should have called me, why did you never call me Xon? I'm your mate, your partner, right?"

I nodded but couldn't say anything with her hands clamping my cheeks together, if she pressed any harder she'd break my cheekbones.

She breathed in heavy and kept shouting. "Why in God's name did you take on Carter by yourself? If he showed up at your house and started to threaten your family, why didn't you call me? I would have run over and helped! Instead you killed him and got yourself arrested with the whole story on national TV!"

I really would have liked to have said something but Sky bulldozed onwards. "Now I know it helped out, Connor is freed from that pain and he's safe with your family but I can't believe you didn't even send a *text* Xon, you acted like you're the one and only mighty Alpha who has to do everything himself! Hell, you could have gotten Shane, he would have helped too!"

I nodded again, gazing at the bright red-purple flush to Sky's sculpted cheekbones, her flared nostrils, the curl of her mouth and her heated roses and honey scent flushing my nose. She smelled great, she looked great and I wouldn't mind standing here with her yelling at me forever.

Shane, Leo and Javier stood a few feet behind her. Shane had his arms crossed while shaking his head, though he had a wide grin on his face. Javier smiled as well and tossed me a thumb's up. Leo's face was blank as it mostly was despite the brightness in his green eyes.

Sky sucked in air and let me go, turning her back on me with a swift snap of her body. "And that's all I have to say to you Mr. I'm The Alpha Jaxon Reeves! If you don't trust me enough to the Alpha queen at your side then fine! Go marry Melody instead."

I caught her elbow as she moved to stalk off and pulled her against my chest then wrapped my arms around her. I bent over so my mouth was at her ear. "Thank you Sky. Everything you said was right and I deserve your anger. I don't have any excuse for not calling you during that time, the real thing is it was in the heat of the moment and all I was thinking was stopping Carter. The idea of calling reinforcements didn't cross my mind and that's my fault. You can beat me up later but the bell is about to ring and I'm still on probation. So think we can pick this up later?"

Sky snapped at my face so I let her go and stepped back. She tossed her thick braid behind her shoulders and glared at me with silver eyes. "Fine, after school, the park. And if you don't show up, I'll bite off your nose!"

Then she trotted away with her sweet behind bouncing from side to side.

"You asshole." Shane caught me around the neck and jerked me against him, his other hand dug his knuckles into my scalp. "I can't believe you took on a Rogue and left me out of the fun! Now who will I get to disembowel and tear off heads?"

Javier blanched and covered his mouth as his honey-colored skin whitened. He wrapped his arm around his pouched stomach. "Shane, please, I told you before I did not want the details."

I grinned and twisted myself out of Shane's grip. "Sorry but like I told Sky, it was the heat of the moment. Besides there wasn't enough room to have another wolf in the fight. Otherwise we'd have completely destroyed my house."

Javier stared at me with huge brown eyes. "So you really fought him to the death in your living room? I avoided the news coverage if I could because I'd rather hear it from the source but everyone on the bus was talking about it so I heard some rumors."

The bell rang loud and clear, the crowd of students all herded to enter the building.

I waved my hand at him. "I'll tell you all after school, okay? Come on Leo."

I held out my hand and he leapt to grasp it tight.

Shane rolled his eyes even as we all headed into the school together. "You're still too touchy-feely Xon. I'll get used to this no hitting Pack you've created but if you try to hold my hand I'll bite it off."

I huffed, rolling my eyes. "We can play fight as much as you want but if you get too excited, I'll bite something off you."

Shane's eyes brightened, his blue eyes shifted a touch of olive. "Maybe you can show me some of those taekwondo moves then I can challenge you to be Alpha again!"

I growled at him but it was more playful than anything. "I don't mind giving you a few pointers but you should know it's against the Law for you to be Alpha."

Shane's brows furrowed. "Games aside, what the hell do you mean by that?"

"Toni told me." I said. "Alpha of the United States Law is that if an Alpha loses the fight against a challenger, he can't be Alpha again. So because you lost to me Shane you can't ever fight to be Alpha. You'll never be an Alpha, period."

Shane's knuckles popped and he swore under his breath. He shrugged and tossed me a small hard grin.

"Whatever. I had my reign and it was enough. Now I don't have to worry about keeping bastards in line, you'll do it for me. We're late to class, so see you after school."

He was right, the late bell had rung and I was still holding Leo's hand. I picked up the pace and went to American Literature about six minutes late.

"Sorry Ms. Cannon." I said as I opened the door. "Sorry I'm late. Leo's here too."

The classroom abruptly silenced, like pressing the mute button on a loud TV show. Everyone stared at me and the scent of the classroom morphed with the sharp stinging scent of piss, fear. Ms. Cannon stepped back from the doorway, she touched her throat like I was about to rip it out.

I sighed. I let go of Leo's hand so he could go to his desk. He nuzzled my shoulder and neck before moving away, giving me a deep green-eyed glance. I only couldn't smell him because of the heightened piss scent in the classroom, taking over everything.

I said, loud and sincere like my speech on the bus. "Everyone, I'm not a wild man-eating shifter. Yes, it's true that I killed another shifter. It's also true that it was the father of my best friend. What's not true is the idea that I'll kill anybody else. I'm not interested in killing; I don't intend on becoming a serial-killer. What happened was something I had to do and it's over now. So treat me like a regular person and not some psycho because I'm not. That's all."

With that, I took my seat and looked at Ms. Cannon to continue class.

Ms. Cannon coughed, still pale and sweating. She started to teach, her voice shook at first but eventually became steadier. Greg Johnson, the kid next to me, didn't attempt to pay attention but stared at me. I looked away from him at Leo. Leo met my eyes and shrugged one shoulder.

I paid attention in class and did my work, ignoring everyone staring at me and I smiled calmly at Ms. Cannon whenever she looked freaked out if she came too close to me. Class over, everyone rushed to leave, except for Leo and a girl I had never talked to. I recognized her smell as inhuman and my nostrils flared to take it in. Burnt fruits and fresh fungus.

She walked up to me before I could leave and held out her hand. "Vanessa Finney. I'm a Chiropteran, if you're wondering at my smell. I shift into a flying fox. The largest bat in the world and the only type of bat shifter."

I shook her hand. "Jaxon Reeves. May I ask why you're introducing yourself to me? I mean, we've never talked before."

"To congratulate you." She said, shocking me completely. "I've never been comfortable living here with that Rogue wolf, never. I once tried to ask Richard Forrest, the Dominion, to chase him away or even to kill him."

She winced and shook her head.

I laughed. "I guess that didn't work out well."

I remembered very well my first encounter with Mr. Forrest, both at school and then meeting him out in the forest.

Vanessa crossed her arms over her stomach. "No it didn't and my parents are both human, so there's no way they'd talk to him about it."

Now my brows rose. "How can you be a shifter but have human parents?"

I knew I did because I had been attacked by a werewolf but I never heard of prey shifters attacking people.

Vanessa answered. "You heard about the shifter vaccine right? They keep making new strains to make it safer but the fact is sometimes it backfires. There's several types of vaccines, one in which the virus is alive or it's dead. Sometimes if the virus is alive, it's supposed to be tweaked so it's harmless, so that it can't actually infect. Well my vaccine's virus wasn't quite castrated enough and once it came in, the black strands of infection started. They tried to stop it but it was too late. I changed into a giant flying fox right there on the doctor's table."

"Wow." I said. "And how did your parents take it?"

Vanessa shrugged a shoulder. "It took some time getting used to it but we've handled it. Arthur Finney, my father, is the human guidance counselor here. So he gets to talk with other student shifters if their parents are humans. Like I was saying, the fact a Rogue wolf lived here was frightening. He could haul off and start trying to hunt prey shifters whenever he wanted to. While it is against some Laws for shifters to kill other shifters, Rogues just don't have that control like Pack wolves do. Whenever I came across him he'd always stare at me but it was never like sexual, it looked hungry. He'd lick his lips like I was some sort of tasty turkey. It freaked me out. But now." She smiled, eyes twinkling. "Now he's gone and I don't have to live in fear anymore. So thank you."

She hugged me close then left with a wave.

Leo and I looked at each other then as the warning bell rang, rushed to our next class. Mine was Algebra II with Mrs. Ellis. When I got there Mrs. Ellis wasn't inside but everyone stared at me. So I had to do the same speech telling everyone I wasn't a crazy man-eating shifter. My former friends Aydan and Regan looked drop-dead afraid of me. I didn't try to comfort them, I had new friends now and like I said, they would do them and I would do me.

The Asian guy who smelled like herbs and cashew came over to my desk.

He introduced himself. "Dylan Zhu." After we shook hands, he said, "I really can't believe you killed a Rogue wolf. Like, you were Changed like what, last month?"

I grinned at him but shook my head. "Nah, I was changed on the first. Two weeks ago."

Dylan's eyes bugged but then he grinned back. "Damn, that's really something else. And look at you, you don't have a mark on you. You must have had an easy time of it."

I shook my head again. "No, it was tough but I managed to win. I guess you're okay that I killed him?"

"More than okay, I'm glad." He laughed with a deep boom in his chest, it didn't sound human, it was too low and raspy compared to his speaking voice. I noticed some people look up and stare at him. "That guy terrified me, and my family. We're prey shifters, we come from China and it's not the safest place for gaurs anymore. We're running extinct over there because of all the forest molestation and illegal hunting, so we moved around to find a best spot. We settled here in Lakeside Village because of the closeness to the Blue Ridge Mountains. We were happy for a minute but then the Rogue moved in. Unfortunately, we don't have the option to uproot again."

I asked, "I'm guessing he'd act weird around you guys?"

"He stalked us if we were in the forest at the same time." Dylan shuddered. "He never attacked but like I said, getting followed around by a giant white wolf was frightening as fuck. Yeah we have horns and all, but yeah, I'm glad he's gone. So thanks."

He held up his fist and I knocked it with mine as Mrs. Ellis came in, looking harried and rushed.

"Sit down please." She said, plopping her things on her desk.

"See ya." Dylan said with a wave and went back to his seat.

Mrs. Ellis apologized for being late then got class started right away. She was nothing like Ms. Cannon and didn't act afraid or cautious of me but treated me like a normal person. I appreciated that and it made class go much more smoothly for me.

After that, I had lunch. Leo met with me at the top of the stairs. As we walked down the cafeteria went dead silent, everyone staring. I sighed, not really wanting to give another speech. Before I could decide what to do, I was bum-rushed by a crowd of shifters I hadn't talked to before, all laughing and cheering, a few hugged me. I recognized all of their smells from earlier and now they introduced themselves.

The gazelle siblings were named Calvin and Callie Lucas. The tabby cat twins were Julio and Julienne Pereira. The seawater smelling male was named Santiago Velazquez, apparently he was a dolphin. Then the only one I already knew of, Dave Powell the SSGA president. Like the other two shifters, they all wanted to thank me for killing the Rogue and ask me what it was like. Dave Powell suggested that I join the Shifter Student Government Association. I turned him down politely.

After that was finished, I got some food with Leo and sat down with him.

"It's been crazy." I sighed heavily, pausing to stuff some pizza into my mouth. "All the shifters keep thanking me every class. It's getting a little tiring but it's cool at the same time."

Leo nodded with a peaceful look in his eyes and I noticed the smallest tilt to his mouth. It was a smile, tiny but true, real. I grinned and tousled his hair. I didn't want to call out that he was smiling in case it made him stop but the sight of it really did make me feel a lot better about the whole thing. Yeah, I was glad that Carter was gone so he wouldn't hurt Connor anymore but I didn't think about how his death would affect everyone else. The humans were pretty horrified but the shifters felt like I had done them a big favor.

Leo nudged me and when I looked at him, he tilted his head behind my shoulder. My former crew sat at their table, all staring at me.

I rolled my eyes and turned back around. "Forget them Leo. They're probably pissing their pants about bullying me now that I'm a so-called murderer. Afraid that I might want to extract revenge on them."

Leo nudged me again and I looked over to see that Daewon slowly advancing towards me.

"Hey," I said, standing up to face him. "Been a while."

Daewon nodded, a small smile on his mouth now. "Yeah...You've been busy. The guys, they were a little scared of you before but now knowing you can rip off heads they're completely petrified."

I crossed my arms over my stomach. "Now I don't think the police would actually reveal all of that, I mean, that's a real gory detail I don't think the public would know about."

"You kidding?" Daewon scoffed. "Maybe the police wouldn't but this is a small town and people talk. The way

I see is that anybody who was tasked with getting the body out of the house told some people about it who told others or maybe they're the ones who talked to the reporters. Either way, everyone knows now. I'm surprised no one has approached you for an interview yet."

I shrugged. "I don't know but because what happened is considered shifter politics, humans don't really have the right to ask me about it. I wasn't even supposed to be arrested or charged. Luckily it'll be taken care of and I won't have a record."

"Yeah, you've got the Stone Industries CEO in your pocket." Daewon whistled high and sharp. "Still don't know how you managed to pull that one off buddy."

I grinned for a moment, thinking of the Alpha of the Stone Pack, Toni who has done so much for me.

I said, "It's a long story but yeah, I do know him. We're kind of friends, he's helped me out a lot. Anyway." I glanced over my shoulder where it looked like Leo was starting to steal off my tray. "I'm going to finish my lunch. I guess I'll see you around."

"Yeah," he said, holding up one hand. "Maybe once things have calmed down, we can hang out more often again."

I nodded. "Definitely."

I went back to my table. My tray was empty. Leo looked up at me with wide green eyes that seemed to say *oops*.

"You rascal." I rustled his hair and took a sharp bite on his ear, not enough to damage him but it probably ached. "Now I'm going to be hungry the rest of the day."

Leo wiggled and buried his head into my chest, his arms around my waist. I hugged him back then tugged on him as the bell rang.

"We've got class; I'll see you after school."

Next was U.S. History with Mr. Malone. I had barely gotten in the door when the horse guy with the hat and sunglasses rushed towards me, his hot tangy scent flushed my nose.

"You really did it!" He gasped. His teeth were very large for his mouth and tall, shaped like rectangles. Horse teeth. "You actually killed the Rogue!"

It had happened too many times for my ego to try and stand firm.

I grinned at him. "Yeah, I did. I'm not saying it was easy or anything but yeah, I killed him."

His fists clenched but they were hidden in thick leather mittens and he jerked his arms up and down in pure excitement. "Excellent! I was afraid to death of that wolf but not anymore, he's good and gone now."

I paused then asked, "How come you've got so much of your body covered up? Hat, sunglasses, the mittens. My next class I have your sister Karen and she's not like that."

"Oh. HA!" He laughed; it was loud and hoarse, abrasive, like a horse neigh.

When everyone stared, he blushed.

He said, "I'm Kelsey, and yeah, Karen is my twin. Oh yeah, my telltale has gone haywire. It's a disease shifters can get but its pretty rare. A lot of my Equine form has taken over my human form. I have the ears, eyes, and the teeth of a horse. At this point my fingers are basically hooves. I've got explicit permission to cover up like this but."

Kelsey shrugged. "If the telltale doesn't stop progressing, I'll either be a disfigured half-human half-horse creature or decide to stay in my horse form for the rest of my life."

My eyes bugged. "Is it contagious? I mean, can other shifters get it? I never heard of shifters being able to catch diseases."

"Sure we can." He said with another neighing laugh. "We don't catch the diseases that humans catch just the same way a human can't catch our diseases. A human doesn't have a second form to get a telltale disease, right? Well, with our heightened healing capabilities, we can't get influenza or pneumonia. But no, what I have isn't contagious. From what my herd's shaman says it'll either go away on its own or you know, take over my body completely. Eventually my human form just won't exist anymore."

I bit my lower lip. "Wait, my Packmate, Javier Méndez, he's an excellent Healer. Let him use his heat on you and what?"

He was shaking his head.

Kelsey said, "I know all about the wolf heat healing process and a wolf's heat only works on wolves. The same way you wouldn't use animal medicine on a human being, a wolf can't pass on his heat to other shifters. It doesn't work like that. Thanks for the offer but if this Javier was to put his heat into my body, it would probably act more like poison than heal me."

Before I could respond, Mr. Malone cleared his throat from behind the horse-turning guy. "Enough talk. Kelsey, take your seat. Xon, to your seat."

Kelsey dipped his head at me then went back to his desk at the back. Mr. Malone moved from the doorway to let me in and while the entire class stared at me, this time I didn't give a speech. I sat down.

"Alright I've got to make a small announcement," said Mr. Malone, standing stiff in front of his desk. "As we all know, there was a certain incident yesterday involving one of our own."

I blinked several times, surprised that Mr. Malone was coming right out with this. My other teachers were either afraid of me or tried to pretend it never happened. The class was quiet, listening attentively.

"What I want is for everyone to not treat Jaxon Reeves any different. There is something called shifter politics, which simply means it's shifters business. What Reeves got into the other day has nothing to do with human beings and to try and make it about yourself by being afraid of him doesn't make any sense. If you'd rather keep to yourself then fine, I can't force you to be friends with him.

However, I will ask that you not ostracize him or treat him like he's the plague. Is that clear?"

No one said anything but there was a loud hard clapping sound like hooves clacking together, so I knew Kelsey was in my corner. I had pain for him about his telltale disease and that I had no way of helping him out.

Mr. Malone's eyes narrowed. "When I speak, I expect an answer. Now let's try that again. Are. We. Clear?"

"Yes Mr. Malone." The class chorused together. Everyone knew if they didn't he wouldn't mind writing up the entire class with detention.

"Good. Now let's start." Mr. Malone started to teach class and I paid attention with a small smile on my face.

Next class was Psychology with Ms. Hughes. I ignored the class going silent and staring at me but it was Melody who jerked and braced herself against the wall like I was going to lunge at her. Her skin washed out ghostly pale and her blue eyes stretched wide all around. Even from across the room I could smell her pissy scent of fear.

Mrs. Hughes stood up from her desk, also staring at me. "Jaxon Reeves, should you even be here?"

I sighed. "Yes, I can be here. I'm not arrested and I'm not going to jail. I'm living my life like normal. Like I've been saying all day, I don't intend on killing anyone. I'm not interested in that. The shifter I killed, well, it was something that had to be done. So you guys really need to calm down. Alright?"

Mrs. Hughes spluttered at first then protested. "That's really inappropriate talk Jaxon Reeves and I think you should go to the office for threatening the students!"

"Oh come on!" It was Jarrod Fletcher who stood up, his hands slapping the desk. "Cut him some slack! This guy came out on top of a death battle with a Rogue wolf. You ever fought a Rogue wolf before Mrs. Hughes?"

Mrs. Hughes' flushed red but still tried to defend her position. "I don't know what you mean by that and besides, the fact is he's a criminal and I don't think its appropriate that he's in class and threatening everyone."

Karen stood up next, her fists clenched and her ears had lengthened enough to poke out of her hair, hair that was growing longer than it had been a minute ago.

She spoke in a rough raspier tone, much hoarser than her normal voice. "He was saying that he *wasn't* a threat if you were even listening. Besides, like the deer said, us shifters are pleased about what Xon did. He got rid of a very dangerous problem, a Rogue wolf who really could have gone wild and started to kill everyone. Rogue wolves are like lit time bombs, that Hawkins wolf was moments away from losing control. So leave Xon alone and let him be a student here, he's never hurt a human being and he said he doesn't intend to."

I couldn't believe that these two were sticking up for me. Maybe because I had done away with my human glue, maybe because I was truly an Alpha and I had done something that helped out the shifter community, now things were different.

Mrs. Hughes slammed her hand on her desk. "Jarrod Fletcher and Karen Nash, you two both have detention. As for you Jaxon, I'm calling the principal to have you removed from my class because quite frankly I don't feel comfortable with you here."

Jarrod and Karen both opened their mouths but I put my hand up, silencing them. "Forget it you guys. She's the teacher and she has her rights too. Let her call Principal Hamilton, it's fine. You've already got detention, don't make it worse on yourselves. I'll wait outside."

I stepped back into the hallway and closed the door, leaning against the wall with my arms loosely crossed. If I focused, I could easily listen in on Mrs. Hughes conversation but I decided not to. After about five minutes, Principal Hamilton power-walked her way down the hall.

I stood up from leaning on the wall, raising one hand in greeting. "Hi Principal Hamilton."

"What is going on Jaxon?" She puffed, arms crossed. "I thought we had made ourselves clear about not getting into anymore trouble."

I didn't get to answer when Mrs. Hughes came out of the classroom, her chin lifted.

She spoke firmly, "Lisa, I don't feel comfortable with Jaxon Reeves in my class. He's threatening the entire classroom and he shouldn't even be in school after what he did, not the next day."

Principal Hamilton sighed then said, "Helen, what happened yesterday isn't any of our business, we have nothing to do with it, that's what shifter politics is about. Xon is not in trouble so he has every right to be in the classroom and to continue going to school."

Mrs. Hughes's fists clenched, her face flushed bright pink. "He's a murderer, he killed a man and he can just as easily kill the rest of us. I don't feel safe with him here; I won't teach with him in there staring at me the way he does!"

My eyes widened and I almost spoke but then I remembered that I had frightened Mrs. Hughes more than once while adjusting to becoming a werewolf. I even walked out of her class. Now that it was all over the news what I had done to Carter Hawkins, she really had every right to be too scared to want to be around me.

Principal Hamilton glanced at me. "Do you think this accusation is fair Xon? I know Mrs. Hughes reported you several times but you seemed sincere about not causing anymore trouble and no one else has reported you today."

Before I could say anything, both Jarrod and Karen came out of the classroom and began to plead my case. Mrs. Hughes got upset and ordered Principal Hamilton to give them a two day suspension.

Principal Hamilton put her hands up until it was silent, then said, "The fact is Helen, what you're trying to do is discriminate against Xon for being a shifter. He did something that only concerns the shifter community and I understand you feel unsafe but if you continue to force the issue and refuse to teach with Xon in your class, this will have to be taken up with the shifter representative on our school board. I assure you that the question of getting Xon removed from the class won't be what's on the table but instead your ability to cope with having shifters in your classroom. Do you understand what I'm telling you Helen?"

I understood perfectly. If Mrs. Hughes was going to kick up a bad enough stink about me being in her class, rather than them kicking me out, it'll be her job on the line.

Mrs. Hughes lips pressed together so tight her mouth turned white. "Understood." Her voice was thin and shaking. "Students, back into class."

Jarrod, Karen and I went back into class, and the two both clapped me on the back with smiles. I smiled back and sat down at my seat. For the rest of class, both Melody and Mrs. Hughes ignored me completely, like I might as well didn't exist. It was a little saddening that my teacher was treating me like that but the school year had really only just started last week and it would be silly to ignore me for that long. She'd get over it eventually I was sure. As for Melody, she was my ex-girlfriend and I had loved her as much as I was able back then. But now I was a wolf, and had Sky. Melody had broken up with me for being what I was, and she was terrified of me now. I didn't think there was anything else I could do about it, and resolved to just focus on my own life, Sky, my parents, Connor and my Pack.

When the bell rang, I walked down the hallway to use the bathroom first. As soon as I walked in, I smelled that overwhelming pungent smell, and fear naturally clenched my gut. I froze as Mr. Richard Forrest stepped back from drying his hands at the air-blower. He had a scar cutting from his forehead down over his eyebrow to his cheek, red and rippled like a welt. His eye itself was misty gray, blind.

If I had any doubts that the giant bear I had met in the forest that attacked my Pack had been Mr. Forrest, all such doubts evaporated. And so did the fear. As I looked at the wound I had dealt the King Ursine, and the fact he had backed down, that fear just filtered away. My dominance filled up the bathroom, like boulders piling up and I breathed easily.

Mr. Forrest looked at me, dipped his head in respect and left the bathroom without talking to me.

With that settled, I did my business then I headed to the park to meet with my Pack. After about ten minutes we were all there with Sky still annoyed with me.

"Sky." I took her hand but let go when she swiped at me with sharpened ebony claws. I sighed slowly. "I said I was sorry for not calling you to help but listen, it won't happen again. Carter is gone and if there is ever to be another emergency I promise I'll have you on speed dial. But hey, look, Connor is great, the Pack is safe and Mom is healthy. Instead of being angry you weren't there, can't you be glad that everything is alright?"

Sky's lips tightened but then she nodded and tossed her braid behind her shoulder.

"Fine." She looked at me with bright honey-gold eyes. "So you're sure you're alright? Did Carter hurt you?"

"He beat me up pretty well." I said with a shrug. "But I healed so I'm good."

"That is one particular quality about you, how quickly you heal," said Javier as Sky hugged me. "Alphas, true Alphas, they have a supernatural quality that even normal wolves don't have."

I looked at him as I swung Sky gently from side to side, my arms around her waist while she clutched to my shoulders.

I asked, "You mean its abnormal?"

"It is only for Alphas." He said. "And if that wolf stops being Alpha, it goes away."

"Well what is it?" Shane leaned against a tree, crossing his bulky arms. "We already know that Xon is a weirdo as it is." He tossed me a quick smile then looked back at Javier.

I had to acknowledge that defeating Shane in wolf form had really changed him. Fighting in human form didn't do it, couldn't do it. Shane's wolf had to understand that my wolf was stronger, and that he needed to submit. Shane's aggression was defeated because of this, and so now he could smile, and kid around, and be more like a teen, and not an uber-masculine violent asshole.

I turned back to Javier. "Yeah. What about this only Alpha thing?"

Javier said, "One thing is how the Alpha of the Pack is supernaturally strong, I mean even more strong than strong. If a wolf is ten times as strong as a human then an Alpha wolf is thirty times as strong as a regular wolf. And this strength rises in power. The UAC wolves are incredibly strong. These wolves can kill Ursine if they wanted and even other large predator shifters, such as tigers and lions."

I took this in, I nodded then said, "Well, I want you guys to all officially meet Toni and the Stone Pack. It's because of him I managed to make it this far anyway. You guys down for that?"

"It's Friday," said Shane with a shrug. "Might as well."

Javier and Leo nodded.

Sky took a bite out of my collarbone, her teeth nipping in a gentle prick. "Alright. How will we get there?"

"I'll drive." I said, putting Sky on her feet. "So let's walk to my house. Maybe Connor will come with us."

"Yeah, so how's the little punk anyway?" Shane fell into step next to me, with Sky at my other side, then Leo and Javier behind us.

"He's not a punk first of all." I said. "Secondly he's fine. He's glad that Carter is gone and is happy that my parents are willing to let him join our family."

Shane's eyes widened. "Whoa, what? Join the family? Like...adoption?"

"I don't know if they'll make it legal or not." I said. "But Connor doesn't have other family and as far as I'm concerned, he's my little brother. So he's living with us from now on."

Sky smiled at me. "That's so nice of you Xon. That's one of the things I lo-like about you so much. You're so kind and sweet and gentle."

Shane rolled his eyes and gagged himself. I glowered at him.

I said, "I don't like violence Sky. I was raised not to let my fists do the talking. That even though I'm large and I'm powerful that it's spoken word that's the greatest weapon."

Shane snorted. "Of course he'd teach you that. Wouldn't want his only child following in his footsteps, huh?"

I gritted my teeth but calmed down before I did something I'd regret. Sky slipping her hand into mine helped me speak in a normal tone of voice.

"That's in the past."

We were at my house now, so I got inside, calling out, "I'm home."

"Xon! Xon!" Dashing down the stairs like a green fireball, Connor launched from the fifth step onto my chest in a dive-hug.

Laughing, I caught him and hugged him. "Hey Connor."

Sky, Leo and Javier crowded around him, all wanting to hold and smell him, know for themselves that he was alright. Even Shane passed his hand over Connor's shoulder, which made Connor smile at him.

Shane looked around the house, eyes slightly narrowed, and his nostrils flexed several times. "It smells clean but there's something underneath. It's...nasty."

"Death." I said in a quiet voice just in case Mom was around. "It's the smell of death."

"Xon, is that you?" Mom came down the stairs then her eyes widened. "What's this? You brought all your friends home."

"We're going to Mountain Ridge." I told her. "I want to introduce them formally to Toni."

Mom nodded, wrapping her arms around her stomach. Pain flashed over her face and with it a sickening old blood-like scent. She was hurt.

"Mom?" I peeled away from the others, taking a step toward her.

"I'm fine." She said, stepping up one stair. "Go ahead and go. Your Dad is at work; he might not be back till much later. I'll see you when you come back."

Then she went upstairs and her bedroom door closed. I looked at Connor.

He shrugged. "She's been a little funny all day I guess, not that I know what your mom is like normally. Just in bed then she'll come down and eat, throw up and go back to bed. That's weird, right?"

Again I thought if Mom was pregnant and my stomach wiggled. What would it be like to suddenly have a little sibling, a baby in the house?

I bit my lower lip then said, "Let's get in the car. I'll call Toni to let him know we're on the way."

I did so while I got my Pack in my car. Toni picked up and I told him what I wanted to do.

"Hmm..." He was quiet for a moment then said, "Alright, you can visit. I'll accept the killing of the Rogue wolf as your gift."

I blinked rapidly then turned around to watch as I backed out of the garage. "So I don't need to bring anything else?"

"No. See you in thirty." He hung up and I put the phone down.

Sky and Javier asked Connor about what happened and his feelings during the ride to Toni's house, Leo stayed silent while Shane interjected with questions about what the fight was like. Soon enough I pulled outside of Toni's

A. E. Costello 423

mansion and parked. I noticed that the eight car driveway was full and there were several people lounging outside.

I got out as the front door opened and Toni came out onto the stoop. My Pack came around me, waiting.

"I welcome the Lakeside Village Pack in peace," said Toni with a small dip to his head. His hair was dyed back to platinum, no more black roots, and he had shaved, with a smooth clean jaw.

I glanced at Javier, I had no idea what to say next.

He whispered, "Say, I visit the Stone Pack in peace."

I repeated it, trying to sound as serious as possible.

Toni burst into laughter. "What's with the stiff face Xon?" He clapped me on the shoulder then looked at Sky at my side. "And who's this?"

"Sky Cloud." She said. "I'm the Alpha queen of the Lakeside Village Pack."

Toni's gray eyes glittered with some thought that disappeared too quickly for me to examine and his scent was clean, I couldn't use it to tell what he was feeling. One day I had to learn how to mask my scent too, it was really cool.

He said in his normal rough voice, "And the rest?"

"Connor Hawkins, as you know." I said. "Then this is Leo Dawson, Javier Méndez and Shane Armstrong." I gestured to each with my hand so Toni would know who I was talking about.

"Nice to meet all of you." Toni said, lifting his hand. "I know I saw you when I came to referee the fight but there was no formal introduction. How's your leg Shane?" He lifted his chin to the tall blonde teenager.

Shane huffed from his nose. "It's fine. According to Xon, you said I can't ever be Alpha again."

"Yeah not in this Pack." He said, shocking me. "If you move somewhere else and join a new Pack, then sure, you can try for Alpha there. It would be ridiculous to say that if an Alpha loses a fight then for the rest of his life he can't ever be an Alpha."

"What if Xon dies?"

"Hey!" I stared at him.

Toni chuckled then said, "If Xon dies because you killed him, you still won't be an Alpha because it was an illegal attempt to gain power. If Xon dies for other reasons that have nothing to do with you, you still won't be Alpha because you lost the fight to gain that position in the first place. Besides, Sky is here, she can still be Alpha without him."

"I don't think so."

Stepping around from Toni was Leah, the red-headed Latina who had started it all. She looked right at Sky with her bright blue eyes. Her scent was the orangey citrus of amusement and the sharp oily scent of confidence, or cockiness. That lemongrass and vanilla scent that so confused my wolf was in full affect, yet Sky's roses and honey scent was on my shirt, my arms. My wolf shook his head wildly. Too much, it was too much.

"Leah," I said quietly.

Leah stood directly in front of Sky, revealing that she was several inches taller, Sky's head came to Leah's chin.

Leah scoffed. "She's so tiny, I don't think she could really handle such a strong important position without any help."

I blinked but whatever I would have said was cut off as Sky spoke, her voice already roughened with a growl. "You may be taller than me Leah but unless you fight me you have no idea how strong I am."

"Ah, no." I grasped Sky's arm and tugged her away from Leah who's eyes tinged with the bright yellow of her wolf. "Let's not okay. Here Sky." I pushed her over to stand on the grass where I saw Ethan and a few others. "Talk to the nice Stone Pack people."

I then went over to Leah, grasped her arm and pulled her away. "Are you trying to a pick a fight or something?"

Leah tossed her red hair behind her shoulder but it wasn't the same as when Sky did it, something about it didn't make me smile like Sky did. I looked back at Sky and noticed Sky was watching me and Leah. No, more like glaring at us. In fact, it was just Leah she was looking at. It was a hard heated ugly look. What the hell did Leah do to Sky in the first place? I hadn't ever told Sky about her, I never told Sky about my wolf's conflicted feelings and now Leah was rude to her on their first meeting.

"She looks pissed huh." Leah murmured quietly, huffing a small laugh. "She thinks I'm intruding on her territory."

I raised my brows. "On *her* territory? What do you mean?"

Leah looked at me, as if trying to decide if I was serious or not. She laughed again, more amused this time. "It's a female dominance thing. As the only female in her Pack, in her mind, all of you males belong to her and are under her control. Brenda was the only female for a while and I heard some horror stories about her chasing off other females until Toni stepped in. Even so she doesn't like other females much."

I could believe that. "I don't think Brenda likes anyone much."

"I think she likes Toni," said Leah. "They're always together and I know they sometimes sleep in the same bed together too. True, it's platonic, but I still think there's more going on." She slid me a look. "Kind of like us."

I blinked, trying to understand what she was getting at. "Us?"

Leah smirked and touched my face. "I wonder what Sky will do if I kiss you right now." Her eyes glittered at me. "Do you want to find out?"

Now I was confused. Was she coming onto me because she liked me, or just to make Sky jealous?

"Uh…." was all I got out as Leah leaned in, her eyes on my lips.

Darting across the lawn in a millisecond, Sky grabbed a fistful of Leah's red hair and yanked her head back, damn near breaking the other girl's neck.

"Get away from him you bitch!" She snarled more fiercely than she did in wolf form.

"He doesn't belong to you puta!" Leah screeched back, swinging out clawed hands.

Just like that, the two females were fighting. And they didn't fight like regular human girls, who slapped each other and pulled hair, they were slashing and biting and kicking and basically trying to force the other to the ground, which, if one was on their back with the throat bared, they lose. The snarls and growls they were making sounded ferocious, like they wanted to kill each other. Is this normal behavior?

Shane was laughing and Javier seemed to be a little amused himself, Leo and Connor looked worried. I wanted to step in, but with the way they were bucking and swinging around I was more likely to get decked in the face then break them up. But to be honest, it really seemed like Sky had a good handle on things. I didn't know everything about Sky's past, but she knew how to fight.

A few other members of the Stone Pack were milling around, shaking their heads or smirking. Even though Leah seemed to be on the losing end so far, none of them tried to break it up either.

"Ok she-wolves, that's enough."

Toni, sounding equal parts amused and annoyed, walked up. He easily reached his hands in, somehow managing not to get hurt at all and grasped both of the girl's necks and pulled them apart. Their bodies stiffened up as always when the scruff was grabbed, but they still cursed each other, faces sweaty and breathing hard.

Toni looked at me knowingly.

I put my hands up, backing away. "I swear I didn't do anything. I swear!"

"What's the problem, why are you two fighting?" asked Toni, looking between them.

"Xon is *mine* and you need to stop coming around him, he's MINE!"

Sky tried to swipe for Leah and Toni dug his fingers tighter into her neck, making her go rigid and she yelped with the discomfort.

"And Leah, what do you say?" asked Toni, looking at the older girl.

"She's so annoying, acting like I'm trying to steal away her man, if Xon didn't like me he would tell me to go away! She needs to back off." Leah growled, not able to move with how tight Toni was holding her neck.

Toni looked at me. "Then you're the deciding factor. Who do you like more, Leah or Sky?"

I was flabbergasted. "W-what? You can't ask me that!"

"Well you can't leave them both fighting over you and never pick a winner." Toni pointed out. "Just know if you pick Leah, you'll have to join our Pack. Not saying that should sway your decision, just pick the lady wolf you like more."

I looked at them.

Leah was giving me a simpering coy gaze, trying to entice me with sexy looks. As for Leah, she was a very pretty girl and when I was a human, I had been interested in her. It was her looks that had me talking to Leah back then, even though I had Melody back home. Leah was the reason I was standing here today, she was the wolf that ended up making me a wolf.

Sky was glaring at me hard, demanding I pick her. I remembered how me and her always seemed kinda drawn to each other and we had kissed more than once, even had made out. We had slept together as wolves, showered together.

My wolf scented Sky's roses and honey, and turned towards her. He finally made his choice, and so did I.

"Whoever you don't pick I'll take." Shane said, laughing. "Truthfully I've always had a thing for real redheads." He laughed again.

I gave him a disgusted look while Leah glared at him with a blush on her cheeks.

Toni closed his eyes with a sigh, then opened them, looking at me again. "Don't leave the ladies on a hook Xon, let's go."

"Sky then." I said, knowing I did like her more, both me and my wolf. "Leah and I can just be friends."

"Great," said Shane with a curved smile. "Come on Leah, let's find a place we can be alone."

Toni let the she-wolves go. Leah growled loudly but instead of fighting Shane, she stalked away back into the house.

Toni rolled his eyes. "When you six show up you make Leah behave like she's a cub again. That Shane is a fool."

"You get used to him after a while." I said, putting my arm around Sky's shoulders as she stepped close to me and leaned her body on mine. I liked the feel of her, warm and very soft. "He likes to have fun."

Toni looked at me and Sky cuddling. "Don't get in anymore trouble Xon." He warned. "Especially now that you're in a pair."

I figured that was the same as being a couple, so I nodded. "Sure."

After that, a few of the Stone Pack members introduced themselves to us, including Ethan who immediately challenged Shane. The two grappled but when Shane nearly broke Ethan's neck, the fight was stopped with Shane as the winner. Ethan looked downcast and I realized that just because he had a lot of muscle didn't make Ethan dominant or necessarily make him stronger than those who had less muscle.

While the Lakeside Village Pack socialized with the Stone Pack, I consulted Toni.

I asked, "Why did Sky and Leah immediately start to fight like that? I know Sky, she's not violent, and she's never been the first to attack. She's a protector, she's defended when one of us gets hurt, but...this was wrong."

Toni shook his head. "Not wrong Xon, natural."

I stared at him.

A. E. Costello 429

He chuckled. "You really do know nothing about wolves. Listen, Leah had a claim on you, one that she continually tried to connect to your wolf. Let me finish," he said when I opened my mouth. "Rocky attacked you back then because Leah was coming onto you. Rocky and Leah were in an on-again off-again relationship, and at the time, they were technically on. So, Leah's actions is what brought about your wolf. We moved here, and you became an amazing strong wolf in a quick amount of time. Leah was attracted to that, and tried to get you to come back to her, as after all, you were initially attracted to her in the first place."

I nodded but said nothing, waiting for him to finish.

He said, "Now you and Sky have more or less mated. Sky's instincts were correct, Leah was a challenging lady wolf. Remember, even if Sky's normal personality is not to initiate violence, she is a wolf first. Those two she-wolves had to fight to make it clear who got to be with you. And just to let you know, if Leah had won the fight, you would have lost your affection for Sky."

My jaw dropped then I growled, "That's not true. I lo-like Sky." I bit down hard on my lower lip.

Toni waved it away. "Human love and wolf love is different Xon. Even if your human side believes yourself in love with Sky, but your wolf recognizes that Leah won the right to be your mate, your emotions would have gotten very confused and split very quickly. Like I said before, the wolf comes first. That would have been nasty to go through. Anyway."

Toni shrugged. "It didn't happen. Sky won the fight, so Leah's claim is broken. Sky protected her right to be with you, so those confused conflicting emotions your wolf has been giving you, those are gone for good now."

I let out a big sigh of relief, and my wolf's tail wagged. He was also grateful. Neither of us enjoyed the bouncing feelings between Leah and Sky. Now it was over. I thanked Toni for his help and counsel.

"No problem Xon," he said, smiling and clapped my shoulder again. "Now you can consider the Lakeside Village and the Stone Packs as allied. I've helped you, and you've helped me. We're on equal footing. You may go in peace."

Smiling back, I said, "I leave in peace."

So with that, we left the Stone Pack and went back to my house.

Dad was home and blinked to see us all. "Kyra told me you went out but I didn't think you'd bring everyone back. Ready for dinner you guys?"

I glanced at my Pack. "You guys okay for staying?"

"Let me call my parents," said Sky, taking out her cell phone.

"I guess I should too." Shane shrugged and got on his cell phone.

I brought Leo, Javier and Connor into the living room. Eventually Sky and Shane joined us, both cleared for dinner. Dad cooked enough to feed us all and I cautioned Leo and Connor on eating with manners and using their forks. Mom didn't come down to join us. I was worried about her but didn't want to ask in front of everyone. Dinner over, Javier volunteered to do the dishes and then I brought everyone upstairs to see my room.

Dad caught my arm before I could go inside. "Xon, remember the rules of the house."

"Dad, you and Mom are both here. I won't do anything. C'mon, don't embarrass me okay? Um." I paused then asked straight-out. "Is Mom pregnant Dad?"

Dad's eyes stretched wide. "W-what? Xon, what gave you that idea?"

I looked to the floor, unable to stop the flush burning my cheeks. "Connor told me she's been throwing up after she eats. And you wouldn't tell me if she was on her period or not. So I thought that-"

"Son." Dad placed his hand on my shoulder and squeezed, so I quieted and looked at him. He shook his head at me, his eyes warm and sad at the same time. "Your mother had a hysterectomy after having you. That means its impossible, both for her to have periods or get pregnant. Do you understand?"

I asked, "So she doesn't have a womb anymore?"

Dad nodded. "That's right. So its impossible. I took her temperature when I came home, it's a little feverish so she's gotten down with a cold. Thanks for being worried about her but I gave her some meds and she's sleep, so she'll be fine in the morning. Okay?"

I nodded and hugged him for a moment then went into my room. I smiled to see Leo, Connor and Javier in my bed, looking very comfortable. Shane was at my computer, looked like he was on a website about surfing. Sky was relaxing on my bean bag.

The three on my bed held out their arms to me, so I got on and playfully tussled with them. After a few minutes, I tired out and slumped down on my back, closing my eyes. It had been a long day and a lot had happened in the short weeks since I had become a wolf. I became an Alpha, I won a fight against a King Ursine, I killed a Rogue wolf and I had a girlfriend who I already couldn't see living without.

Sky got on the bed too and laid on top of me, resting her head on my collarbone. Her body was soft and melted against mine.

I grunted and said, "Sky…my parents are home."

"I'm not going to do anything." She kissed my chin. "I want to get that nasty girl's scent off you."

She wiggled back and forth over me, spreading her scent on me.

A scream made me jerk up right but I held Sky close before she fell down. The scream came again, it was my mother. I stood off the bed and set Sky down then rushed to my parent's room.

"Mom!"

She was on the bed, writhing and she screamed again.

"She needs a hospital!" Dad's deep voice shook and his face sharpened with tension. "Kyra, please, tell me what's wrong!"

He was trying to calm her down but she swat at him with a sharp curse. Mom's back bowed on the bed, her hands gripped the bed sheets and she let out a pained scream that had the echo of a howl on the edges of it.

Hearing that howl made my spine tingle.

I said in a low tone, "No Dad. I don't think human doctors would know what to do. She needs a wolf Healer."

"So she's going to be a werewolf?" he asked me, his eyes wide and aching.

I winced as Mom screamed again, rolling onto her stomach and screaming into the pillows, her body curled up and bucked. Mom wasn't used to pain, not pain like this. Dad had tears coming down his face.

"I don't know." I responded, taking a sniff of her. "She still smells human, and like Mom. There's no werewolf smell to her at all."

Mom's scream died off and she went limp but she was still breathing, the pain had caused her to lose consciousness.

Dad stared at me, his eyes wet. "So she's still human? She's not Changing?"

"I don't know." I said. "Let's take her to Dr. Norris in the morning. She's sleep, so let's leave her."

Dad sighed, his breath heavy and shaking. "Alright."

He wiped his face dry and breathed in deep. "I'll watch over her. If she gets any worse, I'm taking her to the hospital." He spoke over me as I opened my mouth. "If she's still a human being then I want human doctors to look at her."

I nodded and said, "Goodnight Dad."

I turned and saw my Pack gathered in the hallway, watching and listening.

"I don't know what's wrong with her." I said as I led the way back into my bedroom. "But like I said, she smells human to me."

I covered my mouth as I yawned and my eyes burned. I needed to sleep.

"Go to bed Xon," said Sky, touching the hem of my shirt. "Your mother will be fine. She could have a stomach virus. I had one of those when I was human and the pain of the cramps was enough to bring me to my knees. She'll get some medicine at the doctor and she'll be fine."

I nodded and took off my clothes and got into bed. Connor, Leo and Javier quickly joined me, naked too.

Shane's brows twisted up high. "You're really all going to sleep naked in the bed like that?"

I nodded, my eyes closing again. "You don't have to stay Shane, it's fine. Sky, your parents expect you, right?"

She said, "I'd rather stay."

I opened my eyes as I heard her bra opening. I watched her get undressed then Leo scooted to the side so she'd take her place next to me. My bed was a king-size but it was nicely full to capacity. Even if Shane wanted to join in there wouldn't be enough room. Not unless someone got on top of him.

Shane stared at us and his fingers clenched and opened, like he couldn't decide whether or not to make fists, to be angry or not.

Javier sat up and held out his hand. "Come Shane. This is Pack, we are family. The need for wolves to feel fur, feel the skin of their Packmates is normal. You are fighting it, I know but put away that human fear. Accept the love of the wolf."

Shane hesitated but then took off his clothes besides an undershirt and his boxers and got in, ending up with Javier mostly on top of him.

He wiggled then growled, "It's uncomfortable. It feels like my skin is about to crawl off."

Javier answered with a soft giggle. "It is because you have clothes on my friend. The clothes are the barrier between skin touching, the wolf can not take that."

Shane growled again but to my surprise he took the clothes off and let Javier hold him.

Shane was quiet then said in a low voice, "It feels so…normal. Natural. This doesn't make…any…"

He didn't finish as he fell asleep that fast.

Sky chuckled then gently kissed my mouth. "Go to sleep Xon. We'll be here in the morning."

I nodded, cuddling her close to me. Her arm was around my neck with her leg tucked between mine. Connor had his arm around my waist with his leg also in between mine, so he was touching Sky as well. Leo with his long arms easily reached over Connor to touch my hip. Javier was pressed close to Sky and Shane, with Shane the farthest away from me. Laying here like this with my entire Pack, I had never felt this warm, this comfortable, this safe.

I kissed Sky again, getting comfortable, and fell asleep. I didn't know how long I had been sleep when my door blasted open, and my eyes flashed open. I jolted up as my father dashed to my bedside, and he stretched his arm over to reach me, shaking my shoulder. His stench of fear flooded my nostrils.

I asked, breathing hard. "Wh-what? What is it?"

"Your mother." He said, his voice thickened. "Come now."

13

August 16th
Saturday

I gently lowered Sky's arm from around me, and untangled myself from Leo and Connor, then got out of bed. I pulled on shorts and a T-shirt and followed Dad to their room. Mom laid on the bed, she shivered with deep heavy wracks. Her body was covered in sweat, enough sweat to dampen her clothes and the sheets. She made low groans of pain in her throat, her eyes jerked underneath her eyelids. Even more than that, it was her smell that made me cover my nose.

"She smells weird." Connor said from behind me, my Pack had all gotten up when I did and followed me. "Twisted."

He was right. Her normal human scent smelled twisted, like it had been invaded with another scent that didn't match, making her smell odd, abnormal.

"Kyra," said Dad, touching her shoulder with a gentle hand. "Can you hear me?"

Her eyes opened and far from my mother's normal brown irises, they were the bright intense yellow of a wolf. Then she blinked and they were brown again.

"Fuck." I said it low but then said louder, "Dad, she's got to come to Toni's. She needs to see Dr. Norris."

"The hospital." Dad insisted when Mom screamed, her mouth stretching wide to let out the desperate pained sound, she writhed on the bed, and gripped the sheets, her body buckling. "It's closer."

As Mom's eyes shifted to yellow again, I said, "The human doctors won't know what to do. She needs wolf medicine. She's got to see the Healer."

"Xon is right Mr. Reeves," said Javier as Dad looked to protest. "There is something very wrong with your wife and only a wolf Healer would know how to deal with this. We should hurry."

"Get dressed." I instructed my Packmates. "Dad, we've got to go. I'll call Toni."

I went back to my room with everyone else and got on the phone while they all put their clothes on.

Toni growled in my ear. "Do you have any idea what time it is you bastard? The sun isn't even up yet. I'm hanging up."

"Toni wait." I said. Clearly this wolf was not a morning person. "Mom, she's sick." I told him everything.

"Fuck." There was rustling of sheets. "Alright. I'll get Will over here. Bring her, quickly. No need for a gift."

He hung up.

I went back to my parent's room, Dad was helping Mom get dressed. She wobbled and weaved like maybe she was drunk. She mumbled as if she was talking but it was garbled, I couldn't understand. Soon we were all dressed and it ended that my Pack went with me in my Subaru Forester and Dad drove with Mom in his Ford Ranger.

"What do you think is wrong with her?" I tried to sound calm but my pulse was beating underneath my tongue and my stomach swirled.

Sky put her hand on my knee while Javier said, "I do not know Xon. She did not smell like a wolf but she did not smell like a human either. Her eyes changing color does not make sense, if she was a wolf she would have Changed. There was no sign of the infection on her either, the black markings that appear on the skin. I honestly have never seen anything like this before."

The rest of the ride was done in silence and by the time I parked outside of Toni's mansion the car's dashboard blinked that it was five in the morning. As we all got out, Dad carrying Mom, the door opened. Toni stood there, wearing sleep pants and an open button up shirt.

He headed to the basement, saying. "Come to the infirmary."

Downstairs looked like a hospital and not the training field it had been for me. The cots were lined up along the walls, each with its own bedside table with a lamp and pitcher. One cot had the covers turned down. Dr. Will Norris stood there with a lab coat on.

Dad laid her down. He told the doctor all of Mom's strange behavior and the fact her eyes had changed color several times, finally asking, "What's wrong with her?"

"Hmm." Dr. Norris touched his chin then said, "Okay, let me talk to her."

Dad gently shook Mom's shoulders until she opened her eyes, they were brown like normal.

"W-what's going on?" She looked around, seeing my Pack, Dad, Dr. Norris and Toni surrounding her. "Am I back in Mountain Ridge?"

"Yes," said Dr. Norris, taking out his stethoscope. "Let me listen to your breathing."

Instead she smacked away his hand, looking angry. "Who do you think you are? I want to go back home."

"Kyra, let him help," said Dad in a soft soothing voice but stopped when Mom sent him a seething glare.

"He's not a real doctor." She sat up and moved as if to get off the bed but we all stopped her. She glared at me. "This was your idea, wasn't it?"

"I have an MD in medicine," said Dr. Norris. "I'm fully accredited to practice and I'm the Stone Pack's Healer. Please, let me examine you."

Mom's mouth firmed up like to protest, so I said, "Mom, your eyes turned yellow."

She stared at me, her mouth flopping wordlessly.

I nodded. "A wolf yellow Mom, not human at all. Please, let Dr. Norris see what's wrong."

Mom closed her eyes tight but nodded. I watched Dr. Norris listen to her breathing and her heartbeat, take her pulse and blood pressure. He shined a light in her eyes and in her ears. He recorded everything on a chart he made with her name on it. Then he drew blood and disappeared into another room for a little while to test it.

Toni took Mom's wrist and even when she pulled back, he rubbed his nose back and forth over her skin, not touching. His nostrils flared as he breathed in her scent and he let her go with her glaring at him.

He said, "That's a very odd smell."

"How dare you!" She pulled her clothes tighter to her chest. "I didn't get to take a shower and it's not like you smell that great either!"

Toni glanced at me but he looked amused more than anything.

He said, "I didn't mean your physical smell. I meant your base scent. It's strange."

Mom glared at me then at him. "I don't know what you're talking about."

"The base scent is the scent of a person's...being I guess," said Sky. "A base scent is like the scent of being a human or being a shifter. Mr. Reeves's base scent is human. Xon's base scent is wolf. Your scent Mrs. Reeves...it's neither. I don't understand it either."

"It smells weird," said Connor as Mom paled under her brown skin, turning her a ghastly yellowish color. "It smells like...it's wrong. You shouldn't smell like that."

Mom swallowed hard and looked at her hands, curling them into fists. "So you're saying that before...I smelled human. Now...I don't smell...right anymore."

Dr. Norris came back with the vial of Mom's blood tucked in his breast pocket and her chart in his hand, scribbling on it. He took the seat next to Mom's bed and looked at her then at Dad before back at her.

"I have my diagnosis." He said with a long breath. "But it's still strange. It doesn't make any sense."

"Spit it out Will," instructed Toni. "Don't jerk them along."

"You have what's called the man-beast disease," said Dr. Norris, looking Mom in her eyes, then looking at me and Dad. "Its when after being bitten, the Change merges human and wolf DNA, turning the infected into what we call a man-beast."

"That's wrong though," said Toni while my family gasped. "If she was a man-beast she'd have Changed *into* a man-beast. A crazy deformed creature, a monster half human half wolf. There's no cure for it and she'd be put to death."

Cringing, Mom leaned against Dad who clasped her against him. They both gasped with horror.

Dad said, "No, I won't let you kill her!"

"That's what he's saying," said Dr. Norris. "Even if you are a man-beast, Kyra Reeves isn't behaving like one. A man-beast is incapable of speech and is extremely violent. She's calm and normal, so she can't be a man-beast. Besides, she doesn't look like one either. A man-beast looks like a human with a wolf's muzzle and ears, the arms and legs are lengthened with long fingers and claws. It has long shaggy hair all over and the spine is curved downwards. She's nothing like that."

Sky said, "That sounds like the Anthro-form."

Dr. Norris looked pleasantly surprised. "You know about the Anthro-form? And yes, it sounds similar but let's say the Anthro-form is more correctly put together. Man-beasts look disfigured and like I said, are insane. That's why is so confusing about Kyra's symptoms, if she's really a man-beast, she shouldn't be acting or looking like this."

Toni rubbed his forehead. "That's because man-beasts can only Change with the light of the full Moon. Even if Kyra was to Change, if she's truly a man-beast then she can't Change on her own. We'd have to wait until the next full Moon, September 9th, if we really want to know."

Kyra stared at him. "Are you kidding me? You're telling me I'm infected with some sort of horrible disease but you can't even properly diagnose me until next month?"

"I'm sorry Mrs. Reeves," said Dr. Norris, looking at her with a calm but honest expression. "We've explained to you the best we can. The blood sample I took from you was a mix of human and wolf DNA, just like a man-beast blood would be. So while your symptoms demonstrate those as infected, you aren't behaving or appearing like a man-beast. As a doctor I am stumped and as a Healer, my only suggestion is to go home and wait for the full Moon."

He looked at Toni. "I should be there in order to examine her. We'd also need someone strong enough to pass judgment should it be true."

I spoke before Toni could. "What do you mean *pass judgment*?"

Toni looked at my parents before looking at me. "It is UAC Law that all man-beasts are to be killed. There's no exception to that rule, period. It's the Law."

I grabbed Toni's shoulder and shoved him, he moved back one step.

I snarled, "I won't stand there and let you kill my mother."

He looked me in the eyes. His gaze was hard but earnest. "You don't get it, do you Xon? If Kyra is actually a man-beast, she won't be your mother anymore. She'll be an unhinged wild beast, her human mind would be ravaged and destroyed as the enraged wolf's mind takes over. She won't feel any emotions but starvation and rage. And the fact is, when a man-beast is Changed, they are hungry and they'll kill whoever is around. So if she saw you, she'd try to kill you, no questions asked."

"Stop, stop, stop!" Mom pressed her hands to her ears. "Stop saying these things! I want to go home, let me go home. Grant." She grabbed his hands, staring at him with wet brown eyes. "Take me home Grant, please."

Dad squeezed her hands and nodded, then looked at Dr. Norris. "Thanks for your help, but my wife and I are leaving now."

"Do your best to address the symptoms." The doctor said, standing up and putting the chart down. "The chills, that is the shivering and shaking, drinking lots of fluids and getting plenty of rest should help that, but if its too much take a fever reducer. Eating a lot is going to be a part of it, so I can only suggest making sure to have enough food in the house. Being hungry won't help."

"What about the pain?" Dad breathed out slowly. "She is having awful stomach and back pain, she can't even sit still or sleep well."

"You can try taking pain reliever." He said. "But if she really is building a wolf on the inside, the pain is a part of it. It'll get worse, a lot worse as the full Moon nears. Any lasting injury she's ever had is healing, any scar tissue for instance, if she's lost any organs from surgery, such as an appendix removed, it'll grow back as well."

Mom and Dad both gasped, so loud and sudden that everyone stared at them. Mom covered her mouth, tears in her eyes and she stared at Dad with wide eyes. Dad looked frozen, he wasn't even blinking.

Dr. Norris raised his brows. "Did I say something strange?"

It was me who spoke up. "Mom...she had a surgery that removed her womb. Are you saying that-?"

Dr. Norris said over me, "Any removed organs will grow back as the wolf takes over, healing all injuries. If she had a damaged womb that was removed, then the new womb will be fully functional."

He looked at Mom. "Like I said, the pain will only get worse, especially if you're growing a new womb. I suggest to take some time off work to handle it. Also if you get the increased sexual drive, try not to bite or scratch hence passing on some sort of infection to your husband. Hypersexuality can be a problem with infected individuals but how you chose to handle it is up to you two."

I squeezed my eyes shut for a moment, wishing I hadn't heard that.

"Then that's that." Toni's hand on my shoulder had me look at him. He nodded his head at me. "You Changed immediately into a wolf upon infection but your mother is going to have it rough these next few weeks. I know you have school but take care of her."

I gripped his wrist tightly, breathing in. "Thank you and I will."

He lowered his hand so I let him go and he led the way upstairs. The sun was up and shining through the blinds. Several wolves were in the living room, which made me wonder how many people lived in this house besides Toni. Brenda and as well as Wyatt were one of them. Wyatt's nostrils flared, then he looked at my mother. His gray eyes shifted to the bright green of his wolf, his scent flushed hot with anger.

I stepped in front of my mother, peeling my lips back to bare my teeth at him. "Back off Wyatt. Don't even look at her."

He sneered. "As if I want to at look the whore who spawned a shithead like you."

Toni grabbed my arm before I could lunge at him, while it was Shane who restrained my father.

Toni snapped, "Wyatt, enough! I know you miss Rocky but I did what I had to do."

My eyes widened. "What? I keep asking where Rocky is but no wants to tell me. Is he in jail?"

Wyatt took a single step toward me, his entire body vibrating with the need to tackle me and rip me into pieces, the hot burning scent of rage and the raw tingling agony of bloodlust seeping from his pores.

"Great Moon you 're an idiot." He spoke, his voice raspy. "There's no prison that can hold a werewolf, none. When Rocky did what he did, when he tried to kill you and instead Changed you, he was punished. The punishment sanctioned by the Alpha of the United States as Alpha Law."

I moved away from my parents because it was clear Wyatt was ready to attack me and I didn't want them getting caught up in the fight that was sure about to take place. He was finally telling me what had happened, why he hated me so much.

I asked, "Okay, but who is Rocky to you? I mean, what's the punishment?"

Wyatt grinned from ear to ear, his mouth chockfull of sharp machete-curved fangs. "Who Rocky *was* to me? What's the punishment you say?"

Toni said firmly, "Wyatt, stand down. Move away from the door and let the Lakeside Village Pack through."

Wyatt was standing right in front of the door, blocking the way. His hackles had raised out of his shoulders, thick gray fur tumbled down his neck, black talons slid from his nail beds. "Goddammit! You're always on his side Toni, you always let him get away with whatever he does. I'm not taking it anymore."

I lowered my head in preparation for his attack, breathing calmly and keeping my eyes on him. "What the hell is your problem Wyatt? I never did anything to you, I know that."

"I'll show you what my problem is!" Wyatt rushed me and Toni put him in a headlock, forcing him down on the ground and straddled him. Wyatt bucked his body but even though Toni weighed less than he did, Wyatt couldn't get him off, no matter how he struggled while he snarled curses.

I stared at Toni. "What did I do?"

"Wyatt has an issue with you because Remington aka Rocky was his younger brother."

Toni spoke rather calmly while keeping Wyatt incapacitated without any outwards signs of struggle to do so. He wasn't sweating or breathing hard, his body barely moved even as Wyatt kicked, thrashed and bucked his body, even shoving up from the floor. Toni was immovable. It reminded me of when Javier said Alphas have supernatural strength and clearly Toni had it in spades.

Toni said, "The punishment for illegally Changing a human, as well as attempt to kill a human being is severe. As decreed by Alpha Law, I had no choice but to mete out the only sentence. The ultimate punishment."

Wyatt roared, sobbing at the same time. "XON KILLED MY BROTHER! IT WAS HIS FAULT, HE KILLED HIM! XON KILLED MY BROTHER!"

Brenda placed her hand on my chest. Her eyes shined with tears, the first time I had seen her so emotional. "You should go ahead and go. Don't worry about Wyatt, Toni will take care of him. It's okay to leave now."

I wanted to say something to Wyatt, I never meant to get anyone in trouble, especially not cause death. What was I supposed to do when Rocky attacked me? Wasn't it Leah's fault for driving him into a jealous frenzy? Was it really all my fault?

"Let's go Xon." Sky whispered, hands on my back. "They'll handle this."

We left, Wyatt's agonized screaming following us out. My stomach tightened as I swallowed hard. So that's why, that's the reason. Mikhail said he was holding a grudge against me and Toni kept evading answering me. The wolf who tried to kill me and instead ended up Changing me...he had been put to death. Every time Wyatt looked at me he was reminded that I was alive and his brother was dead. No wonder he kept trying to kill me. The last thing his brother did before death was try to kill me too.

Sky looked at me as we got back to the cars. "Do you need me to drive?" Her honey-gold eyes were warm and worried.

"I can drive." I said, unlocking the car doors. "I'll drop you guys off at home, your parents are probably worried, Sky, Shane."

Shane snorted. "You know how many times I come home after like two days gone? Sure, they'll dick at me but I'll ignore them. This is important right now."

"My parents are definitely a little worried," said Sky in a soft voice. "But they know I have a mate and a Pack now, and that wolves prefer to stay together. I'm sure they'll understand after I explain it. It is a Saturday so I'd rather come back with you Xon. I'll call them to let them know where I am."

"Fine." I said.

I was still hearing Wyatt's bellows in my head. He had his brother killed because of me, now I understood why he hated me so much. Sky placed her hand on my knee and I took one hand off the wheel to cover it. My cell rang in my pocket, Sky dug her little hand in and took it out.

I watched her answer it, saying, "Who is it?"

The male voice that came out rumbled like an earthquake, loud and powerful enough the entire car could hear it. My hairs rose all over my arms and the back of the neck.

"I'm calling to speak to Jaxon Reeves, Alpha of Lakeside Village Pack."

Sky handed the phone over, her eyes huge.

I placed it against my ear and held it there with my shoulder, gripping the wheel with both hands but loosened when it bent underneath my hands.

"Alpha Jaxon Reeves speaking. Who may I ask is calling?"

"I am Prince Severo of the Méndez Pack." He said. Right in my ear it was like having a wolf god speak to me, his voice full of dominance in every syllable. This was just through the phone, the idea of being in front of him was enough to make my wolf put his tail between his legs. "After the events that have occurred in Lakeside Village the case was brought to the Alpha of your country, the United States. My Alpha was planning on sending me to check in with Javier Méndez so it was decided that I would also come on behalf of your case. I will be arriving from Spain today this afternoon. I will meet you at the house we have set aside for Javier's use, let's say, one o'clock. Agreed?"

I couldn't exactly say *no I don't agree* so I nodded. "Yes, agreed."

"Good," said Prince Severo. "I must go Alpha of Lakeside Village Pack. I will see you soon." He hung up.

I put the phone down, my hand was trembling like a leaf and everyone else in the car were panting.

"Such dominance." Shane said, breathing hard. "That was just over the phone... I've felt your dominance before Xon and let me tell you, it ain't shit compared to that wolf's voice just now."

I didn't like it but he was right. I rolled my head over my shoulders. "I can only wonder what it'll be like in person. Prince Severo of the Méndez Pack. Javier, is he your uncle or a brother? He is from your Pack, right?"

Javier was quiet before muttering. "He is my cousin."

We were back at my house and I parked then went to help Dad with Mom. Mom swat at my hand when I reached for her then pulled away from Dad. She stomped up the stairs without looking back. Dad watched her go with hurt aching eyes, his strong shoulders slumped, and his face etched with lines at his mouth, eyes and forehead. Watching him, this was the first time I thought Dad looked...weak. He's always been my hero, the one I looked up to and needed advice from. Now I had something else on my plate and I didn't want to worry him with it.

Sky slid her hand into mine and squeezed, then said, "Mr. Reeves, we have something to tell you."

I breathed out of my nostrils as Dad looked at me with those sad damp eyes. I knew she was right, keeping the phone call a secret from my father wasn't a good idea. I told him about Prince Severo.

Dad's eyes widened. "Prince Severo?" He looked at Javier. "Your cousin is royalty?"

Javier didn't meet his eyes, he was staring at the floor like if he did it long enough it would open up and swallow him. His shoulders slouched, his scent drenched with ammonia from anxiety, apprehension and the dank lifelessness of both depression and desperation.

Sky answered. "In a Pack hierarchy, the Prince title is just a position in the Pack, it doesn't mean royalty. It's a high-ranking position, just underneath the Alpha."

Shane clicked his teeth. "The highest level of government in the shifter community is the UAC, or the United Alpha Council. There is no king and queen. Javier's father is Rodolfo Méndez the Twenty-Eighth United Alpha. Javier is expected to become Alpha next after him, so yeah, he's basically royalty."

Dad's brows raised. "But, if that's the case, why are you here Javier?"

Javier said in a tiny subdued voice, head down as if in shame. "I am here because I am not like the rest of the males in my family, I am small, chubby and I prefer to cook and to clean. They felt that if I was sent to be alone I would naturally grow tall, muscular, dominant like them. So they dropped me here alone with no contact so that my wolf will become strong and fierce. Still...that is not the case...and now when my cousin arrives he will see."

Connor and Leo hugged him tight and Javier closed his eyes, holding onto them.

Dad rubbed the back of his head. "Alright. So he's going to be here later on. I have to stay with my wife but let me know how it works out. I mean, he's coming here to kill two birds with one stone, right?"

Sky nodded. "To check on Javier and to address the fact that Xon killed a Rogue wolf. Not to mention the fact that Xon is an illegal Alpha anyway."

Dad sighed and looked at us. "An illegal Alpha? What is that supposed to mean?"

"I'm really too young to be an Alpha," I said.

"That's not it." Sky cut in, making me look at her. "The problem is that Changed wolves aren't allowed to be Alphas, that is, a wolf with human parents cannot be an Alpha. If Prince Severo tells United Alpha Rodolfo that you have human parents, meaning you are a Changed wolf, which he will, then United Alpha Rodolfo will decree you are to be stripped of your Alpha status. Wolves with human parents cannot be Alphas, it's the Law."

Anger riddled up my spine. "That only means that Changed wolves can't be Alphas. So born wolves can but if you're Changed you can't? That's discrimination, it's racist."

Sky's mouth trembled and she nodded. "It is a way to make sure that no Changed wolves can be in positions of power, yes."

I snapped, "Javier!"

The wolf in question jumped but looked at me with wide eyes. "Yes Alpha?"

"Did you know this? Silly question, of course you knew. So why didn't you tell your father about me? Why did Toni even let me become an Alpha in the first place? Why did anyone support me in the first place?"

Javier's round body quivered but he said, "I told you, my parents, my family, dropped me here with no intention of communicating with me. I was to be alone, to grow into my dominance. When you became Alpha, how would they know if they never bother to call me, or check in on me? The only reason they know now is because of the popularity of your name on the news coverage, the fact you have killed a Rogue wolf at such a young age."

He kept talking. "Cousin Severo will undoubtedly tell my father who will then have to bring the information to the other One Hundred and Forty-Nine United Alphas. They will convene on it but gathering for a full convention takes time, sometimes months to gather all One Hundred and Fifty. Besides, they only do a complete gathering for major crimes or global-wide problems. A reasonably small matter of a Changed wolf attempting to be an Alpha is no cause for such a thing. Instead, they will pick maybe five or seven United Alphas to talk it over."

Javier sighed and shook his head. "That could take a week or two but the final decision will be a resounding agree that you are not allowed to be Alpha because you are a Changed wolf, period."

I stared at them both. "So you two are saying that there is nothing I can do. The bigger dogs will simply say I'm fired and that's it? All the hard work I've gone through, what we've done together, I'm not an Alpha anymore and Shane is back to being leader?"

Javier said after a minute, "You will no longer be considered an Alpha Xon. You could still be a Pack leader. They can not say we are not a Pack because we have a Pack scent. What they might do is send a wolf here to become Alpha instead of either you or Shane."

"What if I beat him up?" I asked, my voice roughening with aggression, my teeth sharpened. "If I defeat whoever Alpha they send, then I'll be Alpha."

"No," said Sky quietly. "You'll get in a lot of trouble for trying again to be in a position of power. Xon, it's against the Law, period. They won't let you be an Alpha if you have human parents. The one and only way to ensure you continue to be Alpha is if your parents become wolves, period. You can all be Changed wolves but if your parents are wolves then you can be Alpha."

I sat down abruptly on the ground and they sat with me, placing their calm hands on my body.

"I can't do that." I said, my voice strained. "I cannot force my parents to become wolves."

Dad spoke, his voice just as hoarse as mine. "Kyra is infected Xon...maybe you will have a wolf as a parent. Would have one parent being a wolf and the other human count as still being illegal to be Alpha?"

I stared at Dad, shocked at the words coming out of his mouth. "Dad! We're going to heal Mom; we'll get her better. She won't be a wolf; she doesn't have the disease."

He looked at me with dried empty eyes. "They said there was no cure and we'll only know on a full Moon. And then she'll Change into a beast and try to kill you. It's already hopeless Xon."

I pulled Dad to my chest and hugged him as he broke down into dry wracking sobs. "It'll be okay Dad, I swear it." Tears burned in my eyes too. I didn't want Mom to become what Toni said, an unhinged wild beast, that her human mind would be destroyed and that she'd try to kill her family. "She'll be fine, Mom will be fine. I promise."

A scream rose up from upstairs, Mom, her voice wretched as she screamed out her pain. I let Dad go, he wiped at his face then ran upstairs as Mom kept screaming.

Sky held my face and tilted it down so I was looking at her, though her face blurred. "Xon, it's okay. I know your Mom is infected but Dr. Norris is a good doctor, he'll figure out how to help her. We all need to get showered and get new clothes, then head to Javier's place to meet Prince Severo. So let's take one thing at a time. We won't find out about Mrs. Reeves until September anyway. Okay?" She kissed each of my eyes, gently sipping my tears.

I hugged her tightly, burying my face into her hair and slowly calmed down. She kissed my face and stroked my neck and shoulders until I was okay and I stepped back, ready to be in charge again. She smiled at me. I took her hand then gently kissed her ring finger. She gasped, eyes wide.

I said low, "I really don't know what I'd do without you Sky. You raised me up from being a scared weak pup. And you've kept me strong until now I'm a dominant Alpha. Without you, I'd be nothing."

"Oh Xon." She leaned in and I kissed her.

"AH! Stop it, stop it!" Connor jumped onto us both, breaking us apart, while Leo and Javier quickly crowded in for a hug.

Shane didn't join in but he watched and smiled. After a quick snuggling session, it took several hours for us to eat breakfast, shower and change clothes. I had to shave my hair down and dressed to impress with slacks and a collared shirt. My parents stayed in their room the whole time and I decided not to bother them.

I had done enough to my parents already, in fact, I had ruined their lives. The moment I came home as a werewolf everything had changed and now my mother was physically effected. Carter only scratched her to get back at me and I had foolishly believed nothing would come of it. If Mom really was a man-beast, if she became some crazed monster, there was no way I'd let her die. I'd find a way to fix her.

I closed my eyes tight and prayed for the first time in a while. *Dear God, please, look after my mother. Heal her in the way only You can. Don't let her mind be ravaged by a wolf, don't let her lose her humanity. I'll do anything, please protect my mother. In Jesus name, Amen.*

By one pm, the Pack was gathered at Javier's mansion and waiting on Prince Severo. Javier was a bristling bunch of nerves, pacing from one side of the living room to the next, his hands flexing at his side, breathing quickly and his eyes spaced wide. Just watching him was making my stomach jerk around.

"Javier, please calm down." I said, shaking my head. "It won't be that bad. Just tell him that-"

"NO!" He shouted.

My brows raised and I leaned back, stunned and a little annoyed.

Javier breathed out slowly then said, "It will not be as easy as you think my Alpha. You heard his voice on the phone, yes? Now imagine that ten, no, twenty times more intense. You can not lie in the presence of my cousin, you can barely keep your head up around him. His dominant aura drapes around him like a shield, like a cloak. You get too close and you will naturally be forced to your knees before him. When he sees me, sees that I have not changed at all, that I am still fat, that I still have no dominance, that I am short, that I do not have a deep voice and not a strong masculine wolf, he will be furious."

Sky, sitting next to me, said, "But Javier, it's not like you can force yourself into growing taller or deepening your voice, right? I mean, you're only sixteen, right? You have years more to develop."

Javier slumped to the floor like his legs had collapsed. He clasped his forehead, his back bowed. "You do not understand, the males in my family, they become tall, muscled, powerful, very quickly. If I was like them, I would be six feet tall by fourteen, my voice like the mountains, my muscles naturally thickening. I am nothing the way I should be."

"Dude." Shane grunted, sounding irritated. "If you'd stop purposely overeating and actually come with me to the gym once in a while you'd look the way they wanted. You're fat because you want to be, you know how much a wolf has to eat to look chubby the way you do? It's insane, you're making yourself miserable."

Javier laid out on his stomach, crossed his arms then laid his face down. Leo and Connor both moved to lay with him, cuddled into his sides and stroking him.

I sighed and looked at Sky.

She said, "They know how to comfort each other. Somehow in the short time you've been Alpha they've all bonded tightly." She looked at the floor, her jaw tightening. "Now we need to find a way to keep you as Alpha."

Shane rubbed the back of his neck. "I think that rule is bogus anyway. I was basically an Alpha anyway, if I didn't have human parents then I would have been."

I doubted that. I had human parents but I had made a Pack and became an Alpha within a week since I Changed and met everyone. If Shane had been going to make a Pack, he would have done it a long time ago. Fact is, he can't be violent and domineering then make Pack with wolves. That's not how Pack is made. I had figured that out on my own.

Outside came the low rumbling of a car engine then a door opening.

Javier blasted up from the floor, sending both Connor and Leo flying. Sky caught Connor while Leo flumped against Shane. Shane held him first then pushed him away.

The door was knocked on with heavy loud blows.

Javier stood there, trembling from head to toe, he didn't look like he was about to answer the door.

Shane sighed then brushed past everyone and walked down the hallway to answer the door. It opened and I smelled Prince Severo. He smelled like a wolf, like pure intense hard-core animal vitality. Then he stepped into the living room.

Prince Severo was a giant of a werewolf, standing six-feet-seven, his muscles large and bulging. He was wearing an expensive suit but he had taken off the jacket and rolled up the sleeves, baring massive forearms covered in hair. His black hair was cut expertly and his facial hair barbered. His eyes were stark brown and his aura boiled around him, such dominance like it breathed through his skin.

Behind him was another werewolf who smelled like Severo with the deep warm scent of family blood. He was tall, well over six feet and bulked with muscle. Now I realized what an oddball Javier must seem to the males of his family.

Prince Severo saw me but then he looked at Javier, standing at a meager five feet four and weighed nearly two hundred pounds, his face round and his body just the same. Prince Sevcro breathed out heavy from his nostrils then he strode over, grasped Javier's arm and pulled him into a corner. He immediately started talking in low heated Spanish, every now and then his finger poked Javier sharply in his pouched belly, or flicked him on his soft arms. Javier's head was held down, his shoulders slumped and he flinched, not saying a word. I didn't know Spanish but it was clear that he was being lectured.

I turned to the other wolf who had entered. "I'm Jaxon Reeves, Alpha of the Lakeside Village Pack. And you are?"

He gasped and said, "Of course, I didn't introduce myself. My name's Matías Méndez. Prince Severo is my father." He spoke with a rich Spanish accent but he did use contractions and sounded fluent. He dipped his head in a respectful bow. "Greetings Alpha of Lakeside Village Pack." He tilted his head to the side. He looked at me like he was a pin and I was a butterfly. "Are you really seventeen? And did you really kill a Rogue wolf by yourself?"

I blinked then I asked, "What is your position in your Pack?"

Matías smiled then said, "I believe I asked you a question first."

Sky gripped my wrist in her small strong hand. "Jaxon, answer the questions."

I nodded. "Yes, I am seventeen. My birthday is in June, so I've just turned. And yes, I killed Carter Hawkins by myself, in my house. We were both in wolf form."

"Is it true that you were Changed into a wolf earlier this month?" He spoke kindly, calmly and with a gentle smile.

Sky squeezed my wrist again.

I said, "I was Changed on August 1st. My first full Moon was August 10th."

Matías's eyes widened and his breath caught. "And today is August 16th. Yet you've made a Pack as an Alpha and killed the Rogue wolf. I see."

Matías made a long humming sound then walked away to his father. Prince Severo turned from Javier as Matías went to his side. The two began to converse in low Spanish.

Javier fled to come over to me, his hands spread over my stomach.

I took them and kissed his wrists, saying softly, "Relax, okay? He's just the Prince, he can't do anything to you, right?"

Javier's eyes were rimmed in tears, then he laid his face on my chest as he let out a large sigh. "But as Prince of the

Pack, he is just a step underneath my father." My shirt dampened. "He will tell my father everything."

I patted his soft back as Connor took Javier to his side, his hand gently brushing at Javier's tears. Leo took Javier's other side, wrapping his long gangly arms around Javier's shoulders and leaning against him, rubbing his face into Javier's hair. Shane stood at Sky's other side. Grouped together, our Pack scent enhanced, firmed. Even in the presence of a powerful wolf, the Lakeside Village Pack stood strong, a unit.

Prince Severo walked over to stand in front of me but several feet back. His dominant aura was nothing like Toni's cold wave, it was hot like a volcanic eruption. Get too close and you'll be consumed.

Straightening my back and looking at him directly, I said, "As Alpha of the Lakeside Village Pack, I welcome you, Prince Severo of the Méndez Pack."

"Greetings to you Jaxon Reeves." He said. "My son has informed me of the situation. Now, I have come here on behalf of the Alpha of the United States request to make judgment on your position as Alpha. As you should well know, Changed wolves are not allowed to be Alpha, period. However, you have shown spectacular Alpha qualities, including your pure dominance which is particularly fascinating. I am also stunned and impressed that you killed a Rogue wolf. I did take note that the neighboring Alpha Antonius Stone had let the Rogue live while you Jaxon did the correct thing in killing him. Now, due to the fact that the only available wolf is Shane Armstrong, who is clearly not of Alpha material as well as also a Changed wolf, I will allow you to keep your place as Alpha but only until a suitable replacement wolf is chosen. That concludes my business here."

He then looked at Javier, who cringed. "Javier, take lessons from Jaxon. It is shameful that a Changed wolf is more impressive than you, a high-class wolf with excellent lineage. The next time I see you I expect to see you have

The Other Side 456

grown the way you should. Understand? Matías, we're leaving. Jaxon Reeves, we take our leave in peace."

I held up my hand. "Leave in peace."

Then the two left and just like that, it was over. I could still be Alpha for now even though it wasn't permanent.

I looked at Sky, she held my hand in a tight grasp and said, "One day at a time Xon. We'll get through this. All of us."

My Pack nodded. Now I had just to continue going to school and look after Mom until the full Moon next month.

14

September 9ᵗʰ
Tuesday

The full Moon had finally arrived and all of us were ready to find out about my mother. As a little over three weeks passed, just like Dr. Norris had said, her symptoms worsened. She was in constant pain, eating voraciously and throwing up afterwards. Dad confirmed what Dr. Norris told us about her womb growing back, as Mom had a period for the first time in seventeen years. I didn't ask Dad how he satisfied or avoided her intimate needs. I didn't want to know.

Now that the time had come, we had to tell Dad to stay home just in case Mom did Change and he got hurt by accident. Dr. Norris, Toni, and Brenda were all here in the field before the forest, including my Mom and my Pack.

Dr. Norris said, "It's possible she'll turn into a regular werewolf. I've never heard of a delayed Change but seeing as she's infected it could be possible that the Change wouldn't take over until the full Moon. She might not be a man-beast after all."

At the moment, the full Moon was hidden behind the clouds, leaving us in mostly darkness, yet I could see. Everyone's eyes glowed as the wolf spark flickered gold.

Mom's eyes weren't glowing and she was widening her eyes so she could take in as much light as there was available. Maybe Dr. Norris was right, maybe she would be a regular wolf, her eyes had turned yellow more than once and even her pretty nails had contorted into claws. Dear God, she was going to Change, wasn't she?

"Here it comes," said Toni in a tense tone as the clouds parted. The Moon shined down on us in rays of luminescent silver.

The Change clutched at me instantly, starting from the base of my spine and shuddering up to my skull, coursing down my limbs and working at my insides. I had wanted to watch Mom to see if she Changed, but my eyes closed naturally as the Change shifted my body from human to wolf. When I stood up on all fours as a wolf, I looked over and saw Mom standing on two legs.

Her hair, which was normally black, it was now pale gray, and very thick, like fur, coming down her neck and over her shoulders, like a mane, or a ruff. Her eyes were almond-shaped and her irises the intense yellow of a wolf. She was taller by a foot, her feet and toes had lengthened, her ankles stretched up, leaving the heel of her feet off the ground with the front pad and her toes as the base to walk on. Her arms were longer too, her nails like switch blades. Her mouth was full of fangs but not stretched into a muzzle, her nose blackened and lumpy. It was like she was half a wolf and half human. Her smell confused me too, she smelled like a human and like a wolf melded together to make a new strange scent. It made me take a step back, my stomach quivering. Was this still my Mother?

"What the hell is this Will?" asked Toni, staring at the creature my Mom had become. His eyes were amber and his hands buckled with claws, but he didn't change. He really was strong, the full Moon was out yet he held still back the Change.

Dr. Norris looked stunned, staring. He had shifted into something I had never seen before, also like a mix of human and wolf but nothing like Mom's mismatched parts. It was clearly the Anthro-form that he had mentioned before. He looked a wolf that walked on its hind legs, abnormally long with feet-like paws, and a human upper-body, with arms and hand-like paws, his spine straight, shoulders broad and he was completely covered in thick red-tawny fur. His head was very wolfish with tall ears and narrowed dark green eyes set above a long muzzle. It was like Mom had attempted to Change into the Anthro-form he was currently in but messed it up.

[Mom?] I spoke telepathically to her. *[Can you hear me?]*

She didn't answer, stood still, staring at the Moon as if in a trance. The silver light was reflected in her circular black pupils but she didn't have a gold spark that proclaimed one to being a wolf.

[MOM!] I shouted as loud as I could in her head, but she didn't move, staring up at the Moon, her mouth slightly parted, her body was held loose and relaxed, standing still.

"Will, give me an answer dammit!" Toni growled. "What the hell did she Change in to?"

The other wolves in the clearing were my Packmates and Brenda had succumbed to the Change. Leo, Sky and Javier watched Mom intently, while Connor and Shane kept looking toward the forest, making quiet whimpering noises. I heard the call of the wild too, like a hot feeling in my breast, the wind rustling my fur and the smells of the prey in my nose, I wanted to go running and hunting, but my Mom was holding all my attention. What had Carter done to her with just a scratch?

"That is the man-beast form," Dr. Norris said, swallowing quickly. "But it looks incomplete."

He's talking outloud!

His wolf muzzle was capable of performing human speech, like his wolf and his human form had perfectly mixed. His voice sounded mostly the same, with an extra roughness to his tone.

Dr. Norris continued, "She looks somewhat like that, she's retained so much of her humanity and the fact she's not trying to kill anyone, I can't diagnosis her as having the illness. It comes about from being infected by a werewolf bite or any other contact with our blood, and the infection mutates. Instead of transforming the person into a werewolf, it combines with the human DNA. It'll Change said human into a form like this one, as well as driving them clinically insane. Yet Mrs. Reeves isn't acting like this at all. She seems to be in some sort of trance."

Dr. Norris snapped his furry fingers in front of Mom's face and she didn't even blink. She was breathing slowly and easily, rarely blinking, staring at the Moon.

Connor and Shane both gave short high-pitched yaps of impatience. They were ready to go run.

"Brenda, go with them," said Toni, giving a sharp flick of his hand. "Xon, you can go too."

I shook my head and sat back on my haunches. *[I'm staying with my Mom.]*

[I'll stay] Javier said in my head, but I could see his legs trembling with pent up energy to go run.

Leo nodded and sat down, but he was breathing heavy.

Sky sat next to me. *[Me too.]*

[It's fine, you guys can go. I'll be okay and so will Mom.]

I nudged them away with my muzzle and Brenda took off at a high speed, my Packmates after her. Their happy howls rose up in the air.

Dr. Norris had managed to coax Mom to sit down, though it was just her body moving, her mind was gone.

I concentrated and tried to force my body to change back, but instead received a crushing pain and I yelped. The night was too young and the Moon still had power over me. I couldn't change back yet.

"Relax Xon, we'll figure this out. What's going on Will?" asked Toni, his teeth a little sharp but his voice was still human. "What type of trance is she in?"

"Moon-bound," said Dr. Norris. "It's just she's, well, entranced by the Moon. Like being hypnotized by the ticking of a clock or watching the same pattern over and over again. With the rise of the Sun, the spell will break."

"Will she transform back into a human? Is this permanent?"

Dr. Norris cupped his black-clawed hand over his furred chin, his dark green eyes looking over my Mom. "I think she'll turn back into a human but the next full Moon she'll turn into this placid creature again. Her infection is the strangest thing I've ever seen. She's no danger to anyone and I don't see the need for her to be put to death."

My legs relaxed and I nearly fell over with relief. Instead I trotted over to my Mom and licked her face.

[Mom? Mom are you in there?]

She didn't respond to my touch, she didn't even blink, just stared up at the Moon.

At a loud gasp, I looked over and saw Toni bent over as the Change finally overtook him. He stood up as a wolf and shook himself. Toni's fur was a deep chocolate brown with rusty tan undersides. The top of the wolf's head was graced with bright blond fur, just the way Connor's white wolf had green fur. My head only reached his mid-shoulders, my ears barely graced the bottom of his chin. He was a full grown adult wolf and his thick male wolf scent was strong in this form. The cold wave of his dominant aura stretched out and flexed against me. I pushed back on him, my dominance was like boulders, a huge heavy rock that would flatten anyone who got close.

Toni's amber eyes focused on me, his black pupils full of his gold spark. His voice came to my head. *[Looks like*

A. E. Costello 461

I'll be here with you for this full Moon. Will, can you look after Kyra for us?]

Dr. Norris didn't respond, he was taking Mom's pulse with his long-fingered hands.

Toni groaned deep in his throat. *[I forgot, he can't speak telepathically in this form.]*

I again looked at Dr. Norris's strange two-legged wolf form. He was much taller than he normally was, easily seven feet tall.

[So that is the Anthro-form? It's like Mom's...but better.]

Toni answered, sitting back on his haunches. *[Yes. It's the form that takes place in between wolf and human, melding the best qualities of both. A wolf in the Anthro-form can speak outloud, is faster and stronger. However it is highly contagious. If just the smallest scratch or saliva is passed into a human being they'll immediately change into this form but that'll be the only form they have. No longer human and not a wolf, just forever in between. It's illegal for a wolf to take the Anthro-form in the presence of humans. Tonight though, Will had to take this form if he wanted to be able to examine your mother properly.]*

Toni nudged at Dr. Norris's leg until the giant wolfman looked at him. Toni pointed at Mom then pointed back at him with his paw.

Dr. Norris understood, saying, "I'll stay here and watch her. It's not a problem."

I whined low, I didn't want to leave my Mom.

Toni looked at me. *[She's going to sit and stare at the Moon for the rest of the night Xon. You can leave then Dr. Norris will make sure she gets home safe when the sun rises. You'll see her when you get back. For now, let's go.]*

He dashed away and I ran after him, no longer able to deny the call of the Moon, of the forest.

I howled to call my Pack back, and once we were all grouped together, there was a decision to be made. There was my Pack, then Toni, who was an Alpha, and his Alpha queen, Brenda. Normally I led the hunt, but Toni was older.

Toni cocked his head to the side.

[Lakeside Village is your territory] His voice came to all of our heads. *[We're visiting, guests. You lead the hunt.]*

I led the way, with Sky at my side, then Toni and Brenda, with the rest of my Pack following them.

A distressed call split the night air, *keekee, keekee.*

[Wild turkey.] Toni nudged my hindquarter. *[Sounds like a young one is lost, separated from its flock.]*

I nodded and lead the way, tracking down the call of the turkey. We found it, wandering aimlessly, making its *keekee* cry. It was dark, and the way the turkey's head passed back and forth without focusing on us, it couldn't see us in limited light.

I dashed forward, catching its slim neck in my teeth, and chomping down, killing it effortlessly. Once the twenty pound bird was lifeless on the ground, the rest of the Pack and the guests crowded in. The bird was covered in glossy feathers, which while they didn't have much of a taste, I was able to get pass them into the thick hearty meat easily.

We all slept in a tightly knit bunch after eating, until a strange howl woke us up, loud and long like a wolf but not melodious enough, more like a human's fake howl.

[Will.] Toni stretched his front legs forward with his back legs up in a very cat-like motion. *[Guess we should head back.]*

I turned my nose to the sky where the deep dark of the night was gently fading into pale blue. Dr. Norris had said Mom was entranced by the Moon, so if the Sun was out, she should have changed back by now.

We went back to the field, getting there just as the Sun broke out of the clouds. Mom was laying on the ground in her human form, completely asleep.

Dr. Norris was in human form as well, dressed. We all Changed back to humans and got dressed as well.

"She changed back," he said. "And she's exhausted, so she won't wake up for a while. She spent the entire night staring at the Moon."

"So what does this mean?" I asked, crossing my arms over my chest. "Will she do this every full Moon?"

"Fraid so," said Dr. Norris with a nod. "We should have this talk with her husband present."

15

September 10th
Wednesday

Dad was sitting in the living room when we all got back from the forest, including with the Stone Pack members. Mom went straight to sleep the moment the Sun rose and broke her trance.

Dad listened as he was told what happened with Mom then said quietly, "So…she is a werewolf now?"

Dr. Norris glanced at Toni before looking back at Dad. "In all honesty, she's more like an infected human, like she has a disease more than actually being a werewolf. I don't know if she's contagious or not, I would have to take some more detailed blood tests to see so. If she is, that would have to be declared to the shifter community and her job."

"They'll fire her," said Dad in a low voice. "It's illegal to fire people for being shifters but if she's a walking contagion then they have every right to fire her."

Toni rubbed his chin then took out his cell phone. "Let me call our mystic and tell her about this, maybe she can do something."

Dad asked, "Mystic?"

Dr. Norris answered while Toni walked away on the phone. "A mystic is the Pack magic user. Always female and there is a Queen Mystic for each continent, so there is six. Antarctica isn't counted."

Dad whistled and leaned back. "Magic user? As in wands and casting spells?"

Dr. Norris's eye twitched but he said, "No, not like that."

Toni came back, sliding his phone in his pocket. "Let's get to my place. Ze'eva says she has an idea."

It was up to Dad to help Mom wake up, shower and dress, then took three cars to get to Toni's place. I knew Sky and Shane's parents probably weren't happy that they were missing school but Pack sticks with Pack. If my Mom was really some sort of werewolf now, she was my Pack too. Dad was acting calm but his son was a wolf and his wife was infected. How did he really feel about all of this?

At the Stone Pack mansion, there were plenty of wolves there. I knew which one was Ze'eva from the moment I looked at her. It was her smell that caught my attention first. She had all the regular smells, wolf, female, a personal scent and her Pack scent. But there was one new smell that I had never smelt before. A bright tingling bursting smell...magic.

She glided forward like her feet were moving on air and the Pack shifted aside to let her through. She was thin and wispy, like a starved tree. Her skin was just as gnarled and tough as bark, clinging to her bones. Her eyes were glazed over whitish blue as if she should be blind but she was focusing on Mom's face so intensely I knew she couldn't be. Her body may be old but she was still vitalized, something on the inside of her was burning strong and vibrant.

Mom cringed back but Ze'eva took her hand and felt along her bones, then cupped Mom's chin and turned her face from side to side, staring at her. Then she hovered her hands over Mom's chest, her long white lashes fluttered. She spoke and her voice was loud, booming, coming from someplace inside of her that was vital and strong, nothing like her weary outsides.

"The wolf is trapped inside of her, half formed, caged, tangled within her human blood. The Change was incomplete, it failed to take hold completely."

Dad grasped Mom's wrist and stared at Ze'eva. "So what can you do? Is she going to be stuck like this forever?"

Ze'eva bowed her head for a moment then looked at Mom with a force like she was a telescope and Mom was the star she was looking at.

She spoke again in that fierce powerful voice, "There is one thing I can think of. She can eat the Aygül flower."

The Stone Pack all gasped and whispered to each other.

Mom asked, her voice shaking, "A what flower? What are you talking about?"

Dr. Norris said, "The Aygül flower is for werewolves mystic. It's a great healing plant, yes, but it'll do nothing for a human being."

"It will heal the damaged wolf inside of her," said Ze'eva, looking at Mom. "Do you understand what I'm saying?"

My stomach pitched towards my shoes. "You're saying to turn her into a werewolf. A full wolf."

Dad's breathing stopped for a second and I placed my hand on his back.

Mom stared then shook her head. "No, I refuse!"

"You don't seem to understand." Toni looked at her with black eyes brightening to amber. "You are *infected*, got it? You aren't human and you aren't wolf, you're a diseased freak in between. If you really are contagious, no one will hire you and you won't be able to touch your husband unless you infect him. Your symptoms will continue to worsen with each full Moon as your wolf struggles to be fully born and your human blood continues to fight and tangle the process. You can't live like that, period. You can't go back to being human, the infection cannot be removed like that. You *can* become a full fledged wolf, that'll heal you. Bring you from one form to the next."

Mom's eyes watered. "But if I'm a werewolf then…" She looked at Dad, sniffing and lowered her head as if in shame.

Dad hugged her then looked at Toni. "If she becomes a wolf, then I will too."

I gasped, shocked. "D-Dad! But, you're a human, you wouldn't want-"

"I do want Xon." He looked at me with his eyes firm and earnest. His scent matched, the sharp oily scent of certainty and the mint of truth. "You are a wolf and my wife will be a wolf. My adopted son is a wolf. For me to remain human is stupid. I've felt how strong you are Xon and Kyra's gotten a little stronger than normal as well, Connor is stronger than me. If Kyra can infect me by mistake, then it might as well be when she's a wolf. We'll be a proper family of wolves."

I wavered on my feet, feeling a little lightheaded. Sky and Shane grasped me firmly and the pain of their tight hold cleared the fuzziness in my head.

I said, "Dad if you do this, there's no going back."

Ze'eva said, "Kyra Reeves hasn't made a decision. Will you eat the Aygül flower?"

Dr. Norris said, "Are we even sure that will work? I mean, the Aygül flower is-"

Ze'eva cut him off. "Maybe you have forgotten the history of the Aygül flower? It means Moon Rose. This is a flower that the Moon herself gifted to her children when we became stricken with a horrible disease we could not cure. It heals all grievous wounds and shifter diseases. Yes, Kyra Reeves is a man-beast though she happens to be Moon-bound. That is the only thing stopping her from being a crazed killer. Otherwise we would be forced to put her to death."

She looked at Mom who had tears running down her face. "It is your choice. To be in constant pain as an infected being, or to be completely healthy as a wolf."

"I don't want this," whispered Mom, her voice choked. "I never wanted this."

"I know," said Dad, holding her shoulders and rubbing them in circular motions. "But this is what's happening. I know its hard to see it, but this is a blessing in disguise. Our son is a werewolf and if we're wolves too, that allows us to live together peacefully. Our family has been falling apart and you know it. Now it'll be enhanced, tightened. I don't want you to be in pain Kyra and I know you haven't been happy about the state of our family. This will change everything."

"Argh!" Mom smacked him off her and whirled around to face him. "I don't want to be a shifter Grant! I don't want to turn into some animal and eat raw meat and howl at the Moon!"

She covered her face as she cried but she pushed Dad away again when he tried to hug her.

Sky stepped forward. "Mrs. Reeves. Let me talk to you."

She took Mom's elbow, then pulled her away. Mom struggled but Sky was ten times stronger than her. Once they were in a corner, Sky spoke to her and while I knew it was eavesdropping, I listened in anyway.

"I was Changed into a werewolf when I was twelve years old. I was at summer camp and I got in a fight with an older girl there, Alyse. She wasn't taking me seriously at all and I got so angry that I bit her on the arm, taking in her blood. Alyse coached me through the two months of camp, helped me with my symptoms and during my full Moons. Your son and your husband are here for you. I'm here for you, my Pack and the Stone Pack are here for you. No one is going to let you do this alone. I know its scary and you wish it wasn't happening but it *is* happening whether you like it or not. You have one choice to make Mrs. Reeves."

"You can either do this with your head held high, with your pride intact and as graceful as you are or you can do it crying and whining and kicking up a big fuss. I know you Mrs. Reeves, you are strong and intelligent and you don't let anyone or anything push you around. So make this choice, do it yourself. This is your life and right now, this is what God has called on you to do. You can't live as an infected person, being in that type of pain all the time, unable to be with your husband, unable to work."

"I know you don't *want* to be a wolf but think about it. You'll be able to hug your son again, his strength won't hurt you. You'll be able to be with your husband again. You can keep your job. You have a new womb. You can have everything. It's all up to you. Okay? Let's go back."

With that little speech, Sky led my mother back into the group.

Dad quickly embraced Mom, stroking her hair and shoulder.

He said, "What did she say? Are you okay? What are you going to do?"

Mom sucked in air and let it out shakily then looked at the waiting Pack. "I'll eat the flower. And my husband will too."

"No," said Toni, shocking me. "The Aygül flower is a wolf healing plant. For a human to eat it would be useless. If Grant wants to be a werewolf, we'd have to do that differently. Ze'eva, do we have any Aygül on hand?"

Ze'eva smiled, her wrinkled face parting wide. "With the full Moon yesterday, I had several buds bloom. Yes, I have some." She looked at my Mom who paled. "Once you eat it, your wolf will be healed. That means you will Change right there. As for Grant," she looked at him then at Toni. "I suggest the Kiss of Blood will work."

Dad and I said together, "That sounds disgusting."

Toni grinned. "Well, it's exactly what it sounds like. The Alpha bringing about a wolf in the human will cut his or her lips open until they're bleeding freely and kisses the human. It works best if the human sucks or licks the blood from the Alpha, ingests as much as possible while the Alpha sends the power of their wolf into the human. When it goes well, the human turns into a wolf on the spot. So."

He clapped his hands together. "Let's get back to the forest. Kyra eats the flower, and I'll Change Grant into a wolf. That means Grant is joining the Stone Pack."

No," I said, everyone turned to me. "I'm the Alpha of my Pack," I said. "And if my father is becoming a wolf, he's joining my Pack. That means I'm the one who has to bring his wolf."

Brenda stared at me. "You'd do that Xon?"

I said, "I'll do it."

Mikhail's brows raised. "Damn you got balls kid. The Blood Kiss isn't for anyone, it's not a simple kiss. You really want to be that person? The person who takes the humanity out of your father and gives him a wolf instead?"

I said, "If it means my father is a member of my Pack, then yes. Even if it means I have to kiss him, I want my father in *my* Pack."

Brenda smirked. "You really are the strangest teen wolf. But if we're all agreed?" She looked at Toni, my parents and Ze'eva.

We were, so Ze'eva went to get the flower while my parents and my Pack went back to the field. Some members of the Stone Pack joined us to watch as Ze'eva, Toni and Dr. Norris showed up. I immediately saw the glass cup Ze'eva was holding with the Aygül inside. The rose was only about the size of a large marble, the petals glowed silky white and the thin white stem had no thorns.

Ze'eva faced my mother and said, "To heal you of the man-beast disease, I will crush this rose into a liquid and you will drink it from this cup. The Moon rose will heal you from the inside out. You will still be a werewolf. The Moon rose will not turn someone from a werewolf back into a human being. Once a wolf, always a wolf. Do you understand?"

My Mom nodded, her eyes watery. Then she straightened her back, lifted her chin and the tears dried.

"Yes." Her voice was stern and firm, just like the Mom I've always known.

Dad touched her chin and gently kissed her mouth, then said softly, "Kyra, human or wolf, you'll always be the only woman I've ever loved. And I'm sure you're the most beautiful wolf in town."

Mom actually blushed then swat my father away. "Stop it Grant, there's people watching."

She caught eyes with me then looked away, her blush reddening.

"And as for you Xon and Grant," Toni looked at me then my Dad. "Once Kyra is Changed, you will perform the Blood Kiss. Okay, mystic, you can start."

Ze'eva passed the cup to Dr. Norris, who held it with both hands. She gently picked up the Aygül and it made a soft twinkling sound, with silver sparkles lifting up from its petals. My eyes closed as the wind blew the smell towards me. There was the faint scent of like a rose but it was an ethereal intoxicating smell, like I could stand here and smell it forever.

I opened my eyes and watch Ze'eva crushed the flower in her hand and silvery white liquid trickled down into the glass. It only filled it up a quarter and a little cloud of silver dust rose up. Ze'eva took the glass and offered it to my Mom, holding it at her lips.

Mom closed her eyes for a moment then opened them as she parted her lips. Ze'eva poured the liquid into Mom's mouth. Once Mom swallowed, she bent over. Her human skin melted away, folded off her and left a wolf laying on the ground. Mom's fur was pale gray with a white underbelly and chest. Her eyes opened, the bright intense yellow of a wolf, the same color of my wolf eyes.

"Kyra," said my Dad in a low whisper, staring at her. He took a step forward but Toni took his shoulder and pulled him back. Dad glared at him.

Toni gestured to me. "Come Xon. Let's do it."

Dad swallowed hard and stared down at me.

A. E. Costello 471

I winced then said, "Lay down Dad. You'll fall over when you Change anyway," I said when he frowned. "Besides, I can't do this with you staring at me like that."

Dad grumbled but laid down on his back. I knelt by his shoulders and looked at Toni for what happened next.

Toni knelt on Dad's other side, grew a claw and sliced open my lips, deep enough they split in half until it was like I had four lips instead of two. Blood gushed down over my chin.

"Kiss him Jaxon. The goal is to get as much blood in his mouth as possible. While you're doing that, send the power of your wolf out of your mouth and into him. Quickly before you heal."

I bent over my father and pressed my ruined mouth to his. His hands clasped my shoulders like he wanted to push me away. I used one hand to keep him pinned to the ground while I squeezed my lips against his mouth. The blood streamed out into Dad's mouth. I gathered my wolf, he ran forward and I shoved him out of me and into my father.

Dad spasmed in my hold and started to punch and kick but my wolf was still rushing out my throat and pass my bleeding lips, so I didn't stop. Dad tried to jerk his head away but it was Toni's hand that kept his mouth against mine and he was swallowing my blood as my wolf entered him.

Then Dad's head broke free of Toni's grip, he howled as the last of my wolf slid out, swallowed by him.

Toni said, "Let him go now Xon, it's working."

I gently laid my convulsing father on the ground and stood back, watching as he twisted and thrashed wildly, howls rose from his throat and died, strangled. As I watched, his clothes shredded around him. Dad's skin shriveled and revealed light gray fur underneath. His bones snapped and cracked then reformed, his skull stretched outwards, his mouth and nose melded to create a muzzle. Then with a deep sigh, a large wolf laid at my feet, panting. He was a lighter gray than me, smooth with dark cream under his throat and down his chest, his paws and tips of his ears were also dark cream. He was breathing shakily, shudders making his fur wave.

I stared down at the great wolf my father had become, he was easily three times my size, in fact…I think he was larger than Toni.

I looked at Toni and he was staring at my Dad, his face shocked and unsettled.

"Damn," said Dr. Norris, crossing his arms. "Just wait until Xon grows up."

Dad's eyes flickered open and he stared up at me with bright yellow eyes, the same color of my wolf eyes, the same that now my Mom had. I grinned at him and knelt down, grasping the thick ruff of fur and heaved. Dad's long thick legs stumbled and he weaved. He stood six feet tall to the shoulder, his eyes were on level with mine and he placed his muzzle against my face. My arms couldn't fully wrap around him as I hugged him. I didn't feel fear of him but I truly wondered if he decided to challenge me to be Alpha if I'd actually win.

A low whine made me look over as Mom was getting to her four feet. Dad pulled away from me and sniffed her face and ears, rubbing his muzzle against her. From her size, she would only be a little bit larger than Sky. Again it struck me that I really was only a kid and my Dad was an adult.

"It is broad daylight," said Dr. Norris. "But they need to go on a run, to feel the forest for the first time."

I took off my clothes and shifted. I looked around at my Pack. My parents who were both shades of gray, the midnight black wolf Sky, the white wolf Connor, gold-brown wolf Shane, dark brown Javier and Leo who was light brown. I had worked hard, had fought, had grown from pup to an Alpha in such a short time. And now I had the greatest Pack anyone could ask for.

I tilted my head back and howled, loud and melodious, then ran for the forest with my full Pack behind me. Sky was at my side, then directly behind me was my father and my mother, with Connor and Leo, then Javier, and Shane next to him.

The forest breathed with life during the day. The sunlight held a different form of magic than when under the full Moon. The leaves and the grass vibrated, as water rushed through the veins and roots. Birds flew overhead and hopped along branches, with squirrels racing up, down and around tree trunks. The hot wind blew through our fur, and the Sun warmed our faces. Through the grass, over the bushes, running laps around trees, I led my Pack on a excursion through the forest, before slowing down and heading back to the field.

[How was it?] I glanced at my parents.

[Wow!] Mom's voice fluttered through my head. Her pale gray coat was ruffled from the wind, and her plumed tail swiped from side to side. *[This is...this is incredible! I never...I never thought it was like this!]*

Dad breathed out very slowly and looked at me with his yellow eyes like mine. *[Psalm 145:5 On the glorious splendor of your majesty, and on your wondrous works, I will meditate.]* Dad leaned his muzzle onto the top of my head. *[I've never experienced anything like that before.]*

I ran my head underneath his neck and chest in a small hug before stepping back.

[That's just the beginning.] I told them. *[There's more you'll have to get used to. As for now, we have other things to take into account.]*

[Like what?] Mom lifted her head up as Connor was sniffing her face and rubbing his green-topped head against her shoulder. He was just showing affection, but I didn't think Mom understood that yet.

Sky answered. *[Like the fact that Xon can be a real Alpha now. His parents are both wolves, so it's legal for him to be Alpha now.]*

I looked at my father. *[You are okay with me being the Alpha? If you don't want to follow me, then we'd have to fight or something.]*

Dad chuckled, a deep hoarse sound from his chest, but I heard the familiar human sound in my head.

[Xon, my boy, I still don't have the foggiest idea exactly what's happening here. I was on the sidelines as you went through your Change, I saw the struggles you had. I know how you worked hard to be where you are, I'm not going to take it from you.]

I relaxed at that, and led the Pack back to the field. Our clothes were waiting, even new clothes for my parents who had ruined theirs. We all went back to Toni's place to talk about the new development.

Toni clapped his hands together and said, "With that done, the fact remains that Xon is still on the record as a Changed wolf who is not allowed to be an Alpha. So I'll put in a petition for Xon to become a full Alpha, on the records, legalized and everything."

I grinned.

Brenda said, "He's seventeen, he's too young."

Mikhail said, "Xon is an Alpha in everyway except by Law. I think Toni is right."

Toni looked at me with a short smile. "I'll put it in immediately and let you know what happens next."

I nodded, my chest tightened a centimeter. If I could be a real Alpha, official in the Law then I wouldn't have the cloud of being replaced hovering over my head.

Sky leaned in and I kissed her, with a prayer going up in my head.

Wow God. I kept flipping between believing and doubting when praying, and here I am now. You never left me even when I doubted You. Thank you for never letting go of me.

When I stepped back, my parents were also breaking apart from a quick peck.

A. E. Costello 475

16

September 11th
Thursday

The next day I found myself sitting in a waiting room with my parents, Sky and the rest of the Pack waiting to meet the Alpha of the United States in Virginia. Toni had called early in the morning to tell us the Alpha of the United States wanted to see me immediately and had us flown from Hartsfield-Jackson to Washington Dulles International Airport. There was a werewolf with a sign reading Reeves Pack on it, so we went with him into a huge stretch Hummer.

The giant white building we had been brought to reminded me of the White House. It had flags flying outside that I had never seen before. The cloths were emblazoned with a black howling wolf on the background of a red star. Inside the building, the marble flooring was white with gold flecks. The walls and columns made of silver and porcelain, decorated with gold symbols. Red and purple drapery hung, along with ebony curtains framing the tall arched windows. There were statues of creatures with wolf bodies but where the neck should be there was a torso of a male human, which posed with silver musical instruments to their lips.

A very tall and thin werewolf greeted us inside, wearing a black and white uniform like a butler. However the fact that his cuff-links were made out of gold and his buttons were diamond chips made me think he wasn't a regular servant. We were taken to the sitting room and had been waiting for several moments in silence.

The door opened, we all jumped.

The thin wolf from before said, "Come. The Alpha of the United States will see you now."

The Other Side 476

Then he walked away in an odd loping stride, it was like the way a wolf moves but he was in human form, making it look weird but graceful at the same time.

We followed him into a large octagonal room that was like a court room, with two tables for the defendant and plaintiff, a group of chairs to one side, then a high table at the end for the judge and all around were balcony seats, like for an audience. No one was sitting in the chairs but a male werewolf was leaning on the high table, head down and ankles crossed.

His dominant aura breathed from across the room; like fire, already burning up to my face. Each step I took closer the heat intensified. Connor, Leo, Javier and my Mom all bent down to their knees, unable to move any closer.

The wolf stood straight and looked at me, his eyes were boiling bright red, his gold wolf spark took over his pupils entirely. My eyes stung at first but as I kept looking at him my dominant aura built up, giant heavy boulders melding up into a mountain, blocking him.

His black brow arched then he smiled and his aura receded, so I lowered mine.

"Marshall Brentwood," he said. "And you must be Jaxon Reeves."

I nodded, breathing out slowly. "Yes. I am. And this is my Pack."

Brentwood's eyes cinched. "You are only seventeen. Yet you've made a Pack. Its hard to believe."

He stepped forward and strode into my Pack, looking over everyone and flicking our hair and skin with his fingers, his nostrils flared. Our Pack scent heightened, we stood closer together and breathed as one. Yes, we were a Pack. A real Pack that took time and energy to create. And I was their Alpha.

Brentwood left us and moved back to stand in front of me.

His eyes narrowed. "So, when you learned that Changed wolves weren't allowed to be Alpha you went and Changed your parents. That's highly illegal."

I shook my head and told him what happened with my Mom, that she got infected by Carter Hawkins and how my father made the decision to have the Blood Kiss on his own.

Brentwood crossed his arms over his stomach, staring at us. "And the Aygül flower healed her wolf, therefore allowing her to become a werewolf. I see. And so you think you can stay being an Alpha? You are only seventeen, that's not even old enough to be heard at Pack Meets. Your father is a strong wolf, let him be Alpha."

My fists knuckled at the idea of being pushed out of my spot.

I said with a straightened back, and a lowered voice, "All due respect sir, but I worked hard to become Alpha. I made this Pack. I'm their Alpha, period."

Brentwood's eyes brightened like flicking on an open flame. "I'm the Alpha of the United States and *I* say who is and who isn't Alpha!"

His aura slammed into me like a volcano erupting and lava crushing over me. My knees buckled down but I refused to cower and shoved forward my own dominance, the boulders crushing back onto him. I knew this wolf was in effect my boss, he was in charge of all the Alphas in America but I couldn't let him take my Pack away from me.

A door slammed open and with it came the bright tingly bursting smell of magic. Brentwood stepped away from me and we both dropped our auras. I was sweating and I noticed all of my Packmembers were on their knees, heads bowed and bodies twitching.

I turned and saw who had walked into the courtroom. She was dressed in lavish robes of purple and white, she wore a small diamond tiara. Because of her smell, I knew she had to be a mystic like Ze'eva but she smelled many,

many times more powerful than Ze'eva. If Ze'eva had a magic scent like a small thunderstorm, this mystic's scent was more powerful than a typhoon.

Brentwood said, "Welcome, Queen Mystic of North America, Mahlia Venetura. May I ask why you felt the need to join in these proceedings?"

She spoke in a deep echoing voice, it was completely inhuman and made the hairs all over my body stand on end. "I felt Her. I felt the call of the Moon Goddess. I will examine this Pack."

Brentwood stepped back from me with a wave of his hand. The Queen Mystic flowed forward like her feet weren't walking on the ground but over it, gliding and wavering like she was dancing. She swept around my Pack, touching over skin and hair, breathing us in. Up close, her eyes were just the gold spark and her sclera was black like a wolf's. Her ears were pointed and her red hair tumbled down to her back, thick and heavy like fur.

She touched my chest and leaned in to smell my neck then up my chin. She bent down to Sky and lifted her to her feet, then smelt Sky's neck and temple. I held Sky against me when the Queen Mystic let her go. Sky steadied her legs and lifted her head up.

"I have determined," Mahlia Venetura said in that echoing booming voice. "It would be against the Moon Goddess's will to break up this Pack."

She looked me in the face. Her gaze was more intense than when Ze'eva looked at me. She was seeing right through my skin, past my organs and into that cave where my wolf was then through him, going deeper than anything physical and past the metaphysical.

She turned back to the Alpha of the United States. "Jaxon William Reeves was born to be a wolf and to be an Alpha. He will continue to grow in power and strength. Your position will be his one day and he will bring much change. I forbid you from removing him from his position as Alpha of the Reeves-Cloud Pack."

Stunned couldn't begin to cover it. She knew my whole name, she knew the future and she just changed the title of my Pack. She even gave the Alpha of the United States a direct order. She must be higher in the hierarchy than him if she was in control of North America.

Brentwood lowered his lashes for a moment then looked at me. "The Queen Mystic has spoken. Jaxon Reeves is legally and officially the Alpha of the Reeves-Cloud Pack. Your territory is Lakeside Village. With this, the matter is closed. You are cleared to go home in peace."

Just like that, it was over. Everything that I had struggled to protect and save was mine to keep. My parents, my mate, my Pack.

As we left, I said, "Dad, I think I want to be a lawyer."

Dad looked at me, brows raised. "A lawyer? You never mentioned anything like that before."

"Well if I'm going to be the Alpha of the United States when I grow up," I said with a grin. "I should know exactly how shifter politics works. I mean, I got arrested for killing a Rogue wolf when apparently that's perfectly fine in our community. And Connor was getting abused but no one was helping him. The Queen Mystic was right, there does need to be a change. I don't like how shifters are treated at public schools with being forced to act human and anytime we do something animalistic like growling or whining we get reports. Yeah, I think a lawyer will be a good place to start and help forge better human-shifter relationships."

Javier smiled at me. "And I think I want to be a scientist."

My brows arched. "A scientist? Like studying chemicals and stuff?"

He shook his head. "No. I want to study shifter science, and specifically the mystery of the dominant aura. I also want to prove that someone doesn't have to be tall and muscular to be dominant, that maybe a wolf can be short and chubby but still be powerful. What about you Connor?"

Connor cupped his chin then said, "I guess social worker, for shifters. I hated my life and I kept trying to kill myself to escape it. Without Xon, I would have found a way to succeed. So if I become a social worker I can try and help other shifter kids who need help. Like maybe I can run a home for shifter children or young shifters who cannot live with their families because of abuse. Shane?"

Shane jumped to be called on before he grinned then shrugged. "Hell if I know. My parents keep bugging me to follow in the family business, they're all like bankers, into real estate and stockbrokers, so I've got plenty of money. Reminds me of Stone, he's a huge CEO of his own corporation. Maybe I'll do that. Also I'd like to be the Alpha of my own Pack one day. Sky?"

Sky bit her lower lip, her brows scrunched in thought. "I think I'd want to teach at a shifter-only school. Or if I am at a public school, I'd like to teach classes for shifters by a shifter. Or maybe be a public speaker so that I can teach humans about shifters and how to deal with them. I want to help shifter kind. I wonder what Leo wants to do."

Leo looked around at us then opened his mouth. "Child therapist." His voice was very quiet and cracked but he spoke.

We all stared at him until his face turned bright red with a blush, then we jumped on him into a tight group hug. He squawked like a chicken so we let him go but I grabbed him again and lifted him up onto my chest.

"You're talking Leo! You're finally talking again." I set him down and held his face so I could look him in his eyes. He gazed at me with deep warm green eyes and he smiled. From his face that had so long been blank and expressionless, it was like the sun breaking out of the clouds. Everyone hugged him again until I heard his bones cracking. Leo growled, it was low and hoarse, but the sound signaled he had had enough and everyone let him go.

I caught eyes with Sky and we kissed.

Dad broke us up by stepping between us but he was smiling.

"Enough of that you two," he said. "The car is here to take us back to the airport."

I laid my head against his neck for a second before standing up straight. Dad's scent had completely changed. He had the deep warm familiar scent of family, like my father, but gone was that human smell. He had the forest scent and the thick musk of an adult male.

Mom smiled at us and took Dad's hand, gently squeezing. Since being Changed, Mom had seemed to mellow out a bit. Except for when Connor and I ate all the food again, then she showed her teeth.

Looking at my Pack as the car pulled up, I could only thank God again that I had gotten through all the trials He had set up.

We went back home to Georgia.

"Good to be home!" I called out with a heavy sigh as Dad opened the door to the house, letting us all in.

"It is," agreed Connor and he looked very happy as he said it.

"Come on in," said Mom to the rest of the Pack. "I'll start making lunch."

We hadn't gotten settled when the doorbell rang. From how quickly it came, I had a feeling someone had been watching the house waiting for us.

I opened the door. It was Leah, the red-haired Latina from the Stone Pack, and she had tears in her eyes. Before I could say anything, Sky shoved me to the side, growing.

"What do you want?" Her tone was more like *go away.*

Leah paled and took a step back, but she looked at me. She held out a jewelry box, saying, "This is my gift, should you accept it, I will follow your rules as such until you give my leave."

I took the box and opened it. Inside were gold chandelier earrings that probably belonged to Leah or some other female in the Pack.

I said, "Gift accepted." I handed the box to Sky. "What is it Leah? Why are you here?"

"I came to warn you," she said. "Wyatt is on a rampage. I tried to get here as fast as I could, to let you know."

My gut tightened in a knot. "What did I do now? He's probably pissed that I'm an official Alpha now."

Leah shook her head. "No. It's my fault. I came to Wyatt and tried to apologize for Rocky's death, tried to tell him that it was never my intention for anyone to die or get Changed. He completely exploded, he snarled at me then got his car and drove off."

My brows went up. "If he's driving here, and I've seen how fast Wyatt can drive, how did you possibly get here first?"

"I'm a fast runner," she said. "Wyatt still has traffic and stop lights. I can easily get to your house from the Stone Manor and beat him in a car. Still, you have to be careful. I don't think anything can stop him now."

My father and mother came to the door, looking concerned.

"I heard Wyatt's name," said Mom. "That's the white man who hates Xon, isn't it?"

Leah's eyes watered again and she bowed her head low enough I could see the back of her neck.

"I'm so sorry!" She gasped as she broke down crying. "It was all my fault! Rocky liked me, he always had but he was too possessive and controlling. So I would talk to other men to try and convince him to back off. I had done it several times so when Rocky saw me with Xon, he completely lost it. I didn't want Xon to get Changed or hurt, I definitely didn't want Rocky to die! I was young and stupid and I didn't care about Rocky's jealousy!"

I gently drew her into a hug, rubbing her hair to get her to calm down. As I did that, Wyatt's car squealed to a stop at the curb outside of my house.

I pushed Leah back, saying softly, "You'd better get out of here Leah. I accept your apology, we all do but I don't want you to get hurt in the crossfire."

Dad's eyes widened. "You're not about to fight this guy in our house Xon! One time was enough."

Wyatt slammed his way out of his car and walked up the lane. I pushed at Leah, she tossed one tearful look over her shoulder then with a burst of wind, disappeared. I knew she had run away but she was just like Brenda, moving so fast it was like air itself.

Wyatt came to stand in front of me and held out a watch. It was also expensive but seeing the pale skin on his wrist compared to the darker color of the rest of his arm, I knew this was his own rather than Toni's.

He said, his voice rough, "This is a freely given gift and should you accept it, I will follow your rules as such until you give my leave."

I took it and passed it to Dad. "Gift accepted. Wyatt, why are you here?"

Wyatt looked me right in the eyes. "Rocky can't come back."

I blinked, I wasn't expecting that.

Still, I nodded. "Yes…the dead don't come back."

Wyatt clenched his fists as his hands started shaking, his eyes were damp. "Being angry won't bring him back. Screaming and fighting and cursing, no matter how much I do that, it won't bring him back to life."

I could smell the pain rolling off Wyatt in a thick blood-like smell, crumpled and weak as the pain came from his emotions. It stung my eyes and I couldn't stop them from watering too.

I said, my voice a little wet, "I know. It doesn't work like that."

Wyatt looked over at my Pack, grouped together, our smell strong and enhanced.

He said, "You really made a Pack. A real Pack." He looked at Sky. "And you have a real mate."

I nodded. "Yeah, I did."

"If you died it would fall apart," he said, looking over them. "Your parents have made you their life, you're their only child. A mate cannot live without their other half. Leo depends on you. Javier does have a Pack back home but losing you guys won't be easy. You took Connor in as your brother, you are his family now. As for Shane, no matter how rough he is, a wolf losing his entire Pack is bad enough to cause suicide. You are the linchpin for the entire Pack."

I knew he was right. If I died, everyone else would go with me.

Wyatt looked back into my eyes, his dark gray eyes stormy and his wolf spark subdued. "I'll miss my brother for as long as I live but killing you won't bring him back, being angry with you won't change anything. So…let's leave it at that."

I smiled, glad that he was letting it go. "Alright. Clean slate?"

He jerked his head in a nod. "Clean slate."

Then he turned around and walked away. Seeing the droplets on the ground I knew it was because he couldn't hold back his tears. He got in his car and drove away.

Sky hugged me and my parents looked happy too.

Mom let out a sigh of relief. "I'm glad I don't have to worry about that anymore."

"Me too," I said.

Remembering how fearful I had been knowing that Wyatt was out to kill me, I thanked God for helping Wyatt find it in his heart to forgive me and maybe even to forgive Leah. Sometimes we do things that we can't take back, but being able to acknowledge it and learn to heal, that is crucial to being able to live happily.

I looked over my Pack as they went back to their business, Javier and Mom cooking, Shane wanted to play video games downstairs, Dad teasing Leo, Connor snuggling with Sky, a hot feeling rose in my chest.

A. E. Costello 485

This was my Pack and I would protect them with my life.

17

September 12ᵗʰ
Friday

After everything that had happened, Friday was finally a chance to unwind. My Pack all had to go home, Sky's and Shane's parents were worried, while Javier and Leo needed to get fresh clothes. We got Connor's things moved from his father's house into a bedroom on the third floor, next to my bedroom. Connor was upstairs, so I had a chance to bring up a question that had been continually brushed off.

"Mom," I said. "Why do you hate shifters? You seemed so angry and upset all the time about me being a werewolf. Now you're one too."

Mom put down the hunk of raw chicken leg she had been chewing on and stared at it. On the counter was a bag of chicken she had been seasoning. The look on her face suggested she hadn't realized what she was doing.

"My older sister," she began, putting the gnawed-on leg into the sink. "Your Aunt Kysha. She was attacked by a shifter when we were younger. Just preteens, younger than when you were attacked."

I gasped and glanced at my father but he nodded.

"You never told me," I said. "How has she been hiding being a shifter this whole time?"

"She's not one," said Mom. "They used drastic measures in order to stop a change back then. She had been clawed in the stomach, mainly right into her uterus. They gave her a silver injection to stop the change from progressing and removed her infected womb. Kysha is bitter about losing the ability to have children and even though your father and

I had trouble having you, at least I managed to have a son before losing my womb. To me, I had always wanted my sister to have children first. So in a way, we were both affected by her attack."

"But Mom," I said after a minute. "You have your womb back. If they had let her finish changing, she would have been able to regrow her womb too."

"You also have to understand your mother's religious background," said Dad, speaking up. "Before Kyra became a nondenominational Christian, she was raised by a family a part of the Church of the Human God."

My brows raised. "Aren't those the people who think shifters are demons?"

"Yes," said Mom, going back to seasoning the chicken. "As I got older I could tell shifters weren't demons per se, but with what happened to my sister, growing up with constant sermons about how evil they were, I never had any shifter friends or coworkers, I disliked them, hated them. I struggled to deal with you being a wolf Xon and now I'm one too."

She held out her hand and her pretty nails darkened into black then slid out, curved into talons. Then it slid away as she lowered her hand.

"The pain of growing back my womb was terrible." Mom looked at me then at Dad. "But I've come to appreciate what it means."

I sat up straighter. "Mom?"

"I'm not pregnant," she said but she was smiling then looked away with a blush.

I looked at Dad with raised brows and he shoved me to the side, ordering, "Shut up Xon."

"I didn't say anything!" I laughed and said, "On a more serious note, so are you okay now Mom?"

"I have to be, don't I?" She gave me a calmer look. "I did enough kicking and fussing; now is the time to start learning to adapt to my new life. Mainly dealing with the cost of feeding an entire family of four hungry werewolves.

A. E. Costello 487

I finally understand why you kept cleaning out the fridge. It's like being constantly ready to eat."

I nodded, grinning. "Yeah. And then going for a while without eating is torture. I guess I should get a job and start helping out."

"I don't think so son," said Dad, shaking his head. "If you really meant becoming a lawyer then the only thing you need to be focusing on is hitting those books. I want your head full of education, not the stress of working. Your parents can handle the increase in funds, you start studying."

I nodded, even though I really wanted to help out some more.

I asked, "So is everything okay now? You guys seem to have adjusted a lot better than I did."

"Well we are adults Xon," said Dad. "And we also had to watch you from the sidelines first. The main thing for me is how hungry I am all the time. Now with four wolves in the house, our food bill has gone past astronomical."

I opened my mouth but Mom said, "We can handle it Xon. Like we said, you focus on studying. Getting into a law program isn't easy business and if you're going to be the Alpha of the United States one day, you need to focus."

I nodded then said something that had been on my mind.

"Dad…why did you cut ties with Uncle Jeremiah? How come I never met anyone from your side of the family?"

Dad sighed and said nothing.

"Dad," I said a little firmly. "I wish I had siblings and I do, siblings I never met or even knew existed. But you have a brother and from what I saw, he really cares about you and me. I have an entire side of my family I never knew. An uncle, grandparents, cousins. How could you cut ties with them?"

Dad rubbed his hand down his face and glanced at my mom, who nodded at him and went back to preparing dinner.

Dad sighed again and looked at me. "Look…the Reeves family…my entire family, they're all crooked Xon. I grew up in a home that dominated the streets, drugs, trafficking, weapons dealing, all of it. It was what I knew and I did it because it was expected of me and I knew nothing else. Jeremiah became the leader, he's ten years older than me and I took my orders from him. I did things that I regret Xon, things that will always haunt me. I was the first in my family to go to college and I met your mother there. I…I loved her too much to let her join with the Reeves, to become tainted with what the Reeves family did. So I disowned them and joined her family instead."

"But you kept the names Reeves," I pointed out.

"I wanted his name," added in Mom. "I knew about his past and his family legacy, but I wanted him to know I loved him and I loved everything about him. He was determined to keep them out of his new life with me and here we are."

"Well things are different now," I said. "We're a Pack and now that I know about Uncle Jeremiah, I want to actually know him. I want you to make peace with him Dad."

Dad's eyelashes lowered and he asked in a low voice, "Are you giving me a direct order Xon? As the Alpha, I have to do what you say, my son tells me what to do. Is that it?"

I sat up straighter. After Marshall Brentwood declared me legally the Alpha of the Reeves-Cloud Pack, we kind of just went back to our normal lives. The full Moon for September had passed, so we wouldn't really need to go into our wolf forms until next month. That said, Dad hadn't balked that I was the Alpha and not him. Not until now.

I licked my lips for a second and glanced at Mom. She was watching us then seeing me look at her, just inclined her head. It was up to me.

"I'm not a tyrant or anything Dad," I said. "I still see you as my father so you are in charge of our family, you're the

A. E. Costello 489

head of our household. I'm just saying that I want to rejoin with my family, the family I've never known. If you don't want me to meet everyone just yet, then fine. But I want to formally meet Uncle Jeremiah. He contacted me in prison right away, said he was going to help me get out. He hadn't even meet me before but he cared enough about me to do that. And when you rejected him, he seemed really hurt. Please Dad?"

When Dad said nothing, Mom said, "Grant, listen to him. I agreed to never meeting your family because that was what you wanted. But to meet your brother, if he is trying to reconnect, I think it's a good idea. This doesn't mean we'll join the family business of being criminals, all it means is family should stick with family. Besides, you *are* a werewolf now. He can't really threaten you with anything, right?"

Dad finally nodded and lifted up his head, passing one hand over his bald head.

"Yeah," he said with a short smile. "So I guess I'll call him, come over for dinner tomorrow."

I grinned. "That's great."

So I had convinced Dad to make peace with his brother Jeremiah, and now I looked forward to seeing him again tomorrow.

* * *

September 13th
Saturday

Mom cooked six pot roasts with potatoes and carrots, four pans of cornbread, three bowls of coleslaw. There was multiple jugs of water on the table. It was a meal meant to feed werewolves, and make sure there was food enough for our guest.

At six pm on the dot, Uncle Jerry showed up.

He had on black jeans, a red t-shirt with a black short jacket.

"Uncle," I said, holding out my hand for a shake.

"Good to see you nephew," said Jerry, he shook my hand and he hissed a little at my firm grip.

I quickly let him go, saying sheepishly, "Sorry about that. I'm still learning my own strength."

"What...?" He looked in my eyes then as my dad and my mom came to my side, he quickly looked into their eyes. All three of us held the gold spark in our pupils.

"When...? I know Jaxon is a werewolf from the newspapers, but Jackie...and your wife...when did that happen?"

"Recently," said Dad, putting his clenched fists behind his back, crossing the wrists and pressing them to the small of his back. "It's a long story, but it has to do with the situation that caused Xon to kill Carter Hawkins, the reason he was arrested in the first place."

Uncle Jerry's eyes widened. "What happened? I know the story with Jaxon, but I don't see how come you two had to become wolves."

I said, "You guys continue on, I'm going to get Connor."

I dashed up the stairs to Connor's bedroom. I knocked on the door first and opened it.

"Connor?"

Connor looked up from reclining on the bed, an open marble composition notebook propped up on his pillows. He sat up and abruptly shoved the book and the pen he was using underneath the pillow.

I didn't comment and said, "My uncle is here for dinner. Are you coming down?"

Connor looked at his hands, clenching them in his lap. "Isn't this...I mean, that's your family meeting, right? I don't think I really belong."

"Of course you do." I walked over to him and gently rustled his hair. "You're my family and once everything finishes up, you'll be a Reeves too. If you want that is."

Connor leaned back on his arms, lightly kicking his feet back and forth. "Become Connor Reeves. It's not a bad name. Better than Hawkins…like having some of my father still with me."

I tilted my head to the side. "You are still his son, even if he is dead. Changing your name won't change your biology. All that matters is the choices you make from now on. My parents will do their best to raise you the way they raised me, to not be violent, to speak first, to be kind and polite. I don't know what kind of father Carter made, if he was a father to you at all, but in the end, it's your life and you decide what you'll do with it. That said, I believe you belong at the dinner table because you're my little brother, and my uncle is your uncle."

I grinned at him. "Besides it'll drive you crazy being able to smell that roast and not eating it. There won't be any leftovers, not with three wolves down there. So you coming or not?"

Connor grinned and we went downstairs together. My parents were still grouped in the entryway with Uncle Jerry, and from the sounds of it they were filling him in on everything that had happened these past two months.

Uncle Jerry's eyes bounced from my father to see me then Connor.

"Connor Hawkins," he said as we walked towards them. "Are you really getting adopted by my brother's family? My nephew…I mean, he-"

"Killed my father, I know," said Connor, finishing the other man's sentence. "And I'm grateful for it."

Uncle Jerry's body stilled and his face blanketed with no expression, but being werewolves, we could all smell his emotions. His scent stifled the room with the tingling lemony scent of shock mixed with sour milk of unease. I also heard his heartbeat skip several times, his pulse thudded in his neck.

"The short story is Carter was abusive," I said, making calming motions with my hands. "I removed Connor from the house, Carter came after us and took my mother hostage and tried make a deal to give over Connor in exchange. I refused and ended up killing him. Connor is my brother now, and he wants to stay with us. That's all."

Uncle Jerry slowly crossed his arms like he was trying to move in an non-threatening manner but his scent was rife with the faint weakness of uncertainty, the electric lemon of surprise, thick smoky scent of worry and smooth fruits of relief.

"So that's why you're not in too much trouble with the shifter community," he eventually said. "Because Connor is grateful, then you didn't commit a crime."

"That's not why," I said with a smile. "But yes, I'm not in trouble. Are you hungry Uncle Jerry? We can eat now, right Mom?"

"Sure," said Mom and she gestured to the set dining room table. "Everyone take a seat, I'll get the roast."

We moved to sit. Dad and Mom sat on either ends of the table with Dad at the head, I sat next to Connor and Uncle Jerry sat across from us. This left the chair next from Uncle Jerry empty and I could only imagine that should be Sky's place. However I had kept Sky from her family for so long, and this was about reconnecting with my family, my uncle. There would be time for Sky to met Uncle Jerry.

Mom came back with the pot roast, and set it down as the centerpiece of the table. She lifted the top and the thick savory smell of meat rose into the air. A chorus of rumbling stomachs was like applause for the arrival of the main event.

"Grant, if you could cut the meat please," said Mom, sitting down at her seat.

Dad did get up and started to cut and serve the meat, and I had to give Connor a warning look as it looked like he was about to just start eating it. Once everyone's plates were full with roast, white halved potatoes, soft baby carrots, homemade coleslaw and cornbread, Dad made the prayer.

We began to eat in awkward silence, before I decided to break the ice.

"Uncle Jerry, I want to thank you for coming to bail me out of jail," I said straight to the point. "At that time, I didn't know who you were and I didn't know what was going to happen to me. I don't really know how you found out so quickly where I was and came to help, but I'm grateful. I apologize that was how we got to meet for the first time and so I asked for Dad to invite you here to reconnect with the family I never knew."

"Yeah, right." Uncle Jerry cleared his throat roughly and glanced at my Dad. "I was really glad to get your call and the invite Jackie, but I didn't know it was your son's idea. I should have guessed, you've been adamant about not talking to me anymore, or any of us. I mean, Caleb, Isaac and Levi, they all still talk about you."

Dad's face darkened with his scent clouding heavy and dank, but I asked, "Who are they?"

"Our cousins," said Uncle Jerry. "Caleb and Isaac are the sons of our Aunt Tessa, our father's sister. And Levi is the son of our Uncle William, our mother's brother."

My eyes popped. "I have great uncles? And cousins? Who else is there?"

Uncle Jerry half-smiled then gave my quiet Dad a firm look. "Jackie, what is this? You didn't tell him anything about his family? About us?"

"No," said Dad in a low voice, his eyes on his plate. "I just…I wanted to get away from all of it. I loved Kyra but I didn't love my background, my history. I wanted to be separate from all of it. I raised Xon to be different, to not have any Reeves influence."

Uncle Jerry's mouth opened and Mom said, "Let's not argue or discuss the past. We know that Grant decided having a life away from his family was the best decision for him at the time. Let's focus on right now, and that is that Xon wants to know and meet his family. So start with that."

Uncle Jerry kept his eyes on Dad who stubbornly refused to look up. I didn't want to press my Dad any further than I already had, so I didn't try to force him to be more involved.

I asked, "Do I have any grandparents?"

"Ma is still around," said Uncle Jerry, looking at me again. "Pa passed around eight years ago. You have plenty of second cousins, I don't have any kids though. Guess I should soon."

I tilted my head. "Why?"

"Someone to carry on the business," muttered Dad bitterly, his voice coarse in tone. "If I was still in it…you'd be up next."

Connor asked, "What business?"

Dad's scent burned hot and attacked my nose, like prickling fire and heavy exhaust. That smell was just a precursor to anger and violence. I wondered how to change the topic so Dad didn't quit on dinner.

"I'll tell you later Connor," I said. "Look, all I really want to happen here is for Dad to let me meet the rest of my family, that's all. And hopefully you guys make peace with each other."

"I've never had bad blood with Jackson," said Uncle Jerry in a serious voice, and his minty scent proved his honesty. "I was rightly upset, yeah, because he was turning his back on me, his blood, his history. However he was the first of us to go to college and he found a special woman, so I understood that he decided to make changes to his life. I felt that cutting ties completely with us was just too far. Why couldn't he be out of the game but still take time to visit? Why did I have to never meet my nephew until he was about to do time for murder? This wasn't what I wanted. Jackie, look at me."

Dad did look up and the estranged brothers looked each other in the eyes.

Uncle Jerry said, "I'm happy to be here in your house, eating dinner at your table, talking with your son and your wife and your adopted son. I'm overjoyed to be here, really. I'm not going to ask you to return to the fold, you left with fine acceptable reasons. I want to be your brother again, I want to be an uncle to your sons, I want to be in your life again. Can't you at least let that?"

Dad's eyes lowered for a moment as if he was trying to hide what he was thinking, but his scent gave him away. His emotions of shame, sickly and humid, regret was like thick dirty mud and sadness was wet mud. It was an overall disgusting mix of scents, but I didn't care, because it was like Dad had finally seen his actions through the eyes of someone else.

"I'm sorry Jeremiah." Dad met eyes with his brother again. "Maybe I did overreact, maybe I went too far. If you're willing to let me make up for lost time…then I'm willing too."

Uncle Jerry's face lightened and softened, and his scent bloomed with the smooth fruit smell of relief, peacefulness like soft gentle cotton and the pleased sweet scent of hope.

"I'm glad," he said with a warm relaxed smile.

"Now that's out of the way," said Mom with a kind tone, "Let's see, Xon, why don't you tell Jeremiah about yourself. He doesn't know any of your better qualities."

I perked up. "Sure."

Dinner shifted tone from uncertain and tense, to cheerful and inquisitive, I told Uncle Jerry about my childhood, and I got Connor to tell him about how he came to know me, and what kind of person he thought I was, and I explained a little more about why I wasn't in trouble for killing Carter and told him about my Packmates, Sky, Leo, Javier and Shane. During all of that, Mom continued to bring roast to the table until all six roasts were gone. All the cornbread pans were picked clean, not a single shred of cabbage remained, and we drained the jugs of water.

Mom cleaned up the dinner dishes with Connor helping, while Uncle Jerry filled me and Dad in on our family, he didn't mention anything about being in a gang, but just light-hearted anecdotes. I hadn't seen Dad smile so wide and his laugh so loud in a long time, he seemed to really relax and let himself enjoy the conversation.

As the brothers talked, a smell resurfaced between Dad and Uncle Jerry. It had been very faint and dull when Uncle Jerry first walked in, but now it was thick and heavy. A warm deep scent of family, the scent that blood-relations share. I understand that because they were estranged, the family bond scent had withered away, they had no close ties to keep that scent strong. But now that bonds had been reconnected, and they were reaffirming their brotherly feelings for each other, the family scent had returned. That scent had spread a little onto me from Uncle Jerry and I figured after I spent even more time with him it would get even stronger.

It was getting late, so we all walked Uncle Jerry to the door once the conversation had wound down.

"Well Jackie…" Uncle Jerry turned to Dad, a smile soft and loose on his face. "I'll admit it was a little awkward for me to see you're a shifter now, I wouldn't have ever thought that would happen. So I guess I can't bully you around anymore like I used to but you're still my baby brother Jackie and I still care about you the same way I always did."

"Thanks Jerry," said Dad with a short nod and held out his hand for a shake.

Uncle Jerry took the hand and tried to use it to pull Dad into a hug, but Dad's body was too heavy and dense, so only his arm moved.

Uncle Jerry's bugged eyes and shocked expression made us all laugh.

I said, "He's a werewolf now, so he's too heavy for you to move him by force. Dad, be careful hugging him. You can break bones by accident."

"You hug me then," said Dad with an easy smile. "I really don't know my strength yet."

Uncle Jerry put his arm around Dad's neck and patted his back for a quick moment then stepped back. He clasped his hands over Dad's cheeks, and said low, "I'm glad we did this Jackie. Can I call you later on this week?"

"Sure," said Dad.

"Goodnight Kyra," said Uncle Jerry, stepping back. He nodded at her and gave Connor a small smile. "And good to meet you Connor. You're in good hands here."

"I know," said Connor with a cheery happy smile. "My life is going to be completely different thanks to the Reeves. It was nice to meet you too."

"Bye Uncle Jerry," I said, giving the older taller man a hug without squeezing. "I'll see you again."

"Yeah," he said, blinking rapidly just as I scented the salty tang of tears. "Goodnight everyone."

He left the house and I watched him trot over to his Cadillac SUV. Several guys were hanging around outside, and they all got in, Uncle Jerry wasn't driving.

Dad slumped against the wall once the Cadillac SUV disappeared around the corner and I locked the door.

"That was exhausting," he said with a heavy sigh.

"But you got through it," said Mom, laying her hand on his chest and rubbed her head and cheek underneath Dad's chin, a nuzzle. "I'm proud of you Grant."

They hugged. Watching them made my chest ache for Sky. Connor yawned and laid his head on my abdomen, eyes closing as his body relaxed against mine.

I laughed and hugged him close, then looked at my parents. "I'll turn in now and take Connor up."

"Goodnight Xon," said Dad.

"Sir," I said, and scooped up Connor around his knees and shoulders, carried him up to his bedroom and laid him down. I didn't wake him up, his clothes still being on would irritate him later enough to cause him to get up and get ready for bed properly.

I went to my bed and took out my phone to text Sky.

Xon: Family dinner success.

She texted back instantly.

Sky: That's great Xon! Happy for you.

I smiled and relaxed against the covers, propping my phone on the pillows while I laid on my stomach. Warmth billowed low in my abdomen.

Xon: Wish you were here.

Sky: Same. I'd run over 2 c u but my parents want me to stay home for a while.

That made sense. Sky has been spending a lot of time at my house, and we even missed school more than once.

Xon: I know. I wasn't going to ask. How's Falcon and Raven?

We texted for over an hour, until my door opened and my Dad looked in with heavy brows and his mouth held in a firm line.

I winced then said, "Okay, I'll tell her goodnight."

"Don't let me come back and see you're still on your phone. Goodnight Xon."

He closed the door.

I said goodnight to Sky then left my bed. I went to my window sill and looked out at the sky, the stars, and the Moon. I knelt down, clasped my hands together, and prayed.

Dear God, it's me, Xon. A lot of things have happened, and while at the time I was lost and confused and upset, I realize now You were there that entire time, leading me and guiding me. I didn't pray daily like I should have, and I haven't read my bible at all, so I apologize. I want to thank You for watching out for me, my family and my Pack. There was a time I couldn't decide if I was still Your child or not, but I now believe that no matter what form I'm in, You still care and love me. I love you too. In Jesus name, Amen.

Prayer finished, I stood and picked up my bible from the nightstand. I opened it to a random page, and read the first verse I saw.

Revelation 4:11: Worthy are You, our Lord and God, to receive glory and honor and power, for You created all things, and by Your will they existed and were created.

A. E. Costello 499

18

September 14th
Sunday

My parents didn't believe in wearing everyday clothes to church, so I put on dark slacks, a white collared shirt and a dark blue blazer. Connor didn't have any formal clothes, so Mom dug out my old church clothes from when I was like ten and eleven, which had been well preserved in storage, and he wore something similar to what I was wearing now. Mom also combed and styled his hair but tsked with disapproval about the green color.

All ready, we went to Lakeside Community Church, the nearest non-denominational church in our village and the church I've been going to since before I was born. The pastor, Scott Evans, shook hands with those who entered the building and chatted with a wide welcoming smile on his face.

Mom stopped walking the moment she saw him. Her scent washed sharply bitter and sour, while her face tightened with hesitancy.

"What's wrong Kyra?" Dad asked, placing his hand low on her back.

"We haven't been to church in months," she said, swallowing. "And now...now I'm not even human anymore. What is he going to say? Should I...should I even be here?"

"Pastor Evans loves you and our family Kyra," said Dad firmly. "We've been going here since before Xon was born, we got married here. He's not going to turn us away, he knows who we are. Being a werewolf hasn't changed anything about us, our history or who we are. Come on, don't be afraid."

Mom nodded and straightened her back, then I followed my parents to the pastor, with Connor hovering behind me.

"The Reeves's!" Pastor Evans smiled brightly at us. "Good to see you again, it's been so long and oh…" He smiled at Connor. "Who's this tagging along?"

Dad gestured to Connor to come closer, and I pushed Connor forward in front of me.

Dad put his hand on Connor's shoulder and said, "This is our second son, Connor Reeves. The adoption isn't formal yet, but for all intents and purposes, he's ours."

Connor gasped, just like Pastor Evans, but while Evans's smell was lemony with shock and surprise, Connor smelled the bursting orange of happiness.

"Well that's great," said Pastor Evans, his scent now more cotton and soft with acceptance and understanding. "You've found a great family to join Connor, believe me. So I know things have been rough lately and that probably explains why you've been missing from the pews."

Pastor Evans looked at me, right in the eyes and took note of my gold spark, the telltale of the wolf inside. Then he looked at my Dad, my Mom and Connor, we all had it.

He took a step back but recovered, quickly moving back into his previous stance. While his facial expression struggled to keep calm, his scent fluctuated, and let us all know what he was feeling. The crumpled weak scent of emotional pain, the stinging onion of confusion, the smoky muddy scent of pity, thick dirty mud of regret, sour milk of unease and lastly the bittersweet smell of awe.

He finally said, "Why?"

"Our family was changing," said Mom, her own scent minty with truth mixed with the soft cotton of understanding. "Xon had become a werewolf while out of town, I couldn't really deal with it, though I tried and I leaned on God like never before. Then Xon was making friends and enemies who were werewolves, I ended up getting caught in the crossfire and got infected. Connor joined our family, and he's a werewolf. Then I was a

A. E. Costello 501

werewolf and so Grant made the decision to become one as well. So now the Reeves's…we're all wolves now."

Pastor Evan's jaw nearly hit the floor, and his eyes popped. His scent condensed with many emotions and the smells too crowded to pick out.

Yet then he smiled and his shoulders relaxed. "It seems like God saw fit to give you a new lease in life," he said, making myself and Mom gasp. "That's just what I can tell from that short explanation," he said. "How everything lined up to change you all from one thing to another, yes, there was a reason for that. Sometimes in order to fulfill the destiny God has for you, or to come into the path that God has called you to follow, you need to change."

I said, "I was told that I was destined to bring change in the shifter community, that in fact I was born to be a wolf and to be an Alpha."

"My," said Pastor Evans with several quick blinks. "Now who said that? Ah, well, you can tell me later," he said as there was the sound of the music for the praise and worship to begin. "But yes, I do agree that you three must have a calling that God needed you to be in a new form for. I've never believed that shifters were made by anyone else other than God. God created everything, and we are all His children. Come, go take your seats."

"Thank you, Pastor," said Mom in a thickened voice, and I didn't need to smell her tears to know she had began to water up. She hugged him and he squawked and tensed up, so she quickly let him go with a hurried apology.

He laughed heartily, wrapping one arm around his waist, and his other waving us on. "It's okay, it's fine. You just hugged me too tight, that's all. I'll see you in the pews."

"Wait," I said. "What about the Summers? I mean, have you seen Melody around lately?"

"Ah…" Pastor Evans looked downcast. "I'm afraid they made a decision to leave our congregation. The last I heard, they had joined the Church of the Human God."

I gasped, and so did my Dad, while Mom just looked shame-faced.

The Pastor shook his head but gave us all a smile. "God is God, and He takes care of all of his children. He'll lead them regardless where they choose to go. It's time for praise and worship, so let's get our seats."

"Thank you Pastor. Come on Kyra, Xon, Connor." Dad ushered us forward and handed Mom a tissue from his breast pocket.

"I guess that's all I really needed to hear," said Mom, dabbing at her eye carefully. "Somehow he knew what to say."

Mom was exactly right. Ever since I became a wolf, I struggled with wondering if God had made me, if I was still considered His child, if I even had the right to pray to Him anymore. And yeah. I actually did. Just because I had become a werewolf didn't mean God had no hand in my life. For me to become a wolf in the first place must have been a part of His plan. A plan that would lead me to becoming the Alpha of the United States one day and making changes to the shifter community, some of which I already had a good idea of what needed help.

Thank you God. Thank you for being pleased with me, for showing me how to do the right thing. I can tell now that maybe this whole thing was meant to be, that it wasn't chance. I'll keep doing my best, and please keep showing me the way.

19

September 15th
Monday

When I came downstairs the next morning for school, Connor was dressed too.

I asked, "Connor, are you going to school today?"

He nodded. "I've been avoiding it for like a month. I mean, things are mostly settled now and I miss hanging out with everyone. Besides, I'm a freshman, if I mess this up I might end up getting left back."

I nodded and we went into the kitchen where Dad had breakfast on the table, eggs, turkey bacon and a pile of buttered toast.

"Where's Mom?" I asked while we ate.

"She got called in for a meeting at work." Dad said it calmly but his smoky worried scent gave him away.

I said, "Do you think they'll fire her? She's not contagious anymore, well, I mean, as long as she doesn't bite anyone, she won't Change anyone else."

"I know son," said Dad, pouring us orange juice. "Even if its illegal to discriminate against shifters, she also missed a hell of a lot of work. At this point its way past unlawful vacation. So there's that as well. Don't worry," he said as my own scent thickened with smoke. "We can handle this. Go on you two, before you miss the bus."

"Later Dad." I put on my shoes and made sure I had my bookbag.

"Goodbye Mr. Reeves," said Connor, doing the same as me.

Dad smiled at him and gently rustled his hair. "You don't have to be so formal Connor. I know things are still shaky and uncertain, but you're a son to me, not just Xon's school friend. We're a Pack, aren't we?"

Connor nodded, his eyes glossy and he hugged Dad, pressing his face into Dad's abdomen. Dad hugged him back then we all heard the churning of the bus going by.

"Run Connor!"

I ran out of the house with Connor behind me. The bus was stopping at the stop sign where Jarrod and Gavin were getting on. I skidded up and gently grabbed onto the side of the door, and waved my arm to let Connor on in front of me, before getting on next.

The chattering of everyone else died away at the sight of Connor and myself. Connor had been missing from school since the day I killed Carter, he had been getting his life re-organized, leaving his father's house and moving into mine. His father's house and effects had to be sold, and there was still things to be taken care of before Connor officially had the last name Reeves.

Connor took a seat by the window in the front and I sat next to him, loosely crossing my arms over my chest.

Whispering filtered through the bus, and while I normally try to ignore the gossiping, this time a few choice sentences came through.

"Isn't that Connor Hawkins? The kid who's father…?"

"He was in the news, yeah."

"Xon's the one who killed his father."

"Wait, he's sitting right next to his father's killer?"

"That's insane!"

"They're not human, neither of 'em."

"I'll get my Dad to start driving me to school from now on."

"Maybe I'll transfer schools all together."

I started to get up and put these people straight, but Connor grabbed my arm.

He said with a shrugged shoulder, "Those aren't the people who's opinions I care about. As long as I have my Pack, I'm okay."

I settled back in my seat and nodded. The rest of the bus ride, Connor and I sat quietly together, while the everyone else continued to voice their ignorant human opinions on things they didn't understand. I can't speak for humans who've been abused but for Connor, having Carter gone for good was the best thing that could have happened to him. Carter had no intention of letting his personal punching bag slash sex toy get away from him, and he scratched my mother, purposefully infecting her, just to make a point. I didn't intend on killing Carter at first, I didn't go to Connor's house with ideas of killing Carter. However it happened, and not only was Connor happy about it, every other shifter I've met congratulated me for it.

As the bus was pulling up outside the school, I muttered, "I guess humans really can't understand."

"The ones that try to can eventually I bet," said Connor as the bus heaved to a stop. "But these guys, they want to draw a line in the sand. Them versus us. It's ideas like that that make human/shifter relations get really tense."

"That's why we have shifter politics, right?" I clambered down the bus steps with Connor behind me. "In the end, it's better to just let shifters deal with their own problems themselves. Humans don't really understand. So I will bring the change that will lead to shifter rights as well as human understanding and acceptance."

Connor opened his mouth to speak but the calling of his voice made him pause.

"Connor! Connor!"

The voice calling his name was quiet, not loud enough to be heard over the rush of students without a werewolf's sharp ears. I had only a second to register the voice as Leo's before Leo jumped onto Connor in a tight hug, nearly knocking the smaller wolf down. Connor gasped but then Javier threw himself into the hug with Sky right behind, the three all tightly hugging, nuzzling him and asking about him.

Shane loped up behind them but stopped by me, not attempting to join the little celebration.

"He seems alright," he said, shrugging.

"He's going to be fine," I said with a grin as Connor blossomed under all the attention, his face reddened and his smile cartoonishly wide.

"And you?" Shane looked at me, his sky beach-colored eyes looking straight into mine. "No one is shutting up about this whole "Xon is a murderer" shit. It's been an entire month already, you'd think they'd get over it by now."

"A month's not that long," I said, though it did seem like a long time ago.

A lot has happened in a short period of time. August 1st I had been attacked by Rocky and subsequently Changed into a werewolf. I went back to school just the next week, I met the Wildebeasts, got knocked around by Shane until I finally won our fight, got attacked and stalked by Wyatt more than once, saved Connor from Carter, managed to keep my Alpha position, Sky protected her right to be my mate, and even my parents had become wolves in the Reeves-Cloud Pack. Looking back, there was no way these things could have come to pass without God's helping hand. Even when I thought He was ignoring me, those were the times He was closer to me than ever.

The warning bell ringing made the tight-knit group break up as it was time for class.

I said, "Sky, can I talk to you for a minute?"

"Sure," she said with a bright smile, her honey-gold eyes warm and relaxed.

"I'll walk you to class," I said, gesturing for her to lead the way. "Leo go on without me," I instructed when Leo took a step toward us. "I'll see you at class, alright?"

He nodded. Javier gave me a one-armed hug around my midsection, and everyone went their separate ways, besides Sky who was walking me away down the long sidewalk path that curved around the main building down towards the gymnasium.

"I have Aerobic Dance first," she said with a shrug. "So what did you want to talk about?"

I crossed my arms over my chest and scuffed my shoe for a second before stopping.

"Well, I know you can get possessive when it comes to other women," I said. "But I need to talk to Melody."

Sky frowned and her scent blistered hot and spicy. "What for?"

"Because I never really got closure with her," I said. "She seemed really afraid of me and I don't think its right to leave it like that."

"Is she even worth it?" Sky stopped outside of the open gym doors, her eyes paled in color but not yet silver.

"She was once the most important girl to me," I said honestly. "And I think in respect to our past relationship, then yes."

Sky turned her face away without saying anything. Her scent soured sickly sweet with disgust.

"You're mad at me." I stated quietly.

Sky sighed heavily and tousled her thin micro-braids then tossed them back over her shoulders as she looked at me.

She said, "I do understand. You have your own code of respect and what's honorable and a strong sense of what's right and wrong. To you, leaving your ex-girlfriend terrified of you isn't right. To me, I think that's excellent. So I get it, it makes sense to you to set things completely straight. So I won't stop you…I just don't want to smell her on you later."

"I won't hug her or anything," I promised as the late bell rang. "I've got to go now, and you too. I'll see you after school."

"Yeah." She leaned on her toes with one hand sliding behind my neck and we shared a kiss.

School went surprisingly fast until forth period, and when I walked in, a strange bald man was behind Mrs. Hughes desk. He had a dry acrid smell, like a waterless desert.

I stepped closer and he looked up as his nostrils flared to take in my scent. Running along his neck from each side of his jaw was a patch of greenish black scales. He was also hairless, no hair on the head, no eyebrows, even his eyelashes were very thin and fine.

Some sort of Saurian. Like a crocodile or alligator.

I asked, "Who are you?"

"Mr. Lopez," he said. "I'm replacing Mrs. Hughes."

I took a step back. "She left? Or was fired?"

"Well I can't go into details," he said with a short smile, revealing very wide and very sharp teeth. This guy must have spent so much time in his other form that its leaked into his human form. Like how Carter had the eyes of his wolf. "But yes, I'm the new psych teacher. Is that okay with you?"

"It's fine," I said, and saw Melody in her seat, her head lowered so she could only see her desk, and her body turned to the side towards the windows. "Excuse me."

I walked over to Melody and tapped her desk.

She jolted and stared up at me, with huge blue eyes and her scent flooded with fear.

"It's okay," I said, raising one hand calmly. "I wanted to get some closure with you. Listen, I'm not mad at you and you don't have to be afraid of me. I know becoming a wolf changed things between us, and we didn't have a friendly break up. But that doesn't mean I'm going to attack you or that I hate you. We're going to be in the same school for another two years and I don't want to ruin your experience by being afraid of me the entire time. I'm cool with you now Melody, so relax, alright?"

Melody slowly nodded then shifted her fingers together. "Oh…okay. But…your uh…new girl. She's not too friendly towards me."

My eyebrows raised. "Sky? You know her?"

Melody looked at me. "We have first period together, Aerobic Dance. And she's not very, well I'm pretty sure she hates me, let's put it that way."

"Well Sky can be aggressive towards other women," I said with a nod. "But she won't hurt you either. I'll tell her to cool off though, okay? So we're fine."

Melody sighed and nodded.

I said, "I'm willing to let bygones be bygones Melody. We made our choices, and now we have to deal with them. I'm not the same person I was during the summer. I'm

A. E. Costello 509

someone else now and I'm moving forward. So you should too."

Melody nodded and I waved then went back to my seat.

I ignored whispers from humans about Carter's death but if one decided to talk to me, I let them know about the implications of a Rogue being killed, and why I wasn't supposed to be arrested. At lunch, Dave Powell, the President of the Shifter Student Government Association, hailed me down.

"I still think you would be a great president Xon," he said. "So I thought I'd try to bring it up again over food."

I said, "Actually…I'd like to join."

Dave's eyes widened, and he made this bird-like trilling sound in his throat. "Excellent!"

If I'm going to be the Alpha of the United States, I should know what it's like to be in charge of a body of people, even more so than just my Pack.

Dave was elated to show me the ropes, and by election time, I was voted unanimously to become president by all the shifters. Connor was formally adopted by my family, and became Connor Reeves. He let his green hair grow out so it was back to his original blond. The humans eventually let the thing about me killing my best friend's and now adopted brother's father go, as the shifter community had already moved on from it.

With the Reeves-Cloud Pack secured under my leadership, I looked forward to my future.

Epilogue

Four Years Later

I rang the doorbell to my parent's house, then took out my phone to check Shane's text that him and Leah were running late.

Sky at my side smoothed down her maternity shirt over her mound, and fussed at the hemline.

"Quit it babe," I said, dropping a kiss on her forehead. "You look great."

Twin howls rose up from within the house.

"I'LL GET IT!"

Following the howls came thuds of rapid footsteps, and the door shook as two bodies collided into it. I smiled at the scrambling to unlock the door before it heaved open.

"BIG BROTHER!"

I knelt down and scooped up my twin sisters as they dove at me, and stepped inside the house with Sky behind me.

"Xon, Xon!" The girls chorused my name eagerly.

I kissed the girls' foreheads and set them down.

"Faith, Hope," I said. "You two being good for Mom and Dad?"

As she came into the entryway, Mom spoke over their assurance, "No! They drive me crazy! Sky, you sure you ready for this?"

Sky smiled and nodded. "Yes, I am. Xon and I have been married for a year, and everything is going really well with For Shifters By Shifters, so we agreed to start our family. Who is here?"

Loud cheering blasted from the basement, loud enough the door shook a little.

Mom rolled her eyes. "Connor, Leo, Grant and the rest of his crazy Reeves. Also the newest Pack members have arrived."

"Yikes," I said, wincing as Sky threw me a glare. "I guess we're unfashionably late, besides Shane and Leah. How are the new members getting along with everyone?"

"You know," Mom smiled. "Connor is the life of a party, and he gets everyone else to relax and loosen up. Leo won't stop talking either. Ever since he's started speech therapy, he's an unending chatterbox."

A. E. Costello 511

I grinned but the doorbell ringing cut off the conversation as Faith and Hope rushed to answer it.

"Shane, Shane! Leah, Leah!"

"Hey," said Shane, entering and using his arm to give a hug to both girls, then Leah hugged them. "We're a little late, but I got the gift."

Shane offered a wrapped box to me. "Greetings Alpha of the Reeves-Cloud Pack. Here is a freely given gift and should you accept it, I will follow your rules as such until you give my leave."

I took it and nodded. "Gift is accepted. No one else from the Stone Pack is coming?"

"Nah," said Shane with a shrug. "They've got their own thing. Brenda gave me a little mouth for coming here instead of staying with them, but Toni said it was okay for now. Of course once I'm Alpha of the *Armstrong* Pack, then that'll be different."

"Armstrong-Gomez Pack," said Leah with a short snap of her teeth.

"Let's not argue," said Mom, ushering Shane away. "Go and join the rest of the wolves in the basement, the game is on. You too Xon, I'll take it over from here."

She took the gift from me, and Leah and Sky went with her towards the living room.

"Leah only wants it hyphenated because you do," said Shane as we headed into the basement. "It'll be the Armstrong Pack, period. Doesn't that sound more intimidating and powerful?"

I didn't get to answer as greetings went up from all the wolves in the basement. The eight newest members immediately rushed to greet me.

"Hey, hey," I said, giving out hugs and nuzzles, gentle bites to ears and tousling hair. "I'm right here."

Out of the eight, two were in elementary school, two in high school, and the other four were the parents. I had already been notified that another new werewolf family would be on the way in a few weeks. The Reeves-Cloud

Pack was growing faster than I could comprehend, Mom with the twins and Sky with my son on the way.

Leo called for me from across the room. His raised voice was hoarse and hesitant, but he still did it.

"Xon, Javier's on video-chat!"

I came over and sat next to Leo, he adjusted his phone so I could see Javier.

"Greetings Alpha," said Javier in an eager tone. "Leo hasn't stopped updating me, so I think I know everything now."

I laughed and said, "Alright, how about you then? How's Spain treating you?"

"It's a lot better now that my research was acknowledged as fact by the Queen Mystic of Europe," he said. "You know, if a Queen says something is true, the UAC and other heads of state accept it. So my father told me last week that he understands what I've been talking about this whole time."

I nodded. "About the dominant spirit of a wolf is sentient or something like that?"

Javier used his free hand to wave it side to side. "Not fully sentient, like having a full consciousness or being a second person, but yes, those who have the dominant spirit, or pure dominance like you Xon, it'll seek to defend the top position as an Alpha, so when that Alpha, such as my father for instance, has a son, that spirit will destroy the son's wolf from becoming dominant in an effort to protect it's own existence. That's why out of the sixteen children my father had, I'm the only boy and I have no dominance."

I sat up straighter, a cold thrill striking down my spine. "What about Junior? Will my wolf's spirit do that to him?"

Javier said, "Well maybe there's a way you can stop it or reverse it. The next thing I'm researching is how a wolf who was born with a lack of dominance can be taught it or earn it. Ah!"

A. E. Costello 513

The door behind Javier opened, and I saw a male face that quickly darted back as he must have seen Javier was on video. Javier turned to face us, a huge smile on his face.

"I got to go," he said.

"Javier, you dog!" I shouted. "Who is that!"

Javier smiled again, winked and said goodbye. Leo put up his phone.

"Was that Javier?" Connor broke away from the game, which had turned to commercial, and dropped onto the couch next to me.

"Yeah," I said, cupping up Connor's head, and leaning into his neck. He smelled of himself, cinnamon and clover, with the Reeves family scent over it, and the scent of the Reeves-Cloud Pack. The sad scent his father had stained him with had finally been erased.

Connor grinned at me. "You scent-check me like every time you see me, you know that? I'm better now, that part of my life is over. Do you know how many shifters know me at college? They're always like, "hey, you're in that crazy powerful young Alpha's Pack, can I talk to you?" It drives me nuts."

I chuckled and shrugged. "Well, I'm glad you're making friends. I had a lot of shifters at my back in high school too. Besides, the more shifter cooperation the better."

Leo said, "Definitely. That's one of the things they teach at in my seminar course."

"Child therapy right?" I stretched my arms up over my head. "You've finished your speech therapy classes?"

"I'm learning how to make my voice louder and more efficient," he said. "So yes, I'm studying to be a child therapist while I'm in speech therapy."

"And now we can't make you stop talking!" Shane jumped onto the couch, nearly knocking the entire thing over as we leaned back then thudded forward. He wrapped his arm around Leo's neck, and tightened. "So you wanna join Stone Industries with me? I could use a guy to fetch my coffee in the morning. You can practice saying "yes sir" and "no sir" all day long."

Leo, face purpled, wheezed, "I'd rather not."

"What did you say?"

I left Leo and Shane roughhousing to join my Dad who was coming from the cooler with several fresh bottles of Cola.

"Hey," I said. "How's everything?"

"Being Shifter Advocate isn't what I went to school for," he said with a wince. "But the company pays me well to relate and deal with shifter employees. At first, I was really awkward, but after supporting a shifter's case and helping him exercise his rights, I started to feel better about it. Especially that even though discrimination against shifters is illegal, Kyra still got fired back then because of her Change to a wolf."

"Yeah," I said. "But she's fine staying at home to raise Hope and Faith."

"For now," said Dad with a wry smile. "The girls are young and are driving her crazy. Once they're going to school, I'm sure Kyra will want to get back into the workforce. Maybe she could join Sky at her organization."

"BOYS!" Mom's shout came from the basement door as it opened. "FOOD'S READY!"

I patted my Dad's back. "Let's go eat."

Everyone was herding up the stairs, but Dad held my arm to hold me back.

"Son," he said.

I looked at him, brows raising. "Hmm, Dad?"

"I just want to say that this entire thing is still crazy for me," he said. "Being a wolf has a new interesting surprise every day. I get new respect for shifters who have to deal with it from birth, or who had horror stories from being attacked. That said, when we were going through everything…I rubbed my knees raw from praying. Yet, God never abandoned the Reeves family, even when I thought He had."

A. E. Costello 515

I nodded and said, "I know. No matter how depressed I got or how doubtful I became, God never once stopped believing in me or abandoned me. When I felt like I was in situations that I couldn't handle, I got through because of God's grace. I went from a weak-willed pup to a strong dominant wolf and in doing that, became a man. No matter what happens, I'm always a child of God. Now let's go eat."

Dad grinned. "Race you!"

He ran up the steps, with me following, calling up, "Hey! The Alpha should always go first!"

A. E. Costello 517